PRAISE FOR *GUESTHOUSE FOR GANESHA*

"Over the course of this debut novel, Teitelman paints an intensely beautiful world in which different cultures merge in surprising ways. Although it centers on what may seem like an odd pairing—a Jewish mortal and a Hindu god—the novel weaves the two characters together in a very natural way, as Esther, withdrawn from those around her, is shown to need Ganesha as a protective, loving companion. Teitelman's deft execution as she explores this relationship is a major factor in why this unusual novel works so well. Throughout, her writing shows a finesse that's as compelling as the story it presents, employing a lyrical prose style when focusing on Ganesha and a more decadent tone during Esther's parts.

A rich and moving story about an unlikely pair.

—*Kirkus Reviews*

"A parable, a prayer, a piece of magic realism, Judith Teitelman's *Guesthouse for Ganesha* begins with the (improbable; wondrous) visit of Ganesha, the Hindu elephant deity, to strife-torn 1920s Köln, setting us off on a journey of love, grief, understanding. A feat of (and feast for) the imagination, the novel unfolds in ways at once heartfelt, surprising, inevitable. You will not be sorry you accepted this invitation to voyage."

—Howard A. Rodman, former president of Writers Guild of America West, screenwriter of Savage Grace and Joe Gould's Secret, author of *Destiny Express,* and the forthcoming *The Great Eastern;* professor at the University of Southern California

"This young woman's journey through love, betrayal, dislocation, adaptation, terror, and spiritual discovery is unlike anything I have read before. It is both heartfelt and unexpected."

—Bill Stern, author, curator, and executive director of the Museum of California Design

"In *Guesthouse for Ganesha*, Esther Grünspan embarks on a journey, leaving her native Poland to arrive in Germany in 1923. She does not know that her journey has only begun—a journey of the heart and the spirit, a journey not only across distances but across time. So too the reader embarks on the journey through this vast and lyrical debut novel that will expand our view of the world, our consciousness, and our compassion."

—TERRY WOLVERTON, author of *Insurgent Muse: Life and Art at the Woman's Building*

"The story grabs me, Esther's journey is compelling and beautifully told. I love that something feels withheld from her story, I'm drawn into her character, fascinated that she is 'emotionally hardening' before my eyes. Yet there are these beautiful moments of her softening, succumbing, listening. I like the historical milieu, this eerie calm before the maelstrom of war, where an outsider can catalyze such irrational (and violent) race hatred. These pages are beautiful . . . it feels like Judith has breathed them into being."

—LOUISE STEINMAN, author of *The Crooked Mirror: A Memoir of Polish-Jewish Reconciliation*

"Judith Teitelman's remarkable imagination produces the thrilling illusion of several layers of different lives. The way she honors her main character's indifference to human contact and emotion and then poetically leads her to a redemption is an act of cosmic chutzpah."

—SASHA ANAWALT, author, educator, and director of art journalism master's programs at the USC Annenberg School for Communication and Journalism

"Lyrical and moving, *Guesthouse for Ganesha* weaves a story of daring and courage in a world rent mad by war and destruction."

—GARY PHILLIPS, editor of *The Obama Inheritance: Fifteen Stories of Conspiracy Noir*

"*Guesthouse for Ganesha* by Judith Teitelman spins a mythic tale with a heart so big it takes two continents and four countries to hold the story of Esther Grünspan, a seamstress whose needlework is as pierced and perfect as the needles in her heart. Teitelman weaves a tale of a seventeen-year-old girl jilted at the wedding chuppah with such extraordinary tenderness and grace. The reader cannot help but rejoice in Esther's beautiful, broken spirit and in the way Ganesha wraps her up in his caring love, gradually melting the ice that is her armor and awakening her spirit to live again decades later. Teitelman is a masterful storyteller who knows and loves her characters deeply, and Esther's courageous rebirth captures a kind of universal longing in all of us to heal our broken hearts."

—KERRY MADDEN-LUNSFORD, author and director of Creative Writing at the University of Alabama, Birmingham

"Have you ever read a book that begins with the great Indian elephant god, Ganesha, dancing through the night with a spunky young German woman? Judith Teitelman's *Guesthouse for Ganesha* is a truly original novel. I was immediately hooked by that image, with its blend of magic realism and a down-to-earth heroine who must grapple with abandonment and her own capacity for fortitude, all under the compassionate gaze of Ganesha, who observes and guides her with his 'surveillance of souls.' Teitelman yokes holocausts—both historical and personal—to compassion and possibility, giving us the timeless writerly gift of immersing this reader—and I'm sure many others—in a journey of renewal both archetypal and unprecedented."

—JANET STERNBURG, author of *The Writer on Her Work*, *Phantom Limb*, and *White Matter*, and photographer of the monograph *Overspilling World*

GUESTHOUSE FOR GANESHA

GUESTHOUSE FOR GANESHA

A Novel

JUDITH TEITELMAN

She Writes Press

Published May 2019
Printed in the United States of America
Print ISBN: 978-1-63152-521-6
E-ISBN: 978-1-63152-522-3
Library of Congress Control Number: 2018962788

For information, address:
She Writes Press
1569 Solano Ave #546
Berkeley, CA 94707

Interior design by Tabitha Lahr

She Writes Press is a division of SparkPoint Studio, LLC.

This is a work of fiction. Names, characters, places, and incidents either are the product of the author's imagination or are used fictitiously. Any resemblance to actual persons, living or dead, is entirely coincidental.

For Doug, who inspired.

Aaron, who sustained.

Terry, Maia, and Kerry, who encouraged.

"Beth" (or "Bet") is the second letter of the Hebrew alphabet and, subsequently, of all Jewish-language alphabets. It is also the first letter of the Torah—marking the beginning. It represents the beginning of duality, where there is both a giver—the Creator—and a receiver—the created world.

The literal meaning and form of the letter "Beth" denotes a house, underscoring that the created world is meant to house the spiritual within it.

This being human is a guesthouse.
Every morning a new arrival.

A joy, a depression, a meanness,
some momentary awareness comes
as an unexpected visitor.

Welcome and entertain them all!
Even if they're a crowd of sorrows,
who violently sweep your house
empty of its furniture,
still, treat each guest honorably.
He may be clearing you out
for some new delight.

The dark thoughts, the shame, the malice,
meet them at the door laughing,
and invite them in.

Be grateful for whoever comes,
because each has been sent
as a guide from beyond.

—Rumi

PROLOGUE

Dance, He whispered ever so softly.
Dance . . . without memory . . . of your heart being sundered.
Dance . . . never knowing . . . sorrow and pain ever kissed your lips.
Move! Feel again! Recapture yourself . . . who you were at three
when your song was pure . . . and electric with possibilities.
Come . . .
Dance with me.

He peered down at her with eyes the color of fawn and looked clearly into her soul. His trunk gently touched her right cheek. With His one free hand, He carefully lifted her out of bed. Esther took no notice that her linens and quilt were thoroughly soaked or that instead of her muslin nightdress, she was wearing layer upon layer of diaphanous silk.

She floated into His four arms and let Him guide her around the room. Though it was no more than the size of a small closet, somehow there was space enough for leaps and twirls. To an outsider's eyes, they made an awkward and ungainly pair: she, barely five feet tall and slender as a rod; He, towering at eight feet with a voluminous belly and extraordinary countenance. Still, their partnership was graceful and fluid, and the music—an interweaving of bells, horn, tablas, and sitar—seamlessly melded with their steps, as though the composition had been created solely for this dance.

Esther felt safe. A feeling long forgotten. It was as though she were once again in her mother's womb, floating in warmth. When the cabin door blew open, they danced onto the deck, now more than ever moving to the motion of the waves not far below. They journeyed in contented silence, words unessential. This was the liberation of movement, the release of the past and all that had held her captive. After some time, dancing in great abandon, Esther even lost sight of her partner as she whirled and twirled without benefit of support.

It was a beautiful, crisp fall night. The first calm sea experienced since leaving port. The four days prior had been stormy with giant swells, and most of the passengers had severe seasickness. But tonight the sea, and with it the ship, were at peace and gliding easily across the deep.

A young couple decided to take advantage of the night's tranquility and went for a stroll around the deck. They came on a barefoot Esther spinning and leaping, completely oblivious to her surroundings. Fearful she would soar over the railing, the man grabbed her, and immediately Esther began to mumble, incoherently it seemed, about a man—about an elephant—about freedom.

"My God," he yelled. "She's burning up. Get the doctor!"

Within minutes Esther was back in her bed, covered in cloths filled with ice. The ship's doctor forced a few pills down her throat.

The pure bliss of the past few hours dissipated; her teeth chattered without control, and her body shook violently. Soon her being began to relax as the drugs seeped into her bloodstream, their power taking dominance over that which had brought her to such a state of joy.

A tear formed in one eye and slowly rode the curves of her face before she drifted into a deep sleep and whispered, "Tadeusz."

CHAPTER ONE

*E*sther Grünspan arrived in Köln with a hardened heart as her sole luggage.

An uncommonly sweltering September day was her welcome, as well as a language that sounded like her native Yiddish yet foreign in structure and comprehension. A formidable determination guided her actions.

"*Stantsye, ikh darf a stantsye.* Lodging, I need lodging," Esther demanded of the first person in uniform that crossed her path. "*Vu ken ikh opzukhn stantsye?* Where can I find lodging?" Her articulation was clear and direct, emphatic. Quizzical, the man's eyes skimmed this plain-faced young woman from her faded, long-sleeved cotton frock with white rounded collar to her scuffed, lace-up shoes. Small in stature with thick blonde hair pulled away from her face in a tight bun, she was unadorned and clearly out of place.

"*Was? Ich verstehe Sie nicht*! I don't understand you," he said, waving her away and pointing toward the train terminal.

Without a note of thanks, Esther headed in the direction he indicated. Once inside the terminal, she strode through the cavernous building to consider every booth, kiosk, and stand until she found a corner counter with a large sign overhead announcing

INFORMATION. This was close enough to the Yiddish *informatsye* for Esther to push her way to the front of the line, disregarding the glares and loud protests of those in her way. She paid them no heed. Patience was no longer a part of her framework. It had been displaced by entitlement and self-preservation. The recent, devastating turn of events—Tadeusz's action, his rejection—and such a public spurn—of her, of them, of all their plans—had shaped an impossibly conceived scenario. Esther's one priority now was Esther.

She repeated her request to the man behind the counter three times. Each time she enunciated every syllable more precisely, then more slowly but colored by rising frustration.

The official, while clearly annoyed, noticed her youth and asked, *"Wie alt sind Sie?"*

Alt? Esther thought quickly, *alt*—old. Just like in my language. Although the other words made no sense, she correctly assumed he was asking her age.

"Zibitsn," she said.

The man shrugged his shoulders, rolled his eyes, and turned to help the person next in line. Esther leaned over and grabbed the pen on his desk. In clear, thick lettering she wrote the numbers one and seven on her palm. Standing on the tips of her shoes, she stretched her left arm high and held it up close to his face.

With a snort, he reached into a pile under his desk and thrust a piece of paper in Esther's expectant hands. She looked intently at the page's Gothic script and line drawing of a building.

This must be a place for young people to stay, she deduced, for next to a name and address 16-22 was printed. A map of the area with a large X seemed to mark its location. Expressing no appreciation, Esther turned quickly, jostled the three people beside her, and ventured out into her first metropolis—a location as far away from all she had ever known as her meager resources enabled. A place with an assurance of anonymity and seclusion.

If she could still muster gratitude for anything, it would be for this.

And in the only way anguish can be subdued, if not entirely vanquished, Esther never stopped moving during those first self-exiled months. She couldn't. She could not allow herself to sit idle, not even for a few minutes, for if she did, memories of him, of them, of what was, would deluge her mind. Emotions that she now strained to destroy or deny ever existed would take over, and she would be rendered helpless, powerless, as she had been and as she promised herself she would never be again.

She devoted her time to establishing a formula for sustenance. Sewing was her foundation. While she strove to grasp the rudiments of German speech, her willpower propelled her to walk up and down the streets of Köln seeking work. She entered every dress boutique and tailor shop she could find with samples of her handiwork as calling cards.

"*Schauen Sie*—Look!" she ordered those she met, holding up one of her tasteful blouses for inspection. The caliber of her skill and artistry supplanted language barriers.

She was rewarded with small assignments from four tailors after just two weeks. Basic tasks—shortening a dress and repairing a pants cuff—were soon replaced by more complex responsibilities, for her mastery was revealed in the simplest exercise. Her stitches were precise, her hems and seams were even, and the presentation of each project was flawless.

Stitching, basting, pleating, hemming, altering, darning, tucking, grading, embellishing, blocking, mending—these activities were second in nature only to breathing for Esther. Daily she sewed from the first hint of light to its last shadow to ensure her new clients received the quality work of which she alone was capable. No matter if her eyes burned, her neck strained, or her fingers ached without respite.

Here, in the windowless room cramped by a single bed, rickety table, rough wooden chair, and hot plate at the noisy, dilapidated youth hostel, Esther's stoic nature took root—growing deeper and thicker by each day's passing. She barely spoke, except as needed to secure a sewing assignment, purchase necessary supplies, or tell one of the other residents to quiet down. It was a raucous building, filled with too many young people, constant comings and goings, stair stompings, door slammings, and shouting. For much of the day, with her focused concentration on work, she was able to ignore any distractions. Such sounds were common to someone who had grown up in a home with twelve siblings. But when she couldn't, Esther found her nerves rattled, her posture tested. At these instances, she forbade the pent-up tears behind each eye to fall and quashed all but the most basic thoughts if one dared enter her head.

After darkness fell, she spent the better part of the night trudging along the riverfront. In 1923, Köln was a chiaroscuro palette of grays and blacks with a few patches of deep brown or the darkest blue breaking through the visual monotony. Most structures housed three stories; a few had four or even five. Although some were stout like marshmallows, and a handful of others were lean as poles, each was indistinguishable in design, color, and pattern from its neighbor. Esther faded easily into this cityscape, apart from the occasional streetlamp illuminating her face's stony glaze.

On these walks Esther contemplated how long it would take the cold, fast-moving Rhein to swallow the torment that she, as yet, could not fully ignore. The memory refused to dissipate: every feather, overcast, and edging stitch in her simple white dress; the posies in her hands; family and friends gathered in the town center, their excited chatter overlaid by *klezmer* music as the musicians frolicked; and she, standing unaccompanied under their tenderly crafted *chuppah*. Waiting. Until too much time passed. Until she could no longer remain there—alone. Surely the weight of Tadeusz's abandonment would supersede her ability to swim.

Over successive evenings, Esther marked a route that covered six kilometers in total. Once established, her steps never varied, every evening the same. She always headed toward the river via Trankgasse near the Kölner Dom, the city's glorious cathedral, and then crossed over Hohenzollern Bridge. When she reached its crown, water on either side, only sky above, Esther paused to relish the cool breeze of the river blowing on her face. One of the few joys she permitted herself.

From there she went north, where she plodded the full length of the cobblestone path that followed the Rhein's left bank. Her movements were precise, not unlike her stitches. Each step she took landed in the exact center of the unvarying stones. A low, wrought iron fence ran the river's expanse, providing a demarcation of choice. Her choice. To stay on one side or cross over to the other.

At the furthermost edge of Rheinpark, the area defined by its thick row of uniform trees, Esther would stop, squeeze her eyes tight, inhale deeply—and consider. A few minutes might pass or just a handful of seconds. Inevitably the mantra "He cannot prevail, he will not prevail" would resound in her thoughts. With a toss of her head, she would then turn around to retrace the course. Some nights she traversed this route twice, sometimes more. She moved steadily. Eyes most often directed downward with fixed attention on the patterned cobblestone. Esther never cared to look around to explore, for there was nothing of significance to see.

At the close of the day after darkness reigned, her evening unfolded exactly like the one before and the one that would follow.

Until—

—the fourth of December, a bitter Friday twilight with the promise of snow four months after Esther's arrival in this city. It began like the others: Esther treading, once again, the familiar course that bordered the Rhein. However, tonight her pace was limp. As she walked, she stretched, one arm extending long and high above her and then the other. She rounded her shoulders up and down and back and forth and rolled her head from side to side until her neck cracked. She pulled on each finger to extend the ligaments, and when she reached the last digit, she returned to the first. The weariness of her heart had been compounded by what had been a tedious day creating ten flawless buttonholes on each of two dozen long-sleeved white shirts for the members of a youth band. She was lost in thought, eyes focused on her feet and the cobblestones, as she reviewed the deft movements she had taken to ensure every stitch's identical length, when—

Esther stopped abruptly.

—she glanced up to take care she didn't overstep the sharp curve in the path and saw, juxtaposed against Köln's muddy landscape, streaks of luminous color burst through the trees barely fifty meters away. Like a beacon.

"*U va! Vos iz dos?* What in the world is this?" Esther said out loud, startled. Quickly she looked around to see if anyone had heard her or saw what she saw. She was alone. Focused again on the phenomenon before her, she thought: I've not seen this before here, or anything like it—anywhere!

Just ahead, in the grassy area near the north edge of Rheinpark, stood a small, poorly constructed wooden stand. Its only defense against the open sky was a square canopy of fabric—a cacophony of vibrant, garish colors—supported by four thick poles at each corner. Tiny mirrors and tinted glass were stitched throughout the material, along with fringe, sequins, ribbons, tassels, and beads.

Utterly incongruous in the surrounding dim setting, this was a vision from a dream gone awry—a sight she could never have possibly conceived. Intoxicating smells—pungent, sweet, musty, sharp, woody, comforting—wafted from within the stand. Esther inhaled deeply. Such a bouquet impelled further exploration.

She moved closer to peer inside and saw that the interior of the stand's makeshift plywood walls was covered in a motley array of printed pictures of people—or were they people? Strange characters! Perhaps these are images from a theatrical production taking place somewhere in the city? Esther mused. Or maybe a circus? Certainly nothing like this had ever come through Przeworsk.

Most of the images were of scantily dressed figures in brightly colored sheer fabrics. Some had far too many hands and arms, one had too many heads, and one face possessed three eyes. There was a picture of a woman who was completely blue and an image that seemed more monkey than man. Larger than the others was a rotund man with the head of an elephant.

Both women and men were heavily made up, with most covered in strange elaborate jewelry. Many wore outrageous headdresses. Whether seated on one large, stuffed cushion or on an ornamented throne or standing in front of a glowing orange background, all were encircled by a variety of objects, some recognizable, others not—books, shells, musical instruments, candles, bowls, crescent moon, pillows, swords, snakes, fruit, flowers—too extensive and too confusing to register on first look.

Esther's eyes widened, and she began to feel lightheaded. The lone man in the back of the booth smiled at her, exposing a stained, cracked front tooth. Thin, dark-skinned with thick black hair and a deeply angular face, he also looked like no one she had seen before.

In imprecise German with a peculiar accent, he asked, "*Würde Sie, einen Samosa mögen?* Would you a samosa like?"

Intrigued, though not knowing what he offered, she nodded, and he began to fry a small, doughy turnover. The strong smells that had originally lured her inside now overpowered the modest space.

As Esther waited, she once again scanned the gallery of images that filled these crude walls. Truly an archive of the bizarre, they were at once compelling and absurd. Her eyes came to rest on the elephant-headed man. He, alone, captivated her. Esther felt, in the oddest of ways, he was calling out, seeking her notice—demanding attention.

This man's—

Is it even a man? Esther wondered.

—large animal head and ears, wide mouth, four arms, broken left tusk, and huge protruding belly bordered on the comical. His body, seated with one leg folded inward and the second resting on the ground, was loosely draped in sheer yellow and red fabrics. He held a highly wrought axe in his upper right hand and some type of flower in his upper left. Another hand held a thick rope, while the fourth was outstretched, its palm facing toward her.

Esther inched closer and squinted. She observed that a mark, similar to a single cross-stitch but turned upright with short lines like flags on each end, was carved on his palm. A mouse staring at a tray that overflowed with what she thought were cookies sat near his left foot. The scene was outlandish but alluring nonetheless.

Esther took a step backward to grasp this image full on and stared steadily into the elephant-headed man's eyes. It was only a picture, this she understood; nevertheless, she was struck by a gentleness and profound compassion. She descended into his eyes. Consciousness of time and space evanesced. A forgotten sense of warm, soothing calm wholly embraced her. All feelings of suffering and loss dissipated.

And . . . I . . . looked deeply back into her eyes . . .

*In that penetrating gaze . . . I learned what had passed . . . and
saw what was to come. Her life's path could not be evaded . . .
but I knew from this point onward we would travel together.*

The man handed her the warm pastry, transporting Esther
back to the stand. She began to nibble the savory treat filled with
new tastes and impressions—she recognized potato and perhaps a
pea—when an abrupt shudder coursed through her body, as though
a hidden switch had been flipped on at the core of her being. Her
eyes began to water, and she let out a quick breath.

No doubt, she thought, from the heat of these unusual spices.

It was too soon.

She would not . . . no . . . could not understand . . .

I watched her walk away . . . and toward her future.

Back in her room at the youth hostel, Esther could not oust the
image of the elephant-headed man from her mind, nor could she
escape the feeling he had invoked within her.

She paced back and forth between the bed and the chair.
Three equal steps in either direction. She twisted her hair around
her index finger and chewed on the inside of her right cheek. Normally after these evening walks to the riverfront, she would simply
go to bed, exhausted from the day's work. But this night sleep would
not come. When she attempted to lie down or just sit, her legs would
tremble as though they had somewhere to be.

Oy, gevalt—Good grief, Esther thought. This is crazy—*Meshuge!*
If I can't sleep, I'll work. That's what I'll do. There is much to get
done, and I'm certain sewing will set me right. It always does.

So though the light in the room was poor, she began the next
day's assignments and gathered needles, threads, and fabrics. Esther

first lined up the necessary materials as she did each morning: measuring tape, shears, pins, seam ripper, and thimble. She matched the cloth with the proper thread, in thickness and color. Threading a blue strand in her milliner's needle, Esther began to baste a pleated skirt. But the gathers kept bunching, so she put that project aside and turned to another. Then another. And then one more.

Surprisingly, needle and thread were not able to bring composure. This had never occurred before. But all was not the same, something had shifted—of this Esther was sure. Yet she was not capable of putting into words what that difference implied or what exactly had changed.

For the first time since Esther had moved to Köln, she felt the need for someone—most especially one of her sisters—to talk to, to share what had happened. To help her understand.

"Am I going mad?" she asked out loud.

Questions overflowed—

Why do I feel so strange? It's like my head and body are no longer connected! What was that place? Those pictures? Did the stand even exist? Was my imagination playing tricks on me? I was overstrained from the day's work, after all. Perhaps it was some type of dreaming while being awake?

All the while knowing she had had no dreams since leaving Przeworsk.

It's so very late now, really the middle of the night. Perhaps that's why I can't concentrate on any of my assignments, she ruminated. For even the most straightforward task, re-seaming a pair of men's trousers and adding cuffs, seemed beyond her abilities. She kept making mistakes. Repeatedly she pulled the stitches out and began the process anew. Her slender, normally dexterous hands would not stop shaking; her fingers refused to cooperate.

"*Nit vider*—Not again!" Esther cried out after the fifth time she pricked herself. "*A chorbn*—Disaster!"

What is wrong with me? she wondered. This is crazy. Silly, silly me!

After two and a half hours passed without progress, Esther put down her needles and thread. "Enough!"

I must go back. I don't know why, this makes no sense at all. I must revisit that place. Perhaps I need to return for no other reason than to assure myself that the stand and the experience were, without a doubt, real.

For a second time that evening, she put on coat, hat, gloves, shoes, and scarf and, at a swift pace, retraced the nearly three kilometers to the site of the stand. In the middle of the night, the riverfront was devoid of people, serene. Until Esther was close to a hundred meters from the location she sought. From this distance she heard cries—screams—that became increasingly pronounced with each step forward.

Moving as stealthily as possible, Esther ran to the edge of the nearby park and hid behind a tree.

"*Helfen Sie mir!* Help me! Help me!" A male voice shouted, "*Bitte!* Please, please help me!"

Esther's body stiffened. Like stone. She could only watch as two Polizisten ferociously beat and kicked and pounded the same man who had so kindly offered her the doughy treat a few hours earlier. These supposed officers of the law shouted epithets at him:

"*Dreckiger Ausländer! Mistkerl! Arschloch!*"

"*Geh' zurück in deinen Dschungel!* Go back to your jungle!"

And they laughed and joked. Each goaded the other on.

Esther had never witnessed such violence. While able to acknowledge the horror of what was taking place, she willed herself not to physically react. Honing stoicism served her well here, allowing her to smother compassion and the desire to shout out, to let the man know he was not alone. For to reveal herself would only bring peril to her, and likely, even worse to him. So Esther shut her eyes tightly and tuned out all sounds. Her mind traveled back to the evening's earlier encounter and the sensations it invoked. This is the place she would like to remain.

As the man lay on the ground, writhing and bleeding, one of the officers poured gasoline, lit a torch, and set the stand ablaze—intensifying its color and vibrancy for a few moments until it, too, became black and gray and ash like the environment. Like all of Köln. Like Esther herself.

Charred bits of fabric and pictures flew in the wind.

All too soon, not a remnant remained—only a vision, a taste, and an enduring longing.

CHAPTER TWO

I followed her.

Not with footsteps or binoculars . . . camera or recorder . . . but with consciousness . . . proffering a depth of understanding known by too few.

It was a surveillance of souls.

She as yet could not acknowledge I was with her . . . but knew on the deepest level within that I shared her path. Draped in a bitter aloneness . . . defiant of memory and emotions . . . at times . . . of course . . . she would falter. And . . . every now and again . . . she would feel my soothing presence . . . when his face emerged in a crowd . . . when anguish rose . . . when her hand trembled . . .

We developed a rhythm . . . an arrangement of notes and scales . . . actions and thoughts . . . that united our distinct dispositions and . . . seemingly . . . disparate desires.

I remained at a respectful distance. Always . . . watching . . . observing . . .

Without reproach or judgment . . . as I knew her story and her destiny and accepted her choices . . . but was pleased when she sensed my murmurs extending help and guidance . . . and compassion . . .

I knew her mind and her every thought and continually applauded her fortitude born of that mortally inflicted wound . . . abandonment.

But there were no tears . . . never any tears . . .

Just an ever more indurate heart that stiffened her jaw . . . forming a chronic grimace on her lips.

Esther endeavored to get by. She subsisted on a meager diet—mostly bread, cheese, and beans—and wore the same three dresses in rotation, always neat and clean and stitched to perfection but without trimming or frill. Her one pair of shoes, sturdy and brown, would carry her far; her russet coat, hat, and gloves were certain to make it through quite a few winters, for the weather in this city was mild.

She worked tirelessly to build up her tailoring business. Early success with those few tailors had encouraged her, yet the need to secure work remained an ongoing challenge. There was much competition in a city as large as Köln, even for a skilled and gifted seamstress. Relentlessness was central to Esther's character, and she honed her shrewdness.

In addition to contacting tailoring businesses and dress shops, she used a portion of the small reserve of money she brought from Przeworsk to print leaflets. These Esther distributed in the neighborhoods with the largest houses and most expansive lawns—the areas of Köln where the air smelled the sweetest, for aromatic linden trees—

*Ah . . . the tree of truth . . . of course. Waiting . . . for its time
. . . to reveal . . .*

—lined each street, and pots with flowers and herbs bordered windows. The scents were reminiscent of her birthplace, and while Esther's rigid stance would slacken with each breath, she struggled to maintain her focus on what was before her rather than what had been—with him.

And she forced herself to resist reflection on that unsettling encounter and bewildering image. There was work to do.

She knocked on countless doors, and when she had the chance to see someone other than a maid, generally the woman of the house, Esther would hold out samples of her exquisite handiwork and say, "*Preiswert.* Fair price." If the person tried to turn away without inspection, Esther would insist, "*Billig!* Cheap!"

Not yet possessed of the most persuasive vocabulary, she would turn the garments inside out and with her fingers trace the perfect seams, refined collars, cuffs and pleats, and blind-stitched hems. She would point to the top of the pants sample to show there were neither gaps nor bulky lumps at the center back waist.

Esther would then give the woman the price sheet the hostel's caretaker had written out for her—in exchange for the repair of two shirts in need of new sleeves and a tattered pair of overalls. Her services were for the lowest prices possible. She had investigated local tailor shop menus and costs and had slashed their standard rates by nearly half. If she got this far, more often than not she would get a straightforward assignment with a quick turnaround to prove her abilities. Esther never failed to meet deadlines and always exceeded expectations.

While researching the local competition, Esther chanced on one tailor who agreed to give her German lessons twice weekly. In exchange, she cleaned this woman's shop on Tuesdays and Saturdays, refolding fabrics and stacking the pieces in order of texture, weight, and color—dark to light—and patterns—large to small. She reorganized spools of thread, as well as the buttons, needles, and myriad notions and supplies strewn throughout the floor after projects were completed. As part of her regular duties, she scrubbed floors and washed windows. The tailor had no interest in Esther's forte; she cared only that the shop was cleaned to satisfaction and orderly. Whenever she was told to ready clothes for a customer, Esther struggled to not look closely at the mediocrity of this tailor's output.

I can do better with closed eyes, she would think. To discourage herself from expressing such thoughts out loud or making suggestions, she would bite the inside of her right cheek. Esther had only one goal: to achieve a flawless command of German. To simply learn the basics of this complicated language would in no way suffice. She was confident fluency would lead to business success.

An advantage for her work . . . yes . . . but only one benefit among those even more vital . . .

"*Jetzt*—Now. *Nähen*," Frau Schneider said, as she redirected the lesson from basic food shopping terms to sentences about sewing. As a rule, each session focused on only one topic, but this Tuesday they had moved swiftly through the discussion of how to purchase fruits, vegetables, and basic necessities, and time remained.

"*Lassen Sie uns*—Let's review sewing tasks. This is most important, of course.

"*Hmm. Wo soll ich anfangen?* But where to begin? Where to begin?" Frau Schneider's speech was slow-paced as she tapped her fingers on the wooden table. "*Vielleicht*—Maybe. Hmm. No, no, you're not ready for that. Too advanced."

Esther bit down hard on the inside of her right cheek.

Oy, gevalt—Good grief! This woman is so slow, she thought. So much more could be accomplished in these hour-long sessions. But I can't let her see me fidget. Or have her perceive that I'm frustrated by her pace. Frau Schneider is not a professional teacher, after all. I have to remember she is doing me a favor, even if I must clean her wretched little shop. I could never afford a real language class.

"*Ach so*! Here is one—how many centimeters would you like the hem?"

More often than not, Esther emulated the words without error. She learned quickly. Typically, she would only need to repeat a sentence or term no more than three times to grasp its meaning and successfully replicate the enunciation. This language came easily to her. German shared an extensive vocabulary with her native Yiddish; its greatest challenges were syntax and alphabet. Esther worked diligently to prevail over what seemed irrational sentence structures with the pertinent verbs lined up in formation at the end. She did have a foundation—slim as it was—to fall back on. Her first two years of schooling, at ages four and five, had included a mandatory German class once each week. During those years, Poland and Galicia were still part of the Austro-Hungarian Empire, and German was the official language. However, when the government changed, few in her *shtetl* had any use for it, and what had been learned was quickly forgotten. Now, from the recesses of her mind, Esther found she could forage remnants of correct pronunciations and tense formulas.

With repetition, diligence, and time, an acquired fluency would soon enough be her reward. Each day while she sewed, or walked to and from appointments to pick up or drop off assignments, or lay in bed longing for sleep to arrive, she would practice words and terms, sentences, and grammar patiently, over and over and over again.

Her determination to perfect this new language kept her mind occupied during the times she was not concentrating on the particulars of a sewing issue or strategizing new ways to secure projects and make more money. It served as a distraction and aided her underlying challenge of forgetting.

As the months passed, Esther's fortification continued to grow tall and thick around and within her. She remained unwavering in her resolve to survive at all costs—to continue on, as though to spite life itself. Forward motion was essential. Stagnation would imply that his action—Tadeusz's unbearable act, devoid of heart or consciousness—had wholly consumed her. And that was unacceptable.

She held fast to her mantra, "He cannot prevail, he will not prevail." A potent reserve of strength arose from her depths. The person whom she had turned to—leaned on—shared everything with—was gone. She had to carry on self-reliant, without wants or desires. This is the better way, Esther would think. I have no need for another—ever! In the bitterest way, I've learned that people so often—most often—disappoint.

Thus she remained in self-imposed solitude, not interested in friends or relationships of any sort. She spoke only when absolutely necessary, and then mostly about cloth and color, size, shape, and measurements, or about supplies, those items essential for sewing, eating, or bathing.

However, not surprisingly, every once in a while, Esther's thoughts would roam. When they did drift away from thread and needles and their utilitarian uses and inventive potential, it was toward that most perplexing evening, just four months after her arrival, and the encounter and image for which there were still no words of explanation. This was the only reminiscence she allowed herself. And then, for only a few moments. Nothing more. There was work to be done.

Esther never returned to her childhood home of Przeworsk, Poland, not even for a brief visit. No longer able to offer hearth and home, it was now only a place of lost innocence and bankrupt hopes. Her image of that once beautiful, fertile town, personifying the assurance of unlimited possibilities, had dissolved into a wasteland of disappointments.

She had written to her parents soon after arriving in Köln to inform them of where she now lived, and every few months she sent a brief note to assure family members she was out of harm's way and had settled into a new life. These were as light and hopeful as she could feign.

"*Alts iz git.* All is good." Esther closed each message with these mendacious words. "*Kh'bin zeyer tsufriden do tsu zayn.* I am happy to be here."

Toward the end of her first year in Köln, Esther answered a late afternoon knock on her hostel room door. Strange, she thought as she placed the skirt she was repairing on the table and took the few steps from chair to door. No one comes here. My rent isn't overdue, and clients don't know where I live.

She turned the knob, cracked open the door, and looked out. There, on the other side, was Tonka, the youngest of her twelve siblings. Sweet, impressionable, adventurous Tonka. Esther's favorite. A dark-haired version of herself.

"*A vunder*—Surprise!" the young woman shouted. And jumped up to engulf her big sister in an embrace and cover her face in kisses. "I've missed you beyond words. Home is impossibly lonely and dull without you. We all miss you enormously."

Esther's arms never left her sides, and her stance remained stiff, rooted in place.

"*Vos tustu do?* What are you doing here?" she asked, her face taut, her Yiddish without expression.

"Oh, Esther, our lives are not the same without you. Not a day goes by that we don't talk about you. Talk about how much we miss you. *Azoy fil*—So much! How everything is different—wrong—without you. We want you to return home." The words and hopes cascaded out of Tonka's mouth. "Nothing would make me happier, nothing would make any of us happier, than for you to come back to Przeworsk with me. You know we are all extremely sad, devastated really, about what happened. To this day, we can't believe what Ta—"

"*Her oyf*—Stop! Don't mention him, that name, to me—ever!"

They were still standing on either side of the doorway, and the potency of Esther's voice carried down the hall, tempting other lodgers to peer through slightly opened doors in curiosity.

Appalled by this invasion, Esther yanked Tonka inside and said, "You can spend tonight, but you must leave in the morning. Just when the sun comes up. Can't you see"—pointing to the piles of clothes all around—"I'm very busy and I have no room for you? There is no time to entertain!" She stomped her foot as churning emotions deep within—loss, grief, desolation—strained to rise to the surface. The floor reverberated in all corners. She bit down hard on the inside of her right cheek.

"*Ober, Ober*—But—" Tonka pleaded. "Please, dear sister, I only—"

"*Nayn*—No!" Esther shouted. "I will hear no more from you." She turned her back and picked up the skirt and needle.

Stunned by her sister's reaction, Tonka cowered in the corner, distraught. Who is this person? she wondered. How could my once vibrant sister, my adored Esther, have become so hardened and aloof? So harsh? It will be impossible to persuade her to return home. Tears swathed Tonka's face.

No more words passed between them that evening. A weeping, despondent Tonka left before sunrise and carried home the news of Esther's changed character. Her parents and siblings felt impotent. They had no frame of reference as to how to respond, to help, or how to react. All behavior—first Tadeusz's and then Esther's—was out of character, and they were baffled.

Nevertheless, her family continued to regularly reach out as best they could. Her parents and siblings sent cards and letters often, filled with stories of life from their *shtetl*. Mostly, Esther let these missives pile up in a corner, unopened. But one day, there was an unusually thick envelope, and she decided to skim the pages. Her mother was the author of this letter, and she wrote exhaustively about how generous the butcher had been in saving the fattest chicken for their Sabbath meal and details of the honey cake—with recipe—Aunt Fannie had made for Jakob's recent birthday. "I know you won't be surprised, but Rose is refusing to study. She gets so easily distracted, and now she's falling far behind in her schoolwork, most especially mathematics. Might you have any suggestions? Estherle, you were always good at getting her to focus." Her mother went on to portray with great amusement how the wheelbarrow had broken, once again, and that they had scraped together their *zlotys* to have a new one constructed.

With a grunt, Esther tossed the letter on the mushrooming pile. She had read enough and returned to repair the inseams of the tweed pants that must be delivered by three o'clock. When the mound of letters, cards, and notes grew too high and spilled over, she put them out with the rubbish.

No one in Esther's family understood that a heart—her heart—once so full and bright and vital, filled with the desires and the dreams of tomorrow, could be decimated by a single act—and that of someone else's doing.

Ah . . . it is so very difficult . . . so challenging . . . the most challenging situation many would say . . . when someone's action . . . a spontaneous irrational act . . . dictates events and directions that change the course . . . the hope . . . in fact the destiny of another's life.

It was not possible for her to go back in time . . . amend history . . . change that moment . . . that split second when fear took command . . . grabbed his head and his passion . . . shook his soul to its core and his life . . . her life . . . their promise . . . was lost.

It was Tadeusz's fear that redirected Esther's life course. His fear of love . . . true love . . . that which humans most desire and that which can cause the most pain. Far too often . . . fear supersedes truth.

Fear is a dark mask that buries perspective and reason and . . . yes . . . even true love . . . and repeatedly leads one astray . . .

That mask had taken possession of Tadeusz.

Certainly . . . in some cases it is part of a divine plan . . . however . . . more often it is fear that sets a course far afield of what our Dharma . . . true destiny . . . had planned. To flee because of one's fears . . . to run away from that which terrifies yet is most desired . . . this is surrendering to The Fates.

Of course it is understood . . . as a consequence of Tadeusz's action . . . Esther's heart would be affected . . . that her heart would become frozen . . . for it is the center . . . the very core of life.

And it is no accident of divine design . . . that the heart is the first organ of the body to be created . . . and the last to die.

One night, not long after Tonka's intrusion, Esther could not sleep. She could not get comfortable, and her thoughts would not quiet. She lay first on one side and then the other. She tried her back and her stomach. No position led to slumber. She tried to distract herself with grammar and new vocabulary, but her resistance was low and her energy spent. Her mind attempted to direct her back to the encounter on the riverfront, the makeshift stand and the striking image of the elephant-headed man, but she shook her head sharply and tossed herself to the other side of the bed. No, Esther thought, squeezing her eyes tightly, no time for such nonsense. I must sleep.

Out of her control, other images floated to the fore and took command of the here and the now. Sounds drifted back to the day—that day—that moment—when everything changed.

Esther recalled the faint but evocative strains of *klezmer* music as though it had all occurred yesterday.

Without effort—

And with my assistance . . .

—she was there.

In accordance with the customs, musicians would lead the wedding procession to the town's main square, where the marriage would be performed, stopping at the homes of the bride and groom to accompany them on this journey of promise. Invited guests, and most likely those who were not, would join in along the way, announcing to all the festivities were underway.

However, as Esther and Tadeusz lived at opposite ends of their *shtetl,* and in consideration of the elder members of their families who could not walk far or long, they strayed from tradition slightly. They decided separate sets of musicians would lead each to the wedding site. Though all considered this logical and practical, Esther and Tadeusz secretly cherished the idea that for this one day, Przeworsk would be theirs and theirs alone. Everywhere and everyone enlivened with their celebration and music and beatitude.

Esther stood in the front room surrounded by the female members of her family and close girlfriends. She looked tiny and delicate in the simple, flowing white dress with the laced neckline she had designed and lovingly sewn, imbuing the sheer fabric with her passion for this wonderful young man who had chosen her. The one who completed her sentences and shared her heart. It had taken more than five months to finish the dress to her satisfaction, but she spent the time savoring the moment when he would first see her wearing it. Her sisters had wanted to help, but she was the more talented seamstress—adamant that every stitch be the same as the next—not always graciously refusing assistance. Though rarely revealed, Esther was resolute about getting what she wanted, the way she wanted it.

All the same, caught up in their excitement for her, she did yield to their demands that they participate in some way. On the morning of her wedding, after giving each sister a tight hug, she let them braid her thick blonde hair with sheer ribbons of white and yellow and fashion the bouquet of white posies she now caressed in her hands. While the girls fussed over her, Esther's gaze rested on her and Tadeusz's *ketubah*—their marriage contract—with the Tree of Life's branches that she had adeptly drawn to frame the Aramaic words ensuring the husband's obligations of protection, commitment, and honor.

She smiled deeply as images of Tadeusz framed her thoughts: their encounter—the bakery—*dos ershte bagegenish,* first date—their picnics—saunters—the lake—first kiss—his homemade *hamen-tashn*—her borsht—laughing, always laughing—shared dreams and plans—meeting her family—meeting his family—their meadow. The time was nigh.

When the lively melodic tones of the fiddler and accordionist arrived at the front door, beckoning her outside, she eagerly joined in and let them lead her forward. Walking slowly but deliberately, Esther felt every crunch of the fallen and dried September leaves below her white-laced slippers. The path was animated with a rich palette of reds, browns, and greens. When they were within sight of the square, Esther beamed, delighting in the red rose petals strewn along the way.

As she took her place, Esther glanced around quickly and saw the *badkhn* give her a large, warm smile. The deeply lined face of their revered *rebbe* wore a solemn expression. Her family members, all fourteen of them, standing side by side, displayed a range of sentiments that matched their individual characters, nearly forcing a loud chortle she had to strain to conceal. *Klezmer* music encircled them all.

Then she waited.

Expectantly.

Beneath the canopy they had created together—for this day—for their ceremony.

The *chuppah's* covering was of hand-spun, hand-woven, thick white cotton, interspersed with tiny threads of colorful silk Esther had managed to scrimp from tailoring jobs for wealthy customers. Five centimeters of blue thread from a man's dress coat. Ten centimeters of light violet from one summer dress. Nearly twelve centimeters of a golden yellow from another. Threads from party skirts, trousers, fancy shirts, and frilly cuffs were scattered throughout, creating a playfulness and gaiety Esther felt echoed their union.

The poles were made from branches taken from spruce trees in the woods close to their town. Just by the meadow alongside the lake where they had picnicked and swum, first kissed and made love. Tadeusz had selected four branches of similar height, weight, and shape and spent hours meticulously sanding them smooth. He had oiled them until they glistened.

This was all done in the evenings at Esther's family home, where they had sat by the fire with the sisters sewing or knitting, needlepointing or weaving, and with her brothers regaling them with jokes and songs and tall tales of misguided exploits.

The bends and curves of the branches were purposely not straightened, for Esther and Tadeusz believed they more accurately reflected the unknown. Those twists and turns that made life an adventure and not a preordained path of complacency.

The cloth had been tied to the poles with streaming silk ribbons of purple and green—their favorite colors—braided together. It was an unnecessary and frivolous extravagance in the years that followed the Great War, but one Esther refused to do without to complete her vision. Her visual metaphor of their life and their future.

As she waited, Esther dreamily reviewed the events leading up to this day and all that their future held before them. She did not notice the passing time and that the second procession, and with it Tadeusz, had not yet arrived. As her mind journeyed over the past few months, it struck her he had been acting preoccupied, even perhaps somewhat distant. But she had been so excited and consumed with the myriad wedding details, on top of her sewing work and other responsibilities, she barely took notice.

When she saw him on Friday, right before *shabbes,* he was his usual loving and joyful self. But in parting, Tadeusz had gently touched her right cheek and said, "*Vos vel ikh ton on dir.* What will I do without you?"

Too full of the plans for the weekend ahead, she had merely thought he had misspoken, intending to say "would." Or perhaps she had misheard him.

Standing quietly, Esther realized she should not have arrived at the *chuppah* first—Tadeusz was supposed to be waiting for her. They had carefully timed the musicians for this to work out. As she watched her brother run off to investigate and began to hear mutterings from the guests, Esther felt a pain surge through her.

Jakob came running back. He shouted, "He's gone! *Tadeusz iz gegangn!* Tadeusz is gone! He's packed his bags and he's left!"

Then he added, "And Sarah"—revealing the name of the daughter of the town's wealthiest merchant—"*Sara iz oykh antloyft*! Sarah's gone too!"

When the truth of the news registered within her, Esther's body hardened, her vision glazed over. She fought back the tears and took in a sharp breath that would not be released for years to come. One hundred eyes watched her, searching—for a reaction, an emotion, a response. None could be found. Only two people would know the irreversible devastation to her soul.

Holding head high and still clinging to the small bouquet, Esther walked back to the family home, neither quickly nor slowly. She went to the room shared with four of her sisters and decisively closed the door behind her.

She was left alone, her sisters sleeping on the floor with coverlets in the front room, the whole family speaking in hushed voices and tiptoeing when moving from table to chair. It was as though a death had occurred and they had begun sitting *shiva.*

These are the days of mourning for the Jewish people. Or perhaps . . . it is for my Father . . . my dear . . . dear Father . . . Shiva . . . worshipped by so many . . . as destroyer . . . not unlike what you call death . . . but . . . also worshipped as the restorer.

Destroyer . . . restorer . . . like two sides of a coin . . . death . . . life . . . same . . . same . . . just the same . . . always the same . . . but different.

During the next two days, her family listened intently for any movement made in the room. There were few: an occasional turn on the bed or a slow walk across a creaking floorboard. She did not, could not, respond to offers of food or drink.

Esther left during the deepest part of the third night. She crawled out the bedroom window with only a satchel and an integrant of her dignity.

The next morning a makeshift shrine was found on her otherwise empty bed. There lay the bouquet of dead posies and a scrawled note saying—

Kh'vel shraybn.

. . . .

I will write.

The centerpiece was the result of her handiwork of these past days: a neat pile of deliberately and methodically torn colored paper. Each piece the same size and shape as the others—just like Esther's stitches.

It was the remains of their *ketubah.*

Once in a while, Esther experienced a pang or cramp in her chest. Sometimes palpitations. She grew accustomed to these and did her best to squelch their effect. *Ach,* Esther would think, such a nuisance.

Time did not lessen their influence; she just became better and better at denying their presence.

> *This is an illusion. Things adjust . . . shift . . . but never go away. The energy of true love is eternal.*

CHAPTER THREE

An image . . .
painted of memory and dust.
A feeling . . .
and a hope (that could not be) imagined.
Despair dissipated . . .
momentarily.

....

As soon as she received payment for her first significant proj-ect—to design and sew a *bar mitzvah* suit for the local grocer's son—Esther was finally able to leave the hostel. With these few additional *Reichsmarks,* she moved into a rented basement room in the Metscher family's crowded home, which offered a larger space and somewhat more privacy. Located on a highly trafficked street in Köln's inner city, and with three young children, the setting was loud and boisterous, frequently bordering on chaotic. Not dissimilar to the environment of her childhood home. Although their own resources were slim, this family was kind.

"*Schließen Sie sich uns bitte zum Abendessen an.* Please join us for supper," the mother would bid. "We have plenty of soup and bread for all."

On occasion, Herr Metscher would inquire, "Would you like to sit with us this evening? There is lots of wood, the fire is warm, and we thought we would play cards for a while."

"*Danke, aber*—Thank you, but I have much work to do" was Esther's standard response. Sometimes she would add details about a particular assignment—the need to lengthen the sleeves of a man's suit jacket or put ruffles on a little girl's party dress—but always she declined.

The solitary companionship of her four walls beckoned. This place did not make her nostalgic. Esther was clear that part of her life—family—was complete. Home was now without definition, and this was her preference. She was determined to expunge her past identity. She studied to perfect her German in all spare moments. Her pronunciation became impeccable. The precise structure of sentences remained the challenge, for there seemed to be no rationale.

"The verb goes where?" she questioned repeatedly. "Here it is at the end of the sentence, and here it is in the middle?" In spite of the language's convolution, she practiced tenaciously. Esther's commitment to pass as a native—to begin anew—never wavered.

And of course, she was driven to persist through her expert sewing talents. Besides her own customers, she pursued an opportunity to apprentice with a master furrier. Although the training was without pay, and often she had to start as early as five in the morning, Esther knew such a distinctive skill in her repertoire would give her a necessary edge over much of her competition.

Her strategies impressed me. Unbeknownst to Esther she was putting the elements in place that would serve her very survival . . . in the future.

Never pause—never rest deeply—never be idle. Thoughts, memories, reflections had power and could overtake her, bringing back the searing pain of loss—the loss of her beloved—with renewed force. So in lieu of rumination about what had happened—and the whys of Tadeusz's action—she soldiered on, submerging her history, as best she could, with a fusion of grit and necessity.

Work was her salvation, and she kept herself as occupied with as much of it as possible for as much of each day and as late into each night as her fingers would bear.

In spite of this, on the scarce chance there was an interlude—and this might possibly occur while walking to the market or heading home from an appointment with a tailoring customer—solitude engaged her. Only then would a recollection float to the fore.

One would imagine that this memory . . . this thought . . . would be of him . . . of Tadeusz . . . of the love shared . . . of the love lost . . .

But at this time . . . during these years . . . that story was buried too deep to mine.

Esther's thoughts strayed to a singular evening, nearly two years ago, one with a distinctive palette of gray, black, and ash in setting and in circumstance. One that embodied wonder and a spark of recognition, although perception without comprehension. For in the midst of that evening's bleak twilight, like a flare within a foggy sphere, had stood a garishly decorated, rickety wooden stand emanating color and vibrancy and energy not previously known or possibly imagined that had drawn her like iron to magnet. The crowded space filled with exotic, intoxicating scents. Over the entry, a scrawled sign introduced *INDISCHES ESSEN*—INDIAN FOOD. Images covered the walls—a portrait gallery of the odd and the bizarre and the obscure and the indefinable and the impossible. And one in particular—

Me

—that stood out to her, that whispered to her, that softly spoke her name and sang her truth.

Did it really happen? Did the stand in fact exist? And what is it about the elephant-headed man that I can't get out of my head after all this time? Esther would wonder, for experiences like that were not natural. So very strange, for it was merely a picture and nothing more.

Or was it?

I make such connections with many . . . in fact . . . with each and every one of you . . . and often . . . but most do not feel my energy . . . or simply ignore.

Yet . . . with Esther . . . the bond formed was indisputable and resonated throughout and between our realms.

So much had passed; still, she was certain it was more than just a sweven. She had not imagined the scene, the experience, or most especially, the connection made there. Of this she was adamant. While highly skilled and inventive with pattern and thread and capable of making smart party dresses out of odds and ends, bits and scraps, Esther was not worldly or sophisticated. She could not be considered a woman of vision, or one of magical thinking. Esther had only ever lived a practical life, an ordinary life. One secluded and confined within borders of daily tasks, necessities, and demands.

I would sometimes be a tad mischievous . . . when I could . . . when I thought it would help ease her ache . . . for just a moment . . .

When no one else was around . . . I would encircle her with gentle whiffs of my home . . . the food . . . the air . . . the cities . . . the land. These times would surprise her . . . take her off guard . . . yet ignite her senses . . . revive her . . . they would not let her forget. And then . . . she would . . . ever so slightly . . . smile.

Once, and only one time, on a day when she had finished her assignments early, when she had purchased needed supplies and had just picked up a customer's black silk pants and dress shirt to be mended, Esther took this unique interlude without obligation to investigate further. To test herself and remembrance. To find answers without questions. She was a few blocks from the Köln *Bibliothek*. She had passed the narrow, stately brick building often; it was at the edge of the neighborhood, on Josef-Haubrich-Hof. She had considered venturing in more than once, but always her days were otherwise filled with responsibilities.

This uncommon day, curiosity guided her through its heavy wooden doors. Esther wanted to know more—to learn something, to learn anything—to understand her strange, if not irrational, interest, this calling to a place and a land and a concept disconnected to the realities of life.

Not surprisingly, the *Bibliothek's* selection of geography books—those of other countries, most particularly countries outside the European continent—was wanting. She wandered up and down the aisles without result. The undertaking soon daunted her, for she couldn't understand its systems or organization. Frustrated, Esther marched over to the large, imposing desk and the woman seated behind it and asked, in a too loud voice, "*Können Sie mir helfen, ein Buch über Indien zu finden?* Can you help me find a book on India?" She remembered to add the word "please" after the fact.

"What kind of book?" the librarian inquired. "*Geschichte Indiens?* India's history? Cooking? Architecture? Travel?"

Esther shook her head at each topic.

Only when the librarian suggested, "Perhaps a picture book," did Esther finally nod. This will make the most sense, she thought. For it was an image—a fantastical image—she could not get out of her head.

The librarian went into the stacks and returned with the one book in residence on this faraway place in space and imagination called *Indien*. It was thin in size and content.

Esther carried the book to a corner table at the back of the library. She sat down and slowly turned each page in hope of finding what she was seeking, although not at all confident she knew what that was. A few of the pictures, mostly of landscapes and oddly designed structures, offered an impression of the stand that remained alive and vital in her mind's eye. But Esther could not find anything that resembled the curious portraits she recalled more vividly, most particularly of the one that was half man, half elephant—

Me . . .

CHAPTER FOUR

A-U-M
"A" represents the waking state . . .
"U" the dreaming state . . .
"M" the state of deep sleep.
AUM in its entirety,
followed by a moment of silence, represents the Shanti—
the peace beyond understanding.

Aum Shri Ganeshaya Namah
(Praise to Lord Ganesha)

. . . .

I am Ganapati . . .
son of Shiva and Parvati.
Lord Ganapati . . . Lord of the Ganas . . . the celestial ones . . .
who watch over all . . . protect all.

I am Vighnahara . . . Remover of Obstacles . . . I am Siddhipriya . . .
Bestower of Wishes and Boons . . . Buddhinath . . . God of Wisdom
. . . Swaroop . . . Lover of Beauty . . . Uddanda . . . Nemesis of Evils

and Vices. And . . . I am Kaveesha . . . Master of Poets . . . I have one hundred and eight names.

Most know me by Ganesha . . . Ganeshe . . . God of the People.

But . . . truly . . . sadly . . . most do not know me at all . . . or even acknowledge my very existence.

There are countless stories . . . legends really . . . describing how I came into being. Explaining my unique form . . . part human . . . part elephant. Some say I came through my mother's loins . . . others through her mind . . . that I came of a wish . . . a desire . . . to bring harmony and prosperity to all who reside here . . . Calm.

But . . . I came through a sound. A sound so pure and clear and true . . . it has been known so far to only a very few . . .

AUM was my birth canal.

And I came out dancing at the first flicker of dawn . . . dancing with a joy and a passion and a freedom not yet to be matched. I long for partners in my movements . . . but the time has not yet arrived. So I dance . . . for universality . . . for unity . . . for the supreme God force present within all things . . . within all.

I smile broadly, ecstatically.

When I dance. . . I dance for all . . . as I am here for all . . . I am here for you.

I have been here a long time . . . and I know I must remain here longer still . . . for this is the Kali Yuga . . . and I am needed here now more than ever. For this is the period of the greatest . . . darkest evil of man unto man. The time when avenues of possibility and opportunity and hope appear to be cut off . . . with only despair and desperation emerging in one's path.

But truly . . . this is only an illusion. It is all an illusion. Yet I remain visible to those willing to see me . . . to let me guide them on.

Esther saw me . . . although she as yet does not know who I am or why I am here for her. Deep within her . . . she recognized me . . . and carried me forward to accompany her . . . to support her . . . to help her triumph over that which took place and that which is to come.

This is the Kali Yuga . . . and the destruction and horror that lies in wait for her will be more immense than the human mind can fathom . . . more than the celestial ones could conceive. And we remain in the darkest part of that night . . . when even the stars sleep . . . when the forces of ignorance are in full bloom . . . and the subtle faculties of the soul are obscured.

The depth of Kali's rage strikes each corner of the globe.

And . . . can strike in the very core of one's life . . . testing heart . . . testing faith . . . as with Tadeusz.

Ah . . . Kali . . . the black one . . . the dark one . . . Kali Ma . . . is the mother . . . the goddess . . . of destruction and dissolution. She . . . alone . . . commands transition.

And in contrast to the way I dance to hope and triumph . . . She steps out with Her left foot . . . sword in right hand . . . and dances to death. Burial sites and cremations are Her platform. And Her followers . . . yes . . . She has many . . . dance with Her. Playing their flutes and pungis and kabbas and banging their tablas in revelry . . . in awe . . . of Her power . . . Her force . . . kicking up the ashes that follow Her everywhere. The footprints of Her destruction.

Her disciples . . . sing in ecstasy . . .

"Because You love cremation grounds
I have made my heart one
so that You
Black Goddess of the Burning Grounds
can always dance there.
No desires are left, Ma, on the pyre
for the fire burns in my heart,
and I have covered everything with its ash
to prepare for Your coming.
As for the Conqueror of Death, the Destructive Lord,
He can lie at Your feet. But You, come, Ma,
dance to the beat; I'll watch You
with my eyes closed."

Ah . . . six million . . . twelve . . . no . . . the numbers will be unfathomable . . . the loss . . . too expansive . . . the pain . . . cavernous . . .

And for so many . . . so very many . . . for those who will remain . . . those who will endure . . . it will appear to be the end . . . the end of everything . . . the end of this world.

I take a deep breath and sigh, faintly.

But there is no end . . . no real end . . . in the same way there is no real beginning. It can be said . . . in all candor . . . that the end of the world never is and never can be anything . . . but the end of an illusion.

Yes . . . Kali brings forth destruction. Yes . . . this is true. But this includes the destruction of ignorance . . . the end of unconsciousness. She maintains our world order and blesses and frees those who strive for knowledge . . . for verity.

For Kali's force . . . and Kali's will . . . alone . . . bring forth renewal.

Oh Kali . . . my Kali . . . is so reviled . . . so misunderstood . . . so terribly misunderstood. So many perceive Her as hideous . . . evil . . . unforgiving. But while She kills and destroys . . . She also creates and nourishes. Kali is the Goddess of Time . . . a concept few understand.

She is the Goddess of the transformation you call death . . . the power of time that devours all. But we must learn that when time is transcended . . . there is only the eternal night of unbounded tranquility . . . bliss. By Her magic we see good and we see bad . . . but in truth there is neither.

The world . . . this world . . . this whole world . . . and all we see . . . it is the play of Maya . . . the veil that lays over all.

So . . . now you know . . . now you see . . . death is not an end. This is important . . . it is key. This is truth. Death is merely transition.

There will be no end for Esther and the others . . . a passage . . . perhaps . . . a shift . . . but not an end.

Life . . . IS . . . precious . . . sacred . . .
Life is an illusion . . .
Kali is destruction . . . dissolution . . .
Kali is renewal . . . rebirth.

CHAPTER FIVE

Unceasing days of darts and darning, seams and hems,
yokes, eyelets, scallops—
backing and beading, pinking and pleating,
ribbing and ruffles,
appliqué and overlay,
for dresses and skirts and camisoles and capes—
pants and shirts and vests and suits,
cummerbunds and sashes—
made of lace and velvet, cotton and wool,
silk, on rare occasion, silk
Buttons and zippers and snaps and ribbon—
Thread connecting all.
Thread weaving through fabric and days—
Thread—
Ceaseless days—unceasing.

....

ours accumulated. The sun rose and set. One season gave way to the next. And whether stormy or snow, rain, hail or warmth, each day passed much like the one before it.

1925 came and went, without singularity or punctuation. As did 1926 and the years that followed—

—until 1929, that is.

Esther's resolve—to survive, if not surmount, her deep-rooted anguish—never wavered. Embitterment and ire maintained their grip and continued to fuel and define every action and all decisions. The world she had composed was basic but functional, for her needs—her only needs—were straightforward: tailoring assignments with fabric or fur and thread, sustenance, shelter. In no case, however, was work easily acquired. Even after these many years. Even with concerted and innovative efforts and expanded contacts. New hurdles appeared. Challenges abounded.

> *And always . . . she endeavored to conceal the emotions . . . the memories that lay within. But she could neither hide . . . nor deny . . . herself from me. I helped when I could . . . placing a Pfennig or two . . . sometimes a Reichsmark . . . in her path or holding the scale up when the grocer weighed the cheese. More often . . . I watched her actions closely . . . understanding her choices . . . her strategies . . . her need to do all on her own . . . by herself.*

> *And then . . . but not to my surprise certainly.*

A time did come, as Esther approached her middle twenties, that to struggle on her own no longer felt compulsory. Perhaps it was the tedium of routine or an outcome of too many years of hurt and festering spite. Conceivably it came about through an unacknowledged loneliness, suppressed below epidermis, muscle, and bone. Regardless of its source, Esther grew exasperated by the daily difficulties of living with others, most especially a family with loud children. Yet she could never gather the capital necessary to secure separate living quarters.

At this juncture I watched her marry . . . Abraham . . . a man she did not love but who was devoted to her . . . and did not know the difference.

He was a quiet, simple man, a cobbler with his own small shop on Kämmergasse. Esther had passed it a few dozen times when on the way to a furrier for whom she sometimes worked. She ventured inside the day she needed assistance with a client's pair of shoes.

"*Hallo,*" Esther said. "*Können Sie mir helfen?* Can you help me?" She tried to gain the attention of the man bent over a large machine at the shop's rear.

"*Bitte!*" she added, remembering to append the expected politeness.

When he did not immediately turn around, Esther shouted "*Hallo*" a second time, loudly and with impatience. Her sharp slaps—three times—on the wooden counter rebounded against the walls and quiet.

Startled, the man looked up. When he saw Esther, his eyes twinkled playfully. A smile formed on his face, one seemingly without end.

No man since Tadeusz, or before, had looked at her in the way Abraham did upon this first encounter. Esther, surprised by his overt attraction, simply said, "I have a pair of shoes that must be covered in this fabric, to match this dress. Can you do this?"

As though he had not heard her request, he said, "*Guten Tag,* my name is Abraham. This is my shop."

Esther did not introduce herself, merely repeated her need and added, "Can you help me?"

But her mind moved quickly. This is interesting, she considered.

"*Ja, ja,* of course I can do this. But please. What is your name?" Abraham asked.

"Esther. *Mein Name ist* Esther Grünspan."

"It is your first time in my shop. I would have remembered you," Abraham said, a tremble in his voice emerging.

Esther ruminated. He is not so horrible to look at, and he owns this shop. He must be very successful. And our work is complementary. There are many possibilities a union of this kind could offer. Most especially financial. I would not have to work so hard all the time.

Outwardly, Esther's actions were businesslike; coquetry was no longer in her lexis of words or emotions. Abraham was not put off by her manner. He stammered, "*Vielleicht*—perhaps—perhaps I could take you for a meal sometime?"

She responded with a nod, no smile, no hesitation. Just an affirmation—to herself, really, more than to him—that this was the direction in which she needed to head.

A date was set for the following Sunday.

"*Erzählen Sie mir von Ihrer Familie*. Tell me about your family," Abraham said carefully, his manner formal, as though he had rehearsed what to say and how to say it. They were seated on a bench across from the Kölner Dom's ornate public entrance. Esther had never allowed herself to consider the cathedral—she had only ever hurried by—and was distracted by its immensity and the spires, pointed arches, and sumptuous carvings that covered its façade. Abraham had to repeat his question before she realized he was speaking.

"There are thirteen of us children," she replied. "Only five boys. At twenty-three, I am the second oldest. I come from Przeworsk, in Poland, and mine is a family of exceptional tailors. For generations. I have lived in Köln now for six years."

"*Warum*—Why did you come here? What led you to this city?"

"It is of no importance. That time is no more," she said as evenly as possible.

When Abraham made another attempt to learn more, Esther had to bite on the inside of her cheek in order to not snap at him. Be polite, she scolded inwardly. I will be polite, I can be polite, she thought, as if in response, but he has no need to know what has passed.

Abraham decided it best not to question further. Out of respect. He was a kind and gentle soul, truly the sort who would go out of his way to help an elderly woman cross a busy road or give a hungry beggar his last bite of bread. He prided himself on being understanding and accepting.

This man seems a bit slow, Esther observed, perhaps even foolish. But I believe he will be useful. *Ein reicher Mann!* He must have money if he owns a shop and can maintain it. I am sure his resources coupled with my earnings will make for an easier life. I am ready for some help. I have worked so hard for so long, and I am in the very same place! I'm sure I can manage him, and I can tell he is attracted to me. He will be lucky to have me! He will not find anyone more capable than me.

Studying Esther out of the corner of one eye, not wanting to stare, Abraham, too, reflected on the situation. She's a peculiar one, this woman. She is not a beauty or especially warm, but she conveys a force of will I have never experienced. It is at the core of her. I can't imagine where this comes from; she refuses to share her circumstances. She is not like me at all, and I find this very appealing.

Her background and story were irrelevant to their future life together, so he never tried to learn more than these threads of her past. Abraham was simply grateful he had found this woman and she accepted him.

Conversely, Esther learned all there was to know about this man.

"*Und Sie*—And you, what of your family?" she asked, thinking it proper to inquire.

"My family name is Klein, so I am Abraham Klein," he said, smiling, "and I am twenty-six, three years older than you. This is good, no? I was born and have lived all my years in Köln. In the same four-square blocks that make up the Jewish Quarter, just a few streets west of here, west of the Kölner Dom. I'm an only child. I am sad to tell you both my parents have passed away. My father, Anshal, died seven years ago, and my mother, Orly, not even one year ago. I learned my trade, being a cobbler, from my father, who had learned it from his father before him. I inherited the business from them. To this day I live in the same apartment in which I was born, above the shop. Mostly what I do is work. No relatives, both my parents were only children too. My one close friend, my childhood friend Gunter, moved to Hamburg with his new wife two years ago. That is where her family lives."

Like her, he was alone. Unlike her, it was not his preference.

Their courtship was minimal; both were too busy to take a long break from their respective responsibilities. So the customary process of getting to know one another took place once weekly. They would meet promptly at three o'clock on Sunday afternoons in front of the grand bronze doors on the Kölner Dom's south façade. From there they would take a stroll. Side by side. Eyes most often directed ahead. Hands never held. Shoulders never rubbed. Occasionally, Abraham would bring flowers or a scented soap. In response, Esther would oblige a smile and a *"danke."* The first time he brought a gift, her "thank you" was automatic, two words spilling out of her mouth without significance. But then she added, "That was thoughtful" in an awed tone, for such attentiveness had become an alien gesture.

These outings quickly became routine in activity and conversation. For this, Esther was grateful. She had neither the interest nor the wherewithal to charm or entertain.

"Have you been busy?" Abraham would ask each time they met. Right after he said how pleased he was to see her. Always with a broad smile. He did not compliment Esther on her clothes or appearance, but his eyes would twinkle. "Has the week gone well?"

Esther's usual reply was terse. *"Ja, ja."* But every so often she did add an account of a particular assignment: "This week I repaired a stole with real mink. The owner had stored it in a metal box near the furnace, can you imagine? How stupid! Of course, the hide dried out and pieces of fur fell off. I was able to restore it perfectly. More beautiful than it was originally."

Abraham nodded. "I'm sure it is better than when she received it, no doubt as a gift from her husband." He smiled at Esther. She tipped her head slightly, and they continued walking.

Silence between them was common but not uncomfortable. They were not awkward with one another. They shared an ease of understanding that this was how they must proceed.

If assignments were few that week, Esther's days were spent with the tasks necessary to secure work. This demanded more effort than the sewing itself, for the stress of no wages and the need to draw on her reserves compounded all activities. Although her expenses were few and she was frugal, the realities of a hand-to-mouth existence never left her thoughts. She paid bills promptly and with each payment set something aside, if only one *Pfennig*. Any savings was better than none, she surmised. The weeks Esther made no money were when she was most confident the path pursued with Abraham was correct and necessary.

Most Sunday walks comprised no more than a three-block radius circumambulating the Dom. On a few occasions, they ventured farther to explore the sights and shops of other neighborhoods, but soon discovered they were most at ease in the territory both knew best.

"Let's walk along the riverfront," Abraham proposed each week at some point during these afternoons. "It's very close by, barely a ten-minute walk," he would add. And each week, Esther refused.

"*Aber*—But this is the most beautiful part of our city," he said, mystified. "I don't understand."

"The water makes me dizzy" was her thin excuse. I don't need to explain, she thought. If I'm truthful, I don't understand myself what happened there. Better to leave it alone and stay away.

Abraham, so wanting to please, would merely shake his head, throw up his hands, and lead them in another direction.

Nevertheless, on the Sunday that was his birthday, Abraham said, "*Bitte*, Esther, it would give me much pleasure to walk along the Rhein today. I haven't seen the river in too long or the park. Have you visited the park? When I was a child, I often played there. I have many happy memories. *Bitte*, it would be such a special gift."

Esther closed her eyes, inhaled deeply, and thought: If this is to move forward, I suppose I must.

"Just this once," she said.

Esther had not returned to the riverfront since that bizarre and perplexing encounter. She did her best not to think about what had occurred and was mostly successful as her days overflowed. Her one visit to the library to seek out answers had not enlightened her, and she pushed the experience aside when she could. It was only when she didn't fall asleep immediately that the memory returned. Only when she lay awake, staring at the ceiling or into her pillow, did her mind drift in directions she couldn't control. Esther had no interest in returning. She had purposely avoided this part of the city, for it brought up questions for which no rational answers could be found.

Yet here they were slowly meandering along the riverfront, retracing the route Esther had trod her first months in Köln. As they walked, she observed that the background was no brighter; the setting was still gray, even though this was the middle of the afternoon in a summer month. She focused her attention on the cobblestone path and where next her foot would land.

But barely half a kilometer along, Esther lost her concentration. A large, iridescent butterfly flew toward and around her and then, executing an elegant figure eight, returned. Enthralled, her insides swooning, she could not take her eyes off of it as the delicate creature danced in front of her face for nearly one full minute before flying backward and vanishing into the patch of flowers ahead.

Ah . . . the butterfly . . . symbol of the soul . . . released from earthly connections and trials . . .

"Look at that," Abraham said with awe. "What an astonishing creature."

Esther could not speak. Her thoughts directed her back to that December evening, six years prior. Only the second time in her life when incident overshadowed reason. The first—that fateful day when she was left alone under the *chuppah*—had ignited her flight to Köln. The consequences of this second event were as yet unknown.

She pushed hard on her brain to invoke the experience. To bring forth a clear image, grappling for a vestige of the peculiar food stand that had stood out like a beacon in the bleakness. The happenstance that sparked something deep within her she could neither understand nor forget: the image of the elephant-headed man who seemed to gaze right back at her—within her—and seemed to know her—when she looked at it intently. But it was just a picture. How could—?

Abraham noticed Esther's distraction and pained expression. He asked, *"Sind Sie in Ordnung?* Are you well?" Distressed by her reaction, he thought the water might indeed be making her dizzy.

"Perhaps it's a slight headache. If it is fine with you, can we once again walk near the Dom?"

"*Natürlich,*" he replied. "Of course, of course. *Es tut mir leid*— I'm sorry, I guess we should not have come here after all." He led them away from the riverfront.

"Shall we get some dessert now?" he asked. Esther nodded in relief. This was part of their Sunday routine. At some point along their usual route, they would stop at one little café or another, the location never mattered, for a coffee and a piece of *Apfelstrudel,* her favorite. Abraham always accommodated. His interests were clear, and his affection continued to grow despite Esther's emotional remoteness.

For Esther, however, love was not a factor in moving forward with this man. What must happen would happen.

When they were married by the local *Bürgermeister* in Köln's town hall four months to the day of their meeting, Esther knew she did not love him—could not love him. She knew she could never recover the magnitude of truth and sensitivity she had once known with Tadeusz.

During the brief ceremony, Esther bit down hard on her cheek. Her right cheek. The last place Tadeusz had touched her. The last time she had seen him. The metallic taste of blood exploded in her mouth. Her chest palpitated. Still, physical pain could not supplant what churned within her. As she stood here, in this setting, the memory of a parallel scene engulfed her. But today she was without the tenderly fashioned *chuppah,* the bouquet of white posies, the audience of family and friends, the decorated town square. Most distinctly, the groom who stood beside her was not—him.

No! Stop! What am I doing! This can't happen, she shrieked inside. Stop! Esther inhaled sharply, holding her breath so as not to shout aloud, to expose herself. Calm. I must remain calm. This is the way it must be. I know this. I can't continue alone. But—

She could not look in Abraham's eyes. She focused on the tip of his narrow chin, which was not far enough below his huge, gaping smile.

At the required moment, Esther managed a soft "*Ja*" and the appearance of a smile.

A pragmatic move . . . a marriage of shoes and clothes, boots and furs.

Esther was confident she could not love again—not anyone—not even the three children she would birth over the next eight years. The consequences of a marital obligation she could not otherwise circumvent.

The firstborn, Tova, a slight colicky girl, arrived only nine and a half months after their wedding day, bringing tremendous joy to Abraham and nights of cries and wails for Esther. More work and more responsibility. Her irritation mounted. While Abraham tickled and cooed and sang to this little one before he disappeared for the better part of the day to his shop, Esther changed diapers and nursed. Baby care sandwiched between tailoring assignments and appointments, and shopping and cooking and cleaning.

When Esther asked for help: "Can you pick up some beets for the soup?" Abraham's standard reply was, "I'm sorry, but I really shouldn't close my shop to run an errand. That doesn't make sense. You can easily go with the baby."

How can he believe his work is more important than mine? She bristled. What nonsense! Even with many more responsibilities and less time to sew, I am paying many of our bills. And I am more talented.

In rare instances, perhaps when threading a needle or reinserting the bobbin in the sewing machine that was a surprise wedding gift from Abraham, Esther's eyes would catch sight of the fragile band of gold that encircled the second finger on her right hand. A pang at the base of her insides would assail her. It was unfathomable that she wore another's ring. It was supposed to be Tadeusz's. Only Tadeusz's—the one he had molded for her out of a melted-down family heirloom, the gold from a cracked and broken watch once worn by his grandfather.

Why?

If the question began to take flight, Esther shoved it aside in the same manner she swept up dust with a broom. She propelled all thoughts and feelings back where they belonged, consigned to history. No lingering thoughts of "what if?" were allowed. Esther had duties to carry out—to this semblance of a family she had created—to this child. Her child. Her responsibility. Although her instincts for mothering were not of the most loving nature, her experience as the second eldest of thirteen siblings ensured she had the abilities to fulfill basic needs. She refused to dwell on what had been and what could have been. Should have been. To reflect would only bring sorrow and, with it, weakness. This she would not abide.

Erroneously and regrettably—for all concerned—Esther's thinking about this union had never factored in children. Additional money had been its singular priority. Now she reprimanded herself. Why didn't I think the whole thing through? So foolish! I wanted to ease my money issues, not increase expenses as a brood surely guarantees.

Repeatedly, she rejected Abraham's advances unless sheer exhaustion made that effort too great. Eight months later Esther found herself burdened once more. This time, however, she attempted to take charge of the situation.

I stood by her when she tried to abort this one . . . unsuccessfully . . . the remedies of her ancestors not obliging her desire.

I remain saddened that not even motherhood . . . tiny babies born of her loins . . . souls her body carried and nourished for nine months . . . could fill the cavernous hole carved within her.

And that cavern would grow ever deeper as events fomented . . . outside . . .

CHAPTER SIX

Each day . . .
the same . . .
as the one before.
Always the same.
But . . . now different . . .

....

Sunday, the fifth of March in the year 1933, brought Esther additional labor—nearly twenty-two hours of it. Though jovial once she arrived, Miriam, a chubby child born with a full head of curly black hair and an insatiable curiosity, surely resisted the passage and caused all manner of pain and suffering. Perhaps the child knew instinctively she had not been desired. Perhaps she perceived her mother's truth and heavy heart: that this woman, chosen to care and nurture this tiny being, had attempted to terminate her pregnancy—Miriam's life.

But cells and spirit conspired.

And—perhaps, Miriam had a foreboding sense of events evolving.

Her entry marked a turning point. For on this very day, within hours of her appearance on this plane, the course and direction of a country, a history, her people, all people, shifted.

Elections. A new Chancellor enabled, and a dictatorship underway. Inconceivable in the land of Goethe and Steiner, Beethoven and Bach, Nietzsche and Hegel. Incomprehensible in a history steeped in innovative production, enlightened thinking, visionary perspective, and thoughtful discourse.

Ah . . . power and greed and evil can . . . and far too often do . . . supplant consciousness.

Entrenched in the daily toil of keeping family fed and clothed—for now anyway—as regards Esther and Abraham and neighbors and customers and all those around them, this immeasurable shift in perception and priority was subtle, imperceptible—

—for now anyway.

There was neither respite nor resources to dwell on the politics fermenting around them.

And there was certainly no rest for a young woman who had just given birth, with a two-year-old in the adjacent room crying for attention.

CHAPTER SEVEN

Only able to breathe bitterness and regret . . .
and taste loss and misery.
Emotions were frozen . . .
Feelings submerged.

....

Days bled into months, and then years.

Time did move forward, the wheel did spin, but—alas—Esther's motives for marriage and partnership were not met with the comfort and security she had envisaged. Instead, she found herself in the winter of 1937 with four mouths to feed rather than just her one. This husband was in no way the provider she had hoped.

A kind, easygoing man, Abraham was friend to all throughout Köln's Jewish Quarter, ready with a joke, some local gossip, and a generous nature. Never without his heavy apron, soiled with oil and its palette-like array of thickly layered colors and polish, he bumbled about with the wood lathe and metal tools of his trade more often than not falling out of one or the other of two pockets. To Esther's distress, he spent much of each day kibitzing with the street's other vendors, no matter if he had shoes to repair.

"*Später*—Later" was his common response. "All in good time. Work can wait a while. We must laugh while we can."

And far too often, Abraham would replace a broken shoelace without charge or buff a pair of boots for the price of a smile.

"*Nein, nein,*" he would say with a shake of his head when performing what he considered a too easy task to accept payment. "*Kein Problem.* The pleasure is mine."

Esther knew the neighbors took advantage of him, yet her complaints never aroused a reaction. Consequently, she was forced to continue to work exhausting hours seven days each week. Her bitterness swelled.

In spite of this, Esther accomplished her obligations adequately. She served plain warm meals with some meat included in the fare a minimum of once weekly, and a roof—albeit an insufficient and overcrowded one—remained over their heads. Their two-room apartment three floors above Abraham's cobbler shop provided shelter, although not a modicum of privacy. They all slept in the smaller room, swollen to capacity with wall-to-wall beds and a crib crammed in front of the one closet. The larger room was continuously in use for cooking, eating, bathing, and—most importantly—Esther's tailoring. The space necessary for her work took precedence. An intricate choreography of timing, structure, prioritizing, and urgency made their life possible. Demanding, but functional.

The one covered toilet, shared among five families, was outside in the building's rear, abutting the supply shed. With two small children, Esther spent an interminable number of hours descending and climbing the stairs, sometimes with both girls, to use this inconvenient but necessary facility. Her legs grew strong and her frame sturdy. Over the years, her physique began to resemble the golem-like condition of her emotions.

Yet, even now, the sporadic pang—in her chest, her heart, her core—would compel attention to the fact that nothing was completely forgotten or lost to time.

A young girl's heartbreak . . . never leaves the woman . . .

During these moments—these flashes of weakness—Esther would think. Reminiscences of him, Tadeusz, would overcome her. Then, as if in tandem, her mind would lead her to that other him, the elephant-headed man, raising all those questions without resolution. *"Genug! Genug!* Enough!" she would shout, startling anyone standing near her, for nothing outward had occurred. She forced her attention to return to whatever project was at hand.

The children had decent clothes, although not a large variety; Esther used the bits and pieces left over from various sewing projects. With limited choice of materials, the girls' dresses were identical down to the number of backstitches. They did not appear to mind, although Miriam was quick to make hers distinctive by pinning on one shoulder a small piece of ribbon or lace scrounged from her Mama's sewing box.

"Es ist meins! That's mine! Mine!" she would squeal in delight when something pretty caught her eye.

Abraham made sure both had one solid pair of shoes, no matter how quickly his children's feet grew.

And when Tova's, and then Miriam's, little hands became supple, Esther began the process of teaching them to sew. As her mother had done for her, and her mother's mother before that, she used the approach passed down as tradition if not birthright. The most basic stitches at first, certainly. However, flawless technique was sacrosanct from the onset of their training.

"Haltet die Nadel gerade. Hold the needle up straight. Don't let the thread go limp. *Niemals. Never.*

"If the thread goes limp, you can't control it. Perfect stitches are about control. All about control.

"Und Geduld. And patience. Be patient. Don't ever forget you must stay patient."

Then Esther would continue, "Breathe into each stitch. Breathe evenly or your stitches won't match.

"Breath in. Breath out. Count—three in, three out, three in, three out.

"Don't change your breathing pattern unless you change the stitch.

"Each stitch has its own distinct breath, its own life. And each must be the same.

"*Identisch.* Identical.

"There is no room for error.

"If they are not the same, the fabric won't lie flat. The seam will buckle. The hem will ripple. Then you must take it out and start once more. And then again, if that is necessary.

"Until it is uniform—*ganz exakt*—exact. The puncture of the needle must disappear.

"It must be as though the thread was always there, holding the pieces together.

"*All die Teile zusammengehalten hat.* Holding all the pieces together."

Esther took few joys from these children's small achievements: their first steps without assistance; words tentatively formed; eating on their own; or, as they grew older, solving a basic mathematics exercise or writing a simple sentence. Esther's manner, like her tailoring principles, was strict. She had little patience for childish activities.

"*Hört auf!* Stop!" she would shout if the children grew too loud or became overly rambunctious. "*Tut das nicht!* Don't do that!

"Go into the other room and stay out of my way!"

Esther never slapped her children, but each rebuke was like a hornet's sting on tender flesh. In spite of her coldness and actions, the children loved their mama fiercely. Through their shared blood, the girls sensed the anguish that ran deep within her and, while not comprehending, they felt compassion.

When scolded, Tova and Miriam would scurry away and whisper between themselves, distressed one or the other had made Mama unhappy.

"Why did you make Mama mad?"

Mostly, it was Tova saying this to Miriam, the more boisterous of the two. "*Schwestie,* little sister, why must you always make our mama mad?"

Tensions often ran high, and laughter rarely emanated from these two rooms.

Every now and again . . . when it felt necessary to do so . . . the thing that must be done when the time was opportune with neither parent in the room . . . I would leave a cookie or two

... or a small toy ... for the children's pleasure ... for their amusement ... and of course ... for mine. Naturally I would have a few cookies myself.

As is so often the case ... these children understood. For ones so young are still connected ... they still remember.

The children sensed my presence and my purpose clearly and without question. Certainly ... they greatly enjoyed these small treats ... never sharing their discoveries with either parent. Just smiling ... consciously ... amongst themselves ...

Early on, the children understood whom to run to when Miriam scraped a knee or Tova needed help with a shoelace or button. Abraham welcomed any excuse to play with his daughters rather than work, and whenever Esther asked him to distract them, he responded eagerly, "*Ja, ja,* no problem. For the children, of course. Anything for our little girls."

A devoted father, true to his name, Abraham provided his children with hugs and dabbed away their tears. He sang silly songs and played games. He was the parent who took his daughters along the riverfront each Sunday afternoon for ice cream. They looked forward to this weekly delight with great anticipation.

In winter or warmth, the girls would put on their favorite flowered dresses, the ones with the ruffles at the hem, white eyelet aprons at the waist, buttons down the middle, and short puffy sleeves. Esther had provided wide seams, so as they grew, the dresses could be let out easily and worn for years to come. Miriam, not surprisingly, would pin a small piece of lace at her collar.

"Mama, Mama, will you come with us today?" she always asked. "*Bitte! Bitte,* Mama!"

Each week Esther would shake her head, and her youngest daughter would pout. And Abraham would say, "*Mein Liebchen,* you know the water makes your mama ill. It is better she stays here. Come. We will have fun."

Before leaving, Miriam and Tova would wrap their arms around Esther for a hug, which she obliged. Then each girl would grab hold of one of Papa's hands and, as best they could, drag him down the stairs and along the street. The route to the Rhein was the same, and its observance was inviolate: down their own short street of Kämmergasse filled with family-owned businesses on the ground floor and apartments above; past their school and the little park where they played when Mama and weather permitted; east on Agrippastrasse and then Nord-Süd Fahrt, waving at neighbors and only pausing to smell flowers that may be in bloom or pet a small dog that might share the path.

Their first stop would be the Kölner Dom, the spiritual core of this ancient city, and its expansive cobbled square. The girls never tired of the Dom's beautiful façade or its skyscraper-like spires that commanded all views. Convinced it was a structure that had magically appeared out of their picture books, they loved to invent stories of the fairies that lived behind each of the carved cornices, up near the clouds, or of the sculptures over the archways that came alive at night when the rest of the city slept. With its location adjacent to the train station, they fabricated tales about visiting gremlins and sprites—and *dybbuks*, particularly if the day was cold and gray or rainy.

Here, nearly every Sunday afternoon, entertainers could be found, usually one or two musicians who hoped to make enough money to live on for the coming week. Most often German folk songs were sung. On occasion, a fiddler or accordion player performed Yiddish *klezmer*. No matter what was played, Miriam and Tova loved music, and the girls danced without inhibition. They did their best to entice their papa to join in. "*Bitte*, Papa! *Bitte!* Please, come dance with us!" they shouted, voices melding, as they whirled and twirled. "This is so much fun!"

Abraham reveled in their joy. But—as the seasons began to shift, the relaxed atmosphere on the square also transitioned. A tension surfaced and began to spread and deepen. The presence of *die Polizisten* became increasingly conspicuous. They watched everyone and everything a little too closely. Harassed the musicians without provocation, threatened the crowd if it grew too large or too noisy.

Tova and Miriam appeared oblivious to anything but the music, and for this Abraham was thankful. However, he would shorten their time on the square, saying, "Come along girls, let's get ice cream." They never resisted. As much as they enjoyed the music, they liked this sweet treat more.

They would head to the Rhein and stroll along the riverfront. The girls counted bridges, barges, and boats until they reached the vendor where ice cream could be purchased and savored— chocolate for Tova and strawberry for Miriam. Both chose the cones patterned after the Dom's cobbled square, or so they thought. These were the ones that were exceptionally sweet. Above all, they relished the special hours with their adored and adoring papa.

Thankful for the solitude whenever Abraham took the girls, Esther would stay home to attend to household tasks and sew. Continuously sew.

There was no true respite to her week's drudgery, only—

CHAPTER EIGHT

They say... on this day:
No sowing, plowing, reaping...
No grinding, sifting, kneading, baking...
No shearing wool or washing wool or
dyeing wool or spinning wool...
No writing two letters or erasing two letters...
Certainly, no weaving of two threads or
sewing of two stitches.
And yet... there is no rest possible...
and no divine reflection.
No reflection at all...
of what or why or how...
or what if or why not or how come...
Borukh ato adonoy eloheynu melekh ho'olam
asher kidishonu bemitzvosov
vetzivonu lehadlik ner shel shabbes. (Omeyn)

....

Esther's most cherished possession, the only thing she still held dear from her youth, was the *kiddush* cup that had once belonged to her precious great grandmother. Made in Galicia by a master silversmith, this elegant goblet, barely the size of her palm, included a *shabbes* prayer engraved in Hebrew letters around its rim. It remained the one attachment to her former life, that other reality that refused to fade with time or allow memory to erase.

She recalled the day she received this gift. Bubbe Royza visited the house in the early morning and came directly to the corner of the table where Esther sat spooning up the last bits of her *krupnik*.

"*A freylekhn gebortsog,* Estherle! Happy Birthday! Today is your thirteenth birthday," she said, leaning down to embrace Esther.

"Thirteen," Bubbe Royza exclaimed. "*U va*—So wonderful! Reaching thirteen years is an achievement that must be recognized. Regardless of whether you're a boy or girl. It's not right that there's nothing special for girls like boys have with their *bar mitzvahs.* As your brothers will have when they reach this age. Today, you are ready to stand up, be counted and, most importantly, be account-able. For today, you are an adult.

"On this occasion a gift must be given, and it must be signif-icant. We don't have much, our family, really not more than the basics. But," she continued on, beaming, "there are a few keepsakes we have clung to over the years. To share with you, the next gen-eration, our legacy."

At these words Esther flushed. When her elder sister, Lifcha, had turned thirteen, she had received the treasured tablecloth elab-orately embroidered with roses, lilies, and corn poppies by Bubbe Royza's own mama. What might I get? she wondered. Could it possibly be—?

Esther watched with keen eyes as Bubbe Royza reached into her dress pocket and pulled out the coveted silver *kiddush* cup and placed it on the table in front of her.

Esther jumped up and wrapped her arms around Bubbe Royza's robust frame.

"*A sheynem dank! A hartsikn dank!* Thank you so much!" Esther shouted.

No present could have been more fitting or made Esther happier, because for her, from earliest remembrances onward, the Sabbath was sacred. A pause from work and lessons. This con-stant day of commemoration and freedom was a refuge from the week's pressures, a safe haven enabling contemplation and renewal. There was a comfort in the evening's structure and coordination: the Sabbath meal, prepared with close attention to rituals; the two candles lit within eighteen minutes of the sun gently kissing the horizon; the special prayers sung that separated this day from all others; and the shared wine from the *kiddush* cup. The meal always included some special savory treat, the only one of the week. And there would be her family, all fifteen of them, gathered around the huge wooden table, for this one night covered in lace. The evening overflowed with laughter and food. They caught up on gossip and the events in each other's lives. For Esther it was a period of blessing and gratitude that continued until the first three stars appeared in the sky the next evening.

> It was . . . of course . . . a Friday evening in the period before
> the sunset . . . the coming of the Sabbath . . . when Esther met
> Tadeusz . . . and the spark ignited . . . and the story began . . .
> and destiny unfolded . . .

Thus, the *kiddush* cup, and with it the Sabbath, remained the pivotal bridge from Przeworsk to now.

Although Esther did not keep kosher, nor follow the practices and rituals associated with a Jewish life, her observance of the Sabbath constituted the cornerstone of activities. It was the one consistent element to any week she had ever known. As a child, she had believed in it as a covenant with God, but her experience—of unbending hurt and heartache—had made her disavow all existence of possibilities other than what was right before her.

Abraham was a third-generation German, raised without religion but not without Jewish roots and culture embedded within his soul. He was content, if not relieved, for Esther to arrange their lives and manage the children's upbringing, religious or otherwise. It was clear who ran the household and kept all in order. He did not argue or question decisions made.

Their lives were centered in Köln's Jewish Quarter, an area mostly crowded with old and crumbling buildings, some the remains of Romanesque architecture. The apartment and shop were situated two short blocks from the *mikveh*—the ritual bath—on the east toward the river, the butcher and his slaughterhouse equidistant on the north. The city's largest synagogue was only one street away to the south. They did not belong to this synagogue or to any other. They attended no community meetings. Esther had no interest in such gatherings. Her preference was to be self-contained. Maintaining distance ensured her desired privacy, or at least as much isolation as was possible when one had to manage the lives and requirements of children.

Esther did not take the children to synagogue even during the High Holy Days, those ten days of awe in the fall that heralded the New Year and new beginnings and culminated with atonement for past transgressions. There were no more new beginnings for Esther. No celebrations in anticipation of what was to come. She was clear that amends and expiation were the responsibility of others.

Still, every Friday afternoon, no matter how busy, Esther put aside her tasks and assignments to prepare the Sabbath meal. Gefilte fish with horseradish sauce was a staple, accompanied by a potato or noodle kugel. She included one side dish of carrots, turnips, parsnips, beets, or celery root, depending on what looked freshest at the market that morning. And most weeks she made a noodle soup with vegetables or chicken, as finances allowed. The abundance of aromas flooded the apartment.

Without exception, the menu included one indulgence: doll-size challahs for Tova and Miriam, something her adored Bubbe Royza had made every week, one for each sibling. Even though one large challah was more economical and would feed everyone, Esther remained faithful to this one tradition from childhood. These little challahs and the *kiddush* cup were the only links to her past.

Well . . . the sole connections she dared or could concede.

Since their apartment did not have an oven, it required juggling and logistics to take the miniature yellow-braided mounds of dough down the street to be baked at the bakery—and one mark, twenty *Pfennig* for the baker. Friday afternoons, after carefully molding these loafs, Esther made this time-consuming, not inexpensive trek. Truthfully, although the children delighted in these challahs, Esther knew she made them for Esther.

"Mama, Mama, it's Friday afternoon," Tova and Miriam sang in unison as they ran into the kitchen area. "We're here to help. We want to help."

"*Seid still!* Be quiet!" Esther demanded. "*Ja, ja,* it is Friday afternoon, and you are here to prepare for *shabbes* as you do every Friday. I understand this. But you do not need to be so loud. If you continue to shout, you must leave, and you will not get your challahs."

The girls immediately stopped talking. For while both had many chores as soon as they were strong enough to hold the laundry basket or push a mop to scrub the floor, assisting with meals was *verboten.* According to their mama, there were too many opportunities to break something or burn themselves, too many chances to add an abundance of salt or pepper and ruin a meal. Only on Friday afternoons were they allowed in the kitchen area to assist. If they were good.

After five minutes of silence, Esther said, "Okay, fine, go prepare the Sabbath table. Don't break anything!" A smile claimed her face as she thought of making these same preparations with her own sisters. A momentary reflection. Her attention quickly turned to the details of the meal, and she ignored their prattle.

"*Schwestie, hol' die Servietten,*" Tova ordered. "Get the napkins. Only the napkins. The plates are too heavy for you. I will set them where they need to go and then you place the napkins beside each plate, on the right. Okay, here, take our little pitcher filled with grape juice. Hold it with both hands so you don't spill. The one with wine, I will put above Papa's plate." Tova then positioned the plain wood-turned candlesticks Abraham had made in his shop on either side of a small vase at the table's center.

"It's my turn to put Mama's special goblet on the table. This week it will go closer to my seat. And look, I picked a flower—" Miriam said excitedly.

"From Frau Lang's garden! You have to stop that. She'll be so mad if she catches you again!"

"It was just so pretty," Miriam said, hiding her face in her hands.

Tova and Miriam knew everything must be fresh and orderly. For on this evening the angels were greeted. It was important the family received the blessing of the good angel and only the bad angel's "Amen."

"*Sholem aleichem*—May peace be upon you"—

—would be sung, opening up the heavens and welcoming the angels. With all seated around the table as the sun began to set, candles would be lit, *kiddush* blessings said, and the meal consumed.

Then dishes were cleared and washed, and all would ready for bed.

No telling of stories or laughter and no break for rest or contemplation. For Esther, Abraham, and the children, the Sabbath could not continue through the next day's sunset; Saturday could not be a day off from work and responsibilities. And it could not be a day of reflection, most especially not for Esther.

CHAPTER NINE

Yet . . . of course . . . not all of this country's
history has been without blemish.
Not all days past overflowed with compassion . . .
with beneficence . . . with tolerance . . .
toward one . . . toward all.
Aberrations pullulate,
for that is what happens here . . .
and so we learned—
one man's view, through
sixty-five thousand words, denouncing a people . . .
a tribe . . . a religion . . .
Instigating an aggression—
Counseling government to act . . .
and to cleanse . . . and to rid . . .

. . . .

"Mama, Mama," Miriam shouted, "*eine Parade! Schau,* Mama. Look, Mama, a parade is coming!"

The little girl was at the narrow window in their front room, jumping up and down, chortling with excitement.

"Look at all the pretty balloons! There are red and white balloons. Look! And black balloons. So many balloons. They are coming right down our street. They are coming down Kämmer-gasse, Mama! Look at all the people! Who is that man standing up in the car? Why is he standing? Can we go, Mama? Can we go downstairs? *Bitte,* Mama, please, Mama, please!"

Miriam waved joyfully out the window. She wanted to be a part of the scene below. Mimicking the people lining the parade route, precisely like the man in the car, she raised her right arm straight outwards.

Esther seized Miriam by her shoulder and smacked her bottom. "Get away from the window immediately and go to your room! *Jetzt*—Now!"

Bewildered, Miriam burst into tears and ran to her bed.

What did I do wrong? Why is my mama always so mean? she thought. Grabbing her cherished little bear and holding him tight, Miriam hid under the covers and continued to sob. "It's a parade. It's only a parade."

But it was not only a parade, and Esther understood this beyond question.

In the few brief years since Miriam's birth, daily life as it had been—Esther's world—began to change. At the outset, it was subtle. Barely discernible. Often it was more a feeling than anything else, observations she might attribute to her imagination. But then there would be an off-hand remark from a passerby or an offensive name shouted by a young child.

"*Untermenschen*—Subhuman" was oft repeated.

For the most part, Esther could ignore such occurrences, ascribing them to a person having a difficult day or youthful ignorance.

*This was all so understandable . . . for often . . . so very often
. . . one does not wish to see what is before them . . . that which
is transpiring . . . the true nature . . . reason . . . reasons . . . for a
situation . . . for a circumstance . . .*

Slowly, randomly, rules and restrictions were imposed on daily activities. Laws came into effect that declared when or where or whether Esther could shop or ride the tram or take her children to play in the park. Under these circumstances, sporadic as they were, there could be no denying, no refuting, what was taking place.

Well—at least no denial for Esther, whose internal armor heightened her already acute sensitivity. Abraham maintained a state of practiced obliviousness. He went about his daily activities—helping a customer when one ventured in; watching or, more accurately, playing with the children; and puttering about, here and there—as though no change was upon him, his family, his community, his people.

For Esther, the inconsistencies and irrationality ensured that each day presented more challenges to navigate than the one before.

The corner grocery store where she shopped no longer consistently stocked basic staples and supplies. Tempers flared.

"*Nein!* These are mine," the gray-haired woman insisted as she held fast to the small bags of sugar and flour. "I picked them up first. And the baking powder is mine too. Take your hands off them."

But the brunette refused to let go. "We have not had bread in our house for four weeks. My family is hungry. I have young children. And I saw these before you. You know I did. You pushed me out of the way. Who knew such an old crone—*ein altes Weib*—could be so strong?"

Esther had not seen salt on these shelves in many months. Or onions and garlic. Potatoes and celery were also rare. Butter and cream had become fantasies of the imagination. It was no longer possible to offer the miniature challahs at their Sabbath meal, and when Miriam groused, Esther did not contain her frustration. "I will hear no more from you!" she shouted and demanded the little girl leave the room without eating.

Fruits and vegetables appeared sporadically. When they could be found, they were inevitably the ones most bruised, damaged, or speckled with brown spots. Her sewing supplies were no longer carried in any of the nearby shops. So Esther traveled by tram forty-five minutes each way to purchase threads, buttons, zippers, straight pins, marking chalks, and fabrics.

It became more difficult to keep customers.

Only the week before the motorcade, Esther had lost a valuable client, one of the wealthier ones. Frau Osterhoudt was not a longtime client, but she was one who, for the past three or so years, had provided Esther with consistent work and interesting projects. Not simply to hem a skirt or mend a shirt, the most common assignments. Often, her services were retained to sew complete outfits for one of Frau Osterhoudt's four daughters. Once, she had Esther create a coat from rabbit skins, with silk lining. Payment was prompt and more than fair, and she praised Esther for her superior craftsmanship and exquisite detailing. Whenever Esther dropped off or picked up clothes, she made sure to bring Miriam along; Miriam played with the youngest daughter while Esther measured and pinned. But when last at her front door, Frau Osterhoudt refused to let them in the entryway. She snatched her clothes from Esther's basket and said, "Here is *Ihre Zahlung*—your payment!" She thrust a fistful of bills into the empty basket.

Taken aback, Esther did manage to say, "I have time this week to repair—"

But the door slammed in her face before the complete sentence was formed. Obviously her services were no longer favored. No opportunity to inquire why. No explanation provided.

It became harder to manage from one day to the next without feeling as though the business Esther had established would be taken away without notice. As though nothing were truly hers anymore. Maybe it never was. Perhaps it had all been an illusion, for there was no reason or rationale to what was occurring, no justification for how some people were acting or how other people were treated.

Indeed . . . darkness prevailed . . . and light had forgotten its timepiece . . .

The situation felt all too familiar. For not that long ago, still within memory's clutch, Esther's world had been ripped away.

Granted, then it had happened in an instant, and this time, so much was taking place in subtle actions, often indiscernible and seemingly intentionally so.

As the temperature grew colder, an oppressive fog gathered in the mornings and refused to dissipate throughout the day. The weather mirrored the atmosphere of fear that had begun to form. First, as a mere rustling, its intensity and volume increased each day. Fear was not in Esther's vocabulary, nor part of her consciousness. She felt impervious to its force. It was not something she understood, nor an emotion she intended to engage.

> She did not know or perhaps did not . . . could not . . . acknowl-
> edge . . . that fear . . . escalating and overpowering fear . . . had
> been around her before . . . had been around her then . . . and
> was the root of her unrelenting pain.

A few times, when especially bothered, Esther attempted to speak to Abraham.

"This morning, I went to the market and there was not one piece of fruit to buy. Just potatoes. This is the fifth day in a row with only potatoes. And I couldn't board the tram to shop in another part of the city. They are now refusing to stop on our streets. It is *unglaublich*—unbelievable—what is happening."

His response was dismissive. "There is nothing to worry about, dear Esther. This situation is only temporary. *Alles ist gut.* All is good."

Abraham's casual indifference to these circumstances included the daily mantra "All is good, all is fine." There are no worries. Nothing bad could possibly happen. He said these words as much to himself as to anyone who would listen.

Esther muttered to herself, That man infuriates me! He does not see what is right in front of him, what is all around us. He will be the end of us. I must take care of myself. And the children. This is clear.

The one emotion she could muster was anger, and it fueled her actions. Constantly tensed muscles and a hot, flushed feeling kept her clearheaded and hyperconscious of her surroundings and everything that must be accomplished.

And more sensitive to my presence...

"*Genug von ihm*—Enough of him!" Esther stopped speaking to her husband except when conversation was essential. When one child or another needed water or milk, if it was available, or when she wanted them out of the apartment to get her sewing accomplished without distraction. Conflict rose in this already stressful household. Miriam began to have trouble sleeping, and nightmares came when she could finally sleep. She regularly complained of headaches and stomachaches. Tova, in contrast, shared Abraham's light-hearted, nothing-bad-can-befall-us attitude and became her sister's protector.

Miriam returned home one day crying loudly. "They called me bad names at school again! They won't leave me alone! Why won't they leave me alone? I haven't done anything wrong! Not to anyone—ever!"

Tova shushed her little sister and mimicked Abraham: "Don't worry, *Schwestie. Kein Problem.* Not a problem. Everything is fine."

Through her tears, Miriam asked, "Can we play in the park this afternoon? That would be fun. It's so pretty there."

"I'm sorry, *mein Liebchen*," Abraham said. "Today is not a day when they let us go to the park. But come here, your papa will give you a hug. I will make you feel better. And here is a special treat, a bonbon."

Miriam took the candy but chose to give her little bear the hug. She whispered in his ear and held him close.

Observing this exchange, Esther snorted. As if we have an extra *Pfennig* to spare for candy! What is he thinking?

Abraham did his best not to think. He continued to be every neighborhood child's greatest ally and softhearted to the shrinking number of customers who came his way. He never worried about money. Never worried about the family's next meal. Never worried about anything. He was more interested in pleasing as best he could. Friend to all—that was Abraham. But Esther wasted no days with friends. Friendship had not served her well in years past, and she saw no need now.

She was primed for the tests to be confronted. Esther's core ensured these young children, who now constituted her family—her responsibilities—would have, at the very least, the basic necessities as long as they were in her care. Esther may have lost most of her desire to love and nurture, but her resilience remained unshakable.

CHAPTER TEN

A symbol appeared . . .
ubiquitously.
One of the oldest in existence.
Prevalent throughout the world . . .
a cross quadrupled . . .
a cosmic pinwheel.
More potent than words.
Arrogated from the original Sanskrit . . .
meaning: conducive to well-being.
Appropriated from the right-handed emblem of . . .
purity . . . auspiciousness . . .
innocence . . . supreme devotion . . .
Ganesha.
Assumed from the left-handed emblem of . . .
destruction . . . strife . . . devastation . . .
spiritual dissolution . . .
Kali.
This . . . is the one they used.

. . . .

She excelled at options. Found alternatives. Located more for less. Esther still shopped in the Jewish Quarter's shops but, after some probing, became acquainted with the burgeoning black market. It became not so difficult to find what she needed, as she only had to listen closely to those who whispered and watch the ones who pointed with their eyes. She found them hanging out on street corners. Leaning against buildings. They were the ones who pretended to be engaged in conversation. Or folded and refolded stacks of newspapers. With their assistance, she discovered those who offered what was no longer available in regular stores—at a price, of course.

It all came down to money.

This was paramount. One did not need friends or family. Only money. Butter, milk, flour, even cheese and eggs—anything and everything were within reach if one had money.

As her client base shrank, and despite Abraham's negligible contributions, Esther figured out new ways to hoard money. She scrimped more *Reichsmarks* from every tailoring assignment, cut corners to put aside every possible *Pfennig*. Most fortunately, she had saved a considerable sum. And she felt no qualms hiding these funds from Abraham. She placed coins behind the flour on the highest shelf over the sink. The paper bills were unseen at the bottom of her sewing basket, below a couple of layers of fabric, and in a slit skillfully cut into the top right corner of the mattress on their bed—her side.

She provided necessities, if even on the most basic level. He bought candy.

CHAPTER ELEVEN

Herr Wolf said, "We are going to treat the Jews like flowers;
only we won't give them water."
The garden had been rich and lush,
overflowing with color and texture, life and song . . .
And dance . . . there was always dance.
A vibrant panoply of personalities that welcomed visitors . . .
families . . . friends . . . lovers . . .
to gather and talk and play and laugh
and sit and breath and be.
Until the day sustenance was slowly denied.
And the garden . . . silently . . . painfully . . .
began to shrink . . . began to cry.
Not comprehending . . . for there were
no cogent answers to the why.
Then the Hummingbirds came.
Instead of transferring life-bearing pollen . . .
only blood dripped from their knife-like beaks.
There were now buds that would never bloom,
and seeds that would never rest. . . .

. . . .

With her small basket curled under her right arm, Esther walked down this street just as she had a thousand times before, prepared to get vegetables and perhaps some meat for the evening meal. Typically Miriam accompanied her, slowing her mother down as she looked at a bird flying by or a squirrel on a tree or asked question after question. But this morning the little girl had chosen to stay with her papa and play in the shop with Tova.

For this, Esther was grateful. No explanations would be necessary. Because starting on this day, it was no longer possible to ignore or deny everything was now different.

The air was thick and apprehensive. The street, mostly bare of people. The few she did pass looked down or away or within. Overnight, prominently and brashly displayed in many shop windows—those shops she regularly frequented—appeared bold signs that proclaimed: *Keine Hunde, Keine Juden!* No dogs, No Jews! *Juden Verboten!* Jews Forbidden!

A few shops, the ones she recognized as possible to enter, had *Juden* emblazoned in yellow across the full expanse of their windows.

Esther stopped. No movement possible.

Although she stood for just a few seconds, an eternity passed.

She remained still, and strong, and tall. She gathered her full stature, establishing a figure that ascended far above her nearly five feet.

With control, she slowly and warily looked around. Up and down this street she had come to know so well. She blinked and acknowledged that the familiar had melted away.

Esther turned and retraced what little remained of her original steps—back to their too small apartment three stories above Abraham's shop. And then, she sat.

Time, once again, lost its influence.

At some point, Miriam and Tova ran through the door. They shouted and sang as they came in the kitchen, still joyful from the afternoon in Papa's shop and the chance to play.

"Mama, Mama, *was gibt's zum Abendessen?* What's for dinner? What's for dinner? We're hungry!"

Esther turned to them and responded with a stony glare, "*Drek—drek mit laber!* Dirt with liver!"

In the Kali Yuga . . . humanity toils . . . righteousness . . . morality . . . virtue . . . ethics . . . diminish . . . and evils . . . evils abound . . .

The situation escalated, more rules, more restrictions, more humiliations that culminated in the branding of the yellow Star of David required on all their clothing—*"Jude"* broadcast in black imitative Hebrew script at its center. This became mandatory for everyone over six years of age. To facilitate identification, they were told. To what end, they were not told.

Truth obscured.

The streets became filled with brown-shirted soldiers—boys, in actual fact, barely out of school, most, no doubt, still in school—marching up and marching down. Goose-stepping. In unthinking conformity.

Spiritual degeneration.

With only one hour permitted each day for shopping of any kind, fewer meals had to stretch further.

Darkness.

The reduced periods allotted to travel by streetcar and tram limited Esther's ability to pick up her tailoring assignments and return them in a suitable fashion. Her business suffered, just as intended. Politics, actions, and attitudes conspired against her—against all of them.

So much darkness . . . in action . . . and in thought . . .

Although restrictions abounded, the rules and requirements and orders seemed to change daily. Attacks and charges were ambiguous. There were constant shifts in regulations, momentary lulls in persecutions. Mixed signals sent consistently. Vacillating policies. Any semblance of normalcy was not possible.

And ignorance . . . of an unfathomable magnitude prevails.

In comparison to many around them, Esther, Abraham, and the girls were among the fortunate. A couple just down the street that had long owned the neighborhood drugstore was accused of tax evasion and forced out of business. The wife resorted to cleaning houses—when she could find the work—and her husband set up a shoeshine stand. Others in the neighborhood—those who worked in offices, restaurants, retail shops, factories—began to lose their jobs. All given excuses. No basis in fact.

Sporadically, men in the neighborhood were rounded up and taken away. No one knew where. The destination never revealed. No questions allowed. More often than not, these men did not return. The few that did were battered nearly beyond recognition, too frightened to speak.

The sound of synchronized boots against gravel became routine. *Sturmabteilung*—Stormtroopers—marched through the streets. They shouted anti-Jewish slogans and sang jingoistic songs:

Die Fahne hoch! Die Reihen fest geschlossen!
SA marschiert mit mutig-festem Schritt
Kameraden, die Rotfront und Reaktion erschossen
Marschieren im Geist in unseren Reihen mit—

. . . .

Fly high the flag! The ranks be tightly closed now!
SA is marching, bravely and firm
Comrades shot dead by Red Front and Reaction
In spirit march within our ranks

And always the catchphrase: "*Sieg Heil!* Hail victory!"

Random searches took place. *Die Polizei* took whatever they wanted. No recourse.

Daily now, Tova and Miriam were taunted in school by their classmates—without provocation. Names were called. Hair pulled. Rocks thrown. These children went unpunished. Then—teachers began to ridicule the girls.

"Tova, you don't seem to know any of the answers this morning." Fraulein Richter inquired, "Didn't you read your assignment last night? It was only a few pages."

When Tova, cheeks flushed, slowly moved her head from side to side, Fraulein Richter continued, "*Wirklich?* Really, again? Class, once more Tova is the example of how not to be a good student." Her classmates snickered. "Go stand in the corner!" And that's where she stood until lunchtime, more than one hour. Red-faced.

Far too often these girls returned home in tears and ran to their papa for comfort.

The family's decent landlord assured them that the roof would remain over their heads. And her actions supported these declarations; when *die Polizei* came by to ask if there were any Jews in the building causing trouble, she said, "*Nein, nein.* Not here," while she swept the sidewalk.

This support, coupled with steady loyalty from a handful of customers—many of whom were young, bold Germans—allowed Esther and Abraham to continue to scrape by.

More struggles. New challenges. Increased frustrations. Constant juggling. Yes. But they got by nonetheless, when so many around them were losing everything.

Then all efforts became compounded when Esther found herself pregnant for the third time. In the middle of one night when exhaustion overtook her, and she could not resist Abraham's pleas. And, yet again—after she mixed the herbal combinations recommended by the neighborhood's *Hebamme*, the midwife, this time adding more pennyroyal than was recommended, more evening primrose, more parsley, and the rest—her attempt to terminate the pregnancy was unsuccessful.

With Zami's birth, Miriam began to have tantrums. She was used to being the baby of the family, her father's pet, and became resentful of the new arrival. This little thing brought only noise and distraction and took away the attention of her precious papa.

Esther watched and listened acutely as the situation around them developed. Her senses were heightened. Adrenaline elevated. Although she had never laid down her guard—not since she had arrived in Köln—she found herself, once more, immersed in strategizing the methods and means that would ensure survival. She was stunned by what had unfolded, though it was difficult to shock someone who, for so many years, had mostly been going through the motions of life. Someone who had already known a bitterness that strangled her inner core.

Evenings, after the children and Abraham had gone to bed, Esther would sit in the kitchen area close to their radio and listen to the speeches of a man who described an *Über* race. His discourses blamed the Jews for all the misfortunes that had befallen Germany and the world: "—the personification of the devil as the symbol of all evil assumes the living shape of the Jew—definitely a race, but—not human." In this way she learned of the latest restrictions leveled against the Jewish people, considered the scapegoats for all of the world's ills.

The noose slowly tightened—

Setting . . . and circumstance were now ripe . . .

CHAPTER TWELVE

Molded over the millennia . . . shattered in one night.
Imbued with healing properties and mystical strengths.
With the abilities to cure and to calm.
Every color of the rainbow . . . every size known to man . . .
Such con—struction turned to total de—struction.
First one home . . . then the next . . . one business . . . then two.
Synagogue after synagogue . . .
one after another . . .burnt to the ground . . .
shattered . . .
broken . . .
shreds of life.
All transformed into shards of broken glass—
crystal . . .
Kristallnacht.

....

T he abrupt silence woke her. Like the moments right before a large quake when the earth takes a slow, deep, measured inhale, or the stillness that occurs as the tide retreats into the depths, calculating the force necessary to return to shore with embroidered dominance and impact. Though deep asleep, the absence of sound announced the looming arrival of a not unanticipated, though much-dreaded, caller and thrust Esther into a state of hyperconsciousness.

Some say it was initiated by a long designed plan, one implemented after years of vengeance against those singled out by the propaganda machine as enemies within the state. Others insist it was a lone incident, one young man's desperate reprisal, a visceral reaction to too many injustices inflicted on his family. Regardless of its root, the incendiary spark incited rampant destruction throughout the land. In the brief span of a few hours, hundreds of synagogues were burned, thousands of Jewish-owned businesses destroyed, and nearly one hundred Jews murdered.

That same evening, more than thirty thousand people of Jewish lineage were sent to camps. Concentration camps. Such a benign term, "to concentrate." It assumes a gathering, a place to focus, absorb, meditate, muse. And the concept of "camp" does not elicit the type of activities that were to take place there. But at this time, the true objectives were concealed, the full extent of the horror to be carried out not yet revealed.

As the onslaught of heavy boots pounded down the pavement, and the sounds of shattering glass and screams encircled them, Esther scooped the baby out of his crib and jumped onto the children's bed. Both Zami and Miriam were sound asleep and yelped when she woke them. Tova was curled up under the covers, whimpering. Abraham tried to comfort his little girl, but no words would form. Even a more educated man, a scholarly man, could not have found the sentences that, woven together, would provide a logic or rationale for what was taking place on the streets below.

For the remainder of the night, Esther and her family huddled in a corner of the bed in the small room, clutching each other. They listened anxiously as the shops on their street were ravaged. And they took in one sharp collective breath when they heard men smash the large window of Abraham's cobbler shop below and enter to complete their task. For too long they were unsure whether their apartment door would be broken down, whether this night would be their last. For the next seventy-four minutes, the sounds of unbridled anger and hatred overwhelmed them: fists against walls—boots against counters—wood against wood—metal against wood—shoes flung into the street—ripping leather—shelves shattering—equipment smashing.

And then—quiet.

Amidst her sobbing children and distraught, enfeebled husband, Esther heard me whisper . . .

It is time.

CHAPTER THIRTEEN

Esther—
so aptly named.
Hidden...
from herself.
Veiled...
to the world.
—facilitates deliverance.
No accidents...
No coincidences.

....

*I*n the morning, as she surveyed the damage before her, Esther's composure stood in stark contrast to the frenzy and despair of those in the neighborhood. She moved slowly up Kämmergasse, balancing each step on the glass mounds that blanketed the street. Every shop window was shattered. Half the interiors had been burned. The air was thick with ash. Screeches echoed between the buildings, still in pain. Produce, staples, supplies, equipment, and clothing were strewn all over. She watched some neighbors cull through the ruins in search of anything salvageable. Others swept, their brooms no match for the mountains of rubble surrounding them. Esther spoke not a word.

Clearheadedness, decisive action, and forward motion were now her trinity.

She did not bother to conspire with Abraham. She knew full well he would hold her back. Resist her efforts. These past few years he had given no credence to her observations, to her warnings. Even now, after last night's calamity, with head shaking, he only said, *"Diese verrückten Regeln*—These crazy rules, this insane government, it can't continue. This is a passing craze. Worse than others, maybe, but this too will pass."

And he laughed, as though all that was taking place, all that had taken place, was merely some type of prank or a joke—destroyed businesses, broken windows, smoke thick in the air, hysteria all around, and worse.

Just a joke.

Nothing seemed to upend Abraham's buoyancy. He did calm the children, who were in a constant state of distress. And he distracted them. This was the most important benefit.

He must keep them out of my way, she thought. It's time to leave, and I must plan for all of us. This situation is impossible. It will only get worse, like some incendiary device on verge of erupting. Of this I am confident. The fragile seams of existence—my life—are rapidly unthreading. I must figure out a fail-safe departure. And soon! I can't be bothered by the children's whining. Or Abraham's foolishness.

But—depart to where?

As she gnawed on the inside of her right cheek, Esther ruminated: Is there somewhere safe? A sanctuary where such madness does not dwell? Where people—all people—are free to live their lives? To simply go about daily activities and responsibilities and interests without risk that all could be taken away at a whim—no notice, no warning? Could such a place possibly exist?

As these reflections swirled in her mind's eye, the makeshift stand, its alluring colors, textures, whiff of exoticism, and those surreal, etched-in-memory images of alien beings appeared—the elephant-headed man in the center. *Ach nein!* she thought, pushing them away as quickly as one would a hair that had gotten into an eye.

There's no room for fantasy, she admonished herself. Pragmatism is crucial. I must devise a realistic plan I can manifest. I have money, the amount is substantial, but the question is: how best to use it?

Esther had heard about people from the Jewish Quarter who had emigrated. They had left the country, left the whole continent and its myriad trials and miseries behind. Some had ventured to Palestine, some to the United States, even a few to China. Desperation was a powerful motivator.

She did have her sister Lifcha in the United States. Someplace called Chicago, she believed, deep in the middle of that country. Lifcha had married when Esther was nine. Her husband was a young dairyman with big eyes and bigger ambitions. Right after Lifcha and Isidore wed, they sold most of their possessions, negligible as they were, and arranged for travel to the place that promised the realization of dreams, particularly economic ones. Their intention was to return to Przeworsk, yet twenty-three years later, that had not come to pass. The pledge had not been honored. Evidently challenges abounded there too.

Although her funds were significant, Esther knew if she did try to emigrate—anywhere—it would take every *Pfennig* she had worked relentlessly to accumulate just to get travel papers secured, if that was still possible, and pay for passage. She would arrive— wherever—without anything. She had no doubt she could subsist on her skills and talents, but to once again start all over with next to nothing, this—this was unacceptable.

Esther shook her head firmly.

To return to Przeworsk was certainly not an option. Nothing remained there. Not for her. Moreover, from the bits of news she had heard these past few years, the poverty was oppressive in the remote town. On the scarce occasion when mail would still come through, she learned of her family's hardships. Her parents and siblings barely made do. These letters included requests to send money, and once she did consider obliging—a small amount—but then thought better of it. Esther had no confidence the money would arrive, certain most correspondence was confiscated, particularly envelopes that looked as though they contained more than one slip of notepaper.

I've worked hard for everything I have earned, she thought while experiencing a twinge of compassion for these people from her early life. But it's mine! This money is mine!

Esther persevered. There will be a way out, I'm sure of it. There is a solution, and somehow it will be revealed to me.

Evenings found her hunched over a map of Germany, the large, detailed one with explanations Tova had needed for school. Esther traced her fingers over and over the territory of this vast country. She remained unsure—confused as to what direction to take. Where would it all ultimately lead?

And what was she actually seeking?

Abraham watched her wordlessly. He did not understand her obsession with that map. Her back and forth pacing across their crowded space accompanied by her incessant muttering made his eyes roll. Or he would sigh. This woman had begun to repel him, and after his darling little boy was born, his Zami, Abraham no longer tried to touch her. Any pretense of affection from Esther was long gone. He spent a greater part of each day in his shop. Not that his work had increased. He preferred to keep his distance. He set up Zami's crib in a corner and took care of his son's every need. Tova and Miriam preferred to stay with him. It was more comfortable for them. Their mama barely spoke, and when she did, it was most commonly, "*Geh' weg.* Go away. I'm busy."

Her responses to questions were rough and curt. Her commands hurtful.

Still, she never made light of her familial responsibilities. She was focused and vigilant on their needs as much as her own. For throughout all of her mulling and planning, the question hovered— what about the children?

Esther became emboldened after the events of that horrific night of broken glass. Intrepid. Adamant nothing or no one would obstruct her momentum. She had no idea where that path would lead or what lay ahead, yet she remained firm in the conviction that she would not be a victim.

Although she had lived in Köln's Jewish Quarter for nearly fifteen years and each Friday, without fail, prepared the Sabbath meal, Esther did not identify as a Jew. She ate pork and shellfish, on the rare occasion they were available and affordable, and combined meat and dairy as she pleased. She had not studied Hebrew or the Torah or the circuitous history of the Jewish people. She knew only the prayers associated with the Friday evening meal, and those she understood more as part of a weekly ritual than as a sacrament. Esther was not religious in any way and had no belief in any kind of higher power or a Holy Spirit—

She was not yet ready . . .

—most especially when she considered the circumstances that incited the move to Köln and away from her heart and dreams and desires. How could a God—if He existed, or She, or for that matter, They, who really knew?—have let life unfold as it had? It was pure conjecture, all of it.

Judaism as a culture, as a community of sorts, was rooted within Esther's family and its generations. But it remained on the periphery of her life, barely in the backdrop of her thoughts and actions. As a religion, a philosophy of principles and practice, a belief system, it did not signify, not at all.

Why should I suffer for something I don't believe in? Esther often thought as the restrictions tightened and the hardships multiplied during these years. I am entitled to live as others live—as one should live—without designation or label. But the realities of this current situation are clear. Too many assumptions, preconceived ideas, and prejudices are rampant. The need to maneuver through this landscape is taking all my wits.

Esther realized it was most essential to rely on her intuition, her instincts—

And upon me . . . whether she acknowledged it . . . or not . . .

—and she began to excel at determining when and what to avoid or ignore, whether to venture down a certain street or to look in the eyes of a particular person.

In order to once again move freely about the city and accomplish necessary tasks, Esther artfully put snaps on her yellow stars so they could be discreetly removed or quickly replaced as the situation necessitated without revealing patches or hanging threads.

She began to use public transportation, ignoring the large signs posted declaring *JUDEN VERBOTEN*.

Who is to say who I am or what I am when I get on a streetcar or a tram? she rationalized.

Without exception, Esther dressed modestly, with hair pushed back into a neat, tight bun. And—she moved with purpose. When she ventured out, away from the Jewish Quarter, she observed people still walked freely and talked and laughed; they met friends and drank coffee at cafés, carried packages and went about their business seemingly without a care—barely half a kilometer from her neighborhood.

Esther saw how easily she blended in. Without that yellow Star of David shrieking its pronouncement on the skin of her clothes, no one took notice of her. There were no sideward glances. No looks of disgust or pity. No mutters under their breath. No walking to the other side of the street so as not to cross her path. Here she was simply a woman—a German. Another human being going about one's day. Her indistinct features and thick blonde hair did not proclaim her part of one ethnic group or another. She was merely a member of the species. It especially helped that her accent was flawless. Like a native.

> I ask . . . what is identity after all? What is it . . . truly? The way one dresses? How one wears one's hair? Inflections of speech? Features? Characteristics? Mannerisms? Personality?

One afternoon, as she turned from the main street into another neighborhood's market with its abundance of fruits and vegetables and household supplies, her sweater slipped from her shoulders to the ground. Before she could bend down to retrieve it, a young man in a brown uniform picked it up. He handed it to her and said, *"Bitte meine Dame,* let me assist you."

"Vielen, vielen Dank," Esther responded.

"Nein, nein, the pleasure is mine."

She did her best to contain her surprise that what just took place was not the most normal of exchanges.

The uniformed man gave her a warm smile before he walked away.

Ach, ja! Esther thought.

In an instant, a light switched on and a door opened wide.

From this point forward, Esther's plan developed methodically, with the same singular focus she applied to any assignment: each step like a new stitch that had to precisely match the one before and lead the one to follow.

Esther realized that it would not be necessary to journey far. Only enough of a distance where she would be assured no possibility of recognition. These days travel was neither common nor popular. The majority of people she encountered in a day's activities did not have the resources to ride the local tram, let alone a train to another city. The most critical boundary she would have to pass would be the one that defined her present identity.

Her contacts in the black market proved indispensable. The same individuals who had helped her obtain essential sewing or home supplies and grocery staples no longer available in her neighborhood shops now introduced her to those who could supply identity cards, passports, and visas. They provided precious information. Through this network, Esther met an extensive group of people who were resisting—defying those working hard to destroy them, re-insisting in all ways resourceful and inventive that their lives were their own to live—and she listened intently to everything they told her. The stories of people who had changed their identities and gone into hiding were of most interest. She absorbed their recommendations and experiences.

And she heard stories of many—far too many—who had simply disappeared.

Esther discovered good fortune was on her side.

Me . . . of course.

By what seemed miraculous—

Or so one might conjecture . . .

—she learned a longtime client had joined the newly formed Resistance. One afternoon, as Esther lay out the clothes to review her tailoring repairs, Frau Göttlieb asked about the sheer fabric Esther had used to line a skirt and a distinctive stitch bordering a buttonhole. Then she said, casually, *"Wenn es Ihr Wunsch ist*—If leaving is your desire, I can assist you."

"Really?" Esther reacted with suspicion. "How is this possible?"

At first, Frau Göttlieb's response was merely a slight smile, followed by, "Even in times of war, the wealthy and the privileged will demand their luxuries. They will not look too closely at the one who provides this service, most especially if the work is exceptional. It is not—*sehr schwer*—so very difficult to hide when one does not want to see what, or in this case who, is right before them.

"Of this, I can assure you."

Such wisdom . . . and . . . without question . . . Esther's masterful tailoring skills would provide a camouflage few could emulate.

Such a perspective astonishes me, Esther thought. Who could have imagined those interminable hours sitting in front of the family fire night after night, from age three on, perfecting a stitch neither too long nor too short, would someday be the thread between life and death?

The Göttliebs were an affluent, well-regarded Köln family with ties to government, both local and national. Their position and stature gave them access to confidential information and the most up-to-date news. They had no reason to align themselves with anyone outside of those in power. Apart from their consciences. They were appalled at the disintegration of life and liberties taking place all around them and went out of their way to treat everyone in their employ equitably and equally. And to provide any special covert aid they could.

Frau Göttlieb took Esther and her plight on as a personal crusade and was generous with her assistance. She knew Esther could not work much with all that was needed for her departure preparations, so she provided a large sum of money to cover all expenses and then some. Frau Göttlieb took advantage of her extensive contacts and personally arranged for Esther's new identity papers. These would include birth certificate and baptismal documentation. She knew the best sources, and there would be no question the papers would be official with appropriate stamps and dates and signatures. The documents Esther had purchased from her contacts on the black market were good. These were flawless.

As they were making the final arrangements on the paperwork, Frau Göttlieb asked, *"Welchen Namen hätten Sie gerne?* What name would you like? Who do you wish to become?"

Esther smiled broadly, astonishing Frau Göttlieb, for she had only ever seen this woman as stolid. Completely controlled in action and thought.

This one question pleased Esther down to her core. Amid the horror and hardship, she was given the rare, but oft-desired, opportunity to become someone else, a persona new and different. She thought for a long while, culling through the widest range of possibilities and options, before finally she blurted out, "Etta— Etta Göttlieb."

She chose to keep her initials, not unlike bookends holding the full passage as one. With this change, Esther Grünspan would, for all intents and purposes, cease to be. Really, this had already occurred on that fateful day in Przeworsk—the day Tadeusz forsook her, forsook them. The name had remained, the person had not. Exposing a remnant of her humanity, Esther wanted to honor the kindness of her benefactress by taking the woman's family name. Frau Göttlieb nodded circumspectly.

*The irony of course . . . the beauty of this name . . . is that it
means literally . . . God's love . . .*

To fully form Esther's new identity, Frau Göttlieb provided
her with a small Bible—the New Testament—that could easily fit
into her handbag. She also gave her a rosary of dark wooden carved
beads and a delicate Holy Mother medal on a thin gold chain. Most
importantly, they spent three and a half weeks of afternoons studying catechism. Esther was a diligent student and learned quickly.
Then again, there was no question her life, literally, depended on
this knowledge.

Wuppertal, a small factory town less than forty kilometers
north of Köln, was chosen as the location to embark on her new life.
Recently formed through the merger of seven small communities,
this city was filled with new inhabitants, and Esther would find
few obstacles to blending in. In addition, Wuppertal had quickly
become known as a center for manufacturing textiles; thus she was
ensured there would be reliable need for her expertise. Here she
could continue to earn a living. Arrangements had been made for
her to move into a serviceable one-room apartment, and Frau Göttlieb shared two contacts that would, upon arrival, provide Esther
with sewing assignments and begin to advertise her talents. There
was a wealthy enclave—mostly composed of factory owners—
whose wives were sure to be delighted by the addition of a skilled
tailor in their small town.

Through a contact of Frau Göttlieb, Esther learned about a
transport to England—for children—that would take them away
from Germany and from danger. There were more than a dozen
charitable organizations that oversaw the arrangements, and Esther
registered with each. Her children's names were put into a pool, and
relief was all she could muster when Tova and Miriam, now ages
eight and six, were selected to join the *Kindertransport*.

Oh no! Oh no! This is dreadful, she thought, upon learning
that Zami, barely one year old, was considered too young to go on
the *kinder* train. The officials could not guarantee there would be
people on the other end—in England—who would agree to care
for babies.

"What will I do? I don't believe he will survive if I leave him with Abraham. Or any other family who stays here. Köln will not be safe. I can't possibly bring him with me. So much ahead is unknown, and being with a small child will likely impact my own ability to endure."

"*Aber*—But, Esther, you really must reconsider," Frau Göttlieb insisted. "Your son will be safer with you. Children under six years of age don't need identity cards, and people will be far less suspicious of a woman relocating with a young child. His very presence will act as a helpful cover. He will be an asset, and he will provide comfort. You will appreciate you are not completely alone."

What she did not say, although most definitely thought, was that as a circumcised boy—if exposed—Zami would intensify the potential of danger. Esther was well aware of this fact, and as a mother and a human being, struggled with herself to consider this little boy as anything but a liability. But above all other considerations, the thread of their bond ultimately kept him with her.

She went about her daily activities as though nothing were unusual, while stealthily assembling the necessary ingredients toward escape. With her new identity and the vital documents secured, Esther turned her attention to final details.

I will not need much, she thought, but I cannot forget the essentials. Sewing supplies, of course, those I can't do without. But how many needles and how much thread? What colors? What sizes? There's so much uncertainty. Just about everything is unclear. Will there be a store that sells what I don't bring? Can I get by with one pair of scissors? Or one large pair and snips? Appliqué scissors are probably frivolous, but what about my pinking shears? I could make a zigzag edge by hand, so perhaps bringing these are also too much. How to decide? How do I decide? So many unknowns! And dresses? Two, no, three at most. I must always look presentable. After a month or so, when I am settled, I can make whatever additional clothes I might need. One pair of shoes will be fine.

Esther's thoughts raced on. I must take care that neither Abraham nor a neighbor suspects I'm doing anything out of the ordinary.

It was not difficult to keep these plans hidden from Abraham. He was not inquisitive by nature, and their exchanges were few. He was mostly in his shop. With Zami, and then also the girls, when they returned from school. They came up to the apartment only to eat and sleep. Often, Abraham slept in the shop. Esther's days were spent almost entirely alone.

The strata of her responsibilities grew thicker.

The clock ticked ever more rapidly.

And the stifling summer heat exasperated everyone.

Around her, stress and anxiety continued to mount between the normal and the abnormal, the straightforward and the extreme, the ordinary and the extraordinary. It appeared as though most people were attempting to adjust to this new normalcy—to repair and retain their lives as best they could. Yet, in actual fact, the situation's deterioration had accelerated like a revving engine.

Esther's single-mindedness in laying out her path diverted her focus away from the people she had shared roof and life with these past eight years. While she made sure the children's basic needs were met, she remained far more concerned with the future—to ensure there would be a future for her and the children—than with the day to day. This explained why nearly two weeks passed before she noticed Tova had a persistent, odd cough that would result in a strange, high-pitched sound. And a fever accompanied the cough, which made the girl's face turn bright red and her eyes bulge. She was losing weight swiftly.

"Ach nein!" Esther shouted. "Tova's got *Keuchhusten*—whooping cough." She knew this illness well, as five of her younger siblings had contracted it when she was fourteen.

You cannot get sick, not now, and you cannot get the others sick, Esther cried out silently. It's not possible. This cannot happen. They won't take you on the train. You must go on the train. If there is a trace or suspicion of illness, you will not be allowed on the train. Oh, what to do? What to do?

And what about me? I have to leave. I must continue with my plans and get away from here!

There was no doctor to turn to. The two in their quarter had been taken away five months before. Neither had returned. She could ask Frau Göttlieb for help, but she was out of town with her family for a short holiday. Even if she had been reachable, Esther was not certain she could or should seek more help. Frau Göttlieb had done so much already, and all at her own risk. Asking for anything more—even for a child—was too much. Especially now, with the complicated issues finally resolved, the strategies designed, and the plan soon to be carried out.

Nein, Esther thought, I must manage on my own. She scanned the recesses of her memory for remedies Bubbe Royza would use to heal her and her siblings when they were ill. Esther had never thought about these before, favoring new medicines for the children. But options were no longer available.

"Swallow these," she ordered, handing Tova four cloves of raw garlic.

"Nein, Mama, *Neeeeiiiiinnnnn!"* Tova shrilled, her face a bright red. *"Igitt!* Yuck! I don't like this! It tastes horrible!"

Tova kept her jaw clamped and shook her head fiercely. Esther had to wrestle with her to get the cloves down her throat. She then forced the girl to suck on thick pieces of salt. "This, too, will help make you better."

"Igitt!" Tova shouted.

Esther recalled Bubbe Royza, and her own mama, had the children breathe in tar whenever they developed colds or respiratory problems. I must give that a try, she thought. The closest location under construction was at the southern edge of the Kölner Dom. Parts of the cathedral's roof truss were under repair. Half carrying, half dragging an exhausted, tearful Tova, Esther got her to the site and sat the little girl on the ground at the corner where the stench of tar was strongest. An open vat was nearby.

"Breathe, Tovele, breathe deeply," Esther said gently, encouraging the girl to inhale the smelly black liquid. "And please stop crying. I know it seems strange. It's not like going to the doctor's office, but this will help you. I'm sure this will make you feel better right away."

At first Tova resisted, but Esther pressed her close. She tenderly held Tova's long hair away from her face as the girl bent over to take in the tar's healing properties.

"Ah, my Tovele," Esther said, lightly stroking Tova's forehead. "You will feel well very soon."

Esther felt a pang in her chest but brushed it aside. Now is not the time for sentiment, she thought. Tova must get better quickly! There is no alternative.

Still, she was unexpectedly gentle with this child. It was one of the few genuine acts of mothering compassion Esther had expressed to any of her children.

After about one hour, Tova began to breathe more normally, and she stopped coughing. Her body relaxed. She snuggled into her mama's chest, content to have a special moment of consolation.

Imagine that, Esther reflected, this old Polish remedy actually works.

And imagine . . . caring and compassion still resided within . . .

Two days before the girls' scheduled departure, Esther informed Abraham about the preparations she had made. "They are going to safety. This is a good thing, and it's all been arranged. There is nothing to discuss."

Before Abraham could object, she repeated, *"Es ist alles arrangiert.* It has all been arranged."

She didn't elaborate on the details or reveal her contacts, but she did underscore their good fortune. "Getting on these transports is highly competitive. Not every child whose name got in the pool was selected. You must understand how extremely lucky Tova and Miriam are. How lucky we are."

Abraham did not understand. "How can you use the word 'luck' when you tell me you are sending the girls away? My girls?"

Abraham shouted—it was the first time Esther had, in their eight years together, heard him raise his voice. "How can you do this to us? *Unserer Familie*—to our family? How can you do this to me?"

She watched impassively as he ranted on. He stomped his foot and pounded his fists on the table, on his chest, on the floor. Tears cascaded down Abraham's face.

In the end, he did not resist. He did not have the ability or strength to resist. Esther's will was implacable.

The night before her plan would unfold, Esther had a dream. It was the first she had dreamt since leaving Przeworsk, sixteen years ago now. Since that juncture, her nights had been as empty of emotion and heart as her days. But this night was different, for her sleep was deep and full.

Esther dreamt she was descending. One, slow, considered step after another. Each step echoing the last. The space before her was ebony but emanated warmth. She felt uneven ground beneath her feet, and the course she followed wound in a steep decline. In some areas the space narrowed or shrank, and she had to bend or twist her body in response to jutting stones. It was unlike anywhere she had ever been. She did not know where she was or what this was or why she was there. She continued to feel and breathe through the dark. There appeared to be no ending and no longer a memory of what came before. No sense or possibility of time. She had no fear. She was confined but liberated, on a path seemingly without destination or purpose. Throughout the night, in the arms of *Maya,* she ventured forward.

A cave . . .

CHAPTER FOURTEEN

Life . . . this life . . . all life is fragile . . . so very fragile indeed . . .

Gossamer that melts upon touch.

*Most of you . . . most of the time . . . hang on by thin threads . . .
delicate silk . . . glorious strands of luminescent silk certainly . . .
but threads nonetheless.*

*You are here in this place . . . in any place . . . at this time . . . at
any time . . . to confront your fears . . . your issues . . . and rise up
. . . rise above. You are here to learn . . . to grow . . . grow strong
. . . mighty . . . invincible. This is your destiny. This is your karma.*

This is truth for all.

*But far too often . . . for many of you . . . for far too many . . . the
difficulties to overcome are too great. Well . . . they appear too
great. For in truth they are not . . . they cannot be . . . for you
. . . yourself . . . have chosen them.*

Yes . . . this is true . . . although in all likelihood you do not recall.

So many lose the path to strength . . .

So many lose the path to truth.

In your human incarnation . . . so much . . . so very much . . . sadly most . . . is forgotten. Numerous blocks . . . countless walls . . . endless barriers are erected. Thick . . . and high . . . seemingly impenetrable.

I could say this is a travesty . . . but it is not.

For at some point . . . at some place in time . . . you will prevail. You will overcome all adversity even . . . and most significantly . . . overcome yourself . . . your limitations . . . your fears. The things that torture you . . . chase you down at night.

Please . . . you must know . . . there is nothing . . . not one thing . . . that is impossible . . . that is insurmountable . . .

Truly . . . truly . . . nothing at all.

CHAPTER FIFTEEN

"*Nein! Nein!*

"Papa! Papaaaaaaaa! *Bitte!* Papa! Mama!

"*Bitte!* Please! Please! Papa!

"I want *nach Hause gehen*—to go home!

"*Jetzt!* Now!

"I don't want to go on the train!

"*Bringt mich wieder nach Hause!* Take me home!

"Papa! Papa! Why don't you listen to me?

"*Was habe ich*—What did I do? What did I do?"

Watching his little girl in such pain, Abraham's heart strangulated; tears coursed down his face. Esther remained as stone, willing the demise of any rebel feeling.

I cannot react, she ordered herself. I must not react. I am doing this to save their lives. This is the only way. There are no other options.

She continues to smother her heart . . . but at times this is essential.

Miriam's screams refused to stop. Could not stop.

Tova watched the scene unfold as if from a distance. At eight years old, she had twice traveled on a train—to go on overnight trips with her class—and although Papa and Mama had not informed them of their destination, she assumed she was going on a similar outing. And *Schwestie* must be old enough now to come too.

This trip seemed to be more of an adventure than those in the past because Mama had roused them before the light and dressed each in five layers of clothing. Additional clothing was stuffed in two tiny suitcases. *Schwestie,* of course, had to bring her bear. She was never without it—would never be without it.

When they arrived at the train station, Tova wondered if a festival was scheduled, for the platform swarmed with children— maybe hundreds. She had never seen anything like it, and while the scene fascinated her, the crowds frightened Miriam. That was when she began to beg Papa to take them home.

"Stop crying, *Schwestie.* Don't worry. Everything will be fine." Tova tried to quiet her little sister.

"It will be a great adventure. We'll play lots of games. And they'll be new games, different than what we have. Last time I went on a school trip we stayed by a large field, near woods. We went on walks and learned lots of interesting things about the forest. We'll have a good time. I promise."

But Miriam refused to listen. A perceptive child, she sensed a finality and with all her weight and will resisted the end to everything she knew and loved to the best of her six-year-old ability.

Esther and Abraham did not contradict what Tova said; in fact, neither uttered a word. Esther had business to attend to. She needed to ensure all the necessary forms were in order. And Abraham could not construct an adequate sentence to explain what was happening and why. Chiefly because he did not understand it himself, nor agree with Esther's rationale that their lives were in danger.

"*Müll*! Rubbish! This is all rubbish!" he muttered to himself, but was in no way capable of surmounting Esther's indomitable will.

Feigning a unified front, they led Tova and Miriam through the various check-in lines, where official papers were inspected, signed, and stamped. The girls were issued numbers on small cardboard signs they were to wear around their necks throughout the journey. To make sure they were fastened securely, Esther pulled out a calyx-eye needle and twine to stitch these to the collars of each girl's dress. She knew this would create small holes, but more importantly, the signs would not fall off.

Tova did not recall she had been given a number to wear like this on either of her previous trips. Perhaps this is a game, she thought. How fun! Everything taking place made it seem like a special occasion.

When they were put on the train, *Schwestie* screamed and cried with renewed vigor. Until all she had the energy for was a slow, low whimper. This would remain her constant companion for months to come.

The train's whistle blew, and within a few brief minutes, metal and glass, wheels and spokes dissolved away to become a nearly kilometer-long sea of thin, outstretched, imploring arms, tiny hands—and desperate tears.

Esther was the first to turn and walk away.

CHAPTER SIXTEEN

Plans, long conceived,
become deed...

....

She left two days later.

With the girls now gone, Esther turned her attention to the unfinished details that would ensure safe flight.

But what does safe in actual fact mean? she wondered. Does it exist? And I'm still not convinced I will be able to conceal myself with a toddler by my side. But I have no choice. I must take my chances with my young boy on the road. It's clear I can't leave Zami with Abraham. Wherever I go, wherever I end up, no matter what might occur, Zami will be more secure with me.

Esther had an inherent sense of duty coupled with protective instincts. Abraham trusted everyone and disbelieved what she knew, without question, had taken root. She was sure harm would befall him but could not muster an ounce of empathy.

"Foolish, foolish man," Esther would mutter under her breath. She did this often. "Fortunately he is no longer my concern."

While Esther packed and made final preparations, Abraham moved through the apartment like a ghost—a dark and brooding ethereal shadow. Engulfed by resentment and pain, he could not forgive Esther for sending his girls away.

No more words passed between them.

Abraham's lone pleasure and only joy was Zami. To feed him. To rock him. To change him. To sing to him:

Schlaf, Kindlein schlaf.
der Vater hütet die Schaf,
die Mutter schüttelt's Bäumelein,
da fällt herab ein Träumelein.
Schlaf, Kindlein schlaf.

. . . .

Sleep, baby, sleep!
Thy father guards the sheep;
Thy mother shakes the little tree,
That pleasant dreams may fall on thee.
Sleep, little child, sleep!

Or *"Rozhinkes mit Mandlen,"* the one his grandmother sang most often:

In dem beys hamikdosh,
In a vinkl-kheyder,
Zitst di almone, bas tsion, aleyn
Ir ben-yochidl yidele,
Vigt zi k'seyder,
Un zingt im tzum shlofn a lidele sheyn.
Ay-lu-lu

. . . .

In the Holy Temple,
In the corner of a room
Sits the widow, Zion's Daughter, herself.
There she keeps rocking
Her only small son, little Yidele [Judah]—
And sings him to sleep with this sweet tune:
Ay, lyu, lyu

He would speak about the games they would play together when Zami grew older and bigger. Oblivious to Esther's machinations, Abraham had no idea that soon he would be alone.

With the baby occupied, Esther arranged her most important belongings in the large woven basket. This flight was one of practicality and necessity. Nothing more. She did not own many things, and most of what she had was of no interest or personal value.

The singular possession that transcended material need was Bubbe Royza's *kiddush* cup. Its connection to Esther's history ran deep; its innate sense of calm and well-being were primal. She refused to leave it behind.

"Oh, my dear, dear Bubbe Royza," Esther murmured as she caressed the engraving that bordered the cup's rim, then tenderly wrapped it in a small square of black felt. She sighed. "I do miss you deeply." But, she continued on in her head, now is not for sentiments. I must be practical. I know you, of all people, dear *bubbe*, would appreciate that. This fabric will protect the cup while traveling. I am confident it will. Then, at some point in the future, it will be molded into a flower to adorn a skirt or blouse. Each item I include must have a purpose. No space can be wasted.

Esther became a master at layering. Over the past month she had brought necessary items concealed within her clothing to Frau Göttlieb's home. A medium-sized suitcase waited for her there, holding one winter outfit each for her and Zami. Frau Göttlieb assured her warm coats and winter boots would be made available in Wuppertal.

Esther did her best to keep the basket light so she would not exert too much effort under its weight. It could not be unwieldy and draw suspicion. Sewing supplies lined the bottom. She put in as wide a selection of needles and colors and sizes of threads as space allowed, along with scissors, tracing papers, stencils, templates, and wheel. An assortment of common buttons and zippers of various sizes joined them, neatly arranged beside a variety of ribbon, pins and pincushions, thimbles, snaps, hooks, eyelets, marking pencils, and chalk. And—the essential tape measure.

Together . . . these materials will be her lifeline . . .

"*In der Wohnung*—In the apartment, you will find all the basic furniture and household utensils you will need," Frau Göttlieb informed her during their most recent visit. "*Eine tragbare Nähmaschine*—A portable sewing machine will be there. It is small, but I am confident you will find it useful. There will also be some bobbins and thread. I was not able to locate a wide variety."

A sewing machine would enable her to work more quickly, and Esther was appreciative. However, she knew instinctively this location would not be permanent, and the likelihood of carrying a sewing machine where next she must venture was unlikely. Esther understood that wherever this odyssey led, a needle and thread would suffice—must suffice. And, beyond question, her clarity and wits. For what Esther was to embark upon, her capacity to bury sad and sorrowful emotions was now a benefit.

> *Life's occurrences . . . its lessons . . . and of course its trials and its challenges . . . had trained her well.*

Finally, the money must be secured.

Esther stitched the many bills she had hoarded into the hems and seams of each piece of clothing she and Zami could bring with them. More, of course, was included in the seams, as their stiffness allowed the fabrics to retain their natural movement.

Interwoven between the *Reichsmarks* in one dress, Esther included a faded black-and-white photograph of her family. Before she closed off the seam, she took one last look at her twelve siblings, standing on both sides of Mama and *Tate*, enshrined around the dining table of their modest home in Przeworsk. The five boys were all crowded together on one side. Jakob, not surprisingly, had contorted his face like a comedic mask. Lifcha, the eldest and tallest, stood directly behind Mama, with the twins, appearing as though they had just been offered candy, in their matching dresses to her left. Esther found herself at the edge of the table, tightly grasping Tonka's hand. She sighed. In a mere five-centimeter square, the image conveyed a history and a legacy. Carrying it into the future was more an act of posterity than sentiment; nevertheless, it felt right to do.

The impulse lingers...

Buried in the bottom left corner of a drawer filled with rags was one black-and-white photo of Tadeusz. He was looking straight into the camera, leaning against their tree in the field where—

No! No memories! This must go, she thought. Esther could barely glance at it without the pit inside her core beginning to churn. It was not as though she needed anything to remember his face, for Tadeusz's image remained a deeply etched chasm not possible to erase—an *aide-memoire* was not necessary to know she must never weaken, never trust, and never, ever let down her guard.

Esther took the photograph, as well as the few in the apartment of herself and Zami, to the kitchen burner, where she started a fire in the iron skillet with a little kerosene. The flames took to the papers easily. Esther watched impassively as their edges curled and then blackened, the images slowly contracting before they disappeared completely. Thin wisps of smoke swirled upward; gray ash drifted to the floor. She did not bother to clean up the mound that formed.

Ah ... the scene ... a reflection of what is to come ...

On the kitchen table, Esther ordered the elements that would inform, and ideally safeguard, her new self—her new reality: identity papers, birth certificate, baptismal documentation, rosary, and a copy of the New Testament. The Holy Mother on the thin chain would soon rest against her throat for the entire world to see and understand her religious affiliation.

Well, she thought, they won't know if I'm Protestant or Lutheran or Catholic, but they will know I'm not Jewish. At that, she snorted. Anything but Jewish!

Esther silently recited the catechism once more to ensure it was fixed in her memory.

She studied these items intently, first individually, then collectively, as though learning the lines for the lead role in a play. Esther

Klein had never taken hold as a genuine identity; she had adopted her married name for purposes of protocol only, negligible as they were. Losing that name caused not a ripple. The full immersion of Esther Grünspan was what mattered.

Esther was now, and as long as need be, Etta Göttlieb.

Next, she laid out the documentation for Zami's new identity, as Hannis.

At one year of age, a name change should not be difficult for him to absorb, Esther imagined. I am lucky he is such a placid baby. Not noisy and talkative as Miriam was at his age, or colicky and sickly like Tova. He is so quiet that at times I forget he's in the room. *Ach!*

In the midst of her myriad preparations, Esther had to remind herself Zami would accompany her. She understood being unwanted only too profoundly but did not regret how she treated this child or either of the girls.

I have been a responsible mother, she reflected. I have remained conscientious when it came to their health and safety. But the deeper reality of my feelings could not be changed. That must suffice.

Jeopardy and countless unknowns might be lying in wait, for this situation guaranteed challenges and trials. Nevertheless, feelings of liberation began to percolate within her. A healing process of sorts felt underway.

I've been stuck these last many years. Marrying Abraham was misguided. The union designed to ease my life's burdens only brought increased labor, effort, and challenge. But that fault can be attributed to no one but me. What was I thinking? Esther shook her head forcefully. I know I should have some comfort with Zami accompanying me, but I am most concerned he will only complicate my movements. Nevertheless, even with all the nonsense going on, he and I will have a freedom that hasn't existed for years.

Above all else, for the first time since arriving in Köln, Esther experienced gratitude. She was grateful for the series of happenstance, chance, and circumstance that led to her ability to pursue this path, to flee in a period and a place when most were trapped without option or opportunity. Frau Göttlieb and her network of friends and associates provided invaluable assistance in making her escape and new identity feasible—making survival possible.

Of course . . . do not forget me . . . my role to assist . . . to help . . . to set all in motion . . . and most especially . . . to destroy what obstacles could be . . . may be . . . will be . . . in her path . . .

On the last day of August, midmorning, a customary hour for Esther to go about the day's errands, she set her plans in motion. While the heat of the summer cast an oppressive coating of sweat and soot, Esther wore three layers of thin cotton dresses and a light sweater without arousing sideways glances or attracting unwanted attention. She looked natural, if somewhat heftier. It was unlikely anyone would take notice. Her neighbors and the local *Polizei* regularly saw her carry bundles of clothing in her oversized basket. They understood this was how she transported her customers' clothes back and forth, and she had been fortunate no effort had been made to stop her comings and goings.

At all times . . . I watched her activities closely and secured her movements. On occasion I distracted an officer . . . or encouraged a Braunhemd . . . a Brownshirt . . . to turn left at a corner . . . instead of right. This day was no exception.

Esther, holding Zami in her right arm and balancing the basket and his cumbersome stroller in her left, climbed down the three flights of stairs to Kämmergasse. At the base, she put Zami in the conveyance and turned right. She did not go into Abraham's shop or glance inside the glass window as they passed.

No goodbyes.

The full transformation took place hidden inside Frau Göttlieb's home, in the storage room without windows or outside light. The steps were orderly and accomplished in silence. The yellow Stars of David were taken off their clothing for the final time, and Esther fastened the gold chain around her neck. From this day forward, the delicate Holy Mother would rest against her throat.

Esther emptied the basket and in each of the two suitcases placed the sewing materials first, neatly layered. Every article of clothing was then tightly folded or scrunched like tissue paper to fit inside. Even with Esther's severe editing, two of Zami's shirts did not fit and would have to be left behind.

No matter, Esther thought, I will make him others when we are settled. No doubt he would outgrow these quickly anyway.

They used the side door that led directly into the garage and the Göttliebs's waiting car. The train station was three kilometers away, and they arrived ten minutes before the three o'clock scheduled departure. A lone officer walked the length of the waiting area and back again without paying their small party undue attention.

No goodbyes or hugs passed between Esther and Frau Göttlieb. No words of thanks. Before embarking, Esther turned halfway around to look at Frau Göttlieb once more and extended a nod and slight smile. A connection of understanding.

The forty-six-kilometer trip took one hour and eight minutes. In their second-class car, Esther chose an aisle seat, indifferent to the passing topography and the transition from one chapter of life into another. Too small to sit in a separate seat without sliding off, Zami sat on Esther's lap with one of her arms secured around him. Although it was his first train trip, Zami did not exhibit a curiosity about these new surroundings, only an interest in playing with the buttons on his recently sewn gray-and-white-striped shirt.

They were to be met at their destination by a young woman in a light checkered dress. She would be wearing a straw cloche hat with a braided black-and-gray band tied around its circumference. Esther found her standing in the north corner of the station as arranged. After the customary welcome and basic pleasantries, she drove them to their new home: a one-room flat on the fourth floor of an old apartment building in the western part of the city not far from the zoo. A key was exchanged, her leave-taking perfunctory.

Esther and Zami, now Etta and Hannis, arrived in Wuppertal without incident.

The incident . . . commenced the next day . . .

CHAPTER SEVENTEEN

In—va—sion!
On a . . .
beautiful fall day.
One country,
brazen . . . domineering . . . potent,
desirous of controlling . . .
another,
previously scarred, already beleaguered.
This, merely the first phase . . .
on the path . . .
to possessing all.

. . . .

The same young woman who had met them at the train station came by the flat late the next morning. This day her dress was of dark blue cotton, although she did wear the same straw cloche hat with the braided band. Word had traveled swiftly through the community of those active in the underground Resistance, and in a soft, matter-of-fact voice she informed Esther of the dramatically changed circumstances in which they all now lived.

"*Sie haben den Krieg erklärt.* War has been declared," this woman said.

Esther did not register one ounce of surprise. Everyone had long anticipated these events. It was only now formally a war, as declared by the government officials. Esther had been at war for years.

The young woman carried a cloth-covered wicker basket filled with a loaf of pumpernickel bread, a half loaf of *Roggenbrot,* a few hard cheeses, and a small portion of salted meat. There was also a freshly baked *Apfelstrudel.*

How did she know? Esther wondered as this favorite treat was handed to her.

My whispers . . . my suggestions . . . can be heard by anyone.
This would be Esther's last semblance of an indulgence for some
time to come.

A map of the city and a dozen tram tickets made up the rest of the basket's contents. The woman opened the map, circled the apartment's location with a pen pulled from her handbag, and pointed out a couple of nearby sights, including the zoo.

"I believe your son will enjoy visiting here. It's a short walk away, and it is a very nice zoo." She smiled at Zami sitting on the bed, but he did not notice. He was occupied with pulling and twisting his pajama shirt buttons one by one. He started with the top button by the collar and headed downward. When he got to the bottom of the shirt, his hands moved back to the top and he began the process over again.

The young woman turned her attention back to Esther. Handing her a piece of paper, she said, "Here is the name and address of the person you must contact who has a tailoring assignment for you. She will refer you to others. Her shop is near this corner," indicating its location on the map.

Her eyes darted first to the room's one small window and then the closed door. "This must be my final visit," she continued, without looking at Esther. "It will not be safe for me to return. Not safe for you and your son. *Es darf kein Verdacht*—No suspicion must be aroused. I am confident you will be fine."

Esther listened intently. "*Ja, ja,* I understand everything you are saying."

The young woman then rose abruptly, turned, and left. Almost vanished, as though never present. She had not offered her name, and within minutes, her visual identity and any distinguishing features were lost to time and history.

Esther moved into action. After indulging in a few bites of the strudel—such a surprising treat!—and feeding Zami a slice of bread and cheese, she put on their most presentable clothes and headed out into the day's thick, repressive heat. In search of this contact and—survival.

Forward motion. Always forward motion. Regardless of what else the conditions demanded, including contending with those who singled out, hunted down, and persecuted human beings merely because they were followers of the Jewish faith or carried the genetic code of a Semitic heritage. Esther had no doubt she could, and would, persevere.

For her real mission was clear. It had not shifted since the day she left Przeworsk and arrived in Köln.

Esther was resolute she would ultimately defy—no, prevail over—Tadeusz, his memory, his deliberate heartrending rejection, and his utter disregard for the truth of who they were to one another. She would endure, and she would triumph over the devastation and pain his actions had inflicted on her.

To what end, of this—truly—she was not clear. Only that she must not succumb. Not ever. Her indomitable spirit and relentless will would not abide this.

I . . . of course . . . would remain by her side.

Swiftly, without drama or uncertainty, a glance or consideration backward, Esther established a rhythm, a routine, and she and Zami settled into their new life. An existence that, despite rations and limitations and the haze of peril in the air, held few risks to overcome and little stress. Just as before, since first she fled Przeworsk and escaped to Köln, days lost their distinction. Each mirrored the actions, movements, and schedule of the one before.

Monotonous perhaps, but it was the monotony necessity demanded.

The flat, in a neglected five-story brick building constructed in the early teens, served her needs: twin-sized beds, a plain rectangular-shaped pine table, two simple chairs—one a makeshift version of a high chair—a compact stove with a single burner, and the sewing machine. Peeling paint speckled the walls like polka dots, and the floorboards creaked in a couple of areas. Otherwise the room was in decent condition. No closet, but a three-drawer dresser sufficed for holding their few pieces of clothing with room to store pantry items like flour, sugar, and beans.

The features that most relieved Esther were its toilet and sink. Situated in a corner, these essential fixtures were separated from the rest of the room by a thick dark green curtain. They could wash up here and not use the large shared bath down the hall. No neighbor would accidentally walk in on her and Zami when his pants were down with circumcised genitals exposed. Frau Göttlieb had made this arrangement. Frau Göttlieb had thought everything through.

And me of course . . . another potential obstacle I could help her overcome.

Esther's lone contact in Wuppertal, her anchor, was a Frau Weir—at least that is the name this woman used for herself. All Esther really knew for sure was that this Frau was stout and businesslike with graying curly hair worn too long, for it got into her eyes as she spoke, her head continuously moving more rapidly than her mouth. Not out of nervousness, Esther decided, for her new employer embraced assuredness in her actions. Most likely it was nothing more than a facial twitch the woman had had since childhood.

As it turned out, there would be no need for other contacts or connections. Frau Weir arranged all of Esther's tailoring and furrier assignments and kept her busy. Esther met her once weekly, every Thursday at precisely twelve thirty, at an overstocked shop on Eddastrasse, nestled between a cobbler and Wuppertal's one milliner. Esther never learned if the Frau was the proprietor or merely an aide. There were no opportunities for questions and, if there had been,

Esther would not have inquired. Just as the store brimmed over with fabrics and notions, pattern books, and quilting supplies, with barely enough room for Esther and Zami to stand, the situation was filled with the consciousness that no questions would be asked, by either party. So their conversations were no-nonsense and efficient.

"*Hier ist die Jacke*—Here is the jacket and the three pairs of pants, four dresses, four shirts, and two skirts I repaired," Esther explained. "*Und, ach! das Taufkleid.* The baptismal gown. The lace was torn in six places, but I was able to re-stitch the pieces. Look. You can't see where the tears were. And I have reconstructed the hem and overcast the seams. It looks brand new. No one will be able to tell it was worn four times before."

Frau Weir fingered each item of clothing. She put her glasses on and inspected the stitches, inseams, button coverings, and linings to make certain that each had been finished to her detailed specifications.

"Ah" and "Hmm," she murmured throughout the review.

While the clothes were neatly presented, they were not ironed. Esther did not have the equipment to accomplish that task. But it never seemed to pose a problem. No doubt Frau Weir had other workers to handle that part of the process before the items were returned to the client. Whether or not they, too, were part of the *untergetauchte Juden*—submerged Jews—those who, during this terror-filled and unsettling period, had successfully faded into the background of daily life, Esther would never know.

Money would be exchanged for the clothes. Not an abundance, but given that Frau Weir could have easily taken advantage of the situation, she paid a fair price for the required work.

"And what do you have for me this week?"

Esther never met a client. Never had to take measurements. Never discussed fabrics or quality or particulars such as button type or zipper length or stitch preference. All specifications were negotiated in advance of these Thursday meetings where Frau Weir reviewed each item of clothing in detail and the assignments to be accomplished.

In response to every tailoring need presented, Esther would say, "*Ja, ja, natürlich.* Of course. I can do that. Not a problem."

No sewing issue was too challenging or complex. Esther knew the *Frau* was impressed with her mastery with needle and thread. However, Esther did not hear a word of praise. Frau Weir never expressed more than a quickly muttered thank you for Esther's efforts. The appreciation was understood. Esther knew her services would be needed as long as the events escalating in the world beyond Wuppertal did not journey closer.

"*Auf Wiedersehen. Bis zur nächsten Woche.* Until next week."

From the tailoring shop, she and Zami would head to the outdoor market to pick up their weekly supplies and food. Even though this city had not yet been directly touched by the war, there were not a wide variety of items from which to choose. Many basics were no longer available, and some, such as sugar and flour, had begun to be rationed. Still, fresh fruits, vegetables, milk, and cheeses were in abundance, as these items were brought in directly from the farmers located in the nearby regions. And Esther had the resources to buy what she wanted.

Money . . . having money was the key to access . . . and would remain so.

Their needs were simple. Zami was not a finicky eater. Unlike Tova who far too often had, with petulance, refused half or more of whatever was on her plate, or Miriam, who had sugar cravings and cried doggedly if she were not given some treat at every meal. Zami was the most easily managed, the quietest, and the most acquiescent of the three children she had birthed. Frau Göttlieb had been right. Esther was pleased he was with her. Although often thinking otherwise, at this moment she did appreciate she was not completely alone.

So Esther purchased what appealed to her, knowing Zami would eat whatever was on his plate. She could not remember a time when it was only about her interests or desires. There was, indeed, a freedom in these circumstances, despite the constraints placed upon her and the realities she had to negotiate.

As the five o'clock hour neared, with one large-sized basket packed with clothes and a smaller-sized basket with food and supplies held securely in one hand and the grip of Zami's stroller in her other, Esther would return to their utilitarian apartment. Work would begin once more. Each week patterned as the one before.

Sewing assignments structured each day, with all other needs and activities woven in and around individual pieces of clothing's unique requirements. Most early mornings found Esther sitting in the chair by the apartment's one narrow window, sewing by candlelight before daybreak and Zami awoke. Sunlight was her light source throughout the day, and when the sun finally set, a candle was lit once again. Most of each day she sewed by hand. The sewing machine, while convenient, was loud and grating, and she made an effort not to disturb the neighbors. A low profile was essential. The few breaks taken were for meals and washing and the occasional need to distract Zami, if he grew fidgety or fussy.

"Hier, halt das—Hold this," Esther said when he seemed to grow tired of rolling back and forth and back again across the bed. She handed him the thick piece of midnight-blue flannel he particularly liked.

Sometimes he would not take the material from her. Instead Zami stared at the candlelight and flapped his left hand wildly. His version of "no," Esther had come to learn.

"Okay, *Hier ist deine Eisenbahn*. Here's your train. You like your train. Don't you want to play with your train?"

There were not a lot of options from which this little boy could chose, but the wooden train, carved by his papa, did seem to placate him. Along with Esther's unending patience and finely honed focus, skills central to quality tailoring. These kept him calm. And too, he had a fondness for long naps that took up a good bit of each day, so there were not a lot of hours when Esther had to consider his needs.

She never ventured far to explore Wuppertal, not even when time became available. Esther did not have a mild curiosity for this city and its potential offerings. She knew she needed to remain as inconspicuous as possible to arouse no suspicions. Equally, she understood that no matter how long in its residence, Wuppertal was an interlude. No reasons existed to learn more than what was essential. And she had no interest in getting to know people other than those who were of necessity.

When Esther and Zami first moved to Wuppertal and into the building, the youthful neighbor directly across the hall had extended herself warmly. This plump woman with prematurely graying hair was talkative. Without encouragement, Esther learned she had lived in this city since birth and never traveled beyond the neighboring countryside. She had a daughter, Winifred—

"*Ein schöner Name für ein Mädchen*—A beautiful name for a girl, don't you think? It means 'friend of peace.' So appropriate for the times we are living in."

—seven years of age.

"My husband was drafted not more than a year ago. I feel lost without him. My daughter and I are fine, of course, but one does get used to having one's man around. I have my work to keep me busy. I'm a secretary at a textile mill, just nearby. It only takes me fifteen minutes to walk there."

Esther observed that every Sunday the mother and daughter attended St. Laurentius, sitting in the fourth pew on the left side, three rows in front of where she and Zami took their seats.

Barely a week after they had moved into the building, this woman invited them to join her for a cup of tea and a slice of *Honigkuchen*. At other times she offered coffee and *Bienenstich*. "I love to bake and always enjoy having company," she said more than once.

But with each offer Esther would respond with a polite but firm, "*Nein, nein danke*. I have much work to do."

She would then walk into her apartment or down the stairs, whichever direction allowed her to be alone and remain alone.

In any given week, she and Zami would journey a five-block radius at most, bringing them to and from their apartment, the tailor shop, the market, and, importantly, church. And back again. There was the rare occasion when she got restless from remaining indoors for too long. This was most likely a Wednesday afternoon when the week's assignments had been completed and the small space became especially stifling. Only in those instances would she take Zami to the little park leading to the zoo's entrance. It was perhaps a ten-minute walk, and the fresh air, no matter what the weather, cleared her head, reinvigorating her resolve.

Zami seemed to take pleasure in these outings, but he was such a remote child that Esther sensed he was never really comfortable or at ease. This little boy rarely laughed or smiled—uncommon for one his age. It was as though he instinctively understood the gravity of their circumstances. More significantly, he seemed to understand he was with a woman who was barely capable of loving him.

Their weekly attendance at St. Laurentius was the most crucial part of the masquerade. Four services were offered each Sunday, the first commencing at seven o'clock in the morning. Esther chose to attend the day's second service at nine. During this hour, the nave would be filled to capacity, and she believed it advantageous to be seen by as large an audience as available. They donned their best clothes, the same ones worn on Thursdays to the tailoring shop. But on Sundays, Esther's head would be covered with a lace cloth that complemented her dress. With small Bible and rosary visibly in hand, they would walk—at a slow pace, for Zami did not yet move with steady ease—up the eight steps to the austere, high-arched entrance as though this were the most natural activity in which they could partake.

Frau Göttlieb had been an excellent teacher. Esther knew when to stand and when to kneel, what words to repeat and when to merely listen and perhaps nod, when to participate in a responsorial psalm, the quantity of coins to contribute to the collection pot as it passed, and how to take the host on her tongue during communion like a true baptized member of this tribe.

Such rituals! Such nonsense, she thought with an internal smirk as she returned to her seat after communion. What a waste of time!

Ah . . . you humans are continually searching . . . seeking . . . craving . . . answers . . .

As such . . . throughout time you come up with ideas . . . philosophies . . . stories . . . intricate ceremonies . . . formulas if you will . . . that provide solace . . . that help you cope with what you consider reality.

And I too . . . by many . . . am merely considered part of that elaborate invention to help you . . . some of you . . . not all humans of course . . . manage what are deemed hardships . . . adversities . . . ordeals . . . misfortunes . . .

These rituals . . . services . . . traditions . . . rites . . . they all appear . . . each and every one throughout the world . . . to be so very different . . . unique . . . to this group or that path. It does not matter . . . the religion or the faith or conviction or creed or philosophic belief . . .

For they all lead to the same culmination: salvation . . . peace . . . deliverance.

For they are really . . . and truly . . . all one . . . one and the same . . .

And let us take notice . . . it is not an accident . . . not a coincidence . . . not merely happenstance . . . that ritual . . . the word . . . lies sheltered within . . . spiritual . . .

Esther favored the days when organ music was included as part of the service and St. Laurentius was filled with alluring sounds resonating against the structure's thick walls and soaring vaulted ceiling. Regrettably this was not frequent, only on certain Sundays when there was a holiday or perhaps a funeral. A few times there had been a soloist who sang one song to which she was especially drawn. A song that reached down to the center of her being and stirred the pot of torpid emotions like no other.

Of course this would be true . . . Oh . . . maiden . . . see a maiden's sorrow . . . Oh . . . Mother . . . hear a suppliant child . . . Ave Maria!

Every now and again during the service, Esther would gently touch the fragile Holy Mother resting against her throat. Her finger would follow its outline, over and over. It was a centerpiece of the costume acquired in this new existence of hers. While she scoffed at any and all superstitious notions, she did consider it something of an amulet, providing protection as she traversed this complicated terrain.

After one hour or so passed, the service would end, and Esther would follow the other parishioners as they lined up to shake the monsignor's hand and thank him for the morning's service and lesson. She made sure to listen closely enough to mention a word or two of the particular passage he had focused on and the morning's topic.

After a *"Vielen Dank*—Thank you very much," a contrived smile, and a nod of greeting to her neighbor, she and Zami would be on their way back to the apartment and her waiting assignments.

Each Sunday passed unchanged.

Esther's facility to act as the situation necessitated served her well. Avoiding or suppressing emotions or reactions facilitated that the needs of a day were met without distraction. No suspicions provoked, no questions asked.

It took little effort to be invisible. Even with a one-year-old who soon became a two-year-old. Even with people on practically every corner with the charge to find you, to grab you, to send you away, it was not so very difficult to maintain a cloak of insignificance. To continuously walk behind thick layers of indistinctiveness that softly melds you into the surroundings, so your coat becomes a doorway; shoes, merely cracks in the cobbled sidewalk; hat, a bird fluttering through the trees.

Disappearing while standing in broad daylight had never been a challenge for Esther. As one of thirteen children, she intuited at a young age that it was essential to learn how to be overlooked, ignored, or passed over. There were too many chores she wanted to evade, too many responsibilities that would take her away from the activities she most enjoyed. Esther learned how to sit at the family table alongside her siblings and be neither heard nor seen. She had done this as a child, day after day for as long as memory served.

It was invaluable training . . . essential preparation . . . and now a lifesaving technique for her present circumstances.

As the product of such a large family, Esther discovered at a young age that people, for the most part, were self-involved and egocentric. Each generally caught up with the noise and thoughts and nonsense in one's own head. Even those with whom you lived. So out in the world—a world where the rules changed daily and chaos took precedence—blending into the environment was like taking perfectly identical, slow, shallow breaths. In accordance with her stitches.

Not unlike the work of a magician . . . people only see what they want to see . . . or what they are led to see . . .

CHAPTER EIGHTEEN

And...
what of the boy?
What... of Zami?
His Spitzname... nickname... always used...
yet without meaning...
devoid of sentiment.
No more... than a designation... a label.
Not... a term of endearment...
nor an expression of love.
Used...
in place of Samuel...
connoting... God has heard.
But... has he?
Never... given more thought than unwanted luggage...
always by her side.
Though... rarely... in her heart...

....

During a period when a multitude of others—it was impossible to know how many—were scrambling for safety, fearing for their lives, and hiding in places that in a more benign time would have been inconceivable to the imagination, this young boy was more than decently fed. A roof covered Zami's small head, and a satisfactory bed was provided for his rest. Water and cloth were readily available to keep him clean. Thanks to Esther's nimble hands coupled with needle, thread, and fabric scraps, there were clothes to wear that kept him warm or cool as weather necessitated.

Physically nourished, yes. In regard to basic human needs, Esther was highly responsible. Efficient.

Emotionally, however, Zami survived with minimal sustenance. As day led into day, he forgot he needed this or that he ever had it. He forgot there was once intense love and support—truly adoration—from his father.

He forgot that he ever had a father.

Esther never mentioned Abraham. Never uttered his name. Nor would she mention Tova or Miriam. She never spoke of Köln or their former life, and definitely not of her life before that. In fact, she rarely spoke to him at all, and most often when she did, it was out of necessity to convey specific commands:

"*Du mußt das essen.* You must eat this."

"Lift your right arm up so I can put your shirt on."

"Hold still, I need to button the last button."

"Take my hand when we walk across the street."

"*Sitz' in der Ecke und sei still.* Sit in the corner—quietly."

At all times quietly. Everything must be done quietly. Zami gave the impression he understood this inherently. At his very young age, he knew not to draw attention to himself.

And he was not such a striking youngster that a passerby would be compelled to stop and say, "What—*ein bezauberndes Kind*—an adorable child!" with enthusiasm.

"What lovely eyes."

Or—

"Such a beautiful smile he has."

Esther did not have to worry Zami would attract notice. His was a face lacking expression, definition, or culture. There were no distinguished or finely etched features. There was not a thick mop of enticing blond curls that suggested a playful spirit. Nothing in his demeanor relayed any manner of temperament. One could never imagine his thoughts; more than likely, he was not thinking anything at all.

Emotionally stunted. Whether this was a natural occurrence or one that grew out of his life conditions would never be known or, for that matter, explored. He was much like clay—a body without spirit. Moldable. A pliant mass Esther formed and shaped and manipulated as situation demanded.

Zami obeyed Esther without question or resistance. He accepted everything she said or required of him.

"Nein" never became a part of his lexicon.

Zami did have a few pleasures: the park was a special curiosity whenever Esther made the opportunity to visit it available to him. There he wandered round and around and among the trees. He ran his hands along their bark. Every so often he stopped directly in front of a tree and moved his lips slightly, as though deep in conversation. But he released no words. Every so often, he chose to roll on the grass—or the snow—down the low incline in the center of the park. Zami did not chortle with the delight of accomplishment Esther observed in most children. But he appeared content to pursue the same activity repetitively without growing restless or bored.

I did my best to bring him some joy when I could ... when Esther was not looking ... which was more often than I liked. As I did with his sisters ... Tova and Miriam ... now and again ... I would attempt to offer him one or perhaps two of my favorite cookies. Zami would mostly stare. I knew he saw me ... it was not a full refusal ... simply a stare. Unlike his siblings who would grab and giggle ... they interacted ...

They understood. Perhaps he did too ... but chose otherwise ...

Zami's train seemed to give him the greatest pleasure. That his father had carved it especially for him was a fact he could not recall. The one-car train was realistic, executed with close attention to detail, including spokes on four wheels that rotated. It had a wooden track, barely twenty centimeters in length, and Zami moved the train smoothly over it. Back and forth, back and forth, over and over and over again.

The little boy spent hours each day in the corner of their single room with his train. Never disturbing his mother. Always quiet. Silent.

Silence . . . his silence . . . is what will save his life . . . save her life.

But the question returns . . . again and again . . . what will be saved?

CHAPTER NINETEEN

Ah yes . . . I understand . . . a human incarnation does confound. When a soul becomes embodied in flesh . . . encased in wrapping . . . this tissue that restricts . . . and confines with boundaries . . . and limitations . . .

When the élan vital . . . the immaterial . . . becomes material . . .

This is when the real challenges begin.

For this incarnation is such a harsh one . . . perhaps . . . no . . . absolutely . . . the most arduous of them all. And far too often . . . for far too many . . . if not for everyone . . . in one manner or another . . . at one time or another . . . it brings devastation and sadness . . . hurt and pain. In all cases there is so much pain . . . so much sorrow.

During this incarnation . . . your incarnation . . . there are countless choices that must be made . . . decisions . . . determinations . . . some . . . too many . . . are fateful . . . to all involved . . . to all concerned. Repercussions abound.

Spirit . . . the divine spark . . . is so very much easier . . . effortless . . . for Spirit is every . . . thing . . . and every . . . where . . .

Spirit is where all is possible.

Please be assured . . . there is a link . . . a connection . . . a bridge . . . between Spirit and incarnation that cannot . . . not ever . . . be severed. This is the central bond that must not be forgotten . . . never overlooked or ignored.

In the human incarnation . . . as in Spirit . . . there resides love . . . deep love . . . true love . . . ever and forever and always . . . love . . .

Such as the love Esther and Tadeusz share. Ah . . . you think . . . you mean shared.

But is it past?

Enduring love between and among each of us . . . each of you . . . all of us . . . and it is the one thing . . . the only thing . . . that continues on . . . throughout each life . . . all lives . . . all incarnation . . .

And the time between.

If love is at the center . . . if love is at the core . . . at the essence of each and every decision . . .

Then truth resides there too.

CHAPTER TWENTY

He lurks . . .
behind every corner . . .
and around every thought.
His presence . . .
woven into each conversation.
No running . . .
No hiding.
For he . . .
is everywhere you turn.
Behind you . . .
when you think you have lost him.
Or beside you . . .
observing every move.
You are never alone.
Though you try to escape . . .
from his influence . . .
and his eyes.
Distance does not aid . . .
and time does not mend.
For neither are real.
For neither exist.

There is only the energy . . .
that sparked the flame . . .
that continues to smolder.
And that energy is pure . . . and true . . . and truth.
It is the finespun thread . . .
you resist . . . and you cling to.
The soul connection.

. . . .

Nine months had passed since they had stolen away from Köln. Nine months on the run, yet never moving. Passing as others— with changed identities, forged papers—in plain sight, but in hiding nonetheless. Submerged with the minimum of life supports.

For no particular reason, as this week was no different or more demanding from the one before, tension escalated. In the past few weeks, Esther had not been able to sleep more than an hour or two combined. Fitful tossing and turning consumed any possibility of repose. Rest—the word no longer held primal meaning. She did not know when she had last felt her time asleep provided a reprieve from her time awake.

In the middle of the night, Esther could acknowledge she was among the fortunate—the lucky ones. She had experienced no trouble since arriving in this new city. She had a roof over her head, secured regular sewing assignments, and got paid money for her efforts. Fair money. Good money, even. During a period when most people, those in similar circumstances—for she was sure there must be others—were barely getting by. Or worse.

People she had to encounter—on the street, at the market, at this shop or that, at church, or on the stairwell to the apartment— had not questioned her story and actions and various plotlines, any of the rationale for traveling away from home in time of war. Her superb tailoring skills forestalled curiosity.

She and Zami kept to themselves, and although she did not initiate conversations, on occasion Esther would hear things as she passed a group of men on the street or while waiting in line to pay at the market. These were frightening reports—shocking accounts, mostly whispered—about battles waged, towns destroyed, and inferences of atrocities inflicted on Jews throughout Europe. Her frozen demeanor provided an excellent mask for absorbing information without reaction.

Even when she was once again in her room, Esther declined to digest any of the words overheard.

More than likely these are merely rumors, she thought. People love to gossip endlessly about terrible things, whether real or untrue. I refuse to accept them as fact. Regardless, they have no import for me. I don't have time to brood over them. I have work to do.

Esther always had work to do, to take care of Esther.

Now, however, was the time to put sewing aside, to put everything aside. For it was a Friday, late afternoon. The cusp of *shabbes*. The Sabbath. A slight break, a pause in all activities and from any thoughts or knowledge of torments, real or potential, must be taken.

Her hands were cramped, and her fingers hurt from too many pinpricks, her work uncharacteristically sloppy all day. The stitches in Esther's back and side overpowered any she wove with needle, thread, and fabric. More were taken out than remained.

Her eyes burned.

Her shoulders and neck ached.

She was drained.

At this moment, Esther felt depleted of the resources heretofore carrying her forward.

But the Sabbath approached, and Esther needed to prepare to greet her. Even under these circumstances, this Friday evening tradition endured—the one link to a normalcy of a life, her earliest life, which she strove to preserve whenever, wherever, and however possible.

The barest thread maintains . . .

This singular practice never ceased to resonate within Esther's core. When the opaque layers of life and responsibilities and heartache and loss fell away, Esther would feel an internal wrench for those evenings with family, when she was a young girl. Or with her own three young children. The time for rejuvenation. She quashed the sentiment but not the habit.

Following her first encounter with Tadeusz—a more fortuitous occasion for such a beginning could not have been granted her—the ritual had taken on a more profound significance. From that day forth, *shabbes* became a weekly declaration of love and the renewal of their commitment to one another.

Until that day . . . in no way forgotten . . . when this bride lost her groom.

While she had established a Sabbath meal and tradition of sorts with Abraham and the girls, Esther only wholly reclaimed this weekly rite when she and Zami were on their own. And when she was certain no one could see in through the apartment's window or the cracks in the door.

Wine was an essential element of this custom, the holy drink. *Kiddush* must be recited over a cup of wine before the meal. Esther was not sure why. It was the way it had always been done, so that's what she did.

Wine . . . the beverage of life . . . of immortality . . . the sign of knowledge . . . of initiation. Symbol of joy. A drink of the gods . . .

Obtaining wine had initially posed a challenge. She did not want to be seen in a store that sold liquor. A lone woman purchasing alcohol was sure to draw attention. Particularly one with a small child. Remarkably, however—

Or perhaps not . . .

—Esther had scavenged a nearly full bottle found in a trash-can not far from the apartment building. Its taste was saccharine, barely passable as wine, but serviceable nonetheless. Over these past many weeks, she had stintingly used just a drop or two to extend its life—and, it seemed, hers too—as long as possible.

As the sun came to rest, Esther removed Bubbe Royza's *kiddush* cup that she always kept near, buried within her clothes, and placed it in the center of the table next to the partially burned candle. Though pieces of jewelry and money were sewn into her hems, this small goblet, now with a few scratches, was her treasure.

Match to wood.

Esther had to strike twice for it to ignite. She took a slow, full breath and touched flame to wick. She drew her hands around the candles and toward her face three times. Covering her eyes with her hands, in less than a whisper, she began, *"Baruch Ata Adonai, Elo—"* but stopped abruptly as the room that had bounded her began to fade away. Zami, lying in the bed, vanished, and all that had come to feel familiar disappeared into a void.

In what seemed an instant, Esther found herself at the edge of an expansive, overgrown field butting up to dense woodland.

She shook her head vigorously and rubbed her eyes. How did I get here? she wondered. And where is here? She touched her arms and legs, which felt solid. She looked to her left and to her right and then gradually turned around in a full circle to gain a view of the scene.

Esther gasped, stunned, as she realized it was the northern end of Przeworsk, a tranquil place where she, her siblings, and friends had played as young children. Hours had been spent here, competing in sports, making up stories, throwing balls, and jumping rope. Often her brothers would chase after the girls with bugs or mice in their hands with the intention to frighten or distress, the way only brothers knew how. An odd expression of love passed down from generations before.

In spite of those incidents, it was an evocative locale that extended memories of happy times.

The field radiated a warm golden yellow. Esther could see buds of buttercup scattered in patches across its full expanse. It was thick and heavy. The narrow paths, long ago carved to ease hauling, were filled in. No one had given attention to this field in a long time.

Yet the meadow was still very much alive and thriving on its own.

Like a forest that immediately begins to regenerate after a fire has passed, war is never entirely successful in its mission to completely annihilate.

Esther heard birds calling to one another in the distance. One silken, blue-speckled butterfly fluttered before her. A zephyr soothed her skin.

The light was soft. The moment, when dusk and dawn meld, had arrived. This was the emergence, once prayed for. What she thought had been forgotten or cast aside. The dawn buried where she could not reach but secretly desired would come—finally—and wake her from the nightmare that for so long now had claimed her. The incident that began in this small town, when he did not join her, when he shunned her, rejected her. For all to see. When the chuppah collapsed around her.

Esther heard a rustling at the western edge of the field and jumped. She thought she was alone—certain she was alone—though unclear how or why she had returned to this place of her youth.

She strained her eyes. There, at the field's edge, in the direction of the setting sun, appeared a billowing cloud of white. Indistinguishable as to shape or appearance, its radiance and beauty unmatched by anything she had seen before. Moving haltingly but gracefully, this image of elation, of peaceful serenity, of true bliss floated imperceptibly across the field and toward her, growing larger and more discernable. Finally, Esther was able to descry a slight figure covered in garments of splendor, a delicate eyelet lace dress that glided over the sharp weeds, as though the wearer drifted on rose-petaled velvet. Everything was in deliberate and measured motion. Esther watched, transfixed.

The field began to fill with sound, an aural counterpart to the vision.

Lekho dodi likras kalo, peney shabbos nekablo.

Come . . . my beloved . . . to greet the bride; welcome the face of Shabbes.

Observe—and remember—

It was the *Lekho Dodi*—the Sabbath Bride—coming to meet her groom and rejoice in the innocence of renewal that would be before her, the joy of new beginnings.

As the figure grew closer, Esther could see that this bride's gown was in tatters, nearly in shreds. Pieces of fabric fell off her body and onto the ground. The sheer veil that rested upon her head covered a blackened face, without benefit of feature or expression. Esther's heart became lead—

Once more—

For on this eve there would be no groom to welcome this bride. Just as he—Tadeusz—her groom—had not been there to greet her.

Night would fall, shadows would take residence, and darkness would descend, remaining her sole partner for time to come.

CHAPTER TWENTY-ONE

Circumstances . . .
became usual.
Daily life . . .
an appearance of routine . . .

....

Like the steps a seamstress must adhere to for the creation of a dress or a shirt, a jacket, a vest, or a pair of pants, Esther and Zami—Etta and Hannis—carried on. They followed a schedule that seldom varied. Esther spent the better part of each day doing what was familiar and natural, truly innate: mending, stitching, cutting, repairing, lining, hemming, altering, and refurbishing.

The bulk of her assignments were to restore old clothes, some tattered and frayed, others barely worn. Often her task was a general request to refresh and renew. Money was restricted, even among the wealthy, but vanity still reigned supreme. So those with ample inventory were reaching into the depths of their wardrobes, dressers, and armoires to find items friends would not easily recognize and therefore would assume to be newly purchased. This was particularly true after Esther took her gifted hand at any item of clothing.

Although Esther met not one of Frau Weir's clients, she became celebrated among them. Who is this mysterious master of thread and cloth? they inquired of one another. Where did he, or perhaps it was a she, come from?

Each would ponder, confident it was an expert tailor most likely trained in one of Paris's most exclusive couture houses, or perhaps one of Milan's. Why this person had only recently appeared in obscure, industrial Wuppertal did not generate a depth of inquiry. Situations of war elicited answers for everything that at other times might have required thorough examination.

One Thursday afternoon as she and Zami stood patiently in the bakery's long line, Esther chanced to overhear the conversation of two elegantly dressed women having tea in the café nearby. The topic of conversation: Frau Weir's shop and how thrilled they were by the exquisite craftsmanship their clothes now received.

"*Genau wie in Paris.* Just like Paris," said the dark-haired woman in the blue sheath with matching shawl. "So exciting!"

"I admit *mit dem Krieg*—with the war and everything—things are a bit hard, but we still need some glamour," she continued.

"Wait until you see the green satin dress I'll be wearing to the Bauers's cocktail party next Saturday. It is gorgeous," said her friend in the fitted black linen suit with the fur collar. "Simply stunning!"

"Tine has a way of finding the most talented people. I've been so impressed. You do know we've been friends since school. Lived a few houses down the street from one another—" As Esther moved forward in the line, the woman's voice grew faint.

Esther smirked. Imagine if they had an inkling of my background and that I am the one who sewed that green dress and the outfits they're each currently wearing.

They would, surely, be stunned if not outraged to learn she was of Jewish heritage from a Polish *shtetl* in eastern Galicia, abutting the Ukrainian border. A woman, no less, who, with relative ease, was passing as one of them. If this fact had been revealed, these women would believe their clothes were soiled and sullied instead of what they were in actuality—sophisticated and stunning.

What is . . . perspective . . . really?

Esther's handiwork grew in such demand she now needed to visit Frau Weir's shop twice weekly and work with greater speed and efficiency. The necessity to feed and bathe herself and Zami did take up time. And Sunday morning church attendance could not be missed. This weekly activity remained inviolate, no matter how many items of clothing required her attention. Sleep was the part of the daily requirements that was most often shortchanged. Esther would, occasionally, grow weary, but her resolution never flagged, and the compensation for her efforts and talent increased.

> *This above all else . . . at this time . . . if not truly at all times . . . this she knew was critical.*

In consideration of the world circumstances in which she resided, a level of comfort was established. A bit of tranquility settled in for her and for Zami. Not that Esther, even for an hour, lost sight of the plight that brought her here, to this place, with this state of mind.

CHAPTER TWENTY-TWO

Then...
in an instant...
everything changed...

....

Tphe day began just like the one before. Like all the days before. Its distinction, up until that moment, was that this day was a Thursday, early morning. In a few hours she would visit Frau Weir and exchange completed assignments for new ones. Eleven months and five days had passed since Esther, with Zami in tow, had relocated to Wuppertal and melded into the city's backdrop.

That had been sufficient time to settle into this new reality, to develop a rhythm, to encase her with an illusion of safety and comfort. Combat and battles raged all over, but within this minor city, life continued on with measured serenity. The war's ravages would eventually catch up to Wuppertal, but during these past months, the cloak of distance and inconsequentiality enveloped them.

The weight and exercise of maintaining obscurity created tension, surely. But this was not a stress rooted in mental anguish, as the conditions would have justifiably elicited. No, Esther did not experience the fear that those in similar circumstances likely shared.

The others. Those *untergetauchte Juden*—submerged Jews. Jews living as gentiles, hiding scarcely below the surface of truth, the deepest kind of hiding. Those who changed their identities, their very selves, to pass—to survive—during these times as one of the accepted, the *Über* race. There were those concealed in attics and in basements and in barns, behind false walls and bookcases, and below floor beams. There were the Jews sheltered by non-Jews for innumerable reasons, many charitable or compassionate, some financial, and more than a few out of guilt—the self-reproach palpable. While Esther shared commonalities with these people, she held none of their insecurities or griefs or doubts. She was not invested in their terror or their plight.

Esther came to these circumstances without baggage of shattered nerves and unending trauma of herself being revealed. The core of Esther had been decimated long before.

Let us not forget . . . her motivations . . . her impulses were born of a particular history . . . a singular rationale . . .

The snippets of news that reached her—when she passed a collection of men on the street talking animatedly, or glanced at the headlines walking by a newsboy, or overheard incidents referenced offhandedly by market vendors—made no mark. Her awareness of the atrocities taking place did not elicit an interest to learn more.

This Thursday morning, Esther had barely climbed the final two stairs on her return from placing the garbage in the bin at the back of the apartment building. As she reached the landing, the neighbor across the hall, the one with whom early on generous offers of cake and tea had been declined, was peering out of her barely opened front door and gestured for Esther to join her in the farthermost corner of their common hall. No more than a polite nod of hello had been exchanged in months. Esther registered surprise but followed her as requested.

"*Sie wissen.* They know," this woman whispered.

There were no greater words of dread.

"They have found out.

"They will come for you. And your son."

"*Morgen.* Tomorrow. At nine in the morning."

Esther listened to the woman's information, her stoicism unmarred. Her face offered no expression. She did not acknowledge meaning behind the words she was hearing. However, Esther's mind began to race furiously—

What could have possibly gone wrong? Where might I have misstepped? Who exposed my secret, and how? *Ach,* there is no time for this! Quickly, her thoughts turned to strategizing options and feasible next steps.

"*Ich verstehe nicht*—I have no understanding of what you are saying" was Esther's response. Then she turned and walked into her apartment.

When the door was gently shut behind her and the latch secured, Esther leaned her forehead against the wall, squeezed her eyes tightly, bit down hard on the inside of her right cheek, and took in a long, slow, considered breath. Her one and only admission to the gravity of the situation.

I embraced her with a warm, gentle waft of air and the aroma . . . the essence . . . of my native land.

On the surface, the day continued on as though nothing had transpired. As though a bombshell had not been dropped and it was now vital to accelerate deliberation and action to save herself. Zami too, of course. This responsibility was hers and hers alone.

Stay wholly present . . . and focused.

Remain in the moment.

Review . . . assess . . . fully grasp . . . the requirements . . . of now.

Thinking forward could not be more than one day; thinking backward as to how this situation came about was futile.

Esther reached for the *kiddush* cup and held it close. She placed it against her forehead and took another full breath. "Okay, *genug*—enough!"

She handed Zami his train and said, "Play with this. And here is a piece of bread. Please, don't disturb me. There is much I must do—and quickly."

He took these items wordlessly and began rolling his train back and forth across the bed. His mother's matter-of-fact attitude provided him a soothing comfort.

With the understanding even less could be transported then when they left Köln, Esther began packing. She would only be able to bring the barest of essentials, those that could be easily carried in one compact suitcase. This would not draw suspicions.

As it is summer, stifling both day and night, only lightweight clothing can be taken, she rationalized. Coats, hats, scarves, gloves, and boots must be abandoned. Far too heavy. And it would look suspicious if I were seen carrying them in this weather. Winter and cold will be handled when the season arrives. Somehow. Next, sewing supplies—my sustenance. These are most critical. Everything else can be made.

The gift of Esther's vocation was that the essential tools were small to miniscule; an assortment of needles and thread can be laid at the bottom of a suitcase without adding consequential weight or requiring much space. Also true of scissors and tracing paper, marking pencils, chalk, pins, and pincushion. A tape measure is thinner than an average belt and easily wrapped along the edges of the case. With these few ingredients, Esther could sustain a profession, an existence, the continued acquiring of money. Clients could be found at all times and in every location. Of this she had no doubt. The other utensils of the trade were not as indispensable and would, in some way, be acquired along her path. However that would unfold.

At the moment, there was no plan, not yet a whisper of a direction, but Esther refused to embrace panic. Self-reliance, self-containment, autonomy, and stoicism embodied the four corners of her nature. Nevertheless, in these precarious times, she understood clearly security could not be attained in isolation.

Esther was savvy, certainly, but shrewdness without partnership could not suffice. Safety was not achievable without the close alliance of dedicated individuals who recognized the iniquities being inflicted on this large sector of humanity. Without connections and the benevolence and support of others, what Esther had embarked upon would have been impossible. These were qualities she believed she no longer shared, traits that were not recollected as part of her composition. If circumstances were otherwise, there was little likelihood that she would have extended herself to others.

Still . . . she was learning . . . she was accepting . . . that not everyone . . . not all others . . . would betray . . . mislead . . . deceive her.

She had no investment in Wuppertal, in this apartment, in her job, or in this life that had been fashioned out of goodwill and fortuitousness. Her sole imperative was continued existence, and whatever she needed to do would be done. There would be a way out. Of this, she was secure.

The need to escape . . . and not be followed . . . the need to disappear . . . and not be seen.

All must be accomplished without a trace left behind, without questions that would find answers.

Esther continued to pack. Her hands moved swiftly as she arranged the materials she would take. Their identification papers, baptismal documentation, Bible, and rosary were, obviously, crucial. Money was stuffed into corners and pockets of every item of clothing—hers and Zami's. Three dresses must suffice. She could easily wear two, as they were lightweight, and only placed her church dress in the suitcase.

Later on I will make any additional clothes we might need, she reflected. In some way this will happen. Somehow.

Esther tightly folded Zami's finest pair of pants and nicest shirt and placed them in the suitcase. He can wear two layers of shirts and pants, she thought. He's such a thin child; the clothing will merely make him look more normal-sized. Definitely not over-weight. That would be suspicious. In this time of rations and few resources, most people look underfed. Except those bureaucrats! She snorted.

Everything must be simplified. The essence of survival had few needs.

At promptly ten minutes past noon, Esther layered the completed assignments for Frau Weir in her basket. With Zami's tiny right hand securely in her left hand, they walked out the door just as they had for the past nearly one year of Thursdays.

Between reviewing the number of pleats to add on this skirt, the possible seam allowance on that blouse, and whether the length of a dress should be at the knee or one inch below, Esther whispered, "*Ich bin entdeckt worden.* I've been discovered."

This fact was conveyed to Frau Weir in Esther's usual, impassive way. Seamlessly woven into their conversation. The news did not elicit an observable reaction; Frau Weir's head continued its characteristic rapid movement with unrestrained hair flying in all directions. She did not flinch, did not look around to see who might be watching or monitoring their actions. There was not a trace of worry that she, too, might be in danger. Even to an untrained eye, it appeared Frau Weir already knew what had occurred and was primed to provide the critical aid. Perhaps she had prepared for this possibility every week. For Esther and for any other secreted Jew she assisted.

"I have *ein Cocktailkleid*—a cocktail dress—that needs to have the ruffles moved from the hem to the neck and the wrists. It may not appear so, but there is enough material. Here, let me draw you a picture of exactly how the client would like it done," Frau Weir said.

She pulled out a pencil and a piece of paper from her desk's top drawer that was already filled with words and a map. She proceeded to simulate drawing on the paper, all the while talking about ruffles and the length of fabric Esther must be sure to gather at the arms in contrast to the neck.

"*Dieser Kunde ist sehr pingelig.* This client is exceptionally fussy," she stressed.

It was evident Frau Weir had done this before.

With measured precision, she said: "You must be at the riverfront at the intersection below Tiergartentreppe where it meets Varresbecker Straße, on the west side of the river, at precisely one thirty-six this coming morning. *Die Polizei* change positions at one thirty, and at this time, if you are extremely careful and quiet, your movements will not be observed. There is not a dock at this location, but the wall is broken, and you will be able to crawl over easily. Even with your son, who must remain silent. A fisherman's boat will be waiting. No one will question his presence. He fishes for eel, and this is when he typically leaves."

Ah . . . eel . . . of course . . . eel . . . the messenger of the gods . . .

"*Wir haben Glück gehabt*—We are fortunate the rains were plentiful, and the water has remained high this year," the Frau continued. "You will be taken down river to Solingen, to a spot a few blocks from a train station. You must purchase a ticket to Düsseldorf—I know you have sufficient money—and, once there, a ticket to Leiden, in Holland."

"*Ja, ja, Ich verstehe*—I understand," Esther said, head nodding, eyes focused on the paper and pencil, as though acknowledging the specifics of this dress assignment. "I can do this easily. It will be beautiful."

"Depart only at the main station, Leiden Centraal. Bombing has been intense in these areas, but the trains are still running, although somewhat more slowly. *Die Reise*—The journey may take you two days. A woman, in her fifties, although older appearing because of her short white hair, wearing a blue knit dress and carrying a large shoulder bag made from the same fabric, will meet you there. She will greet you as an old friend and will take you to your new home. Importantly, she will have contacts for your tailoring work."

And then, as she handed over the last piece of clothing assigned, Frau Weir said: "*Bis zur nächsten Woche.* Until next week."

"*Auf Wiedersehen.* Until next week then."

In keeping with routine, Esther and Zami walked to the outdoor market to purchase one week's supply of grocery items and sundries. She paid particular attention to foods that would travel without spoiling. She also selected items that would perish quickly without refrigeration. If anyone was observing her movements, they must have no idea that Esther knew she was to be arrested.

Arrested—what senselessness! Esther shook her head reflexively, incredulous still at the concept. She was aware that, under current conditions, in these times, what she was doing—going about daily life without observing the defined constraints determined for those of a certain race, those sharing a distinct bloodline—was illegal.

But, truly, where was the consciousness in the governing regulations of the day? Laws are made to serve a country's citizens, to protect them. The absurd rules and restrictions decreed by this present government, laws enforced by those miscreant Nazis, protected no one. They were not to the benefit of humanity.

Is that not what laws . . . guiding principles . . . rules of conduct . . . policies of justice . . . should be? In service . . . to humanity . . . to one . . . and to all . . .

Esther watched the clock attentively. In the best of circumstances, the most normal of situations, it would be a seven-minute walk from the apartment to the designated spot on the riverfront. In this case, twelve minutes must be allotted to allow for any necessary stops to watch and to listen, but not offer too much time to chance encountering an officer on his route heading toward home.

It was nearly six o'clock when they returned to the apartment. After preparing a quick meal of bread and cheese, she ordered Zami to stay in the corner and play with his train.

"*Still!* Silently!" she admonished. Then she took a long breath, looked deep in his eyes, and added, "Please."

Esther began to repack, methodically, for she understood less could be taken than what she originally envisioned.

And it was now apparent what must be done.

A scene must be shaped; a story must be developed; a tale must be told with the barest of information, as though this place, their lives, were part of a play, a scene in a production, and tonight were the culmination. The story's sad but banal conclusion. No questions could be left to ponder; their whereabouts never questioned. It must appear as though everything—absolutely everything—had been left behind. As though this were their final exit, walking out of this door or any door.

At eight o'clock, Esther put Zami to bed and said, "Tonight we're going to play a special game. I'm going to wake you up in four and a half hours, and we are going to go outside. It's very, very important that no matter what you see or what you hear, you don't make a sound. Do you understand?"

Zami looked up at her and nodded. Not comprehending, but knowing this is what his mama wanted and that was what mattered.

"Under no circumstances can you make a sound. Not until the game is over in the morning," Esther said. "I will let you know when."

The next few hours, she worked as noiselessly as possible, walking around in her stocking feet, steering clear of any floorboards that creaked. After she placed the one suitcase by the door, she scattered clothes about the room, pulled drawers out, left dishes unclean in the sink, and piled sewing materials and assignments high in a corner as though thrown in desperation—the backdrop for the acts of a distraught, frantic woman.

As midnight neared, Esther picked up the sharpest scissors she had available. For a few seconds she held this implement midair away from her body, as far as her right arm could stretch. She dared her mind not to think or rationalize, for doing so would acknowledge she had no idea whether the action she was about to take would permanently damage her means of sustenation. Then, using all the force she could muster, Esther plunged the scissors—again—and again—and again—deeply—into three parts of her left upper arm and shoulder and watched as she bled profusely—on the bed where Zami slept, across the floor to the door, and on a sheet she would deposit near the river.

At precisely 1:24 in the morning, Esther, carrying Zami, headed to the riverfront and an indeterminate fate. A clear trail of blood followed them. Left behind was a staged environment of desolation and anguish. It declared to anyone who ventured inside that those who resided here had forsaken their lives.

The note left on the bed was brief but definitive:

Ich bin fertig.
Ich habe jeden und alles verloren, das ich jemals geliebt habe,
und alle, die mich geliebt haben.
Ich kann nicht mehr.
Es ist vorbei.

. . . .

I am finished.
I have lost everyone and everything I have ever loved and those who have loved me.
I can no longer go on.
It is over.

CHAPTER TWENTY-THREE

Embrace the shadows.
Dodge the light.
Don't trust . . .
can't trust.
Lose any thought of an identity . . . your true identity . . .
if you can even remember who you are . . .
while you are here.
Let the apprehension nourish you . . .
so you jump at the slightest sound . . .
and believe they are always chasing you.
Understand that you can never stop . . .
not for a minute . . . and let down your guard . . .
and relax . . . and take a deep breath . . . a sigh of relief.
There is no relief.
No escape.
Not right now.
Keep moving.
Look over your shoulder . . . with one eye around the corner.
Know they are always after you . . .
and will stop at nothing to get you.
Only sleep when pure exhaustion necessitates.

And then for just short bouts.
For they will reach you if you go too deeply . . .
or for too long.
The chase is relentless . . . and they are wily . . .
and conniving.
They are not used to losing.
Hiding is essential.
But not always easy.
Particularly . . . when the hiding also
needs to be from yourself.
When stepping through space . . . and time . . . and blending
into the landscape is not enough.
You remain with yourself . . . and you become them.
When the imminent physical threat is gone . . .
is this ever lost?
Is it ever possible to lose the apprehension? The loss of
control? To not feel hunted?
Walls that are constructed with brick and mortar,
stone or cement, are not as strong as
those built with memory.

....

Seventy-eight exhausting hours later, a spent Esther and Zami arrived at a prim three-story brick house centered on a well-tended lot on the outskirts of Leiden. Trains had been delayed. There were broken railroad tracks. A train had a damaged wheel spoke. Another had been rerouted, which resulted in two unanticipated connections, one that included backtracking more than 150 kilometers to meet up with a train coming from another direction. This was the one that at last carried them to Zuid-Holland and Leiden Centraal.

Because of the myriad problems, trains were overcrowded, making it difficult to move about. The cars were poorly ventilated and stifling during the daylight hours when the August sun held court. For a good deal of the ride, Zami had to sit on Esther's lap, uncomfortable for them both. Tickets and passports were checked a minimum of three times on each train. But no one had questioned their identities, even when crossing the border into Holland. Their papers had not generated suspicion. These documents were as foolproof as could be obtained with the right amount of ready money.

Frau Göttlieb's money, in this case. And her connections. Esther's face and body remained stolid each time the conductor returned her and Zami's papers, while her insides heaved relief and grateful thanks.

Somewhere along the journey—it may have been while waiting at one of the many stations or when sitting for what seemed like time without end as the train moved circumspectly along challenged territory—Zami took to biting the thin skin around his nails. It was a new habit that would not soon disappear.

"*Hör auf!* Stop that!"

"Don't do that!" Esther ordered again and again. The few bandages she had were already in use holding together the gashes along her upper arm and shoulder. So Esther wrapped three of his tender bloody fingers in cloth with tape. This, however, did not discourage Zami from biting the other seven digits and dripping blood. There was no way to avoid his pants becoming dotted with tiny bits of red. At this, Esther sighed and chewed lightly on the inside of her cheek. The wounds in her arm and shoulder were painful and distracting. After a while she grew too weary to try to stop him, so she let Zami do this one little thing that might, in fact, console him.

She stared out the window as the landscape rolled past and contemplated what was to come. Or what might come. Or what could happen. The possible scenarios were limitless. Because of the delays and changes, Esther was sure the connection would not be made.

What options do I have if this plan doesn't unfold the way Frau Weir described? What can I do? What might be possible? Where can I go if the contact doesn't meet me? A hotel? Perhaps I could find a small inn? These thoughts ricocheted inside her head until the train came to a stop and they finally arrived at Leiden Centraal. She gathered up Zami and their one suitcase and stepped out of the train car.

To Esther's astonishment—

But not mine of course . . .

—her contact, the older-looking woman with the short white hair wearing the blue knit dress, was waiting at the station in the designated corner. This conscientious woman, Nadine Vedder, had watched the train schedules, arrivals and departures, and the news vigilantly. As a result of her meticulousness, she was able to greet Esther and Zami with a welcoming embrace, as designed. Esther did not clasp her arms around this woman in response but tried not to stand stiffly or jerk away. Any type of physical human contact unsettled her. Regardless, no one appeared to be observing their interactions.

"Hallo, Hallo, Etta und Hannis! Herzlich willkommen! Welcome! So good it is to see you both!" Mevr. Vedder, or Nadine, as she insisted on being called, spoke German—a formal, imperfect *Hochdeutsch* she likely cobbled together from long-ago school days. And speak she did, without hesitation or, it seemed, breath, in what would become a familiar lilting yet dissonant voice.

"Hierlang, hier entlang. Folgen Sie mir. This way, this way. Follow me," she said, leading them to the streetcar on Schipholweg. Esther grabbed Zami's hand and pulled him along.

"There is the market. We have a market still. A good market too. Every Tuesday and Saturday. *Und hier*—and here," she continued as their transport turned onto Plesmaniaan, "here is where you will find *den Eingang zur Universität*—the entrance to the University. Over there, right across the river, Old Rhine, is the library. Perhaps you know of it already? It's famous. I hope you have a chance to visit this beautiful place. We're so proud of it."

She spoke to Esther and Zami as though to tourists on holiday and not the alleged criminals they were considered, in need of refuge.

They got off the streetcar when it came to a stop at the end of Plesmaniaan and walked two tree-lined streets to Nadine Vedder's home—their new home, in the loosest sense of the word.

Nearly three weeks passed before Esther had an opportunity to be alone in the house. These living conditions presented particular challenges, as she and Zami were no longer in a place of their own. Privacy here was a commodity in short supply. Mevr. Vedder—Nadine—ran a boarding house.

Esther had not known what to expect upon arriving in Leiden. All she knew was that it was a small-sized city with few amenities far enough removed from the bombings taking place in Rotterdam and Utrecht to be considered safe. Frau Weir had outlined how the contact would meet them and that shelter would be made available for as long as possible, if not as long as needed. She supplied no other details, and more specifics were not exchanged. Time and circumstance had not allowed such luxury of information. Moreover, what choices or options did she otherwise share?

What Esther did have intact, what she maintained in spite of all that had taken place and all she would still endure, was a sense of entitlement. While she had gratitude for the help provided and consciousness of the risks these people accepted on her behalf and others, she never wavered from the belief this assistance was justified.

Why should I suffer for something I don't believe in? was her refrain.

Esther's drive never wavered. Not now nor since the moment born of impossible anguish that robbed her self and soul and ignited this pathway in search of—

—what?

If I'm honest with myself, she reflected, I don't know what I'm in search of, what I'm seeking. I only know that it's elsewhere. And in this place of elsewhere, there will be peace, sanctuary.

At the depth of her being, Esther knew the mystifying destination she sought would finally release this unremitting suffering that had informed her every thought and action since that ill-fated day—her wedding day—in Przeworsk.

My home . . . India . . . she knew not why but she knew . . .

I must figure out the ways to make this situation work for me for as long as it is compulsory to be here, she ruminated, chewing on the inside of her right cheek. I must never let down my guard, never become settled. This, above all else, is vital. I can't trust any of them. Not even Nadine. I must maintain control, of my actions and my thoughts. I can't let my mind drift, not to that bewildering encounter back in Köln, not to him, not anywhere. I cannot give in to the threats that surround me. These are other people's issues. Not mine.

The dangers—those known and unknown and unthinkable. Already, so much that had taken place resided in the realm of the unimaginable.

To be in control, she needed to know the layout of the house. Since arriving, she had only ventured from her room to the dining area or the toilet and back again. Now alone, Esther explored the parlor with curiosity. A wood-framed sofa that could easily seat five, covered in timeworn silk damask, dominated the generous room. Twin chairs in matching fabric bookended it. There was a small rocker in one corner with an ornately carved, needlepointed footstool. Once-thick oriental rugs, now thinned and frayed by decades of feet treading upon them, covered most of the floor. An oversized glass-and-oak display cabinet, housing blue-and-white china and figurines, swallowed up one wall. Photographs of people young and old, certainly family members, hung in a random fashion on the walls. Indigo velvet drapes riddled with moth bites, held back by braided cords, framed the room's three large windows. The scent of must, privilege, and years froze in the air. Faded opulence.

All surfaces were covered with lace doilies or runners, and every seat spilled over with embroidered pillows of various shapes and sizes. Esther was drawn to these objects. She fingered each piece thoughtfully, expertly assessing the quality, technique, and complexity of the work involved. It was as though she could channel the women who created these pieces and feel their fingers deftly manage the bobbins and hooks to wind the thread into patterns and designs. One runner had lovely, well-executed turning stitches; a few of the doilies used more simple plaits. One piece had Van Dyke scallops and included an undulating line of picots on its head side.

The quality is not as good as Bubbe Royza's work, Esther mused, nor the motifs as elaborate or unique. However, a few of these pieces are fairly special, she conceded.

At the thought of her *bubbe*, Esther took in a sudden breath and had to immediately press down on her chest, at the center of her breastbone, to maintain her equilibrium. This sharp ache, deep within, surprised her. As quickly as it appeared, the pang abated, and she pushed it aside.

Her heart . . . emotions . . . such possibility still breathes within . . .

These objects, the doilies and runners and delicate pillows, made from thread and silk, linen and yarn—in some measure rather like talismans of her own lineage and history—helped balance her.

Indisputably . . . for Esther it is thread . . . always thread.

As Esther leaned down to more closely examine the footstool's needlepoint stitches, she heard steps behind her and turned, still crouching, just as Nadine entered the room.

"*Hallo,* Etta, *Hallo!*" Nadine sang. "*Genießen Sie*—are you enjoying the day? Outside, it is so hot! How is your shoulder? It is a pretty room, this, is it not? My, how do you say?—*Urgroßvater*—great-grandfather—built this house. His many—eight, I believe—sisters made all the needlework."

Nadine's bouncy manner of speech, coupled with her imperfect school-learned German, contributed to Esther's unease around her. Nadine was generous of spirit; still, Esther's armor was at the ready.

"*Ja, ja, es ist alles gut*—all is good," Esther replied as she unbent her body. "The stitches in my upper arm and shoulder can come out in three days, and then I can get back to work. The doctor was confident I would be fine."

Nadine smiled. With head nodding, she exited the room as quickly as she had entered. She did not give Esther a chance to say anything else, which was in itself a relief. The less she had to participate in any type of dialogue, with anyone, the easier it would be. Most certainly, Nadine played a critical role in preserving Esther's safety; fortunately, remaining wary and continually on alert was second nature to her.

Mindful not to stumble, careful not to trip over stories, experiences, moments, contacts.

Trust could not be found in her lexis . . . yet . . .

Over the coming weeks, Esther did learn how to manage these new circumstances for her own best interests. In addition to Nadine, herself, and Zami, three others resided in the sizable four-bedroom house, and it soon became evident not living alone came with its advantages. Not the least of which was Nadine's daughter Alicja, called Ans.

A mature sixteen-year-old, Ans was industrious and took on many responsibilities for her mother around the house, although she was still in school. She was also sweet and maternal and straightaway became attached to Zami.

"I've wanted a little brother or sister all my life," she told Esther when they first arrived. "It will be so much fun to have him in our home."

Esther did not understand her words, but Ans's mannerisms suggested excitement. This will be a good thing, she thought.

Whenever she could, when not in classes or doing homework or chores, Ans went in search of the little boy. Now nearly two years of age, Zami remained an uncommonly quiet child. He was undemanding of anyone or anything. It was evident he preferred to be with his mama but obliged when Ans came to spend time with him, read to him, play with him, feed him, or attend to whatever he might need. For Esther, to be disencumbered for short periods was a relief.

She was, however, unyielding in her demand that she would be the only one to bathe Zami or help him use the toilet.

"*Er ist sehr schüchtern.* He's very shy," Esther would explain.

"Odd child," the other residents whispered to one another. "Something is not right with that little boy" was their collective belief. Among themselves, when they thought Esther was not looking—or listening, which was most of the time—they exchanged looks or raised eyebrows.

Ans ignored them. With laughter and games, she did her best to draw Zami out, encourage a smile, sometimes a quiet chortle. No matter how strange or indifferent to her actions he might be, she enjoyed spending time with him. It was the closest to a sibling she would ever have, and she doted on him. This young woman had patience and a boundless sense of joy, much like her mother. Ans's personality was too cloying for Esther's taste. Yet, as the girl's German was negligible, Esther did not have to offer more than a nod of her head to convey yes when the request to play with Zami was extended. Without exception, Esther said yes.

> Ah . . . not a surprise to me . . . as her preference was to be on her own . . . and alone whenever possible. This . . . of course . . . was true to her character . . . at least for now.

Esther never inquired about Ans's father, assumed to be Nadine's husband, or wondered what role he might play in their lives. An unspoken agreement seemed to exist among the residents—all women—that this individual was not to be mentioned.

In any case, it is not of my concern, Esther thought. The less I know is for the better.

The house's other occupants held scarce interest for Esther. Sacha Smit, a slight, pretty woman in her early twenties, was a schoolteacher. While she taught four- and five-year-olds in the local *kleuterschool,* Sacha did not share the same affinity or aptitude for working with children as came so naturally to Ans. In fact, she never spoke of her position in terms that implied it was anything more than drudgery. She did, however, light up when the subject was her beau, Claes. He was her inexhaustible topic.

Sacha was deeply in love with this young man from her hometown of Hoogeveen. Barely three months prior, Claes had gone to Germany to enlist in the Nazi party and become a soldier. Motivated by the troops' easy dominance over the Netherlands and his own family's Prussian ancestral roots in that country, he held strong anti-Semitic beliefs. While family and friends had been shocked by his actions, Sacha held only admiration for what she saw as a man of profound convictions.

And unquestionably . . . of most importance . . . of greatest significance . . . this young woman was in love . . . immeasurable love . . .

Sacha did not know German, and thus communication between herself and Esther was limited to nods of greeting when they passed in the hall or hand gestures across the table at meal-times. In short time, both became proficient at signaling for more juice, the bowl of vegetables, or when available, the platter of meat. Esther learned of Sacha's personal tale through Nadine, who loved to chatter at every opportunity.

Although they did not speak the same language, Esther could easily tell Sacha talked incessantly about her man at their meals—or at any time there was someone to listen. Commonality of speech was not essential. Esther could wholly interpret the expression, the desire, and the flush that accompanies profound, impassioned emotion when one speaks of her beloved. This is a look transcending the need for words or expressions of any language. Esther knew its dominance intimately—and its tragedy.

The house's final resident was Ida Van Ostrand, a woman of substantial height and girth who, while only in her middle forties, appeared years older in style and stance. Ida's life journey had not been smooth, and as a consequence, she exuded an uncomfortable bitterness to rival Esther's own. Ironically, by profession, Ida was a seamstress. Although she did have some skill, her abilities did not come close to Esther's mastery or inventiveness.

Ida was the one other resident who spoke German. Like Nadine, she had a foundation of school-learned *Hochdeutsch,* a formal, mostly grammatically incorrect textbook ability to dialogue without ease of casual conversation. Esther was grateful to learn she was not as talkative as Nadine and mostly kept to herself.

However . . .

Ida was the one member of the household who expressed suspicion at Etta and Hannis's—Esther and Zami's—sudden appearance in Leiden and in their home.

"Etta is the friend of my dear friend Matilde, Mattie—you've heard me speak of her—from Germany—Köln," Nadine told her. "Etta's husband died at the Front just a few months ago, and she and Hannis had nowhere to go. You know I have that extra space in the attic. With everything going on, how could I turn her down?"

Ida harrumphed when she heard Nadine's rationale for adding two more people to what she considered an already too crowded house.

"There's a story here," Ida muttered to herself. "The pieces don't fit together. A few layers of truth are absent. What is Nadine not telling us? On quick impression, this woman is not the kind to cull favors from people. She's guarded and keeps to herself. And that son of hers—something is not right here, not at all."

The deep cuts self-inflicted in Wuppertal had limited the mobility of Esther's left hand—her sewing hand—and the doctor Nadine made her visit within a day of arrival in Leiden insisted Esther stop all manual activities until the wounds healed. He was a kindhearted, responsible man who did not inquire about the circumstances of these cuts. His primary interest was that her shoulder and arm achieve complete recovery. Esther thought rest unnecessary and wasteful, but with Nadine's near constant presence, she had to oblige.

The absence of work and busyness and earning money—most especially the latter—made Esther unsettled, more so than anything else she encountered. By the time her wounds healed and the stitches were removed, she was restless, anxious to commence tailoring. The inability to create a stitch was maddening. This was the first period in Esther's life, since she was a young girl of five, when she did not sew or perform some other type of work to earn money.

And money without question . . . was most vital . . .

With mind and hands not consumed by assignments and deadlines and sewing challenges—or marketing and cooking and cleaning, since Nadine and her daughter oversaw those household duties—Esther spent hours on end, protracted futility, in the chair in her attic room. Simply waiting. Willing her wounds to heal. Faster. She struggled to control her thoughts, to keep her mind empty. Free of contemplation. But now and again thoughts would defy her, and memories would appear. Esther drifted among them. Her reflections glided toward family members, individually, then collectively. Her family in Przeworsk. The people with whom she had shared the first part of her life. She thought of Tova and Miriam—their smiles, laughs, and joys—the girls she birthed and put on that train at far too young an age. She did not think of Abraham, whom she never considered a relation.

How are you, Mama? *Tate?* Are you both well? Are you safe? And what of my sisters? My brothers? Gital and Chana and Eli, Itzik, Yetta, Moishe? Frayda, Rose, Chaim, and Jakob? My dearest Tonka? Where are you all? Are you still alive? Lifcha, of course, in the United States must be fine. But all the others? And what of Przeworsk? Does it still exist? And what of my little girls? What has become of them?

"*Ach!* Too many questions!" Esther said softly. "There are too many questions. Would I want to know the answers?"

Even now her conscious mind would not allow her to think of ... to imagine ... Tadeusz ... his story ... their story ... why ...

Nadine did not receive a newspaper, and although there was a radio in the parlor, it was continually tuned to classical music. No one dared change the station. The war was not a topic discussed among the residents around the dining table or anywhere in the house. Nadine would not hear of it. She told everyone who would listen that it was a subject too dispiriting to capture one's attention.

"*Mijn huis moet een toevluchtsoord zijn van de wreedheden die in de wereld plaatsvinden,*" she repeated often. "My house must be a haven from the cruelties taking place in the world."

Yet Nadine thought and knew otherwise. Her activities with the Resistance were, of necessity, covert. Ans did not know of her mother's efforts. Nor did any of the house residents. All meetings Nadine participated in took place during the day when her comings and goings could be attributed to market shopping or tea with friends. Her evenings were spent at home in the parlor near the radio, listening to her treasured music.

Consequently, the events taking place outside of Leiden, let alone those occurring as far away as Poland, were not known. Przeworsk might as well have been on another planet.

Yet it is in my sphere . . . as I traverse all spheres . . . to see and to know . . . all that occurs. It is who I am . . . and when it is time . . . I will help Esther know . . . I will help reveal . . .

There were no updates on whether the Germans had advanced or if neighboring countries had been taken over by their force and will. Even Sacha was rarely able to glean snippets of information from her beloved.

And there was never any mention of the plight of the Jewish people.

Esther's chief task during these weeks of healing and waiting, one that took up less than one hour, was to arrange her and Zami's space in the way most functional for her needs—sleeping and sewing. As the attic was a mere nine square meters, there were not a lot of options. This process involved no more than the need to determine which piece of furniture to cram into what corner.

A narrow winding staircase with a frail wrought iron rail led into the attic, the lone room on the third level above the four bedrooms. The ceiling was low, with a skylight about the size of a porthole. During the day it provided a stream of light in what would otherwise be a dreary, claustrophobic space. Esther stood barely five feet tall, so her ability to move about was not hampered. No door separated the attic from the staircase, and as such, no lock and therefore no privacy. The other residents could wander up the stairs on a whim and on occasion did. Most often it was Ans, in search of Zami.

"*Bitte! Rufen Sie*—Call my name from the bottom of the stairs first, and do not come up the stairs without my invitation!" Esther would implore, barely able to conceal her annoyance.

"*Het spijt me. Het spijt me zo.* I'm so sorry. I forgot. Again," Ans said. "I was only thinking of how excited I was to see Hannis after being at school all day."

In this house, there was not one area Esther could relax in or call her own.

At night Esther and Zami shared the pallet Nadine had wedged into one corner of the room. While Esther decided where each piece would go, Nadine arranged the furniture. She wanted to make sure Esther didn't put pressure on her shoulder or overextend her energies. And although the pallet was painfully hard, Nadine had been kind enough to provide them with extra blankets to lay between their bodies and the straw-filled mattress.

From the parlor, Ans brought up an upholstered chair, a small table, and a floor lamp. Esther had Ans place these pieces in the opposite corner to serve as her workspace. As needed, the pallet would be used for laying out patterns or tracing pieces of fabric.

"So small is this room, Etta," Nadine said. "The parlor would be—Ah, what is the word?—a preference, yes? Do you not think? That room is large, and I could arrange a good-sized space in one corner for you. No one would disturb you."

"*Nein, danke,* but I wouldn't want to bother everyone else, most especially you. I know how you enjoy listening to your music there," Esther said while thinking, of course I don't want to be in that space. People walk through there all the time. No doubt, everyone, most especially Ida, would constantly look over my shoulder and comment on my work. This is not acceptable.

Zami used what little bit of floor space remained to play with his train. Or he would settle on the pallet and stare at the rough walls. Even with such an attentive, regular sitter as Ans, Zami remained the most inward of children, more content to be by himself and with himself than to participate in the outer world.

It fills me with joy that there is one around this young boy who truly cares.

Only when Esther's wounds had fully healed and she had the doctor's approval to start working did Nadine arrange for her to meet with the owner of a local textile mill. It was one of the two mills in Leiden that had a dress shop attached, and this was the more prestigious of the two. Ida worked for the other.

The owner's wife was a former schoolmate of Nadine's who agreed to provide the introduction as a favor in exchange for one of Nadine's antique Delftware plates. It was the large, rectangular platter with the molded white border and delicate Chinese landscape etched onto the centerpiece she had long coveted. Esther did not learn of this agreement or notice that a void had appeared on the third shelf of the parlor's oversized display cabinet. She never knew the elegantly crafted blue-and-white plate had been in Nadine's family for nearly two hundred years nor gave any thought to its personal or monetary value.

Esther never thought to inquire how, without work samples or a portfolio of drawings or photographs to show, she was able to gain entry to Leiden's most exclusive shop. Her inherent sense of entitlement continued to propel her forward—getting what she needed and ensuring she remained out of harm's way.

It is . . . obviously . . . me . . . always . . . me. It is such fun to . . . shall I say . . . influence situations . . . to remove what is in the way . . . to get what is necessary. Yes . . . this is one of my duties . . . but more importantly . . . it is one of my joys . . .

The mill's owner, Hendrik Schoonhoven, did not trust Nadine's raves of talent and skill in reference to the woman now standing in his office. Nadine's praise was, in fact, fabricated. She had never seen a stitch of Esther's work, let alone evidence of her mastery, but she did have confidence in what she heard from Frau Weir. Regardless, entry to Dhr. Schoonhoven's office for the morning meeting was made available exclusively due to his wife's artful arm-twisting and that alone. He was unaware of the backdoor arrangement that had been dealt and the object exchanged in order for her to agree to attempt to make this meeting happen.

With Nadine as translator, for Dhr. Schoonhoven knew little German, Esther recited her qualifications: "I have been sewing for more than thirty years and, for much of that time, have also worked successfully with pelts. There is no tailoring challenge I have not met—be it fabric or fur—to a customer's delighted approval. My work is precise down to the last stitch, my craftsmanship is superb, and my designs can range from simple to elaborate with everything in between. I know you and your clients will not be disappointed."

Throughout the meeting, Dhr. Schoonhoven sat behind his outsized, ornately carved marble desk and moved piles of paper from one part of its surface to another. He tapped his left index finger against a cup. He cleared his throat a few times and scratched his right ear. He refused to meet Esther's eyes while she spoke and murmured "hmm" when she completed her speech. Abruptly, he rolled his chair away from the desk and walked out of the room without uttering a word. He returned ten minutes later with a bolt of sheer teal-green silk, a fabric known within the trade for its slick, watery texture, one of the most difficult with which to work.

"Your test is to design and construct a proper woman's suit. Two pieces. Fitted. Something suitable for a professional office. Mevr. Vedder will be the model, and it must fit her impeccably. With aid of a magnifying glass, I will examine every inch and assess the quality of your work, the construction, your taste, perspective, and the like. My shop sells the very best and nothing else. I do not settle. On your way out, you may pick up whatever else you might need—materials for lining, buttons, matching thread. Anything. I want you back here on Monday morning, ten a.m. Prompt. No excuses!"

"*Ich bin Deutsche.* I am German," said Esther, rather huffily. "*Pünktlich.* Punctual. *Stipt!*" recalling the correct Dutch word. "In all cases punctual! Time is never an issue. Four days is more than enough to complete your task. *Dank u*—Thank you!"

The next days unfolded with continuous drawing, measuring, cutting, and stitching, all by hand, as Esther no longer had access to a sewing machine. She demanded everyone stay out of her way, with only Nadine allowed to come up to the attic room for fittings. Esther took brief breaks during these days, to eat and to bathe Zami. And, of course, to take him to the toilet when she knew it necessary. Regardless of what else occurred around her, maintaining their identity was fundamental. Ans took care of his other needs.

A few times over these days, Ida's curiosity got the better of her, and she would call up from the base of the stairwell, "Etta, in any way can I be of assistance to you? Are there needs you might have?"

"*Nein, Nein.*" Esther responded in frustration. "*Alles geht gut.* Everything is going fine. I need to be left alone so I can concentrate."

Nothing proved too much of a distraction. The finished suit was unadorned, yet elegant—each stitch perfect in size and formation, the lining smooth with hems and seams hidden, the skirt double pleated and flawless.

After Nadine modeled the ensemble, Dhr. Schoonhoven closely looked over every stitch with a magnifying glass, as he had assured her he would. Esther could tell he was surprised but impressed. What's more, she knew he was already visualizing the money he would make from her work.

"What do you think, Dhr. Schoonhoven? Does it meet with your satisfaction?" Nadine inquired on Esther's behalf.

Looking directly at Esther, he said, "*Alstublief*—Please, Etta, call me Hendrik."

From that moment onward, it was tacitly understood work was secured for Esther.

No probing questions of how or where or when she had acquired her masterful skills. No inquiries into Esther's background or history or circumstances. Such quality and talent were rarely seen in small-town Leiden, yet women with strong desires and tastes and resources did reside here.

Nothing else mattered—when there was money to be made.

CHAPTER TWENTY-FOUR

Normalcy...
or...
at the very least...
its illusion.

....

Once more a routine became established, generating constancy and the most base level of security in Esther's life. Structure and focus were her two best allies.

Perhaps the only allies she would accept... could accept...
for now.

Still—she was never truly settled. Esther clung to distrust as though it were an extra appendage trying to work in partnership with the rest of her body. In actual fact, this was the one in charge.

Monday through Saturday, work commenced just before the sun rose and continued long after it rested. There was drawing and cutting, marking and stitching, on silks and linens and cottons, wool and denim, corduroy and gabardine. Just one day after the meeting with Hendrik, a tall, burly man from his company delivered a sewing machine and table so Esther could produce her work more swiftly. Plainly, Hendrik's interest was the earning power of his new employee.

"*Ongelofelijk*—Incredible!" Ida exclaimed with widened eyes, gawking at the man as he carried the coveted machine up the stairs. She had only threads and needles at her disposal with which to work. "*Wie doet zoiets?* Who does such a thing? Etta is not that good!" Jealousy permeated Ida's cells and pores and slowly escalated.

Ida disliked Esther from their first meeting but did not share her feelings. From this day forward, however, she would not stop grousing about Esther to anyone, at any opportunity, with no provocation necessary.

Ida, her actions, her words, her very being, did not faze Esther one whit. Mostly, she ignored her. The other house residents also did their best to stay out of Ida's way. Never much of a pleasure to be around, Ida's escalating spitefulness discouraged anyone from wanting to be near her. Sweet-tempered Ans, with never a rude word or thought for anyone, steered clear of this woman's path. While Esther passed her with barely an acknowledgment, everyone else would turn a corner or duck into a room if they saw her headed their way.

The sewing table and slender upright chair took up the attic's remaining floor space. Esther did not mind climbing over objects, no matter how many times it was necessary during the course of a single day. It was more ideal than working downstairs where she could come upon Ida or the others. As she had always done, Esther kept to herself to the fullest extent possible. When needed, she spoke, engaging in no more sentences than were required, no matter what the topic or with whom. But she did what was expected of her. She punctually paid the monthly sum to cover her and Zami's room and board and kept her section of the house neat. A two-year-old and a burgeoning business did not impact these responsibilities. With Zami, she joined in at mealtimes, as there were no other options. Otherwise she was on her own. This was the way she preferred it—to keep to herself and mind only her business.

*On her own . . . by herself . . . alone . . . she will prevail . . . that
was her mantra.*

In spite of this, Ida was not one to be easily shunned. It was as
though she were on a mission and took every possible occasion to
uncover something that could lead to Esther's undoing.

In addition to meals, each Sunday morning the house's
residents took the streetcar to Pieterskerk, the exquisitely ornate
late-Gothic church across the way from the university library. A
Protestant church. There was not one house of worship for Catholics
in all of Leiden. At first, Esther was taken aback by this newest twist
not accounted for in her planning or Frau Göttlieb's meticulous
preparations. But Esther's stoicism, coupled with instinctive acting
ability, once more carried her forth.

"I was raised a Catholic," Esther informed the house residents
that first morning on their way to church. "I don't know anything
about being a Protestant or the differences with my religion, but a
regular Sunday service is of utmost importance. Nothing is more
essential for Zami's good upbringing."

A Catholic, Ida thought. I should not be surprised. Another
black mark against this dreadful woman.

Nadine preferred the eight o'clock service and would rush
everyone through breakfast in order to arrive promptly. Grander
than Wuppertal's St. Laurentius, Pieterskerk's single complication
was its Protestant rituals. In all other ways, Esther welcomed visiting
its serene setting.

This weekly destination supplanted the Friday evening Sabbath Esther could no longer prepare. And sadly, these visits were
neither relaxing nor renewing, as she had to remain on guard and
attentive to every movement and action, vigilant not to misstep. The
service was in Dutch, a language Esther had only begun to study.
It took all her concentration to try to understand what was said
and to learn the necessary responses and actions at the appropriate
sections. Nadine sat next to her to assist.

Always, Ida made sure she sat in the same pew, too close for
comfort. She spent her time observing Esther's actions instead of
focusing on the morning's sermon.

"Etta, *So eine hübsche kleine Bibel.* Such a pretty little Bible. How long have you had it? Where did you get it? Was it from your family?" she whispered.

"It was my grandmother's. She gave it to me when I was a child. Now, please, be quiet!"

Nadine, Ans, and Sacha would whisper "*Sussen*—Shush" in unison or roll their eyes knowingly at one another in silent frustration and solidarity with Esther.

Unmindful of all around her, or merely disrespectful, Ida would persist: "Oh, I see. Did you get it for your Communion?" Smirking when she asked this.

"*Ja, ja,*" Esther replied, "*Natürlich.* Now, again I say, be quiet."

Ida settled back in her seat but continued to closely study Esther from the corner of her eye.

This is how Sunday's church service unfolded, week upon week. Ida would invariably have probing questions for Esther— about the Holy Mother necklace she wore, about how long she had studied catechism, about where she grew up, about her family, about how her husband had died. Ida asked the same question more than once a few weeks apart, as though she was testing, making sure the facts remained straight, while trying to trip Esther, find a slip-up, see if she would stumble.

Ida never inquired about Esther's sewing skills.

There are those . . . many . . . far too many . . . who live among you . . . whose intentions . . . ambitions . . . aspirations . . . are not of good . . . not of heart . . .

Those . . . whose aspirations are dark and destructive to others. It must be understood that . . . ultimately . . . they are only destructive to themselves.

In this way, September rolled into October, then November. With this dark, rimy month came deep winter. Nadine began scurrying around the house to dig into the backs of closets, on the highest shelves and behind furniture to pull out all sorts of Christmas decorations. Most were family treasures passed down for generations. She spent hours rummaging through these boxes and bags, deciding how to best adorn each room this year. She hummed holiday songs, and throughout each day, whenever she walked past Zami, Nadine would lean down to his height and announce, *"Hannis, Sinterklaas kommt bald! Sinterklaas kommt bald!* Saint Nicholas comes soon!"

Zami's response was a stare. He did not comprehend what she was saying or react to her cheery spirit. Nadine would then kneel down again and say, "This holiday, you will like. It is wonderful, my favorite time of year. No matter what else is happening, this holiday is happiness."

Then, smiling widely enough for the two of them, Nadine carried on with her decorating as though not a care existed—within this house or in the world beyond its boundaries.

Nadine decorated her house much earlier than the neighbors and kept the decorations up longer than others because, as she would say to anyone who asked, "It is just the way I like to do it. It is my home, after all."

It was exactly as she lived all aspects of her life—her way. As much as she possibly could anyway.

Conscious of the events around her. Mindful of everything transpiring. Participating how she could. While holding fast to her spirit . . . and to her truth.

Nadine paid the neighbor's teenage son two guilders to cut down a sizable tree in the nearby woods and help her put it up in the parlor, in the corner where the small rocker with the needlepointed footstool usually rested. Nadine and Ans decorated the tree with dainty glass baubles and tiny bells and stars.

"Would you like to help?" Ans asked Zami, who was lying on the floor nearby, his train held tightly in his left hand. He shook his head, but did take the star she offered him. He placed the train on the ground with the star on top of it, as though a passenger, and rolled them back and forth together.

"Look, look! Hannis likes it," she said, clapping her hands in delight. "It's hard to find anything else he'll play with. It's only the train. Always the train."

Nadine wove red, green, and white satin ribbons throughout the tree and placed glittery pinecones around its base and on the mantle over the fireplace. From the last box, she unwrapped ten ornaments that were considerably larger, about fifteen centimeters in diameter, and mostly spherical. These were made of the same blue-and-white ceramic the display cabinet held.

"Ah," she said, smiling warmly. "Here they are, my favorites. Aren't they beautiful?" She placed the angel holding a wreath at the top of the tree.

"We won't put the electric lights on the tree this year. We haven't had an air raid recently, but I think it best not to take any chances. Everything else will be the same. As much as possible. Ans, please help me place these small pots of *kerstersters,* my adored poinsettias, throughout the house. In the foyer, dining room, kitchen, and each bedroom. Please don't forget Etta's attic. I know it's cramped, but I'm sure Hannis, most especially, will enjoy these."

Ach, thought Esther, walking past the parlor on her way to the kitchen to boil water for another cup of tea. I have no room for such nonsense. And no time! How I wish I did not have to tolerate such silliness. But it seems to be an important holiday with all types of Christians. Silly, silly rituals!

On the fifth of December, the eve of Saint Nicholas's Feast Day, Nadine took Zami's small shoes and Ans's much larger ones and placed them by the front door, as tradition directed. In the morning, Zami found his brimming with candy, which brought a smile to his generally severe countenance. He looked up at his mama to see if it was permissible to try one.

"*Ja, ja,*" said Esther. "It is fine." She then turned to Nadine and whispered, "*Vielen Dank.* Many thanks."

I . . . naturally . . . was so very pleased to see these treats . . . to see him smile. But not one cookie . . .

There was not money for toys or other gifts that year, but the breakfast feast did include *kerststol met roomboter.* Smoked salmon and eel were also part of the table's abundant offerings. Everyone relished their meal, and even Ida seemed to take pleasure in the special treats before her. At least for this one day, her attention was focused on her plate rather than on Esther.

But twenty days later, on First Christmas Day—after the house residents greeted each other in the early morning with *"Vroljk Kerstfeest,* Merry Christmas," after they had returned from the festive church service, and after they had shared yet another feast—Ida turned to Esther to begin the drilling of history and background with renewed intensity. When they were all settled in the parlor to hear Ans sing carols, Ida asked, in her prying way, *"Bitte,* Etta, tell us about your—*Ferien Traditionen*—holiday traditions. How did you celebrate in your family?"

Esther responded coolly, "Our holidays were insignificant really. We never had money for gifts or fancy meals. We were very poor."

Nadine interjected, "Please, dear Ans, please sing one of your beautiful songs."

Ida would not give up, and in between each of Ans's songs, she pushed and prodded Esther further. Finally she asked, "You must have sung songs. *Jeder singt Liede*—Everyone sings songs. What was your favorite?"

"Ja, ja, this is correct," Esther said, thinking quickly, "we would sing," and immediately began—

"O Tannenbaum, o Tannenbaum,
Wie treu sind deine Blätter!"

When she started on the second stanza, everyone in the room joined in.

This was the one Christmas song all Germans learned, no matter their religion or race. Fortuitously, its popularity had traversed borders. Christmas—*Weihnachten*—was well-nigh born in Germany, and *"O Tannenbaum"* was considered the country's national anthem every December. Gratefully, Ida did not seem aware of this fact and felt placated, somewhat, by Esther's ability to respond to her inquisition.

"Du grünst nicht nur zur Sommerzeit,
Nein, auch im Winter wenn es schneit.
O Tannenbaum, o Tannenbaum,
wie treu sind deine Blätter!"

. . . .

O Fir-tree green! O Fir-tree green!
How loyal is thy leafage!
Not green alone in summertime,
But green in winter's snow and rime!
O Fir-tree green! O Fir-tree green!
How loyal is thy leafage!

How loyal . . . indeed. And I like that the leaves and the color
remain loyal . . . steadfast . . . devoted without end . . .

CHAPTER TWENTY-FIVE

The layers . . .
between us . . .
within us . . .
around us . . .
are merely seams.
Binding.

....

December slipped into January, then February, March, April, May. The calendar had reached 1941, and much of Europe and parts of the rest of the world were in the throes of deep, heavy combat. Screams of agony and torment were rising, reverberating through the ether, although not acknowledged by those who could help.

As is everything . . . it was felt in the layer of connective tissue that binds all humans and resonates at the core of understanding.

For Esther and all the residents of the insignificant, distant town of Leiden, deep in Holland, it was, for the most part, life as usual.

Ida did not ease up on her incessant badgering of Esther. This wretched woman remained unrelenting in her search for a tiny crevice in Etta's narrative—her very being an insult. There were no facts or rationale as to why she reacted this way, just a concentrated suspicion and loathing.

Esther's work for Hendrik remained steady and secure, resulting in a substantial accumulation of money. Once more her gift with thread provided options and opportunities others in similar circumstance could not share. Payment was in cash, of course. Esther would only accept cash, which she hid in every nook, crack, and cranny of her attic space and sewed in the seams and hems of their clothes. For she never knew—as happened in Wuppertal—when a hasty departure would be required.

No, no, she thought often, I can never grow too comfortable or relaxed. Especially not with Ida around. What wasted energy she is!

Over these months Zami grew four centimeters taller. He expanded his vocabulary by a few more words in both German and Dutch but maintained his detached, hidden self. Present, but still separate from those around him.

Nadine and Ans were able to preserve their bright, light-hearted selves. This was understandable for Ans, who paid little attention to current events, of national or international significance. School, home, and Zami were her interests. But Nadine, without fail, attended her meetings—now thrice weekly—which provided in-depth reviews of the most recent atrocities happening around the globe. These updates were terrifying and devastating and made her feel increasingly helpless. She never shared what she learned with anyone, most especially not Esther.

How can I, how can we, possibly make a positive difference in the midst of such madness? Nadine thought. How can we help turn things around? There are so many, many afflicted people who need assistance. There is much that needs to be done, but we don't seem to know how or what to do! Our incessant brainstorming sessions have become circular discussions without end or possibility.

Despite the strife churning within, she assumed a cheery disposition outwardly.

Her house was full . . . but her heart was not . . .

Lastly there was Sacha, whose primary activities were working five days a week at the *kleuterschool* and dreaming, thinking, talking about Claes, her beloved. Continually. He had now been gone nearly one full year—the days systematically crossed off in her datebook each night before she crawled into bed and pulled the duvet up under her chin. She used the pen with the purple ink he had given her on her most recent birthday. It was one of the few tangibles she had to cling to. The five letters that had made their way through the sporadic, unreliable post would be read over and over again. Sacha scrutinized each, searching for nuances or possible layers of meaning in the words he used or the structure of his sentences. Certain they would reveal new insights into his thoughts and feelings. While coating these pages with tears and tea stains, she imagined his muscular right hand taking pen to paper, writing his words, and then tenderly folding the page, kissing the envelope's throat.

Sacha slept with these precious sheets, wrapped in Claes's midnight blue cashmere scarf with the thin strip of gray around the edges, beneath her pillow each night. She bound them with a thick satin ribbon of lush crimson. The pages had become tattered and crumpled.

And swathed with love . . .

Sacha spoke of Claes at each meal. Whether anyone wished to hear or not, she shared whatever new information she might have found out, either through the scarce letter or from his parents, with whom she remained in regular contact. Or whatever she could imagine, fantasizing the things he might be doing or thinking or saying.

"Claes must be having dinner right about now, *u denkt niet hebben*—don't you think? The time in Germany is about the same as here, I believe. I hope the food is decent. He has a big appetite."

Or—

"Claes had a night off. I'm so glad that every now and again he gets a night off! He went to have a beer with his buddies in a local pub."

And sometimes—

"*Hij zei hij me een mist!* He said he misses me a lot!" Sacha would shout gleefully.

Esther did not understand the sentences but all too fully grasped the emotion, sentiment, and heart behind each word. She did her best to ensure her facial expression did not belie her thoughts gibing Sacha's pathetic yearning.

At another meal, Sacha shared with excitement: "I spoke to Claes's parents this afternoon. He is doing well. He is in some small town in Poland, where they have arrested many *vijanden van het volk*—enemies of the people—you know, the Jews. I am very proud of him. His work is extremely critical."

Nadine flinched. Grateful Esther did not speak Dutch.

Whenever the conversation drifted to direct information about the war, Nadine had her ire raised. She looked Sacha sharply in the eyes and demanded, "*Einde!* Stop! I will not have any further discussion of that kind in my house!"

Sacha bit her lip, eyes tearing up as though she had been slapped.

"But he is involved in such important work. The most important work," she said. "We should all be proud. I don't understand—" Her voice trailed off.

"*Nee, zei ik!* No, I said! If you wish to keep living here, you must respect my wishes. It is my house, after all, and my rules. Now, let us speak of what is more pleasant. I have an extra ticket to the *Stadsgehoorzaal* for Friday evening. The concert should be lovely. Who would like to join me?"

Turning to face Esther, she said in German, "*Etta, möchten Sie*—would you, this Friday evening, like to join me for the concert?"

"*Nein danke,*" she replied. "I have work to do."

As in the past, Esther turned down such offers—any invitations—because she had work to do. Or, more aptly, work was her priority.

And money.

Ans agreed to attend the concert with her mother. She was the ever supportive, accommodating daughter.

On a particularly cold and blustery Tuesday, late in the afternoon two weeks later, the doorbell rang. All corners of the house and its occupants seemed to collectively jump, startled. Other than during the holidays—when neighbors came to pay a brief visit, extend greetings of *"Vroljk Kerstfeest,"* exchange well wishes for the coming year, and bring their grandmother's or great aunt's special marzipan or *kerstkrans* or the scrumptious little *letterbankets* in the shape of their children's initials—no visitors came to the house. There was no time for socializing.

Nadine hurried to the front door. Peering through the eyehole, she saw a short, nervous-appearing young man. He was wearing a dark gray official suit, though it was indistinguishable in regard to its service. Nadine observed his left leg twitched slightly.

Oh dear, she thought, sliding the door open a crack. This cannot be good.

"Ja," she said tersely. *"Kan ik u helpen?* Can I help you?"

Stiffly, formally, without emotion, he said, "I have a telegram for a Sacha Oudekirk. Is she here?"

Before Nadine could call her name, Sacha slowly emerged from where she was cowering, just inside the parlor.

"Dat ben ik. That's me," she said in a quivering voice, her body intuiting the telegram's contents before her consciousness could possibly envision the words on the page.

Quickly signing her name in a script of illegible scrawl, Sacha ripped open the envelope. Immediately she let out a wail of heart-wrenching dimensions that rebounded against the house's walls and returned to the entryway with force.

All of the residents came running, just in time to see Sacha fall to the ground screeching, "Claes, Claes! *Hij is dood! Hij is dood! Mijn mooie Claes is dood!* He is dead! My beautiful Claes is dead! He was killed! Claes is dead!"

The words convulsed out of her.

Nadine and Ans rushed to Sacha's side and tried to comfort her, but Sacha brusquely pushed them aside and screamed, *"Ga weg! Ga weg! Hij is weg!* Go away! Go away! He's gone! *Hij is weg!* He's gone!"

Yet what Esther heard—at the nucleus of her being, at the center of all her reasons and rationales and motivations for every single action—was,

He's gone! He's gone! Tadeusz is gone! He's packed his bags and he's left! And Sarah, Sarah's gone too!

Every emotion Esther had thought buried at a depth far out of reach, every feeling pulverized, every hope and possibility long ago mutilated, came rising up from her cavernous core in one collective thrust. Nearly knocking her to the floor with Sacha, where she, too, could have shared in the writhing of agony, the pain of loss, the abandonment of truth and love. For this instant, before it just as quickly dissipated, Esther experienced what she had not dared herself to feel, what she had not allowed herself to feel, back then— nearly eighteen years ago now—at the moment of occurrence.

Esther murmured nearly imperceptibly, "*Ach,* Sacha, *wenigstens, zumindest, zuallermindest wissen Sie*—At least, if you have nothing else, at least you know he did not leave you of his own free will. This was not his decision. Not his choice."

Sacha did not hear Esther and could not have understood her even if she had. But Ida, standing close by, took notice of what she said. Ida watched with curiosity Esther's twitching face cloaked in a gray pallor. It was apparent she was struggling to hold back expression.

And, in her mind, Ida questioned, How peculiar. I was led to understand Etta's husband was also killed in the war? What could she possibly be talking about? Perplexing indeed!

That night, the dream returned anew.

Darkness instantly descended all around her. But it was darkness unlike the night that comes with each rotation of the earth.

This darkness grew large and loud and encompassing.

This darkness brought near loss of sight and full loss of clarity.

This darkness disallowed delusion.

Sound, all sound, was heightened. Her thoughts within—elevated, intensely acute. No hiding here. No running.

This time, in the dream, Esther did not try to move, to find out where she was or what this was or why. No movement forward, no backward slide. She did not move but went deeper inside nonetheless. This cocoon's complete embrace was welcome.

Esther was in the cavern of self and understood that it was this place that would feed her, only this place that would save her.

Without benefit of sight, she studied the space encircling her. Walls of uneven damp stone resonated with the calming temperament of possibility and transformation.

Then, suddenly, far in the distance, she heard—

Esther awoke with a start, her body covered in layers of sweat.

She grows ever closer . . .

CHAPTER TWENTY-SIX

Stand straight . . . tall . . . erect . . .
but not rigid.
Shoulders, back.
Chin, ever so slightly tucked in.
Torso, centered . . . solid and attentive.
Arms and hands, relaxed at each side.
Feet, facing forward . . . with purpose.
Eyes, gazed downward . . . half open.
Looking out . . . but seeing within.
Self and soul as one.
Be present . . . clear.
Breathe evenly . . . consistently.
Wait . . . for the music to start.
Begin counting.
At the moment that is yours . . . let the right hand lead . . .
Crossing slowly in front of you from hip to hip . . .
and then . . . toward the future . . . your future.
Palm facing in and then leading outward . . .
in a clean, circular motion.
Knees bend ever so slightly to the left . . .
and then to the right, as the hand and arm
complete their cycle.

Repeat.
This time with more force . . . strength . . . assuredness . . .
determination.
You will know when to add the right foot and have it
lead with pointed toes and high arch.
Leg and knee follow direction at the precise moment . . . their
moment.
The left side is then brought in to sustain balance and flow.
Keep counting.
Move as will necessitates.
This space . . . your space . . . is without
boundaries or restrictions.
Let yourself flow . . .
Leap . . .
Twirl . . .
As will desires . . .
and destiny demands.
What is taking place is timeless . . . and endless . . .
and yours.
This dance is mostly done alone.
Yet . . . at one point . . . out of the corner of one eye . . .
you catch a glimpse of a recognizable form . . .
of familiar energy . . . of directed movement . . .
Striding with purpose . . .
Toward you.
You note presence and strength in each step.
Right arms are outstretched . . .
Palms connect . . .
Fingers interweave . . .
And then . . . release.
You pass.

. . . .

Why Esther . . . you ask?

I understand your query.

Why . . . her story . . . above all others?

Why have I chosen to follow her journey when there have been millions . . . even more . . . who you would say experienced a similar path . . . a shared reality.

Please . . . let me elucidate . . . it is so very important to understand . . . to clearly . . . comprehend . . .

Esther is unique.

I clear my throat. I must choose my words carefully.

Truly . . . all humans are unique . . . you are unique . . .

And I follow all souls . . . whether here in this realm or beyond. I am here for all as I am here for you.

I support each in what she needs . . . he needs.

I know the intricacies of each soul's karma and the perfect path of dharma . . . divine law . . . that will ensure each . . . everyone . . . is triumphant . . . ultimately triumphant.

It may not always appear so. For it is often . . . so very often . . . not the easy course I place before one. Rarely is it a smooth . . . clear . . . level lane neatly carved out. Seldom a straight line without forks or roadblocks . . . challenges . . . raising questions and anxiety . . . anxiousness about the right way . . . the correct way . . . to proceed.

No . . . most frequently . . . time and time again . . . it is . . . it must be . . . a more treacherous trail with steep drops . . . sharp

*inclines . . . boulders to hurdle . . . and crossroads offering too
many paths . . .*

With no clear direction.
*But please understand . . . no matter how difficult . . . no matter
the challenges . . . this is what you need . . . this is what you
genuinely want whether you know it or not . . . or . . . more
correctly . . . whether you remember or not that this is what you
asked for . . . what you came for to support your progression.*

*And it is my job . . . my role . . . my purpose . . . the very reason
why I exist . . . and my great honor . . . to provide each and every
one of you with what you need when you need it.*

Again you ask . . . why Esther?

**I shift on my lotus flower and lean forward on my right leg,
the one resting on the ground.**

*I chose Esther not because of the circumstances in which she
found herself. This is a story told time and again. No . . .*

*I chose Esther because she is a woman . . . a soul . . . who
experienced . . . who truly and deeply . . . to the core of her being
understood . . . understands . . . love. Pure love. The truth of love
and its power and its strength . . . and its purpose.*

*But . . . you implore . . . I hear you shout . . . their relationship
did not work . . . their bond . . . it did not last. It could not have
been real. Tadeusz abandoned her. He denied . . . rejected their
love and she was torn apart . . . devastated. Left all she knew
and ran away.*

And you say . . . a part of her . . . the heart of her died inside.

And I respond . . . but did it?

Do you remember when first they met? Ah no . . . you do not yet know this.

So you cannot recall what took place . . . what really happened. And no . . . not just on the surface . . . the outer skin . . . but within . . . deep . . . deep within . . . at the center of her . . . at the center of him . . . truly at the center of us all.

Please . . . let me take you back . . . back to then . . . back to when it all began.

Envision this . . .

In your mind's eye . . . listen to me closely . . . clearly . . . you will see . . . you will learn . . . you will understand that she felt him before she saw him . . . his essence . . . that is.

She knew him . . .

The one bakery on Przeworsk's main road had been especially hectic that day. When Esther arrived to work after her school day was finished, she found a line stretched out the front door. Most unusual, she thought, even for a Friday afternoon when everyone's preparing for *shabbes*. She rushed in, quickly put on her apron, tied her hair up under her cap, and set about assisting customer after customer without a break. This pace continued until 4:40, when it seemed the last patron had been served and had headed home to prepare their evening meal. Bayla, who typically only worked the morning shift but had stayed on to help, took her leave then. "Mama will be wondering what's become of me. I'll see you on Monday. *A gutn.*" Esther was left alone with the responsibility to sweep up and close the bakery before the sun set.

When the shop door swung open one last time, the tiny bell that usually sounded a soft tinkle seemed to clang as loud as the town's church bells announcing a new hour. But now—instead, it was ringing in the advent of a future she had not anticipated and a history she had long forgotten.

Esther was behind the counter, her back to the door, but at once she felt energy surge, like a current rippling through her. She turned, slowly, tentatively, as if she knew, somewhere hidden inside, in a place long dormant, that once she turned around her life would turn too.

The young man standing before her, simply dressed, was of average height and build, though broad shouldered and solid. A mass of thick, dark, wavy hair framed his head and face. What immediately stole her breath were his penetrating blue eyes, the color of the deepest part of the lake at the west edge of Przeworsk. They were eyes of recognition that spoke a language shared only by two.

"Gut shabbes," he said. "Good Sabbath."

"Gut shabbes," she stammered back, flustered, her heart pounding.

Although Esther was nearly sixteen at the time, the age when her older sister had married, she took no interest in nor saw a need for boys. Her life was too full with school lessons, family chores, younger siblings, needlework, and her Friday afternoon job at this bakery. She had kissed a boy once. When that pesky Milosz had chased her into the woods and practically tackled her for a clashing of teeth and an overabundance of saliva—an incident leaving no appeal for further exploration. And the intricately practiced flirtations her sisters and girlfriends engaged in seemed like silly wastes of energy. Always, Esther had more interesting things to do.

But seeing this boy before her, something new—and simultaneously very, very old—roused in her core. As though a butterfly, finally breaking through its cocoon, were fighting its way out, commanding attention.

"Ikh heys Tadeusz," he said. "My name is Tadeusz." The sound of his voice thrust Esther out of her racing mind and into the present and this moment and this man.

"Enshuldik mir. I'm sorry," she said, turning bright red. She recognized he had spoken but did not understand the words. "Please. What did you say?"

"Ikh heys Tadeusz," he repeated. *"Mayn meshpokhe*—My family— moved here a few weeks ago. My father is the new teacher." Explaining in two brief sentences why they had never met.

In Poland, as in most European countries in the early part of the century, it was unusual for families to relocate. Inevitably people were born and died in the same small village, and Przeworsk was no different. Esther lived in the house Bubbe Royza had, and assumed she would always live there too—never foreseeing the personal turmoil and world events that would impel her journey elsewhere.

Ah yes . . . he bought his challah for the Sabbath meal and went on his way that evening. But both were changed . . . elevated. Enlivened in a way most only dream of . . . in truth . . . most cannot imagine.

The connection . . . their connection had been made . . . understood.

The agreement to meet that these two souls had made long before their bodies gestated from single eggs . . . had been realized . . .

This is destiny. This is the exquisite beauty of truth.

And for a while . . . a short while . . . less than the snap of a finger really . . . they moved forward and . . . danced as one.

I pause and take in a deep breath before I continue.

But as often happens . . . sadly . . . I watch again and again . . . and again . . . as such beauty is undone. I know . . . I understand the human incarnation is a challenging one . . . the most challenging one . . . for there are incalculable temptations and conflicts that fog the mind and deny the truth. More often than not . . . there is one who runs from the other's essence . . . their fundamental nature . . . headlong into their fears . . . and a fate inevitably filled with sorrow and regret.

In this case it was Tadeusz who denied what was . . . who rejected their commitment . . . their story . . . their heart . . .

this most precious gift. And instead pursued a fate that would ultimately lead to transition from his mortal self . . . his end . . .

Well . . . the end of this chapter . . . his chapter . . . this physical chapter.

Always in this changeover . . . clarity is renewed . . . and the impact of action understood. Yes . . . some karma is released . . . knowledge heightened . . . but . . .

I wonder why in the human incarnation . . . why true bliss is so very feared.

Yes . . . Esther suffered with a loss and a pain that at times felt as though her soul had been severed . . .

Yet she gained a force and a will that could not be matched.

Significantly . . . critically . . . she never forgot . . . not for an instant . . . the inciting incident. The distasteful fuel that fed her . . . challenged her . . . supported her . . . and would . . . ultimately . . . be her salvation.

On one level . . . the most simple and surface level . . . it was bitterness . . . anger . . . distrust . . . those emotions only too familiar to the abandoned . . . to the spurned. But at the center . . . at her core . . . it was the knowledge and the truth and the power of love that propelled her forward and saved her . . . on every level . . .

And this . . . this is what truly matters . . . for us all.

CHAPTER TWENTY-SEVEN

No matter how deep...
or how thick...
or how encrusted...
The crux cannot be hidden.
The truth...
not denied.

....

$\mathcal{I}$t was a solitary moment on an early fall afternoon.

Zami had just left on a walk with Ans that would likely include a visit to the nearby park. Esther's assignments from Hendrik were completed, and each piece had already been folded neatly in anticipation of tomorrow's pickup and the delivery of a new mound of fabric, pattern designs, repairs, and alterations.

Such an occasion of quiet repose was scarce. Esther's thoughts, characteristically focused on the matter at hand, as well as the next three tasks to accomplish, now wandered. Reflections bounced like pebbles skipping across a pond. Without grasping how or why, they led her to uncover the *kiddush* cup kept concealed in the left side lining of the small suitcase that had carried their meager belongings to Leiden. This was the first time she had looked at it or touched it since leaving Wuppertal.

Esther held the cup tenderly in her right hand, tracing the skillfully etched Hebrew letters that circled its top with the index finger of her left.

Some . . . times . . . some . . . thing . . . so tangible . . . releases . . . the intangible . . .

Memories and images of a life long departed floated all around, leading Esther to the last Sabbath meal shared with Bubbe Royza and all her family. This was the Friday night before her wedding, only two days away. There had been jollity and much laughter that evening. Blissfully, Esther had gone about her chores, helping with the cooking, the setting of the table, the lighting of the candles, and the serving of the meal. Mostly oblivious to the constant chatter and light-hearted banter taking place around her.

"*Un vos shtelstu zikh for*—And what do you imagine Tadeusz is thinking about right now?" Jakob asked, a wicked glint in his eye. "I believe, most likely, he is thinking about what happens—*nokh der khasene*—after the wedding!"

Tonka blushed a bright red and straightaway hid her face behind a napkin.

"Yakov, *shvayg*! Jakob, you shush! I don't want to hear any of that kind of talk," reprimanded Mama with a scowl.

"Now, Grendel, let them have their fun. We don't get enough *simkhes*—happy events," interjected *Tate* good-naturedly. A broad grin extended across his face. "There are never enough things to celebrate. It's fine if these children get a little silly."

Mama's eyes rolled at her husband. She gave him the look that said "fun is fine as long as no lines are crossed."

Bubbe Royza sat in her favorite mustard-colored chair in the farthermost corner of the large room. Ostensibly concentrating on her needlework's elaborate demands, she smiled softly at the banter occurring across the room.

"Can I see your ring again, Esther? *Zay azoy gut!* Please, Esther! *Zay azoy gut!* Please," begged Tonka.

All the sisters nodded their heads and shouted in unison, "*Zay azoy gut!*"

"*Maskim.* Oh, okay. But this is the last time. You must be surprised when you see it on my finger at the wedding. Or pretend to!" said Esther as she ran to their shared room to retrieve this special object of desire hidden in its small box beneath her undergarments.

"*O, s'iz azoy sheyn*! Oh, it's so beautiful. Simple, but also very elegant," Tonka said. "Did Tadeusz really make the ring all by himself? He didn't have any help? Are you sure? How did he know how to do this?" Tonka asked, always the most inquisitive. Although she already knew the answers, she enjoyed hearing the story again and again.

Esther was patient with her favorite sister.

"I've told you Tadeusz studied welding, so he knows how to heat and melt metals. Even though he had never made rings, or any type of jewelry, for that matter, he is *iz er azoy talantful mit zayne hent*—so very talented with his hands. He had the gold from his grandfather's—*zeyde's*—watch that no longer worked. He knew his *zeyde*, may his memory be a blessing—*an emfindlekher mentsh*—a sensible man, would be pleased with its new use.

"The two rings are not identical, which is custom, but they are made from the same original piece of gold," Esther recounted proudly. "This is what matters to us."

"Oh, Esther," Tonka said. "*Du, du host aza mazl!* You are so lucky!"

No envy could be detected in her voice. Only happiness for her sister and that this special man would soon be a real member of their family.

Esther's thoughts then shifted to a few days later. To the moment when her embittered, aching self tossed that ring into the deepest part of the lake as she headed away from Przeworsk, never looking back.

So engrossed in thought and memory, Esther did not hear Ida climb up the attic stairs; did not hear her say, slyly, "Etta, it was so quiet up here I wanted to make sure everything was okay. Also, I need some light blue thread and recall you using the identical color a few days ago. Oh dear, you look very pale. Are you feeling unwell?"

But Esther did hear—

"Etta—Etta," Ida repeated stridently, *"was ist, das Sie halten?* What is that you're holding?"

Jolted back to the present time, space, and four walls of her attic room, Esther immediately thrust the cup inside her dress pocket. But not before Ida had taken a good look at its distinctive engraving.

CHAPTER TWENTY-EIGHT

And then . . .

....

"Ah—*jetzt verstehe ich*—now I understand. It's all become clear. *Alles.* Every little detail that has puzzled me since you arrived now makes sense. That cup revealed what I needed to know. I've seen ones just like it, with the odd script. Before the war. With others. When there were others—everywhere—just like you," Ida said. Her face expressed a blend of self-satisfaction and triumph.

"*Sie sind jüdisch*—You're Jewish, aren't you, Etta? If that is really your name! Admit it!" The accusation spewed with venom. "*Und, Sie sind hier—versteckt?* And, you're here—hiding? This explains why your story doesn't come together. Why it doesn't make sense when I've examined—thoroughly scrutinized, mind you—the information you've shared.

"It explains why there are few facts about your life before here that you've been willing to share. It explains why you are so secretive. And it explains why, even when we are willing to help, you won't let any of us take that strange son of yours to the toilet!

"And being Jewish is, no doubt, the reason Hannis does not act normal nor could possibly be normal. That would explain why he is such a freakish child. Not acting like a real two-year-old at all. Everyone knows that Jews are inbreeds, after all."

Three weeks had passed since Ida, unannounced, had walked in on Esther as she sat entranced with memories, gently caressing Bubbe Royza's *kiddush* cup.

Three weeks in which Ida had waited with barely a shred of patience, observing Esther's every action more closely than usual.

Three weeks that consumed Ida as she considered all she had witnessed since Etta and Hannis had arrived in this house. Details reviewed over and over in her head, pondering their probable meaning.

Three weeks filled with her struggle during each waking hour to understand the concealed truth behind Esther's cursory answers to questions. Endeavoring to decipher the pieces of this puzzle that had irked her for the more than one year that they had shared a roof and most every meal.

And while she had tried, repeatedly, at different hours of the day, Ida was not able to intercept Esther taking Zami to the bathroom or to "accidentally" walk in on them while inside. Of the two bathrooms in the house, only one had a lock, and Esther was careful to use that one when she took Zami in for his evening bath or to use the toilet.

It was during this time that Ida considered probable options and likely scenarios to explain why this woman had, essentially, appeared out of nowhere and come through their front door.

Not long after Esther and Zami had first arrived, Ida had considered that she could, in fact, be a Jew, escaping what would be a dangerous situation in Germany. But after much reflection, she had concluded this could not be possible, since Etta and Hannis were both light haired and light eyed. They had German features— Aryan features—and Esther spoke the language flawlessly.

How can a German-looking person be Jewish? she had reasoned. Those parasites are neither capable nor educated enough to learn a second language, such as I myself have done. And, as much as I can tell, Etta is knowledgeable about Catholicism and church etiquette. A Jew could not likely have learned that; those people are Christ-killers!

What had chiefly dissuaded Ida was the impossibility that this woman could have such immense talent, such exceptional skills with needle and thread, and be a Jew. This was not conceivable.

Jews were barbaric, uncouth. Everyone knew that.

Without question . . . the motivation . . . the veritable impetus . . . right from the onset . . . has been one of jealousy and resentment.

This . . . the most simple explanation for feuds and wars of a much larger scale.

Now these thoughts were pushed aside. Anomalies do exist in all situations, no doubt even with those Jewish people, Ida reasoned. She was clear this was the explanation—the obvious explanation—and this sham must be exposed.

So, on this particular Monday, Ida cornered Esther in the narrow pantry off the kitchen when she came down to make her habitual afternoon cup of tea. The pantry was in a remote part of the house, and at this time of day, Ida was assured they would be alone.

She repeated her accusation, "You're a Jew!"

Esther did not flinch, her face skillfully devoid of expression. Since the day Ida had come into her room, she had anticipated a confrontation. She was primed. Outwardly, she scoffed and with shrugging shoulders said, "Ida, *Sie sagen die merkwürdigsten Sachen!* You do say the strangest things! How in the world did you come up with such an idea? You have been distrustful and suspicious of me since Hannis and I arrived in this house. And," Esther underscored, "I believe, beyond question, you have been envious of my far superior sewing skills that secured work with the best textile mill in Leiden.

"*Da! Ich habe es gesagt!* I've said it! It is now out in the open.

"Finally! You must stop this nonsense immediately and leave me alone!"

Inwardly, Esther's mind raced.

Verdammt, Ida! she thought. Now what do I do? Where can I go? From the look on your face I see you are confounded. Perhaps I've bought myself a bit of time, but my distrust of you runs deeper and wider than the Rhein!

Esther had hoped to live out the duration of this senseless war in the relative peace and obscurity of out-of-the-way Leiden. It was mostly comfortable. They were settled. Nadine and Ans were kind and generous, and she had no trouble earning a living and paying her way. While saving a substantial amount of money.

A rare and blessed cloak of security . . . in this most insecure of times.

Money! That is it. Perhaps I should offer Ida money to keep her quiet?

Esther quickly shoved the idea out of her head.

Such a proposition would only bring tribulation. I have no doubt, after acquiring a goodly amount of cash, Ida would, in due course, inform the authorities. There is a German-imposed civil government now in charge, and citizens are rewarded for turning in enemies of the state and helping maintain racial purity. Just as in Germany.

The war and its effects were never broached in the house, in any case not without Nadine's rebuke, and Esther did not engage in conversations with others on her way to and from the textile mill. Nonetheless, it was impossible not to observe the city's pervasive atmosphere. Public protests, which just a few months ago had occurred on at least a weekly basis, had all but disappeared; people's voices had been suppressed with severe reprisals. Just as they had in Köln and Wuppertal. Reactions were secreted, like Nadine's associates doing their best to engage in covert actions of sabotage or aiding victims, such as herself, to escape or hide.

In this *zeitgeist,* Ida would be heralded a heroic woman. For her, that would be more important than cash. A pronouncement would also bring serious trouble to Nadine, and this Esther would not abide. Not after everything Nadine had done for her and Zami.

While Esther's thoughts moved like lightning, her face remained blank of emotion, with no effort.

She merely said, "*Und jetzt*—and now—if you will excuse me, I will get myself a cup of tea, which is why I came down here."

With that, Esther picked up her cup and a pouch of tea and turned her back on Ida. She shook her head in what would appear to be disgust and walked into the kitchen to heat up the kettle.

Ida was stunned. Not a flicker of fear had crossed Esther's face. Ida had been positive. She was certain. But then again—perhaps she had made a mistake? Was that conceivable? And there was no greater insult than what Ida had accused.

Ah . . . what is certainty . . . after all? Particularly when it can lead one in a direction . . . one should not venture.

At the first opportunity, when the house was empty of its occupants, when Sacha was teaching at school and Ida had left to meet a client at the other end of Leiden and Ans had taken Zami to the park, Esther approached Nadine. She was working in the garden, planting her tulip bulbs—pointed side up, twenty centimeters into the earth and ten centimeters apart—before the winter's first frost was upon them. This year Nadine had chosen a healing violet in hope for a calmer year ahead.

Esther knelt down beside her and said under her breath, softly but emphatically, "*Ich muss gehen.* I must leave. Ida has revealed her suspicions, and while I believe I was able to dissuade her, it is only a matter of time before she acts upon them."

Esther continued on to relay the precise conversation that had passed between them.

Nadine's face pinched in anger. She had long dreaded the arrival of such a day.

"I have had concerns this would happen," she said.

"Ida is selfish and childish in her jealousy of you. *Und sie ist richtig gemein.* And she is plain mean. So very mean," Nadine continued.

"*Bitte.* Don't do anything yet. Continue your days as though nothing has changed. On Tuesday at my meeting, I will bring this situation up, and we will devise a strategy for your safe departure. You have no need to worry. We will devise a plan.

"You are correct in regard to Ida. Before too long, she will go to the authorities, and then we would all be in trouble. *Sehr großen Ärger.* Very serious trouble."

Nadine turned back to her planting. She stabbed the dirt while muttering, "I should have gotten red bulbs, dark red bulbs. *Of zwart. Dat zou al veel meer fitting.* Or black. Those would have been much more fitting."

It took fourteen days of daily meetings of brainstorming and conspiring and strategizing to devise a workable plan for Esther and Zami. In November 1941, traversing the terrain of Europe was complicated and dangerous. Debates, sometimes heated, took place among the members about the most logical and viable routes.

The critical destination was unquestioned.

Switzerland . . .

I whispered as loudly as I could without revealing face and form.

Swit—zer—land . . .

I enunciated each syllable.

Esther and Zami must go to Switzerland.

But how to get there? the members queried.

After perusing myriad road, train, and topographic maps, listening closely to the shortwave radio's updates on combat activities and other relevant news, analyzing train schedules, and speaking to associates at the few instances when the phone lines did connect, it was determined Esther must first travel to Paris. All members agreed upon this conclusion decisively. Jacco and Ralf had both traveled to this city in the past eight months, and their contacts could be trusted. Within the boundaries of Paris were concealed more powerful and better-informed groups of Resistance members than elsewhere. They were mostly communists but were effective in their efforts and, more significantly, in their results. They had resources and reliable connections for successfully leading people over the Alps into Switzerland, which at the present time was still neutral territory for Jews.

"*Nou, luister*—Now, listen—I am certain she must travel by train," Jacco said. "This type of transportation is the appropriate choice. It will be the safest. We do know many trains are still operating. The schedules, no doubt, will change daily, if not hourly, but in the end it is the most likely system to be consistent with whatever route we figure out. Of course we know it is all a guessing game. At the very least, this is an educated guess."

"I must concur," said Nadine, with everyone in the room nodding their agreement.

"With her Aryan features, Esther is sure to pass without suspicions," she continued. "Or perhaps—it is more her countenance and bearing and that unshakable stoicism than her actual facial appearance that make this possible. She has *een taaiheid*—a toughness—I have not seen in another human being. It is astonishing really. And we must not discount her flawless command of the German language—so much better than mine! Most important of all, I'm sure we can agree, are her impressive, authentic-appearing documents. She could not be better positioned. I am sure Esther will be among the lucky ones."

"I don't think we can be confident about anything right now," Jacco said. "But I haven't lost hope. Otherwise I couldn't still be doing this."

"She must purchase a first-class ticket," Renate chimed in.

"That is throwing away her money," said Ralf. "We don't know how long she'll have to stay in Paris or if she'll be able to work while she's there. She's going to have to keep as much money as she can for all the unknowns she's sure to encounter."

"But we must get her to Paris—safely!" Renate said emphatically. "Otherwise this whole discussion is a complete waste of time. The officials in first class will be less suspicious. For who can imagine a Jewish person in these times would have the kind of money necessary to buy the ticket—or any money for that matter! And Nadine," she added, turning to look at her straight on, "you said this woman has worked all these months at the textile mill. She must have quite a large sum saved, no?"

"Yes, this is true," Nadine said. "Purchasing a first-class ticket will not be a problem, and it's the right thing to do. I believe your assumptions are correct."

Understanding the logic of it, the others agreed, and planning moved forward.

The selected itinerary—Leiden to Rotterdam to Brussels to Lille, then Paris—directed Esther to change trains four times. Not the easiest or most comfortable of situations, particularly with a small child. It would have been more ideal to bypass Brussels, but the April pogrom in Antwerpen had made that a city on the warpath, with the situation unstable.

It was understood the most precarious part of the journey would be traveling through occupied Belgium.

But let us not forget as before . . . as always . . . I journey with her . . .

Arrangements were made. Contacts secured. Times and meeting places confirmed. Tickets purchased—with Esther's abundance of cash. Nearly all of her Dutch guilders were exchanged for French francs.

While life and future were being decided for her—that was the way it felt—Esther went about her work and other responsibilities as though nothing had changed. For so long, going on eighteen years, she had grown accustomed to being fully in charge, independent and self-contained. This crucial need to rely on others was painful to the very fiber of her being. Or at least to the being she had become.

Her ability to trust was gone. But she recognized that, at this time and at this place and in these circumstances, she was fortunate to have such aid fall into place, almost effortlessly.

Someday . . . she will know . . . and she will . . . understand . . .

Ida continued to view Esther with suspicion and cynicism; still, it was easy to ignore her. Esther knew her reaction to Ida's accusation had confounded this malicious woman. At the least, it had procured the necessary time to put plans into action.

Departure was arranged for a late Wednesday morning. The second week of October. During that window of time and that day of the week, Nadine was assured Sacha would be teaching, Ans would be in school, and Ida with a client. Also, her nearest neighbors would be at work. One of Nadine's associates who owned a car would drive Esther and Zami to the station.

The 11:15 train would take them to Rotterdam. There was also a train leaving for Amsterdam at 11:40 and one for Düsseldorf scheduled to depart at 12:05. In the event Ida did try and investigate what direction they were heading toward, Leiden Centraal would be busy that morning. Attempting to trace someone's path would be complicated, and surely Ida did not have the necessary patience. Nadine had a ready story that might not convince Ida of an erroneous denouncement, yet it was neatly structured and would answer basic questions of why and where and how.

By this time, Esther was masterful at packing and was able to fit a couple of different outfits for her and for Zami into the one small suitcase. Only the most essential sewing tools and supplies were included—one pair of scissors, primary-colored threads, a few different size needles, and her measuring tape. As she understood it, the plan was not to settle in one particular location but to arrange and prepare for the journey across the Alps. There, in what would be a safe, stable environment, Esther would reestablish her business. Until then, she would pick up small jobs and assignments as opportunities were presented.

If necessary, she could subsist for a number of months without constant work or any work at all. After purchasing the train tickets, her reserve of cash remained considerable.

Esther left her completed assignments in a neat pile on her bed. Nadine would bring the clothes to Hendrik and collect her remaining fee. It would more than cover their expenses for the last half month spent in the boarding house.

When the car arrived, Nadine hugged Zami, whose arms remained limp and face indifferent. Facing Esther, she knew better than to attempt an expression of warmth. With a tight, serious smile, all she said was *"Sichere Reise.* Safe travels."

Esther held Nadine's eyes for one long moment and dipped her head in a slight nod.

"Danke. Vielen Dank" she managed to say. The sentiment was genuine.

CHAPTER TWENTY-NINE

The (imagined) wall is tall . . . and smooth . . .
without niches . . . or crevasses . . . or landings.
The (conjured) mountain . . . soaring.
The (hoped for) path . . . no longer clear.
The journey . . . relentless . . .

. . . .

"Etta," she said. *"Mein Name ist Etta Göttlieb."*

Esther looked directly into the conductor's severe brown eyes and spoke in her finest *Hochdeutsch.* She knew the Gestapo agent standing to his right was listening intently with the prescribed measure of suspicion. She made sure he heard every word.

"Und dies ist mein Sohn Hannis," pointing to Zami in response to the conductor's inquiry about her traveling companion.

Only answer the questions they ask . . . and only when they ask.

Give no more than is requested.

Be polite . . . but not overly friendly.

Whatever you do . . . do not . . . draw attention to yourself.

Such commanding and perceptive counsel filled her. The voice was unequivocal, and in this situation, she took heed. She didn't understand it, but she could not wonder. All she knew was that she no longer felt completely alone.

The situation was public, and Esther was fully hiding in the open. Simultaneously visible and invisible—a bifurcated world offering no equilibrium or solid ground. Doggedly striving to maintain balance, stay clearheaded and vigilant, while continuously seeing two divergent realities out of each eye: one crystal sharp, hyperreal, the other fuzzy and frighteningly out of focus.

Esther was thankful the train's heating system had broken down and there was nothing unusual about wearing a thick winter coat and gloves inside the compartment. Although it was three degrees Celsius, she was sweating profusely. She remained strong and undaunted, merely out of practice in this type of setting. Fifteen months in Nadine's warm home, even with Ida's overbearing, hostile presence and unrelenting inquisitions, had softened Esther.

And during that period, the circumstances in the world outside Leiden had intensified. The impact of the war was now manifest all along the journey. Security had tightened considerably.

"I have been in Holland, in Leiden, with my younger sister who has been ill. I am now going to Paris to be with my older sister. We will be living with her."

The train jolted; her heart jumped. Esther glanced quickly around the car at the other passengers. No one seemed to take much notice of her or what she was saying. Most were engaged in a book or newspaper. An older man seated across from her, gray balding head leaning against the window, snored loudly.

It took concentration to maintain her balance as the train lurched forward. Gradually. Badly in need of repair, the coarse tracks made the train weave slightly, the ride bumpy, and progress sluggish.

The papers in the conductor's and agent's hands—her acquired identity papers and travel documents—seemed to scream for verity when they were passed between the two men looking for fakes and forgeries. Yes, Esther thought, forgeries they are. But they are the finest money can buy.

"Why are you traveling at this time?"

"Mein Mann—My husband—was killed at the Front last fall, and Hannis and I left Stuttgart to be with my family," Esther responded squarely.

At the mention of her husband's death, the woman on the adjoining seat glanced up with a sympathetic eye.

Throughout this volley of questions, Zami remained his usual expressionless self. He clutched his little train tightly with both hands. Though just three, he knew intrinsically silence was the only option.

"All seems to be in order," the conductor said, handing back her documents.

"Danke schön," she said, and sat back down. The other passengers' papers were scrutinized and approved; the conductor and agent moved on to the next car.

For Esther there could be no sigh of relief. There were four others in the car, and she could not react in any manner that could possibly draw attention. No chance to release a whit of tension with a deep breath or a stretching of arms. She continued to sit stiffly and quietly, pretending to watch the countryside slip by.

She had spent a large amount of her money to purchase these train tickets. Esther was thankful Nadine's associates had the foresight to insist she purchase first-class tickets instead of the much less expensive seats. Esther was confident the inevitable interrogations were not as thorough in this privileged compartment.

Perhaps they, too, have that wise voice guiding them, she mused.

Of course.

It was doubtful that others in hiding had any substantial resources to draw upon or clothes to pass. Esther understood her circumstances were unique. Nevertheless, the prospect of discovery never left her.

However, what had seemed to leave her was—Esther.

She had long forgotten—before this irrational war and hiding and running while standing still—her very self, her wants, her desires, her essence. Who she was at her core. So much of the last nearly two years had been spent fabricating a new reality, a new name, a new identity, and stories of a life she had never lived. Esther had become lost in the process. Like an ingredient in a cake mix folded into the batter where only the slightest hint of its presence remains.

It wasn't until this moment, as the train crawled toward a new locale over yet another division in this interminable road, that Esther realized how worn this subterfuge of nearly two years had made her. Along with the toll taken by the preceding sixteen years. She may have retained her birth name in those earlier years, but that accounted for a fragment of who Esther had come into this world to be.

Of all that had taken place, all she had to endure, losing herself was most painful.

Esther had become mechanical in action and thought. Yes, she had remained functional, always operating at her best, even with the rules and roles of life changing so dramatically. Where once happiness and love, family and friends had been what mattered, the purpose for living had become living. The goal had become survival and only survival.

After all this time, Esther was losing the capacity to know what she was surviving for.

And, most sorrowfully, who was it that would, in fact, survive?

CHAPTER THIRTY

Memory . . . percolates unceasingly . . .
  scarcely below the surface . . .
  of one's thoughts . . .
  one's skin . . .
  one's soul.

Even cement cannot obscure . . .
  what breathes in memory.

Clearly . . . existence is mystifying . . . of this I can agree.

It is multilayered and multifaceted . . .
  intricate . . . complex . . .
  on the surface . . . that is . . .

Only . . . on the surface.

For within . . . inside . . . each of you . . . at your center . . .
  everything is understood . . . all is known.

Remember this at the core of your truth.

Even if you are now so blocked . . . so fixed . . . so rooted . . .
in the here . . .
> *in only what is here . . .*
> *that you can no longer feel veracity . . .*

Know with the depth of your being . . . please know . . .

Memory cannot be shackled . . . or detained.

CHAPTER THIRTY-ONE

Space . . .
offering . . .
a place . . .
a refuge . . .
to plan . . .
to prepare . . .
and then . . .
to pause.

. . . .

*P*aris became about waiting—and delays, and postponements, and plans arranged and rearranged and then suspended. And frustration. It became about patience. Something Esther carried in abundance when constructing a garment, tailoring a jacket, or repairing a fur collar, when the need was to create a stitch that mirrors the one before and then disappears completely. But this situation—after all that had already occurred—did test her.

The original intent, plotted out with great care and detail by Nadine's group, was to spend no more than two weeks in Paris before leaving for the trek across the Alps. It was already late October, and the weather would surely prove to be a challenge in their crossing. As the season advanced, it was certain to become more complicated and dangerous.

> *Alas . . . so regrettably . . . Paris as lovely as it is and always has been . . . Paris with so very many sweets . . . was not the place . . . not at this time . . . in which to linger.*

To stay until the spring and more amenable weather was not a viable option. There was heightened tension in the city. The month before, more than two hundred thousand citizens attended *"Le Juif et la France,"* a maliciously anti-Semitic exhibition organized by French collaborationists at the Palais Berlitz. Demonstrations and rioting followed. Earlier in October, seven synagogues had been bombed. Paris was on high alert. *Gendarmes* were ubiquitous. The Nazis' response to French Resistance activities was to arrest 750 Jews and deport them.

> *To where . . . once more . . . never explained . . .*

Even though Esther easily passed for one considered acceptable and held exceptionally rendered fictitious documents, she did not speak the language. And the French, Parisians in particular, were notorious elitists, intolerant of others. Staying in one place for an extended period could too easily make her a target. No matter how careful her movements. Foreigners were looked at as suspect, and Germans were not considered much better than Jews. So her flawless language skills—which she had worked tirelessly to perfect—became a liability.

It was not a secure situation in any regard. Not speaking French placed Esther in a position where finding work would be impossible. Her resources, while substantial, were not inexhaustible. Her one bona fide security, during these years, had been work.

The arranged contacts—Marc-Philippe Merle and his wife, Yvette—were barely in their twenties, if not late teens. To Esther, mere babies. She was astonished they would take on such dangerous work as safeguarding one considered a fugitive. But what these two appeared to lack in maturity and sophistication, they made up for in keenness and savvy. They were resolute in helping Esther and Zami safely cross into Switzerland. They were not, however, connected in ways that might make it manageable for her to remain in Paris for a prolonged time, if that became necessary.

On the Saturday Esther arrived, they settled her and Zami in a miniscule sixth-floor apartment that Yvette's family owned, but never occupied, in the fifth arrondissement on Rue Clovis not far from Rue Saint-Jacques. It was formerly a maid's quarter, part of a large mansion converted into apartments perhaps a dozen years earlier. One usual step in any direction would take her from the bed to the gas burner to the sink and back again. Two folding chairs and a card table leaned against the wall. The one toilet and shower shared by the floor's four apartments were at the far end of the hall.

Both Marc-Philippe and Yvette spoke impeccable German, for which Esther was appreciative. While Nadine's language skills had been passable, it could be a strain to decipher her sentences. And Ida's German—well, fortunately, Esther no longer had to consider Ida.

Their instructions were brief. Sangfroid and stamina were essential.

"Please be assured our most capable colleagues are working on revising the route and timing so your journey will take place without incident and the outcome will be attained. Almost certainly notification for departure will be immediate. We will keep you apprised of our efforts," Yvette said.

Forward motion . . . as quickly as possible would be essential . . . would ensure success . . . in the end . . . in the end . . .

Marc-Philippe offered, "Here is a map—*eine Karte der Stadt*—of the city. It is best if you do not travel too far."

"The beautiful Luxembourg Gardens are only a few blocks away, an easy walk," Yvette suggested.

"See, it is just here," Marc-Philippe said, pointing to the identifying mark on the map.

"Directly across Boulevard Saint-Michel."

"*Er ist groß und schön*—It is large and lovely—even when the weather is not the best. I'm certain your son will enjoy spending time there. You too, of course. There is a small café in the middle of the garden where it would be safe for you to sit and get a coffee," Yvette said. "And perhaps a cookie for your son."

I . . . most especially . . . was interested in that particular suggestion.

Marc-Philippe continued, "It would be best if you speak as little as possible, and then only as truly essential. You do not want to draw attention to yourself. Germans are not in favor here. Truthfully, that's an understatement. We must avoid any unnecessary incidents. Any incidents at all, of course.

"*Und Ihr Sohn*—and your son—whom you call Hannis, must never say a word in public."

"That will not be a problem," Esther responded. "He does not speak much."

"I will teach you a few useful words and phrases in French. Please write these down and practice. But always, first point to whatever you need. *Besser, Sie benehmen sich weniger intelligent*—Better you act less intelligent—than show you are German."

Marc-Philippe introduced the French words for bread, cheese, meat, and coffee—the basics of sustenance in this country. Fruit was not easily attainable these days, but Esther learned *pomme* and *poire*, for apple and pear, in the event she found any available.

Yvette interjected with "*Et lait. Milch*—Milk—for your son, of course. This is a necessary word to know."

Marc-Philippe finished with, "Importantly, if you encounter any of your neighbors, all elderly women, you must nod and say '*Bonjour, Madame.*'

"That is all that is necessary, but it is necessary."

And please . . . please do not forget la biscotte . . . the cookie . . .

Although told otherwise, after the first week, Esther spent the better part of most everyday walking the streets of Paris with Zami.

Each morning she awoke before the sun rose. There was no motivation to do so—no work to accomplish, no responsibilities to attend to. She lay in bed, staring at the ceiling, until light entered the room. This became a period unlike any Esther had experienced. Other than bathing and preparing a few meals, she had no distractions. None inwardly—

Not any she would acknowledge . . .

—or outwardly, for the space was bleak. Esther quickly become too familiar with the room's patches of peeling beige paint, counting their number combined from the four walls—forty-one—and areas of exposed plaster—seventeen. The room was stifling, and when she tried to open the one small window, she found it nailed shut—with five nails.

She dressed and then woke up Zami. After helping him put on his pants, sweater, and socks and making a breakfast of toast and tea, she walked down the hall to the toilet. Relieved to move her feet more than the one step in any direction the room allowed. It was fourteen steps to the end of the hall. Fourteen steps back. She straightened the cover on the bed and sat down on it. Then she got up and sat in the chair opposite Zami, who had toast in one hand and his train in the other. She chewed on her inside right cheek until it was raw.

Scarcely more than one hour had been consumed.

What a waste, she thought. What a dreadful, ridiculous, unbearable waste this is. What is there to do?

"Enough!" she said out loud. "We are going outside. No matter what they say. I refuse to suffocate!"

Esther put on their coats, scarves, gloves, and boots, and out they ventured.

She found, when walking the streets of this neighborhood, no one took notice of a nondescript, neatly dressed woman in her middle thirties holding the hand of a small, unremarkable child. It appeared most people were heading to or from their jobs or school or shopping or errands, engaged with the thoughts in their heads and the lives they were leading. The surrounding world passed as an impressionistic blur of colors, sounds, and smells.

Even the *gendarmes,* whose presence was prominent and whose charge it was to ferret out those deemed undesirable, offered Esther and Zami little more than a passing glance. Disconcerting to others, perhaps, but not to Esther, who maintained her finely honed confidence of self-protection. She had discovered these past few years that acute observational skills were shared by few. No matter what was taking place in the broader world, daily life generally went on uninterrupted. Until such events occurred on one's own street.

Most days Esther and Zami walked the same series of blocks, in this one regard heeding Marc-Philippe's caution not to travel too far from the apartment. She never explored past Rue Guynemer, on the eastern edge of the Luxembourg Gardens, or Rue de Vaugirard on the north. She became all too familiar with the façades of the various shops selling flowers, handmade paper, clothes, pastries, chocolates, shoes, and books, as well as the many cafés along Boulevard Saint-Michel. Every twist and turn and tree of the Luxembourg Gardens became known. She never strayed from the demarcated paths, never walked on the grass, for that would elicit shouts from the security officers. She never sat at the recommended café for a coffee. It would take up time and be more manageable than staying in their room, but she knew to sit in such a setting for any extended period could bring forth internal contemplation.

Without exception, Esther made sure to stride with confidence, head held high, in no way appearing to wander without purpose or destination.

What Marc-Philippe said about the Parisians was true. They were rude, abrasive, and without patience for anyone who had no knowledge of their precious language. And they were not kind to one another when language was not an issue. Esther observed this fact on her first walk, watching the exchanges of persons she passed. She concluded it easiest to adopt the role of a mute.

At the corner market, one block down from the apartment, where she shopped daily, Esther pointed to the vegetables and other needed items. She pretended to understand when asked questions about quantity, nodding or shaking her head as she intuited what was appropriate. This technique worked reasonably well, even if her purchases were overcharged and she was not assured of getting what she wanted.

Marc-Philippe and Yvette appeared at the apartment every few days, typically at 7:15 p.m., to provide updates, if any were available, on the departure plan's development. Skirmishes were taking place along the route used to traverse the Alps, and there were numerous new challenges in determining secure alternatives.

These two did their best to squelch Esther's possible frustrations by saying again and again, "We are confident it won't be much longer. *Bitte haben Sie Geduld.* Please, please be patient."

Both were distressed by Esther's recounting of her long tours around the neighborhood.

"This is not a good thing to do," said Marc-Philippe. "It is critical that you stay safe, and you are safest inside this apartment."

"It is essential you understand our security is also at issue," said Yvette. "As well as everyone who is helping you and Zami. There are numerous people involved."

"*Ja, ja,*" Esther said, "I know what you are saying, of course. But you, too, must understand I am careful during my walks. There will not be a problem. It is essential we get some fresh air. This room can be unbearable. The days and nights have become never-ending. There is nothing to do here."

> *Activities are needed . . . to distract the brain . . . prevaricate thoughts . . . and memory . . . and truth . . .*

"Can we bring you—*Dinge zu lesen*—things to read? Books? *Oder Zeitschriften?* Or magazines? *Papier zum Schreiben?* Paper for writing?" Marc-Philippe queried.

At each possibility, Esther shook her head.

Then, Yvette uttered the one word that held potency and resonance: "*Nähfaden?* Thread?"

> *Ah . . . the thread . . . sutra . . . as expressed in our Upanishads . . . is said . . . in fact . . . to link "this world to the other world and to all beings" . . . so essential . . . vital . . . thread . . .*

"*Möchten Sie*—Would you like me to bring you a variety of needles, thread, and fabric? Perhaps to create an embroidery?"

At this, of course, Esther nodded vigorously. To create something—anything—with thread and needle would make this wasteful period endurable.

After one week turned into two and then one month, Esther began to attend daily Mass at Saint-Étienne-du-Mont. This striking Gothic church was on the Montagne Sainte-Geneviève, around the corner from the apartment. Mass was offered three times each morning starting at six o'clock and twice each afternoon commencing at four o'clock. On occasion she arrived for the morning Mass at eight o'clock but most often attended in the afternoon. This was a more ideal way to interrupt the day's tedium. Though Mass was monotonous in its own way, Esther found it comforting to once again attend Catholic services.

This feels like coming home, Esther thought. Though strange to call it home. A shelter of calm would be more correct. But this setting has become familiar for me. Likely for Zami too. Perhaps that's what home, any home, affords, after all—ease and comfort.

Her time spent in Leiden attending a Protestant church had never provided a soothing environment. Ida's persistent interrogating aside, not knowing the service's structure remained disquieting. Even as she watched Nadine and followed her actions closely. It had little relationship to the Catholic service, where Frau Göttlieb's training had served her well. During a Latin Mass, Esther knew when to stand, to sit, to stand again; when to kneel; when and what to sing; and when once more to sit. The format never varied, neither in Wuppertal nor here. There was an assurance in its specific unfolding.

Saint-Étienne-du-Mont was an especially beautiful church with much to look at. Its most striking feature was the intricately carved, wall-like screen separating the area where the monks sat from the rest of the church. The double-stair arch that extended upward to the ceiling was a work of magnificence and elegance. Esther committed its elaborate carvings to memory, sections at a time, and used this visual as the image on the embroidery she was creating with the multicolored thread and fabric Yvette provided.

No moment to be wasted . . . no time to be squandered . . . everything must have purpose whether there was a real purpose or not . . . whether there really was . . . far too much time . . .

Getting through these twenty-four-hour periods of the sun rising and then the moon rising, without intention or direction, reason or rationale, tested Esther's mettle like nothing else had thus far. This part of the journey became tormenting to a woman not interested in anything other than activity and forward motion.

Will this not end? Are there no other options? Perhaps being arrested is better than this? Standing, sitting, standing, and then sitting once more. Esther's thoughts raced in directions she could not control. I could lose my mind—I may go mad—if I can't get out of here, if I don't move on soon.

She felt fissures forming on her hardened outer shell, allowing reminiscences of sensations to break through from her depths.

But . . . these small cracks . . . and fractures . . . and splinters . . . avail possibilities . . . and promise . . .

One afternoon, out of escalating boredom, Esther ignored Yvette and Marc-Philippe's admonishments. She put aside her extraneous embroidery project, dressed Zami in his warmest winter clothing, and headed out of the apartment in a new direction.

Today, she determined, there will be no imposed restrictions on the distance we go. We will walk as long as Zami's little legs hold out. If necessary, I'll carry him. Fortunately, he's still small and reasonably light.

For something different, Esther turned right on Boulevard Saint-Michel, heading away from the Luxembourg Gardens and all of Paris she had come to know. Esther brought the map along but kept it concealed at the bottom of a pocket. She did not want to draw attention that might single them out as tourists, visitors, or worse. She took careful note of every major street crossing and easily identifiable landmarks. Her mind's eye marked the route for the return. Esther took care not to make the walk confusing. For the most part, she followed what seemed to be major boulevards and crossings.

Less than one kilometer away, they came upon the River Seine, her first sighting of such a grand body of water since the Rhein.

"Look how beautiful this is," she said softly to Zami, not able to contain herself.

They stood for a few minutes before crossing over the bridge to look out at the river's splendor and expanse. Esther noticed there were many who also stopped. This can't be out of the ordinary, she thought, for the view is breathtaking. Even for those who see it daily.

This river . . . any river . . . draws one in . . . embraces . . . enfolds . . . with the universal potentiality of life . . .

In my home it is the Ganga . . . the Ganges . . . that celestial stream flowing from Shiva's tresses . . .

Just across this river stood one of the most extraordinary and arresting buildings Esther had ever seen. Taking up more than one full city block, this structure—

Is it a church? she wondered.

—seemed to hold court over the river and the little island where it was situated. Esther wanted to leisurely review its façade, with the rose-cut window bookended by two regal towers, but knew they should not linger.

Perhaps another day I will be able to visit, she thought.

Esther and Zami continued down Rue de Rivoli, in awe of its expansiveness. Zami, who generally focused attention on his feet and the ground, seemed to be entranced. Esther had never seen anything like it. Rue de Rivoli was a miles-long and wide commercial street filled with high-end shops butted up against large buildings sharing nearly identical façades.

No doubt this is the city's major business section, Esther mused.

Continuing along the route, a large park came into view on her left. Zami pulled hard on her hand, expressing his desire to investigate, but Esther ignored him and ventured on. She'd had more than her fill of parks, particularly those with grass that you could not walk or play on. These Parisian rules made no sense to her.

After walking for two hours, nearly six kilometers from the apartment to an area where the street became wider still, Esther saw the edges of a crowd that had gathered. As she walked farther, the mass of people grew enormous, and a monumental arch, centered in the middle of the street, came into view. It was hard to discern what was taking place. There were countless people standing around.

Ach so! she thought, it's a parade. Like everyone around them, she and Zami stopped to watch it go by.

A military parade. Not unlike the one in Köln that had passed directly in front of Abraham's shop and their apartment. And they were singing the same song:

"Die Fahne hoch! Die Reihen fest geschlossen!

. . . .

Fly high the flag! The ranks be tightly closed now!

Die Straße frei den braunen Batallionen.
Die Straße frei dem Sturmabteilungsmann!
Es schau'n aufs Hakenkreuz voll Hoffnung schon Millionen.
Der Tag für Freiheit und für Brot bricht an!

. . . .

The streets be cleared now for the brown battalions,
the streets clear for the storm division man!
And towards the swastika with hope are looking millions.
The day for freedom and bread, it dawns!

Only this procession comprised close to a kilometer in length. In addition to the multitude of layers of men goose-stepping in unison, there were tanks—six rows of them with three across—along with soldiers on horseback, soldiers riding in cars with small cannons, and soldiers on scooters. All carrying guns. The crowd, at least eight people deep, stood at attention watching, many with unrestrained smiles on their faces. Shouting in support. Waving enthusiastically.

An older gentleman standing next to them noticed that Zami could see no more than the backs of people's coats. To Esther's shock, and without asking for permission, he swooped the little boy up and onto his shoulders. The man then turned and smiled at Esther, saying something she could not understand. Recognizing Zami was not at risk, she simply nodded her head as though in appreciation.

Zami did not smile or wave or cheer as did the children around them. As did every adult watching the festivities. As had Miriam when she had seen the similar sight in Köln.

But he was bounced up and down as the man joyously shouted, "*Magnifique! Magnifique! À bas les Juifs!* Magnificent! Down with the Jews!"

The walk back to the apartment was routine. It was five thirty, and the streets overflowed with people leaving work or school and heading home. Or perhaps to a local café or restaurant for a meal. This outing had taken them nearly six kilometers in each direction. Esther had to carry Zami the last few blocks; however, she was pleased he had walked most of the way on his own.

This augurs well for all that is to come . . . soon . . .

Esther warmed up a dinner of soup and bread, which they ate quickly. She then put Zami to bed. He was exhausted.

Yvette and Marc-Philippe arrived forty-five minutes later.

"Oh dear," Yvette whispered. "I see Zami has gone to sleep early today. We will not stay long. Unfortunately, there is no news to report at the moment."

"But everyone continues to work hard to resolve this situation," Marc-Philippe said in a low voice. "We will keep you updated and visit again in a few days. Be well."

Esther did not provide an account on any aspect of their adventure, most especially the parade. When they left, she returned to her embroidery to pass the time before sleep took command. To pass the time.

Split stitches. Line stitches. Chain stitches. Picot stitches. Herringbone, stem, and flat stitches. Bokhara couching. Knotting. Fishbone. Point de Russe. Double Leviathan. Mountmellick.

Yvette had supplied her with embroidery floss in an assortment of colors and widths. Far more material than Esther hoped she would be there to use.

But use she did, needing something, anything, to make the minutes and then the hours go by. To distract herself—and the thoughts and memories which could—would—permit feelings and emotions to emerge.

As thus, days and weeks—and more weeks—elapsed.

CHAPTER THIRTY-TWO

Natheless...
with vacant time...
comes space
for...a pause...
an opening.
An ostiole...
delivering knowledge and insight...
that could only be revealed...
through stillness.
When the facility to suppress dissipates.
Then...
and only then...
one truly listens...
and learns...
what one needs to know.

....

The efforts and exercises undertaken not to think or contemplate or wonder were no match for the quiet and the not doing and the no responsibilities and the mindless, senseless walking and embroidery and waiting. They only served to exacerbate the absence in Esther's head. Decades had passed since anything other than a fleeting sentiment had perforated the dense, defensive strata shielding her thoughts and heart. Now, however, the fissures and the cracks and the fractures and the splinters developing on these finely honed layers of isolation and indifference began, by degrees, to expand—and deepen.

During daytime hours, her fierce will monitored any and all thoughts that endeavored to filter through. But when the outside was immersed in darkness and the hour was most still, after week upon week had passed, this control abated.

Then, and only then, did the visitations begin—

CHAPTER THIRTY-THREE

Nothing . . .
and . . .
no one . . .
is ever lost . . .
or . . .
can be lost.

. . . .

H e is not gone . . . you know . . .
Of this you must be secure.
None of them are gone . . . not really.

He is everywhere and nowhere at all times . . .
In the same way that no one is every truly here . . . or only here
. . . here on this plane.

For as you know . . . know in your truth . . . there are many planes
. . . many spheres . . . many realities . . . that exist concurrently
. . . all at once . . . in chorus.

And thus . . . in that same way . . . with that awareness you can know . . . you do know . . . that he . . . they . . . are never truly gone.

This you must acknowledge.

For on occasion . . . and you know this to be true . . . this has happened to you . . . every now and again . . .

You see flashes of light . . . color . . . an outline . . . perhaps a figure. Most often this is out of the corner of one eye or when your head moves quickly and you think . . . you believe . . . you are tired . . . simply tired . . . that your eyes are strained . . . too much stress . . . too much tension . . .

You believe your vision deceives you.

Or you hear something . . . maybe a floorboard creak at a side of the room where no one stands.

Or you feel something . . . a brush . . . a graze . . . on your cheek when there is no wind.

Or sometimes . . . possibly . . . a caress on your arm where there is no cloth.

And you wonder . . .

Because at that moment . . . when the flash of bright colors is glimpsed out of the side of one eye or a sound occurs where no one stands . . . or your skin slightly sighs from what could have been a touch . . .

An image will cross before you . . . a face will float across your heart . . . and memories begin to flood.

And deep . . . deep within you at your core . . . you know.

In that place . . . where you truly know . . . where you are sure . . . where you recognize that he has never gone . . . none of them have gone . . . are gone . . .

None can possibly be gone.

CHAPTER THIRTY-FOUR

The ties that bind.
The thread . . .
that . . .
wends its way through a family . . .
and its generations.
Connecting . . . binding . . . knitting . . .
and mending . . .
one another.
Only colors change discernibly over the lineage . . .
and the images created.
But the thread . . .
endures . . .
mostly without fray . . .
at least as far back . . .
as memory and history allow.

. . . .

Rose and Frayda, the twins, were the first to come. Esther did not take note of the hour. A fitful sleep had gained possession a few hours before. She thought she heard rustling but merely rolled over and closer to a soundly sleeping Zami.

Then a name was called out—"Etka." Only family members ever called her that, a moniker in suspension for so very long.

At first it was scarcely a whisper; then they said it more emphatically, with increased insistence.

"Etka!

"*Mir zenen do.* We are here," Rose and Frayda said in unison, "*mit dir*—with you."

"*Ober mir zenen avek fun dort vu du bist yetst.* But we are now gone," Frayda continued, "from where you are. Please know we are fine. Very fine—now.

"But the past few years have been grueling, humiliating, and overflowing with fear—constant fear.

"*Un der sof*—And the ending—the ending was agonizing."

"They took us to the woods, just outside Przeworsk," Rose said. "The woods where we played as children. Where our children still played.

"Our neighbors—*shtel zikh for*—can you imagine? Our neighbors—*undzere langyorike fraynd*—our lifelong friends—took us to the woods.

"All the Jews left in our town were taken. By then, there were only about eighty of us. Our dear husbands, Isadore and Avrom, were with us.

"*Oykh undzere kinder.* And our children too."

"My beautiful Lilke, just five years old. *Finf yor*—Only five. How could this have been possible?" Frayda whispered heavily, the horror of it still palpable.

"And Benny, my funny, clown-like Benny, and his big brother Fima. Too young," said Rose. "Far, far too young. *Umbanemlekh*—It is inconceivable!

"The gunfire did not stop for a long time.

"The silence has been a relief."

Esther sat up, staring straight across the bed.

My eyes must be deceiving, she thought. The sight before her, of two younger sisters—mere children when she had last seen them and now all grown up—confounded her.

How can it be possible they are here? In this room? In Paris?

Esther was certain she was still asleep. Dreaming. For how could it be otherwise?

*When one wants and when one needs . . . when it is essential . . .
the conceived barriers can be broken . . . communication can
be opened . . . vital information can be relayed . . .*

And then, as abruptly as they had arrived, Rose and Frayda left. Slowly fading out of sight. Esther was left to wonder.

When these appearances became a near nightly occurrence, Esther knew it was not imagination at play.

They came in pairs or in small groups of three or four—they did not come alone, as none had died alone. The efficiency of the Nazi killing machine not wasting bullet, bomb, or vapor.

Surprisingly, the tiny room that barely accommodated two people under more commonplace circumstances never felt confining with their presence. And the visits only took place when sleep should have been the priority. During the night there was no chance of interruption from outside.

Her mama came. Her *tate*. Her sisters Yetta and Gitel and Chana. Then her brothers Chaim and Jakob and Eli and Itzik and Moishe. Occasionally they arrived with their spouses, sometimes the husbands and wives came with others. Jakob's wife, Raina, whom Esther had played with as a child, appeared with her much younger sister, while Yetta's husband, Haskel, whose family had the chicken farm not far from the synagogue, brought his father and an uncle. Itzik's wife, Goldie, came with Chaim's Basha and Gitel's Mendel.

Their children appeared, none of whom she had met or, in many cases, even knew existed. So many children. Esther's communication with family members had been sporadic and lean for nearly two decades, and now she learned how much life—rich, full lives—had continued on without her.

Aunts and uncles and cousins and nieces and nephews came too. For generations, the Grünspans had been a large, proud family spread across Poland, Belarus, and the Ukraine. In the end, there would be so few—only a small number would survive.

Once close and more distant friends showed up, those individuals who, collectively, encompassed Esther's community in Przeworsk. The people with whom she attended school, the many who had benefited from her tailoring gifts, and those who bought bread from the bakery where she worked on Friday afternoons. Along with the ones she passed on the street daily and nodded to in polite greeting.

All these human beings—

All these unique souls . . .

—appeared to Esther to reach beyond the nightmare that had swallowed them whole, to describe in detail how their fate had unfolded.

Train or cattle car had taken many to the camp Sobibor, where a number had passed on after months of hard labor and near starvation. Some, those who had survived the maltreatment and rampant disease, were relocated to Auschwitz-Birkenau and ultimately led to communal showers with hundreds of others. They were met by spewing Zyklon B instead of cascading water.

The ones who had passed most recently—just in the last month—had been taken to the camp Majdanek located near the bustling city of Lublin. The circumstances there were no different.

Still others, those who were young and vigorous, had attempted to escape, to somewhere, to anywhere without the oppressive restrictions and dangers that had seized their homes and their lives. These were the individuals who were captured and sent to work camps in Kazakhstan and Uzbekistan, places with little food and water, daily beatings, and unspeakable abuses.

Esther listened attentively, never questioning, not uttering one word. She recognized that these people had come for her to pay witness, to listen, to digest. The arbitrary nature of the Nazis' actions filled her with shock and nausea. The fact that she felt anything at all was in and of itself momentous.

I sat with them as Esther accepted the certainty of their visits.

Each of them . . . every one of them . . . were all now safe . . . far from harm's way and out of all pain . . . beyond human need . . .

They were truly free.

Still . . . they were compelled . . . they knew it essential to describe their passage . . . the horror of it never . . . not ever . . . to be forgotten.

"*Gey foroys,* Etka. Continue on, Etka. Continue on for us all," each said in parting, offering encouragement and courage.

I embraced them all with spirit.

And at that moment . . . for that one instant . . . I knew . . . she . . . Esther . . . felt me . . . understood me . . . accepted me . . . without question . . . and at the core of her very self.

As the nights passed by, Esther waited, expectantly, but Tonka, her dearest little sister, the one with whom she was once so close, never appeared. For this, she was thankful.

Abraham did not come. Somehow, impossibly, she thought, he must still be alive. Or—perhaps because the bond between them was never veritable—he could not make the connection the way the others had. Did not want to make the connection.

Esther came to anticipate the visits. There was no mourning for those who came, no lamentation for their passing. Just an understanding and acceptance without attachment. Each night she prepared herself for them—these groups of people she now knew would appear.

Only Tadeusz came alone.

CHAPTER THIRTY-FIVE

A part . . .

....

And only he came in her waking hours—
His distinctive voice breaking through the imagined boundaries of space and time and illusion.

Direct.

Sharp.

Insistent.

Imploring.

One word. The forcefulness of his inflection melding two syllables into one:

"Esther!"

There are no limits . . . no constraints . . . no barriers of any kind when it comes to true devotion . . . love . . . eternal love . . .

When two souls have pledged a path . . . designed a plan . . . made a binding commitment to one another.

Even when one seemingly deviates from their vow . . . they will come back together.

Sometimes . . . for a while . . . this may only be fleeting . . . in flashes . . . glimpses . . . feelings . . . but ultimately . . . they will be reunited . . .

For spirit and will . . . and verity . . . triumph above all else.

Tadeusz came at the Sabbath's advent.

At the moment Esther lit the candle, his voice resounded against the walls and corners of the compact space.

Esther looked over to the edge of the bed where Zami lay, head buried in pillow and blanket. They had taken another lengthy walk that morning—akin to them being in training—

As they were . . .

—for an arduous physical trial, and this boy's residual energy allowed for a few morsels of food before falling into a slumber that would permit no possibility of disturbance.

She sat down on the opposite side of the bed and closed her eyes firmly. She took in a quick breath. Esther knew at once what Tadeusz's presence meant, but even the prior weeks of visitations had not readied her for this one.

There was no possible preparation.

More than eighteen years had passed from their time last together. And horrific history had transpired between them and before them and around them since then. Anguish he had birthed, and devastation wrought by overpowering outside forces.

An inordinate amount of time and energy and effort during these years had been consumed with suppressing and submerging and denying and resisting any remaining microcosm of affection that she once felt for him. And it appeared Esther had been successful—

Or so she thought . . .

—for she felt not an ounce of anything as her eyes slowly opened to him standing before her.

"Enshuldik mir. I'm sorry," he blurted out, voice cracking.

"Esther. *Meyn teyrl*—My dear, dear Esther.

"I am so very sorry for everything I have done. For all the pain and all the misery I've caused you. I did a despicable, shameful thing. You did not deserve the way I treated you.

"But everything seemed to be moving fast, too fast. We had only known each other a year. Our connection was so powerful it overwhelmed me.

"I got scared. My fear overcame me. All I could do was run. And I ran in Sarah's direction.

"I never loved her. I couldn't possibly love Sarah.

"Dos voltstu shoyn gedarft visn—You must know that. You have to have always known this. But maybe what you knew only confused you more.

"Sarah was safe. Her family was rich. You know my family never had anything, and I had struggled my whole life. I was tired of going without.

"Kh'ob nisht gekent geyn vayter. I just couldn't bear it anymore.

"I knew the two of us would always have to struggle. I couldn't do it. I guess I wasn't strong enough for you.

"Du bist azoy shtark—You're so strong, Esther. The journey you're on now proves that. I want you to know—as hard as this may be to accept—you were actually better off without me.

"If we had stayed together, if the wedding, our marriage, had taken place, you too would be gone.

"S'iz emes. This is true.

"You need to continue on the path you are on, for you will survive. You will triumph. Perhaps you can't believe this right now, today. *Ober a mol, vestu farshteyn*—But someday you will understand.

"And you are better off without me," he reiterated forcefully.

Esther sat impassively as he spoke.

She attempted to digest all he was saying—tried hard to believe what he was saying. But she could not.

Tadeusz continued, "But I never did stop struggling, although it was in ways I never anticipated—*vayl Ikh hob nokh dir shreklekh gebenkt*—because I missed you unbearably. And knew I had made a shameful error. An intolerable mistake. I constantly regretted what I had done.

"I struggled most because I knew I *gelebt in lign*—lived a lie."

At this last line, Esther stopped listening.

She could not absorb any more of his words. She could not accept his explanations. She simply sat there, immobilized. Waiting for him to leave. This time for good and for always.

Or ... for when she would be ready ...

For all that matters ... truly matters ... all that continues on from one sphere to the next ... the only thing that endures is ... love.

So Esther did not hear Tadeusz describe how Sarah, fragile and mollycoddled, had been captured and taken away to a work camp, where she died soon after. Or that he had initially been one of the fortunate when he escaped to the nearby woods and joined the Resistance. His detailed descriptions of how they fought back were lost on her, as well as his account of the day at early morning, in the moments before sunrise, when his group became entrapped.

However, Esther did hear him say, "It's important you know I was not murdered by them.

"And that it was not an accident. Some might think otherwise or want to think differently. They might believe what I did was a sin. But I want you to be clear about this.

"I had a rope and *un gehat a kavone*—I had intention. I knew what I was doing.

"It was the last act of control in a world gone out of control. A world gone completely mad.

"And my last thoughts, *mayne eyntsike gedanken*—my only thoughts—were of you."

"Stop!" Esther cried out.

"*Genug!* Enough! I will have none of this! *Gey avek! Loz—mikh—tsuru!* Go away! Leave—me—alone!"

No . . . she was not ready . . . she simply was not ready . . .

Tadeusz stood there, stunned. Distraught by her reaction. Tears streamed down his face.

"*Du bist mayn gelibte*—You are my beloved, Esther. I will love you always, across all time and space," Tadeusz cried out as his image began to fade.

For a fleeting moment Esther was embraced by warmth and felt a tender, gentle pressure on her lips.

CHAPTER THIRTY-SIX

And now . . .
I hear you probe:
from whence . . .
does one's innermost puissance . . .
and resoluteness . . .
arise?

....

At a quarter past six, Esther lay down on the bed beside Zami. She covered herself with the portion of the blanket still accessible and, without effort or hesitation, fell into a state of suspended consciousness. They had gone for another extensive walk during the day, and Esther's energies were spent. All she wanted was to not feel anything—anymore—ever again.

Esther did not care if she would reawake. For she understood there were other places and other options.

Not . . . now . . .

This is neither the time nor place.

Within moments of closing her eyes, she found herself once more in the imposing space of stone. Towering walls of irregular damp stone. Large smooth rounded stones, rough squarish stones, oblong shaped stones, amorphous stones and pebbles. An abundance of pebbles.

The location had grown familiar, even intimate, and hidden within its palette of grays and twilight, Esther could perceive gentle hints of color: blue tones and lavenders, shades of dark green, and hues of reds and roses. Restrained beauty. These elements added texture to an environment that had heretofore appeared more one- than two-dimensional. Esther was engulfed in the ethereal realm.

Here was safe haven.

But—where was here? Esther wondered when she awoke.

Early the next Tuesday morning, not much before eight, came one sharp, insistent knock at the door.

Esther, caught up in the morning rituals of dressing and break-fast, started. Not with fright, but surprise. Marc-Philippe and Yvette regularly checked in on them in the evenings. And they had just come by on Sunday.

She went close to the door and in her best, simulated French accent said with measured calmness, *"Oui, bonjour."*

An unfamiliar male voice responded, in German, scarcely above a whisper, "Esther, it is Léon, a friend—*ein Freund*—of Marc-Philippe and Yvette."

They had not advised her to anticipate a visitor or, in fact, told her anything of consequence on Sunday. With those spare words, Esther recognized this situation could suggest ill and give rise to events she had worked so hard, for so long, to evade.

> Let us not discount that I was with her . . . with them . . . as
> I promised always . . . as I would be always.

Esther knew the door must be opened and this man let in.

Straightaway she took note Léon was older than his purported friends by no less than twenty years. He was wide of girth and unkempt. A thick beard and disheveled, longish hair covered his ears. His dark brown pants, black sweater, and thick, fur-lined jacket, while not tattered, were threadbare in places. His boots, which reached just below the knee, were scruffy and had chunky, beaten soles. He held a blue knit cap in hands of soiled palms and fingers with crusts of dirt in the cuticles and under the nails.

At first inspection, his demeanor did not bring Esther comfort or assurance.

But what choices are available to me? she thought. I am at the mercy of situation and circumstance.

Or . . . so she thought . . .

The moment the door closed behind him, Léon spoke hurriedly and bluntly. "Marc-Philippe and Yvette were arrested last night. They're strong, but *les boches*—the Nazi swine—are stronger and will soon break their resistance. *Da bin ich mir sicher*—Of this I'm sure.

"We don't have much time. We must leave immediately!"

Foreboding welled up in Esther's chest.

Sometimes it is necessary . . . for reasons I cannot reveal . . .
I must let . . . it is necessary to allow . . . certain situations . . .
inescapable events . . . to unfold as they must . . .

"Leave? But to where?" Esther blurted out. Her voice trembled. Her mind began to race. She bit down hard on the inside of her right cheek. "Where can we go that is safe?"

"We must take our chances and cross over the Alps," he answered. "*In die Schweiz.* To Switzerland."

Léon swiftly relayed the details of his plan, describing how they would take the train from Gare de Lyon to Lyon. This would likely take seven or eight hours. Or more. From there, they would take another train to Chambéry and then transfer to a local train to Annecy. The final destination, on this first part of the journey, would be a town called Cluses in the southeastern corner of France.

As Léon spoke, Esther noticed how the room, with just this one extra person, became uncomfortable and constrained—claustrophobic. Strange, she thought, especially after these recent weeks of so many visitors coming in groups of three or four or more, where the space never felt crowded or confined. On the contrary, with their appearances, the room assumed an expansive quality.

There need be . . . no distinguishing between the physical presence and the ethereal.

For energy . . . each individual's energy . . . essence . . . whether residing on this plane or another . . . conveys . . . imparts . . . the lightness or heaviness of the weight of veracity each carries.

"*Alles in allem, wenn alles so klappt*—In all, if everything goes as I've planned—it will take no more than one full day and one night of train travel. The trains are still running on time in this area and the route is, mostly, safe.

"To be especially careful, we must not be seen traveling together. You and the boy must be in first class. I'll be right behind you in second.

"At Cluses I'll meet up with you once again and *wir werden unsere Wanderung beginnen*—we'll begin our walk—north. We'll follow a river, *Le Giffre*, which runs through *la vallée du Giffre*. For a while, this area will be flat and easy. We'll come near a town, Sixt-Fer-à-Cheval, that we'll have to avoid. Walk far around it. We can't let anyone see us. But from there, it's only about fifteen kilometers to the border.

"There is a train to Lyon that leaves at 11:15 a.m. We must be on it to make all our connections."

The names, the places, the route Léon mentioned were unknown to Esther. Her head ached—thoughts spinning wild. All aspects of life felt out of control.

There must be questions to ask, answers to know, she thought. Are there options? Other possibilities? Is this, in fact, the safest route? The right time to depart? Then again, is it possible this horror is, truly, finally ending? A few more days and this nightmare, this confinement, will be over—can this be?

Before Esther could manage to form a syllable, Léon demanded, "I'll need the money now."

"*Das Geld*—The money?" Esther questioned.

"*Ja, mein Schatz*—Yeah, sweetheart," Léon began gruffly.

Esther flinched at his coarse use of this word.

"—*Das Geld*. Listen, lady, you don't think I'm doing this for free, do you? Especially not with a little kid. It's far too dangerous. You think I'm doing this for a good time? Marc-Philippe told you how much it would cost, right?"

What he said was true. Esther was aware money would be involved. She and Zami had been able to stay at Yvette's family apartment without charge, but when she first arrived, they had told her there would be "expenses" to get her to safety. However, the exact fee had not been mentioned, and what Léon now quoted her seemed exorbitant. But again, what alternative was available?

Choice is judgment and discernment . . . and need.

"I will get it," she affirmed.

Esther felt Léon watch her keenly as she went to the side of the bed where Zami sat, impassively watching this scene unfold. Wide-eyed, he held tight to his train.

Esther reached beneath the thin mattress and pulled out a bundle of bills. She turned her back and counted.

Facing him once again, she handed Léon a small stack and said, "Here is, *ein guter Teil*—a fair portion—of what you've asked for. It is more than enough to cover your transportation and food. As we make safe progress along the way, I will pay you more. At the conclusion, if we are successful, I will pay you a bonus. More than you requested."

Léon stared at her, dumfounded that Esther had the nerve to not immediately provide what he demanded. Then he snorted and, with a smirk exposing gray and yellowing teeth, said ominously, "*Klar, Schätzchen*—*einen Bonus*. Sure, sweetheart—a bonus. I'll take a bonus. Now go pack. *Schnell!* Quickly!

"Only take what you and the kid will really need. It is nearly six hundred and fifty kilometers to our destination. About twenty kilometers of that we must walk. It may not seem like much, but we'll be walking in snow. *Und es gibt keinen Pfad.* And there is no path."

Léon glanced down at Esther's feet, inspecting the well-worn lace-up shoes with low wedge heels she had not changed in two years.

"Are they warm?" he asked.

"They will do" was Esther's retort.

At last, Léon turned his attention to Zami. "And what about him? Does he have to be carried?"

"He can walk. He is strong," Esther stressed.

Léon said, "Well, he better be quiet. That's what I really care about. We can't have a screaming kid with us. That would nail us completely. *Wir wären erledigt.* We'd be goners."

"*Er ist kein Grund zur Sorge.* He is nothing to worry about," Esther said. "He is always quiet."

Quiet . . . yes . . . on the exterior . . .

What takes place within is not revealed . . . unless one listens closely . . . or accepts what they know to be true . . .

Along the way, every now and again, Esther caught glimpses of Léon watching her at the train stations. He would stand a good distance away, attempting to make himself as inconspicuous as possible. But there was no doubt he observed her every action.

Certainly he wants to make sure I won't get away and then not give him the rest of the money, Esther imagined. But, of course, that is ludicrous. Where would I go? How would I have any notion how to get across the border? *Ach!* It feels so close to the ending of this vileness, but there is more to come. Of this I am certain. There is more to come.

Intuition is a gift that is not often listened to . . . nor acted upon.

The journey, thus far, had been mostly fortuitous and free of grave incident. On each train Esther's documents were scrutinized no less than twice, by the conductor and then by a member of the *Wehrmacht*. Sometimes more. Wearing meticulous dark green uniforms and carrying standard issue *Karabiner 98 Kurz* rifles, these Nazi officers, all barely out of their teenage years, tried hard to rouse anxiety and fear from the passengers. In these circumstances, Esther regained her imperviousness to any emotions. Still, the officers' youth and fervor did produce curiosity—why were they doing this? Why were these young men invested in carrying out this horror? What was the attraction? The need? Had they no compunction? Esther's face reflected none of the thoughts within.

She was never singled out. The immaculately rendered papers she possessed were always returned without an extraordinary depth of probing—at least nothing out of the ordinary, given the times.

Esther's gratitude to Frau Göttlieb never lapsed.

I know someday she would be grateful for me . . . too . . .

Zami seemed unperturbed by the activities taking place in the train car. He spent much of the journey staring out the window or sleeping. The ever-changing, fast-moving landscape mesmerized him. Now and again he would look up at Esther and point to something outside. He did not use words, merely twisting around on her lap to get her attention. Esther would nod, acknowledging what he was showing her. Or attempting to show her, for both hands remained wrapped around his train. He held it close against his chest, caressing it as one would a baby.

It had been anticipated that connections would be delayed, and they were. The Lyon to Chambéry train was two hours late, taking nine hours instead of the anticipated four, and the one to Annecy, which had moved at the speed of a slow turtle, added more hours to the journey than she could count. Now the wait at Annecy was extending past ten hours. Unfortunately, the outpost was uncomfortable and grim.

An incidental town, its station did not provide a wide selection of amenities for travelers. There was a café bar—with three tall stools—that offered coffee and teas and simple fare like cheese sandwiches and biscuits. Some pieces of bruised fruit were available.

Esther and Zami had their share while waiting, and she purchased a few more sandwiches for later. And the one remaining apple. They had been forced to leave Paris so quickly she'd had little time to gather supplies. Esther had not known what would be needed. Léon was not forthcoming with information, only commanding she hurry to meet the Paris train.

Throughout the journey, Esther did her best to ignore Léon's presence. This man did not emit support and comfort. Maintaining as much of a distance as possible for as long as possible seemed the right thing to do.

It was while seated at the café that she saw two *gendarmes* approach Léon. As they were on the other end of the platform, Esther could not hear the words exchanged. But she took note the officers spent more than one hour speaking to him and closely scrutinized his documents. No doubt questioning him. About what she could not know, although Léon did, indeed, look suspect. Esther would have assumed for someone doing this type of work, he would want to make himself look presentable, less scruffy. Endeavor to blend in with the other travelers. More inconspicuous.

She could tell Léon was arguing with the *gendarmes*. Resisting whatever they were saying. He shook his head vehemently.

What if Léon is arrested? Esther considered. Then what would I do? What options would I have?

This would not be a concern she must respond to.

Yet . . . there would be other . . . issues . . . that must be grappled with . . . and triumphed over.

As it turned out, she did not have to reflect on this possibility long, for the train to Cluses chugged its way into the station and came to a stop. At that moment one of the officers waved his hand, signaling for Léon to be on his way.

Esther gathered up Zami and her few purchases of food and drink and headed toward the first-class compartment and their last train ride.

Cluses was shades of gray, ash, and gloom. The town was layered in deep snow. Weeks- and days-old snow, newly arrived snow. Unplowed snow. Streets and buildings were only distinguishable by dark outlines against slightly less dark sky. Diffused rays of light from a handful of windows scattered against the background completed the *mise en scène*.

When the train pulled into their final stop, it was nearly nine thirty in the evening, and the town was dormant.

Léon was waiting for her as she stepped onto the platform, carrying a sleeping Zami. Rushing up to her, he whispered sternly, "*Nicht Deutsch sprechen*—Don't speak German. Don't even open your mouth. I'll do any necessary talking in French. We must get a room for the night. One room, two beds."

Esther looked horrified at this prospect.

Léon, snorting in reaction to the expression on her face, continued, "They have to believe we're a couple. You can sleep with the kid in the second bed. We'll need to leave before dawn, so there won't be much time for sleep regardless. We'll head into the mountains before the sun comes up. I'm sure we won't be able to walk for long each day, not with the kid. It will be safer if we're not seen. We must avoid people as much as possible.

"*Folgen Sie mir.* Follow me," he ordered. "There's an inn across the street."

The aged innkeeper barely gave them a glance through his thick, dark-framed glasses when they passed through the double-paned front door, more interested in his book than customers. From the reception area's neglected state, this place appeared lacking in visitors, paying or otherwise. It was evident availability would not be an issue. Esther's one function during the brief interchange was to provide payment when nudged by Léon.

The room they were led to was no more appealing than the entryway. At least it was sizable, and the two beds, covered in heavy handmade quilts, were one and a half meters apart. Esther lay claim to the one against the wall, at the farthest end of the room, for her and Zami.

Other than removing their coats, Esther decided both would sleep in their clothes. Just as she settled Zami in and was about to get under the covers herself, Léon appeared above her, hand outstretched with one word formed on his mouth: "*Geld.* Money."

Yes, they had successfully reached another target in their crossing. And, as promised, additional funds were now due. Esther went into the bag she had slipped under her pillow and counted out another wad of bills.

Léon grabbed Esther's hand a little too tightly, and for a little too long, as the money was exchanged.

Exhaustion took hold. Léon's snores emulated the sound of a continuously revving engine rebounding against walls, ceiling, and floor. Zami, too, slept deeply, oblivious to the surroundings and concerns of what had passed and what may lie ahead.

Regrettably, rest was not to come for Esther. She could not relax. The approaching day—more likely days—were sure to be arduous and test her intrepidness.

She had grave misgivings—about Léon and about the crossing.

Esther understood the final leg of this journey to the border was only twenty kilometers, a full day's hike under good conditions. She and Zami had walked nearly that distance on a few occasions during their sojourn in Paris.

But these were in no way ideal circumstances.

The extent of snow Esther observed in the short distance between the train station and the inn shocked her. She had never seen anything like it. And this was inside a town. She knew they would be climbing higher. No doubt much higher. To what elevation she could not possibly fathom.

Esther knew nothing about this sort of environment. Knew nothing much about snow. And knew nothing at all about mountains.

Mountains . . . where the Heavens . . . meet the Earth . . .
Where the Gods reside . . .

And where humans . . . oft times . . . amidst strife and difficulty and asperity . . . ascend . . .

To encounter themselves.

With her mind still racing, Esther closed her eyes and by some means was able to drift off. It seemed only a fragment of time had passed when she found Léon leaning over her with pungent breath, hissing loudly, "*Zeit zu gehen.* Time to go. *Jetzt!* Now!"

The next ten minutes were a haze of disorientation. The room had been swallowed by a darkness that provided no sense of space, dimension, or perception. Léon refused to allow the light turned on or to use his flashlight. Zami, not easily roused, was uncharacteristically fidgety and whiny. Léon snarled at them both. After a struggle that startled her, Esther got Zami into his coat and put on her own.

Then, accompanied only by the sound of groaning floorboards in their room, the hall, and the entryway—and with the front door clicking shut with finality behind them—Léon, Esther, and Zami headed off in a northerly direction guided by a pocket compass.

They were greeted by frigidity with a deceptively gentle wind that sliced through their padded layers without effort. The rise of the sun one and a half hours later did nothing to abate the intensity of the environment. Still, they knew they were fortunate there was no falling snow or rain with which to contend.

Their movements were slow and tedious. There was no path and seemingly no direction, except the fact that every step climbed upward.

I must have faith Léon knows where we're heading, Esther thought. There are no other options. Not here.

They did not encounter another person. There was only snow and trees and rocks and more snow. So much more snow.

Sometimes the snowdrifts were as high as Zami's waist.

Twice, Esther had to carry him for an extended distance, his added weight sinking her deeper into the snow with each step. Her shoes, adequate for city walking, were in all respects unsuited for these conditions. In short order her feet were soaking wet. Then they began to freeze like icicles. Esther became anxious. She did not know if this was possible. Humanly possible.

"How long?" Esther asked.

"*Zwei Tage.* Two days. If we're lucky" was Léon's curt response.

No more conversation. All focus was on keeping warm and heading upward. Léon, moving slowly but with a determined gait, led the way. He turned around to check they were close behind every five minutes or so. Esther noticed he mumbled to himself. She didn't understand what he was saying, only that he appeared discontent. She was sure he was swearing often.

After four hours they came upon a hut, almost certainly used by the shepherds who in warmer months would populate the area. Léon said, "*Wir werden*—We'll stay here for the night."

Esther was relieved to stop. But after this morning's trials, she was apprehensive that they would not be able to reach the border. Their trek had been grueling. Torturous in some areas. Although they had only walked for a few hours, it did not seem as though a great distance had been traversed, and Léon appeared frustrated and angry. He, too, had not anticipated such deep snow.

To her relief, the hut seemed to be an arranged stop, for there were a long pallet and a stack of old blankets. Soft cotton-filled bags that could be used as pillows were found in one corner. A compact metal furnace was pushed into another corner with bundles of wood by its side.

Although the inside of the makeshift structure, with its thin walls, did not provide much warmth or protection, Léon refused to build a fire. He was adamant about not doing anything that could attract attention.

Esther sat on a section of the pallet, took off her shoes and socks, and briskly rubbed her feet to bring back feeling. She did the same for Zami, who thought it a game and smiled a bit. She then wrapped their feet in blankets. From her bag, she took out one of the remaining and now precious sandwiches and gave Zami half. Fortunately, Léon had carried his own supply of food and left them alone. Esther did not ask questions, and he did not volunteer any insight on the next plan of action. He paced back and forth. He swore. He rubbed his chin. He grunted. He pulled on his hair. He shook his head. He swore again.

Other than Léon's intermittent rumbles, they spent the rest of the day's light in silence. Zami was content to play with his train. Esther stared out the shed's window, striving to clear her still jumbled mind.

As soon as the sun set off in the far distance, sleep became their one agreed upon action, critical to renew their energies and resolve in anticipation of the next day's walk.

But the next day it snowed without stop, as it did the day following that.

Too dangerous to venture on, they waited. Many times throughout the day, Léon went outside to assess the situation. Coming back inside, his few words—more to himself than Esther—were: "Bad! Really, really bad!"

Then he would swear and go back out again. With gloved hands, he scooped the ever-rising snow as best he could away from the door. But the snow kept falling. Once he had to crawl through the high, narrow window because heavy snow blocked the door entirely.

Esther passed the period when there was light by expertly pulling threads from the edges of the frayed wool blankets. Using her fingers as needles, she patiently wove, filling the blankets' many moth holes. Zami alternated between playing with his train and watching the blizzard through the window. Esther rationed her remaining food, allowing herself and Zami only one small bite every few hours. There was no way to anticipate how long their confinement would last. Luckily, fresh water was plentiful.

She did not speak to Léon. Waiting for the weather to turn more amenable was the issue. There was nothing else to talk about. So much, for so long—for far too long—had been about waiting. And still, everything hinged on waiting. Under these circumstances, stoicism once again served her well.

Every so often, Esther found Léon staring at her. What manner of nonsense could possibly be going through his head? she wondered. She did her best to not think about it, as his looks were disconcerting. His strangeness compounded an already unsettling situation.

Fortunately, each night, even with the uncomfortable conditions and the dull ache of a never easing empty stomach, Esther's weariness took command. Her sleep came fast and deep, more so than could be recalled in memory. And she would remain fast asleep until the morning's sunrays shone through the window.

Except—in the middle of the fourth night, Esther awoke abruptly. To discover the full weight of Léon on top of her.

Her arms were pinned back, clothes pulled up, cotton knickers pulled down. The revulsion of this most personal of invasions froze her mute.

Léon's actions were fierce, his guttural grunts and painful thrusts sharp and forceful.

For Esther—time stopped.

Sound stopped.

The whole sucked into hollowness.

Still . . . she did not submit surrender of her self . . . of her being.

When finished, Léon took in an extended breath, forcefully shoved her over on one side, and said, laughing loudly, "Thanks sweetheart—*Danke Schätzchen, das ist mein Bonus*—that was my bonus!"

He snorted stridently, swiftly grabbed the remaining food and the small handbag where he knew Esther kept her money—

Ah . . . not all of it . . .

—and said, "This isn't going to work. I've got to save my own skin."

Then he strolled out the shed door, no thought or care to what would become of his two charges.

They were not alone . . . would never be alone . . .

Esther was revulsed but shed not one tear. Limbs or thoughts could not move.

Zami had watched the scene from the corner of the shed, where he had escaped to when Léon had jumped on their pallet, jumped on his mama. Not comprehending, he was certain that whatever was taking place was wrong. Very wrong. After Léon left, Zami went to Esther, placed one of his short arms around either side of her neck, and hugged her tight. Astonished, at first Esther tried to push him away, but Zami refused to let go. Finally relenting, she held him tenderly. The first time in his young life that she had ever done so. That he had ever done so. They spent the remainder of the night clasped together.

When the sun at long last rose, it came without snowfall or rain.

Esther, left with only grit and relentlessness, set off to find the border. She bundled Zami up as warmly as she could, dressing him in all his clothes. She wrapped three of the blankets around her shoulders and then searched the hut's four corners to see if there was anything else of use. Léon had taken what he thought was all the remaining food and money, but she discovered the lone apple had slid out of the handbag. She heaved a sigh as they headed out.

They wandered for three days not knowing left from right, north from south. Esther led them upward. At the least she always knew what was upward. They never saw another soul. She did not understand Léon's concern for only traveling at dusk or dawn, as there were no others to be found.

And Esther was desperate to find another, anyone.

She would not stop walking, moving.

As one day led into the next with no noticeable change other than greater height and increased cold, Esther came close to delirious.

Is this how it's going to end? she asked herself. Here—in this ocean of infinite white and unbearable cold? Will this be the culmination of my efforts and struggles? My suffering? All for nothing? No! This can't be! I won't allow it!

Now that it was just the two of them once again, Zami became complacent and more comfortable. The circumstances didn't seem to faze him. He didn't cry or complain. He held his mama's hand and let her carry him when the snow was too deep. Twice each day Esther allowed Zami and herself to take one infinitesimal bite of their apple.

"Roll it around in your mouth, Zami. Suck on its meat. Gently. This way you will release the juice slowly, and it will last longer," she told him. "Try not to chew or nibble. It is better just to suck on it. And don't swallow. Keep it in your mouth as long as you can."

Soon all that remained was the core, a few seeds, and the stem. These they shared in the same manner. Esther tried to make it a game, hoping that would ward off Zami's advancing hunger, her hunger. A distraction.

The snow kept them hydrated. When nightfall arrived, she and Zami would find a tree, place a blanket beneath them and two on top, and curl up together, melding as one.

I would blow warm air on them throughout the night . . . so they would not freeze . . . that was . . . not to be.

And then, materializing from the emptiness of the unremitting white, like a mirage, a depleted Esther saw them—

Three tall, uniformed, masculine shapes in the distance. Each with gun drawn.

She had finally arrived . . . reached the border . . . the invented boundary . . . signaling the end of one reality and onward into the possibilities of another . . .

"*Helfen Sie mir!* Help me! Help me!" Esther screamed, calling forth reserves of energy that had lain buried and dormant. "Please, please help me! *Bitte, Bitte, helfen Sie mir!*"

She saw these men glance at one another, shrug, roll their collective eyes, and shake their heads in unison. They were emphatic.

They thrust their arms outward; they signaled to go away. They threatened with their guns.

Until—

Esther used her final remnants of force and will, ripped open the hems and seams of her layers of dresses and skirts and coat. Money came fluttering out. Into the wind. In all directions.

Then . . . and only then . . . did they come to her aid.

PART II

Brahma . . .
the one . . .
with no beginning . . .
made a beginning . . .
and . . .
can surely . . .
make an end.

CHAPTER THIRTY-SEVEN

Regardless . . .
of what . . .
or where . . .
or when . . .
the thread . . .
endures.
And entwines . . .
securely.

....

With the suicide of the architect who instigated the insanity and resulting devastation, the war in Europe drew to a close.

Esther had been living in a displaced persons camp approximately 150 kilometers southwest of Zürich, for just over three years, when word came in early May that the war had finally ended. The Allies had triumphed. It took one week for the reality of the news to penetrate the layers of toil and suffering now formed like a jagged metal casing over her once soft skin.

Time—at long last—had form.

That which has no dimension or measurement . . . or even truly existence . . . can be formulated and constructed to accommodate . . . to promote . . . action.

Each twenty-four-hour rotation beginning with the first hint of the sun and concluding with its setting was no longer virtually identical to the one that came before or the one that would follow. With this long-awaited and wished for pronouncement, each day began anew with volume and shape, structure and purpose.

Now that commanding vision could be realized. The image, the impression—the divination—that, in spite of all odds and adversities, initiated forward motion and remained her paramount motivator during the years in Köln and throughout the war. The unique fixation that offered solace and strength after her heartrending betrayal by Tadeusz would be pursued. While those surrounding her envisioned a new life in Palestine, the believed homeland for the Jews, Esther only had thoughts of—

India.

A place she knew next to nothing about but one that inexplicably called to her like a small child crying out to be comforted by her mother. That chance encounter—ephemeral, ethereal, inexplicable—on the Köln banks of the Rhein had introduced an image, a sensation, the glimpse of somewhere more different and mesmerizing than Esther could possibly envision.

This, and only this, is what had kept the remnants of her broken spirit smoldering.

"Now," Esther murmured, "this confounding place can be pursued and investigated. At long last, I will be able to do whatever is necessary to solve the mystery of its insistent draw and significance. No more outside forces. No more world events. No more people—husband, children, housemates, officers—blocking my way, my life, my very being. I am fully in control of myself with no one else to contend."

Of most significance, and unlike nearly every one of her counterparts, she had money—a great deal of it in fact—an accumulation of resources her poor Polish family in the best of circumstances could not have dreamed possible. Not a small feat on a war-ravaged continent where she had been among the hunted.

For the first time, truly in decades, since she was a teenager—Esther was liberated.

During these past three years, though free to the extent she was no longer stalked on a daily basis with her very identity a liability, Esther had remained entrapped. For here, in this place of relative peace without threat of bombs or violence or hounding or persecution, it was thoughts and memories that instigated and controlled her web of confinement. Rest too often eluded her. Sleep was sporadic. It was never deep and often troubled. In lieu of the mostly dreamless nights to which she had grown accustomed, Esther had nightmares and flashbacks of encounters and incidents—

One episode in particular...

—that violently shook her out of slumber. Esther tossed and turned and traveled again and again over the distance and misery journeyed. She experienced the feelings and emotions, every one of them, that had been held at bay all those many years by the distraction of surviving and survival. Stress and dread and unfathomable sorrow maintained a firm grasp. Each night, whether awake or asleep, her head burst with thoughts of what had occurred.

A great deal of distance—and safety—now lay between her present path and those two and a half years in hiding. And the events that came before. Esther learned there was no escape from herself—her thoughts—her history—every action that had taken place since leaving Przeworsk—the horrors faced—the denial of emotions—ceaselessly running, often without moving—or being able to move. The endless lying, the fabricating, and the omnipresent loneliness that possessed her and had engulfed her.

And though the war had finally passed, the multitude of questions with all their whys continued to plague her, escalating the need for answers. Feeling consumed, Esther found it challenging to stay in the present, in the moment. To recognize what was real and what was the product of invention.

Before she could pursue the answers to any questions, Esther knew she must first be fully and finally relieved of responsibilities. Her ties to the past must be severed in order to pursue this course—in order to advance.

There was much to accomplish.

With their visitations, Esther had learned most of the details about what had happened to family members and friends in Przeworsk. Still, there were unanswered questions. In addition—

Not surprisingly . . .

—there was a need to verify this information was true. To corroborate these stories would confirm that what she'd experienced had indeed happened. The visitations—these occurrences—took place at the time her umbrage and indignation had peaked; she was vulnerable, weary, mentally unsettled, if not slightly mad. She felt fettered. They easily could have been tricks of imagination.

So often . . . far too often . . . a human being's encounters of a spiritual or metaphysical nature are questioned . . . not necessarily by others . . . but by themselves . . .

The unusual . . . the strange . . . the exceptional . . . the not everyday . . . can be too easily dismissed as a dream or an illusion . . . a figment of one's creative power caused by too much stress . . . sleeplessness . . . blurred vision . . . unclear thinking . . .

Thus Esther, ever the pragmatist and at all times diligent, spent the first few months after the war's official conclusion tracking down, as best she could, who of her family members were still alive. And what, if any, part of Przeworsk remained.

Not ten days after the war officially ended, volunteers, Good Samaritans, came to the displaced persons camp to help assist in locating—misplaced—family. Esther lined up with every other camp resident. When her turn came, she handed the youthful woman seated at the table a piece of paper with notes she had prepared.

"*Ich bin aus*—I am from Przeworsk. It is in Poland, near the Ukrainian border. A very small town, we call a *shtetl*—do you know that word?" Esther said.

"*Ja*, it is common," the woman replied.

"My name is Esther, and my family name is Grünspan. Before the war I had twelve brothers and sisters who lived there. Well, to be correct, my eldest sister had already moved to the United States, so there were eleven. And, of course, my mama and *tate*. Here are all their names spelled out correctly. I've included as many of their husbands' and wives' and children's names as I can recall. There were more than I knew. The address of our home is also noted. We lived near the center of town, just two streets away from the synagogue. Hmm. What else can I tell you? What else might you need to know?"

"Do you have a husband and children in Przeworsk too?" the woman asked. "This list doesn't include those names."

"No," Esther said.

"Okay," the woman said, nodding, "we will do our best to find out what we can."

Three weeks passed before the volunteers returned. Again Esther stood before the same woman.

"I am sorry to tell you this, but we could not locate any definitive information. It is too soon. It appears we were overanxious in our desire to help. While we have volunteers throughout Europe—please know there are scores of people who want to help—we did not anticipate the chaos and confusion that still reigns. There is little infrastructure as yet in place," she said.

"And while we have heard a range of rumors about what has happened to an inordinate number of Jewish people and much of Poland, I prefer not to share them. Rumors are too often composed in one's imagination. The things we have learned are inconceivable."

As it happened, most of what Esther was able to find out came from her oldest sister, Lifcha. She had observed the horrific events happening on this continent from the sheltered vantage of the United States' Midwest. At the onset, when restrictions were first placed upon Jewish businesses and activities—long before the girls were put on the transport to England or Esther's carefully plotted escape to Wuppertal, when the seriousness of the situation was beginning to be grasped—her siblings had devised a plan. It was decided that, in the event conditions got out of control and they lost touch with one another, when they were able, each would make contact with Lifcha. Her brothers and sisters had projected—correctly, as it turned out—even if communication among European countries was not possible, they would be able to reach Lifcha. She, in turn, would be able to make contact with each of them.

It took more than eight weeks after sending off the letter to receive a reply. And it was through Lifcha that Esther learned—

Or more precisely . . . received confirmation . . .

—that of their other eleven siblings, only Tonka, her baby sister, the family's youngest, had survived.

She was the one . . . after all . . . who did not visit in Paris . . . who could not visit . . . because she was still on this plane . . . this material plane.

Lifcha's three-page letter, speckled with what were most likely tear stains, explained that Tonka and her husband, Henig, had been living in Przeworsk when, in the fall of 1940, the town was invaded by the Russians. Their home was destroyed and these two were captured. Tonka and Henig spent the next five years in various work camps throughout Kazakhstan and Uzbekistan. They were moved around every few months. Or more frequently. The fortunate part was that they were able to remain together. Still, the conditions were appalling: severe cold, scarce food, repeated beatings, and continuous heavy labor. Tonka and Henig were young and strong and resilient and were able to survive with their health intact.

They had traveled back to Przeworsk as soon as circumstances allowed. While much of the small town was still intact, their Jewish Quarter had been leveled. And with it, the remains of family and friends and any impressions of the life they had known. Tonka and Henig were now on their way—walking—to a displaced persons camp in Berlin, Germany—their future uncertain.

The letter concluded with:

—meyn teyere Etka, mayn tayere shvesterl, der fakt vos du host ibergelebt, vos du lebst nokh, iz a nes. A matone. A matone fun riboyne sheloylem.

Bite zeyer. Kh'bet dir. Du must aherkumen tsu mayn hoyz in Shikage tsu zayn mit Isidor un mit mir. Un mit undzer Sheyne un Marni. S'iz shoyn di hekhste tsayt, du zolst zikh trefn mit dayne plimenitses. Mir zenen dayn mishpokhe.

Do iz zikher, un s'vet oykh zayn dayn heym. Tomid.

Kh'vel helfn aynordenen dayn rayze-bilet. Shrayb mir in gikhn un loz mir visn dayne plener.

. . . .

—oh, my dearest Etka, my dear, dear sister, the fact that you have survived, that you are still alive, this is a miracle. A gift. A gift from Hashem.

Please. Please! You must come here to my home in Chicago to be with Isidore and me. And with our Shaina and Marni. It is time for you to meet your nieces. We are your family.

It is safe here, and it will be your home too. Always.

I will help arrange your passage. Write back soon and let me know of your plans.

No, Esther thought, no more. I can't go backward. I can't spend my precious resources reconnecting with any part of my past. Surely this would only bring me pain. I refuse to be hurt and lost once more. Esther crumpled the three thin pieces of paper in her left hand and tossed them into the nearby wastebasket.

The Grünspan family—once animated and vital individuals who overflowed with life and all of its potential—had been reduced to three. These threads, their connections were frayed and shredded without a future.

To investigate Tova and Miriam's whereabouts—

Ah . . . wonderful . . . they too are not to be forgotten . . .

—Esther sought the assistance of the International Red Cross. Another resident of the DP camp had told her about this organization that had quickly grown instrumental in tracing the whereabouts of family members separated during the war. These inestimable providers of relief and respondents to emergencies had become vital collators of information on those who were now disenfranchised.

The train to Zürich took two hours and fifteen minutes. Esther located their central office in the business district easily. There was a line extending halfway around the block. But the Red Cross office was well-staffed, and in less than half an hour, Esther was inside.

"*Guten Morgen*—Good morning, my name is Claudine," said the effusive, gray-haired woman to whom Esther was assigned. "Can I get you some tea while we talk? Perhaps some cookies to go with it?"

Such a thoughtful woman.

"*Nein, nein, danke,*" said Esther, "I am fine. Can we get started? *Bitte.* I am here to find out if you can help me locate my two daughters. They were in the transport of *Kinder*. They left on 29 August, 1939. It was the last one to leave before the war began and—"

"Yes, yes, of course I can help," Claudine said, interrupting. "But first I want to say how terribly sorry I am for all the hardships you and your family have suffered." She reached out to touch her hand, but Esther quickly pulled it out of reach. "There are no words that can soothe. I know this. It has been outrageous. Unjust. I know nothing could ever make up for what you have experienced. I am so very, very sorry."

As though she, personally, was responsible for all the evils and ills that had taken place, Esther thought. She struggled to submerge a smirk.

"It would be best if we could focus on finding my girls," she said aloud, striving to maintain her exasperation. Esther chewed the inside of her right cheek. She wanted news as soon as possible.

"It is an awful, awful situation. Really something that is impossible to envision, but—"

Perceiving Esther was about to interrupt, she quickly added: "I promise, I will do my very best to locate your daughters. I can't begin to consider how difficult it has been to be separated from them. I have three daughters of my own and, well—sorry, yes, yes, of course, let us continue. Please, if you could, without too much trouble, fill out these forms. As completely as you are able. Of course, the more details you have for us, the better. But please do not pressure yourself. We understand papers and information have been lost. Of course, with all the stress you have experienced, memories might not be as clear as you would like. We have found it's best if people are comfortable while the forms are filled out. There are many pages. Please—can I get you some tea and cookies?"

Yes . . . of course . . . but only the cookies . . .

Claudine's efforts produced results. With just a few telegrams and one phone call, in a manner of days she was able to confirm Tova and Miriam were, without a doubt, alive.

"I have wonderful, wonderful news to report," Claudine told Esther at their second meeting. "From the information conveyed to us, I have been able to cobble together an outline of your daughters' situation. Upon arriving in England, the transport assigned them to an orphanage called Sunshine House. A mansion, really. Located in one of the most beautiful parts of London, Hampstead Heath. I visited there many years ago. Long before the war, obviously. A wealthy couple that owns many homes throughout England made this one available to the *Kindertransport*. Can you imagine? They were so generous. Your daughters, and twenty-six other young boys and girls from far-flung parts of Germany and Austria, lived together. Endured the war together. The children were supervised by a young, pious couple. Such dedication! Caring to the well-being of these poor children without parents or homes. Their names are—hmm, let me see." She shuffled through the piles of notes on her desk. "Josef and Ruth Simmons. You can be assured their care was exemplary. This must be a great relief." A big smile filled Claudine's face.

Esther took a deep inhale and nodded.

"Oh," said Claudine. "One more thing. I was informed the girls were raised Orthodox. This was the one stipulation of the family who owned the mansion. Those who reside under their roof must keep kosher with the children raised as Orthodox Jews. I'm sure that pleases you."

Raised Orthodox? Esther mused. How ridiculous! That was definitely not something I had agreed to. What in the world were those people thinking? Thankfully, it is not my problem.

"*Kann ich Ihnen helfen*—Can I help you arrange a visit?" Claudine asked eagerly. Making these connections were the highlight of this work. In far too many cases, her searches did not produce joyful results. "We have available funds to assist you with travel costs. I'm sure you are extremely anxious to see them?"

"No," Esther said, exposing no reaction. "No visit. That won't be necessary.

"*Danke. Vielen Dank.*" Esther then turned and exited the office without seeing the stunned expression that shrouded Claudine's face.

Esther was relieved to learn the girls were safe and alive. And she was clear that was all she needed to know. All she cared to know. As with Lifcha, she could not reconnect. She could no longer participate in a life that was not truly her own. Her responsibility to them was complete.

So, what Esther never learned—

What . . . she would never know . . .

—was that Miriam had cried every day and every night the first three weeks after they arrived in England. Crying desperately for her father and holding fast to the dearly loved stuffed bear Abraham had given her when she turned six. The last birthday they had shared.

Or that this little girl, the one who had once been so animated and filled with life, developed a stammer she would never overcome. Nor would Esther learn Miriam was the hardest working student in this group home. She excelled in all of her classes and attended the best schools. But she was also the most shy.

Esther did not know this daughter was among the youngest in the transport of ten thousand and that she continued to be called *Schwestie*. But not just by Tova. Miriam became all of these children's little sister.

Or that Tova, who had been a sickly child, developed colds and fevers regularly and grew into an angry, rebellious youth. Esther would not know that this daughter was an indifferent student who was sent to a trade school in lieu of high school. There she was trained in sewing and tailoring, expanding on the skills acquired at a young age.

Ah . . . this one did not stray from the family's heritage . . .

Esther would never know that Tova lost her virginity at only twelve years of age in the Sunshine House's attic, seduced by one of the much older *Kinder* boys.

She would also never know the children were marched down to the basement during air raids and that Ruth Simmons played classical music—Mozart, Schubert, and Tchaikovsky—at the highest volume possible in an attempt to drown out the sounds of bombs and destruction.

Or that on Friday nights, after the evening meal and before walking to synagogue, Josef Simmons would say a blessing over each child. And on the first night of Passover they were given an orange, the rarest treat during wartime.

These attributes and qualities and characteristics and anecdotes—and so many more—the elements that compose an individual, a life—Esther did not know—or would ever learn.

These girls had been fed and cared for with a constant roof above their heads. They were still alive; she had done her duty.

With all that has happened . . . with all she has endured . . . all she has overcome . . . it saddens me Esther still maintains such a wall of distance . . . and indifference . . . from her self . . . from her soul . . . and from these seeds of her loins.

Esther did concede if she were a different woman, perhaps more like most women, she would do everything and anything possible to reunite with her children and surviving family. But, she often thought, I must be who I am and only that.

At least . . . at the very least . . . she knew herself.

It was clear this would not be possible. For this was not what mattered to her. Not now.

Withal, in a flash of compassion and consideration, Esther found someone traveling to London who agreed to bring a carton of eggs—a luxury—to the two girls. Esther included a brief note that she signed Mama, with ambivalence—and palpitations deep within her chest.

Unbeknownst to the carrier, a few valuable gifts were secreted in the carton. Not unlike preparing eggs to decorate for Easter, Esther had sucked the insides out of three of the eggs. In one she stuffed a wad of bills and in each of the remaining two, necklaces: a rectangular-shaped peridot set in gold filigree intended for Tova and a heart-shaped amethyst bordered by seed pearls for Miriam.

These were not antiques or family heirlooms. Esther had purchased them at a jewelry store in Zürich. If it was important to them, Tova and Miriam could say they had something sweet from their Mama.

Zami, too, had survived.

And in his own way . . . the way that was uniquely him . . . Zami
. . . considered peculiar by most . . . was able to bloom.

The camp Esther was directed to live in, the place the border guards took her to, did not allow children. The explanation was there were no facilities or resources for them. No school or playground. With the help of a local charity, a comfortable home was found for him in a neighboring village. This family he was sent to live with included seven-year-old twin girls.

"This is a good home, a loving home," the social worker had informed Esther. "It is a Christian home. We hope this fact will not pose a problem. Your son will have to follow their practices and rituals. And—they prefer to call him Samuel."

"This is not a concern for me," Esther responded. Inwardly she thought, Truly, of what does Zami know differently? For the past two and a half years, surely from his earliest memories, he has gone to church every Sunday.

Perhaps he is already Christian? Whatever that might mean.

This family, the Stoecklins, appeared to be good people, nice people who said they would care for this little boy as though Zami were their own. He would be the son they had never had.

They wanted him . . . to be wanted . . . feelings Zami had not
known since his father was left behind.

Zami showed no reaction when Esther left him at the Stoecklin family's home. There was neither a cry nor a sound of any kind. His eyes did grow big and his lips separated, as though to shout, but he did not. Pointedly, he did not raise a hand to wave goodbye. Zami turned his back on his mama and ran into the house.

Esther watched silently. So many goodbyes. I have experienced so very many goodbyes.

There was little doubt . . . there was no question . . . by all who were present that this was indeed . . . goodbye.

While she made little effort to find out how he fared, at the end of each month, Esther would receive a note from Zami's foster parents. In this way she kept up with his life, and she did appreciate learning he was doing well. While she desired no relationship, Zami was the only one of her three children Esther had achieved a semblance of a maternal attachment to. Albeit a slim thread.

For although the camp and Zami's new home were not more than one hour's train ride apart, Esther never visited. She could have easily; there were few restrictions on her comings and goings, but she chose otherwise.

By and large, what Esther had done during this three-year period was wait. She waited for this war to end. Waited to regain control—full control—real control—of her life and her life alone. She waited with resilience and with patience. While she waited, Esther sewed and embroidered, stitched and tailored, as she had before.

And she continued to make money. As she had before.

Esther never learned Abraham's status. She made no effort, for there was no interest or concern.

Certainly he had been killed. In all likelihood in one of those atrocious camps she heard rumors of. *Ach so,* Esther would think, on the scarce occasion she thought of him at all. I don't wish him ill, I really don't. I know it was my mistake to marry him. But he was a foolish, foolish man! He refused to believe the situation would get as dire as it did. He refused to listen to me. He refused to leave that silly little cobbler's shop of his on Kämmergasse.

The place she last took sight of him.

That is where he would remain . . . whether in fact . . . or mere memory . . .

Now—

Esther was ready to wholly take care of Esther.

Finally . . . at long last . . . Esther is coming . . . home . . .

And me . . . I am the Gatekeeper . . . prepared to greet her.

CHAPTER THIRTY-EIGHT

Brahma . . . is the great creator . . . the first originator.
  But He is not and does not . . . choose to be . . .
  the only creator.

He gave us all . . . each of us . . . every one of us . . . each one
of you . . .
  the ability and the inventiveness . . . the inner resources . . .
  to envision . . . to imagine . . .
  to initiate . . .

To bring into being . . . into existence . . . a dream . . . a vision . . .
  your vision.

To manifest not only what you have conceived and what you
  have imagined . . .
  but what you know to be true . . .

To be truth.

Amrita . . . the nectar . . .

For truth that transcends . . . mortality . . .

It begins . . . it always begins . . . with a glint . . . a spark . .
a mere flicker . . .
    sometimes so subtle as to be lost . . . to be missed . . .
    to go unnoticed . . .
    or . . . simply . . . as is the case with most . . .
    ignored.

But . . . Esther . . .

Esther saw . . .

and . . .

Esther grasped . . .
    wholly . . . at her very core . . . her essence.

CHAPTER THIRTY-NINE

Now it appears . . .
the seam . . .
so painstakingly and masterfully . . .
sewn . . .
to possess the ends . . .
finally ruptures . . .
and the thread untwines.
But . . . does it really?
For it is the same . . .
truly the same . . .
always the same . . .
just different . . .
merely different.

. . . .

The concurrent planning and preparations underway were for Esther's departure.

Or perhaps . . . more correctly . . . her return . . .

This exit was different from the preceding two times, for in each of those instances, Esther had been running away from all things known and familiar: the first, to secure her soul; the second, to save her life. Now, she headed toward the indefinable, a place beyond description—an enigma of choice.

The destination was clear, at least the general port of call. The exact locale, at present, was still uncertain.

With the assistance of the far too curious, but self-restrained, volunteer in the library a half hour train's ride from the camp, Esther learned a few basic facts. In geographic mass India was bounded by the Indian Ocean on the south, the Arabian Sea on the west, and the Bay of Bengal on the east. And was bordered by countries whose names she could not decipher how to pronounce. Its inhabitants represented a multitude of ethnicities, religions, and languages. She found information on India's history, its economy, its primary resources and businesses, in addition to its government and politics. None of these topics interested Esther enough to spend time reading more than a paragraph or two.

There were pictures of architecture, minor- and large- and colossal-scale, and monuments and scenery and colorfully dressed people similar to what she had found in the Köln library's single slim volume. In this tome, words and terms danced over the pages without significance or definition: Hinduism, Buddhism, Jainism, Sikhism, Zoroastrianism, and Islam. Maharashtra, Rajasthan, Banares, Tehri-Garwal, Goa, and Jharkhand. Cumin, turmeric, fenugreek, cardamom, *garam masala,* and asafetida. *Masala dosa, chana, mung, dal, tandoori,* and *roti.* Page after page after page incited curiosity and intrigue. Esther grew excited.

Foreign. Everything on the book's pages looked far removed from Esther's encounter. From the way the letters of the Hindi alphabet lay against one another to the images they described. Exotic. Intriguing. Astonishing. Outlandish. Unfamiliar—but unfamiliar in the most welcoming manner.

Ah . . . but wait . . . there is one word . . . one experience . . . she will recognize in memory . . . and smell . . . and taste . . .

The word *samosa* leaped out as though in a font, size, and style separate from all else. "Sa-mo-sa," she said aloud, enunciating every syllable. Instantly transporting her back to when this small doughy pie's pungent smells and its savory sensations had filled every pore in her body and every sense of her being.

As before, Esther's eyes began to water.

"*Entschuldigung.* Excuse me. Say again, please. You would like to go where?" The travel agent could not believe he heard correctly.

"*Indien,*" Esther replied. Her articulation matter-of-fact.

"*Wirklich?* Really?" he asked, incredulous. "May I ask why?"

"*Nein.* It is not your concern. All you need to know is that I have secured *die notwendigen Identitätspapiere und Dokumente*—the necessary identity papers and documents. As you must be aware, these are not easy to acquire. Not at this time. The process has been complicated. But all is in order, and I am prepared to arrange my passage. Can you provide me with the pertinent information? If not, I will go elsewhere," Esther continued emphatically.

All the while aware there was no other agent in the region.

"Madame, please know I'm not prying. Surely you can understand my curiosity," he insisted. "India is a most unusual request and not the safest country for a woman traveling alone."

"I repeat, it is not your concern," Esther said, tapping her fingers on the counter in hopes of allaying increased frustration. "Please, I request an answer. Are you able to assist me or not?"

The agent, who had no desire to lose a customer, quickly said, "*Es tut mir sehr leid*—Please excuse my rudeness, I am very sorry. It will take me several days, but I will get the information you are seeking and make the appropriate arrangements. I hope you are aware this will not be inexpensive. This is a high-priced voyage."

"Cost will not be a deterrent."

Over the course of the next three and a half weeks, Esther visited the travel agent's office—two doors away from the jewelry store where she purchased the girls' necklaces—five more times before she received the necessary details. His research required him to explore a variety of routes that would reach the continent. At each visit he described a different scenario with alternate possibilities.

The one constant: Bombay must be the point of entry. This was the only city receiving international carriers on a consistent basis.

Each time, the agent would elaborate on the challenges of getting to India. He described how dangerous it was to travel there, most especially for a woman alone, and that her safety could not be assured once she arrived.

"You must understand that this will be an extremely long journey. Perhaps up to one month. It will be dependent upon the conditions at sea."

Esther rolled her eyes as he rambled on.

Six weeks to the day of her initial inquiry, she walked out of his office with the tickets—train and ship—in hand. Confident she was doing exactly as she must. Still unknowing as to why. The impulse remained a mystery.

Esther told no one of her plans. In all truth there was no one left to tell.

However . . . you must be aware . . . information flows . . . when and where it needs to flow.

The afternoon before the train would depart from the Zürich station to take her to Geneva—then on to Lyon and finally Marseille, where she would board the ship—Esther gathered up the few items that by requisite and circumstance had remained attached to her person for the past nearly six years. These were not unlike a tattoo whose message reflects a name that now only brings forth regret and sorrow.

The need no longer existed to possess or be possessed.

Woodland butted up against the rear of the DP camp. A setting with benches and tables, fire pits and trails that led far into a forest rarely visited by the local inhabitants. On this day Esther headed there with determination and a book of matches.

Agni . . . God of Fire . . . courier of prayers . . . messenger between gods and humans . . . between that sphere and this . . . appears once more . . .

An eighth of a kilometer in, Esther found a clearing with a contained area designed for a campfire. After collecting a handful of twigs, she laid the components of Etta Göttlieb's invented life on the ground next to the pit: birth certificate, baptismal documentation, identity papers. The rosary of dark wood carved beads, now well worn, and the Bible, with bent spine and creased pages, were arranged next to them.

Knowledge . . . purification . . . regeneration . . .

It took eight attempts to persuade the twigs to take to flame. No wind interfered, just weeks of sporadic rain that kept them soft and damp. Esther ripped a handful of pages from the Bible to help the fire take hold and stoke the flames. At last an impressive ring of brilliant reds, oranges, and yellows was established. Into this, without hurry, went these materials, one piece at a time.

To burn . . . externally . . . is not to burn . . .

Words, sentences, purpose, and ruse faded away as the papers turned brown, rippled and curled, then blackened and crumbled. The Bible's cover shriveled gradually. The beads of the rosary coaxed the blaze. Flames rose upward. Smoke wafted.

On top of the burning pyre, Esther placed the delicate gold chain with its Holy Mother talisman. She watched as it melted into a near perfect round ball.

And let us not forget . . . Brahma and fire are one . . .

More endings.

Yet . . . with . . . out . . . end . . .

CHAPTER FORTY

The noise . . .
has dissipated.
That which distracted . . .
and . . .
was distracting . . .
has gone.
Everything that is left . . .
all that remains . . .
is the space . . .
the opening . . .
the gateway.
Inviting . . .
thoughts . . .
susceptibilities . . .
memories.

. . . .

September 1945, just prior to mid-month. For the first time in more than six years, Esther was on a train—in public—as Esther.

She was once again Esther Grünspan. Or, at long last, attempting to find her way back to Esther. No false identities—no forged papers—no intricately fabricated tales justifying the rationale for traveling from one city to another in the midst of war. No story lines rehearsed for hours in advance to ensure the ability to convey particulars—only those pertinent and strategic—with brevity of speech and assuredness of manner.

It was not until she was on the train to Marseille, not until her luggage was securely stored in the rack above her seat, her coat hung on the metal hook next to the window, and her back leaned against the stale, frayed, sunbaked burgundy leather seat that Esther grasped this. Viscerally. And began to feel—to the depth of her core.

She started to shake. At first only mildly, then profoundly.

Sorrow, devastation, rage, abandonment, loss, betrayal, yearning—all these emotions materialized in chorus, took dominion, and flooded over. Such loss of control bewildered her. Tears attempted to form in her eyes, but the actual process of this most natural bodily function had long been erased from her memory.

What is this reaction? What is going on with me? Esther questioned as she wrestled with a blanket to wrap around herself. Is it because I'm entering an unknown situation? Nonsense! These past years have been about the indefinite. Is it that most of my family—those I haven't seen or spoken to in decades—is gone? Is it about those I've left behind? The children? *Ach!* Tova and Miriam—and Zami—are safe. They are all fine. I made sure of that. They are my children, but I know they are better off without me. Is that what initiated this madness? Isn't a mother supposed to do what's best for her children? I don't understand. What's happening to me? Why now?

Her shuddering persisted. A shift was underway.

The threshold awaits . . .

She must understand . . . yet she is not aware . . . that this . . . this of all times . . . this is not the occasion for confusion . . . or dread . . . or panic.

For this is a special time . . . the most special time of each year.

*For now . . . right now . . . is my birthday! It is Ganesha Chaturthi
. . . the fourth day of the brightest fortnight . . . the waxing moon
of Bhadraparda . . . it is during these ten days . . . when I am
worshipped and celebrated by all.*

*It is the most auspicious time . . . the most fortuitous time . . .
for new beginnings . . . for each and every one. For Esther . . .*

*And this year . . . at this time . . . I share my ten days . . . the same
ten days . . . with the Jewish Days of Awe . . . the highest and
holiest of days for the Jewish people.*

No chance occurrence . . . only harmony.

*Distinct belief systems . . . philosophies . . . faiths . . . perspectives
. . . now weave together as one.*

Deep, steady breaths—three counts in, three counts out. This
systematic rhythm composed her. At least somewhat. She slept for
a while. Although not peacefully.

She remained unsettled.

Where did the color go?

When did brilliant blue get mixed with black and become a
muddy gray?

Emerald green—a dreary brown?

Luscious red—a dirty slate?

When did the sharpness and vibrancy of the landscape recede
behind layers of scrim, hiding the nuances of living that had once
been so closely observed and dear?

When had the clarity gone so terribly out of focus? When did
it make me lose sight of the depth of my true nature? My genuine
desires and wants? My feelings?

These are the thoughts that poured through Esther as the ship
eased away from the dock in Marseille. She sat on the deck with the

other passengers—perhaps a few dozen—who shouted and waved to those sending them off and wishing safe journey.

Only Esther arrived alone and remained alone. A solitary figure infused with the bleak isolation of a dark painting.

> I sit beside her . . . I have not left her. On occasion she has acknowledged me . . . my whispered assistance . . . my warm embraces. Still my presence . . . after all these years . . . all this time . . . remains unnamed.
>
> I create a soft wind to sheathe her . . . to assuage the gaping wound that has become more pronounced . . . resonating . . . resounding . . . throughout her being.
>
> That ironic wrong that crushed her heart and slashed her soul . . . and saved her life.

Finally on the way to elsewhere. But with imperviousness lacking and energy spent, the past twenty-some years of inconceivable trials and strain and subterfuge—that which had consumed every ounce of her wits and resources—finally caught up.

Esther crumbled. Fully and completely.

CHAPTER FORTY-ONE

Memory...
fuels the flame...
and...
ignites...
the wrenching heart.

....

Now, and only now, with this interval—the first opportunity to rest and reflect and imagine what lie ahead—self and soul spiraled out of control.

Esther became sickened. Severely. She was thrust to the rim of reality and authenticity, lucidity, and possibilities.

This was not a surprise.

In recent months Esther's formidable, inviolate guard had experienced infinitesimal cracks. What had been buried or vehemently brushed aside was now finding its way back home. After far too many years of triumphant submersion without filtering, the full sum of the mental and physical stress, anguish, and effort never totally experienced or absorbed by her being was coming to the fore at long last.

A breach in the floodgates of emotion . . . true honest emotion . . .
promotes a profundity of discomfort . . . a piercing distress that
. . . in turn . . . in time . . . always . . . without question . . . breeds
disease . . . dis . . . ease.

That evening, the first on the ship's crossing to India, Esther took to her cabin and did not take leave. Not for any meal. Not for one of the numerous stopovers at exotic-sounding port cities where supplies were gathered and refueling took place. Not to breathe freely and deeply of the crisp sea air.

An all-embracing fever—

A gift . . . in actual fact . . .

—had taken hold with concentrated intensity and fury.

A fire within her . . . consuming her . . . with Agni . . . assisting
once again.

A continuous, highly elevated temperature, one of the human body's natural defenses normally called to action to neutralize an infection, also possesses the capacity to alter senses and perceptions. In this case, Esther's senses and perceptions.

It has the ability to unlock a portal . . . providing passage . . .
entry . . . introducing the threshold and a bridge . . . if you will
. . . between Esther's here . . . and my here . . .

I saw the chance . . . the opening . . . a most critical opportune
occurrence for me to be in the very same time and very same
space . . . and place . . . with Esther . . .

To be as one . . . in the indistinguishable sphere . . . to bring her
joy . . . pure joy . . . bliss . . . for the first time . . . the only time . . .
since she was with him . . . that man . . . her man . . . Tadeusz . . .

To dance with abandon . . . and surrender . . .

And . . . dance . . . we did.

The ship's captain and crew of five left Esther to herself, unconcerned she had not made an appearance since leaving port in Marseille. These overburdened men merely assumed, if they considered the situation at all, that as the lone woman traveling without a companion, Esther was most likely not comfortable interacting with others in a strange setting. No doubt food and other necessary supplies accompanied her.

In all probability, the passengers were not aware an additional traveler accompanied them. Most were self-absorbed, since the journey had not been smooth, the weather not so obliging, and each had bouts of seasickness with which to contend. The desire for calm seas was the only collective thought.

Esther is nearly . . . home . . .

CHAPTER FORTY-TWO

Three weeks . . .
time.
All times . . .
Any time . . .
passes . . .
passed.

....

$\mathcal{A}$s the ship eased closer toward shore, the sea grew calm. More than ten hours remained before arrival into port, but a transformation became manifest in the atmosphere. The potentiality of land in the near distance, solid ground—terra firma—began its gravitational pull and, with it, the promise of steadiness and renewal in the next phase of each traveler's journey. This vessel had been christened *L'Étoile,* the symbol of constancy, and true to its name would proffer clarity of direction for those on board.

The steadfast movement forward germinated a keen sense of excitement that seemed to sprout from bilge to keel, gradually embracing the deck that surrounded the bridge and finally extending its reach up to the top of masts, rigging, and sails.

This electric energy had the ability to entice Esther out of the cabin and onto the deck, persuading her to settle on one of the rickety wooden chairs lined up near the bow. Feeling the cool gentle wind on her face invigorated long dormant muscles. Esther took in the setting with a deep extended breath and closed her eyes.

"Where . . . are you traveling to?" a low, assured male voice inquired in what sounded her direction.

Esther's eyes opened instantly and she looked up, startled. Surprised, and more so, uneasy, that someone was speaking to her for no apparent or necessary reason. Other than the doctor who had treated her, not a word had been exchanged with anyone throughout the crossing. With the doctor, not more than a few strained words had passed between them. And those only in response to his questions. The required seclusion for the remainder of the voyage had been appreciated, in fact, a relief.

This man's accent was thick and layered. At first she could not distinguish what language he was speaking nor recognize the words he formed.

He repeated the question. More slowly and precisely, reasoning that perhaps she did not understand him, all the while knowing without question their language was shared.

"Well, Bombay, certainly," Esther responded, puzzled. "This ship is going to Bombay, India, is it not?"

"Yes . . . yes . . . of course . . . it is going to Bombay. Please forgive me if I am being . . . well . . . impertinent. I do apologize. I was asking . . . I am seeking . . . your ultimate destination . . . your true destination. I don't mean to appear rude, but . . . as you must realize . . . it is most unusual to find a woman traveling alone in this part of the world . . . most unusual indeed. Particularly now after all that has taken place. There are a small number . . . just a few of us on this ship . . . a few of us traveling at all. And until now . . . until today . . . you have kept to yourself and . . . well . . . again . . . please excuse me if I am being rude . . . but you have been rather hidden from the rest of us."

This man's cadence was beguiling, unlike any Esther had heard before.

"I have been unwell," she replied. "Quite ill, it appears, and was advised by the ship's doctor that it would be best to stay in my cabin. As much as possible, anyway. My isolation has been necessary to heal and allow me to regain my strength." Esther's voice faltered, the words not flowing with ease. As though her vocal cords were attempting to recall their purpose. She could not bring to mind the last time she had engaged in a dialogue about anything of substance. Or one that was casually social.

For far too long, for more than two decades, any and all conversation had been about necessity. Entered into as a means to an end, to receive information that would carry her forward, facilitate in acquiring what was essential and nothing more. In most every circumstance, all dialogue had related to survival. When first in Köln and through all the ensuing years there, sustenance represented the need for work and lodging and food. Then, when circumstances changed, when the country's troubles escalated and the war intervened, conversing was used for structuring illusion and perception. So no one would guess. None would suspect. No truth would be revealed.

Everything—for so long, anything and everything was simply about survival.

But here Esther was, in the one remaining chapter of this ship's journey with the vessel scheduled to land later the same day, speaking, engaging in an actual conversation with a stranger. About a topic that, at this moment in time, seemed abstract and intangible—her destination.

Esther peered up from the chair and took in his presence.

Towering above her, this man had thick, gray-speckled black curly hair that framed a finely sculptured face, nearly perfectly centered by a long, aristocratically sloped nose. Prominent ears peaked out from behind curls. Kind, compassionate eyes behind oval, silver-framed glasses looked back at her with intensity. A surprising softness and profound caring immediately struck her. Dressed entirely in black with a large gray scarf draped around his neck, he appeared solid—and safe. Radiating comfort.

Taken off guard, Esther was wholly embraced by a forgotten sense of warm, soothing calm.

"May I sit here?" he requested, gesturing to the empty seat beside her. Esther's head shifted downward slightly, a tentative but curious nod.

"Please do excuse me once again. I do not mean to pry . . . but I must admit . . . I am intrigued and compelled to inquire about your circumstances. In addition . . . and I do recognize . . . I do realize I should not be saying this but . . . please let me be truthful. I have spent the past few weeks speaking with the other passengers and have found them to be . . . well . . . a rather tedious . . . ordinary bunch. I know . . . I am sorry . . . I apologize . . . this is not a compassionate or understanding thing to say. But I am regretful in that it is . . . true . . . nonetheless."

At this declaration, he let out a resounding guffaw. His face broke into an unconstrained smile, revealing strongly etched laugh lines around his eyes and mouth, large white teeth, and a dimpled left cheek.

Esther gasped, stunned that someone could express candor with such ease—with unquestioned sincerity. She had forgotten a frankness of this kind existed. It demonstrated how much time had transpired. And how much life and history had passed since an appearance of honesty had been possible or exchanged with another.

Not since—

Perhaps it was this man's approach, almost a childlike purity. Disarming. Possibly it was simply the intersection of chronology and the culmination of years upon years of unexpressed, buried thoughts, denied feelings, ruinous experiences, and unending pain. Conceivably it was Esther's recent exceptionally high fever and vision. In any case, for a reason not to be fathomed, this man's forthright authenticity flipped a switch long in abeyance.

And the floodgates opened to their full extent, and the whole poured forth.

Esther talked, without uncertainty and barely with inhalation.

For the first time—and for this one time only—Esther revealed her story, the full history. She covered family and beginnings in

Przeworsk and did not leave out one facet of the devastation to heart and soul that took place under the *chuppah* on the day when her life's trajectory changed forever. She described the struggles endured in Köln; the miseries of a sad, loveless marriage; the burdens of three unwished-for children; the inhumane, constrictive policies inflicted upon the Jewish people together with those marked as sympathizers. The wartime horrors, the ordeals suffered, and finally—Switzerland.

The retelling was agonizing and not without more than the occasional tear in her eyes. Or the ever-present pang in the core of her being. Again and again, Esther had trouble catching her breath, unable to get the words out. Frequently, she did not know the words to use, did not know if such vocabulary existed.

How to articulate the unimaginable?

How to explain the choreography of a daily life that could be snatched away without warning or rationale, with no security or protection available?

How to put into words the visceral consequences of a veiled identity and invisibility, when you do not understand them yourself?

How to give voice and substance to nightmares of the waking hours—to provide the details of rape and degradation in the Alps?

Fundamental to all else—how to convey the inexpressible— the agony of spurned love—and the mandate it birthed within her to persevere? To move forward and ultimately—survive at all costs?

Survival to what end? she still queried.

Throughout the cascading of stories and words and heartache, he, Marco—for somewhere between the descriptions of her realities in Leiden and then Paris, these two shared their most basic infor- mation—listened with a depth of compassion and a consciousness that transcended her words. When Esther faltered, Marco offered support and encouragement to continue on, always with gentleness and mindfulness.

Occasionally, he caressed her hand or nodded and held her gaze. Compassion enveloped her. After a while he encouraged Esther to walk with him around the deck, the movement helping to secure her calm in the drama's unfolding. Marco knew that this story, the full extent of her chronicle, must be verbalized, and the time was now.

Esther understood this. While bedridden, it had become clear to her that someday, the details of her past and her journey—every detail of those experiences endured—must be revealed and extricated. A thorough examination of conscience was essential. She had begun to feel sorrow—grief—about so much that had taken place. Esther knew that reviewing in depth all that had transpired, everything inflicted upon her would need to be disclosed. Not least of which was an admission of her treatment of others, most especially Abraham, but not leaving out Tova, Miriam, and Zami. Absolution might not be possible, but the weight of this history must be released.

Only now, Esther began to understand there were actions—her actions and her choices—that many would consider sins—perhaps venial, but transgressions nonetheless. These must be unbound in order to advance to this most important part of the passage with clarity of consciousness.

Still, while candid in all aspects of her narration, the fixation that had propelled her life's direction for these past two decades was omitted. For this was the one pivotal element of the story Esther could not rationalize, the facts she could not provide—the one question she, herself, could not answer:

Why India?

What necessity propelled the venture to this country, and why now? What was the motivation for traveling to India? The requisite that overpowered her?

The fundament was not conveyed, because no answer or reason or justification existed. As Esther herself did not comprehend the why, how could she possibly explain it to another? All that was known with certainty was the truth this place existed and that it had remained the central motivating factor continually supporting her. It likely accounted for her very survival.

Better to leave this part unsaid, Esther thought.

So she did not disclose her curious encounter with the Indian food stand four months after moving to Köln. So many, many years ago. Nor her inexplicable reaction.

Separate from this one part of her story, no matter how crucial, Esther asked herself: why now, why here, and most especially—why this man? She had never conceived the recipient of her telling would be a stranger during this ship's passage. Nevertheless, when the words and images and experiences had tumbled forth, an all-embracing relief suffused her.

Esther could not deny there was something oddly familiar about this man—primarily his eyes and those aristocratic features predominated by his striking nose. Inexplicably, she never gave thought to the language in which she spoke nor the language this man conversed in. Only acknowledging that by some means, improbable or otherwise, it was one and the same.

For an instant, Esther's thoughts flashed back to her fever-induced encounter at the trip's onset but shook the image away as purely one of fantasy at play. No matter what had taken place, this man was here. The experience was real, and he was paying close attention to her every word.

This feeling was followed by a peculiar, surprising thought. Perhaps borne of those many years in hiding. Thus compelled, Esther asked, "Excuse me. I'm not sure why I'm asking this. And I'm definitely not sure why I'm even thinking this, but—are you a priest?"

The sides of Marco's mouth turned up, just a little on each corner, his eyes widened and grew round, and his face became covered by a crimson blush. He replied, "Why . . . yes . . . yes . . . I am."

Expressing apology, he smiled sheepishly and said, "Ah. . . *mea maxima culpa.* I hope you understand . . . I am not hiding my identity . . . this is not something to hide. It is only easier . . . much . . . much easier . . . to travel like this . . . to cover a great distance without separating myself out . . . without distinguishing myself from others. I hope you are not offended?"

Esther shook her head. Now she was the amused one.

Marco continued, "Please know . . . please do understand . . . I have been listening as a friend and only as a friend . . . a confidant if you will. I do not believe it is an accident I am here with you . . . a mere coincidence. I do not believe in such things. But also . . . you must know I am not here to grant you absolution or penance for any of your past decisions or actions. I appreciate you are not Catholic.

"However . . . I do realize . . . derived from what you have shared, that you are well schooled in the ways and the rites of the Catholic religion . . . and the Catholic Church . . . perhaps more than of the Jewish faith. I also recognize . . . and respect . . . this has been a survival technique . . . a genius one, in fact . . . rather than an acceptance or an embracing of a faith or way of life.

"I am sure you are familiar with the concept that sin can be considered a tie . . . a bondage of the spirit. And confession . . . or more simply . . . the telling of one's tale as you have done. Sharing with me . . . your story . . . experiences . . . of what took place . . . is . . . has been an untying of those bonds that held you for so very long.

"Please know that it has been my honor . . . it is my honor . . . my privilege to be the vessel by which you could release what you have held on to for these far too many years. Again I say . . . it is not an accident that I am here with you. I believe it has been intended that I would be here . . . now . . . for you.

"And," Marco continued, eyes twinkling, "it is important to me that you understand . . . I am one of the truehearted . . . in no way one of the uncaring . . . indifferent priests that I know you must have encountered. No . . . of my kind . . . I am among the impartial and open-minded . . . the most benevolent." Then he laughed and laughed.

"But I digress . . .

"Destiny . . . if you will. Fate. Providence. Other words that could be used . . . they all mean the same. This is our destiny. There is destiny in all things . . . the purpose for which somebody or something is intended . . . the place to which one is going . . . or is directed to go. Destiny is the ultimate purpose for which something is created or intended. And . . . destiny only ensues when one releases the fears of fate . . . the fears of what might happen."

I believe Marco is the one person who can comprehend to the full extent of his being what occurred at that food stand many years before, Esther thought. Perhaps he will be able to explain what has been to me an unexplainable draw to this country—to India.

She was on the verge of recounting her tale's one missing piece and responding to everything he had just said when a glimpse of land was caught out of the barest corner of one eye. Abruptly, Esther turned and ran to the bow of the ship.

The day was heading into twilight, as was her journey.

Through the dusk, Esther strained her eyes to make out shapes or forms. She had anticipated this moment for so long—envisioned what it would be like, what this place would be like. In a world that had savagely stolen any possibility of dreams and hopes—in a reality where suffering and horrors had become the norm—Esther had clung to this miniscule fantasy of elsewhere and all the prospects it could hold. All the possibilities she was sure it would hold. The draw or motivation for coming here remained elusive, only the necessity had penetrated. The clarity this direction must be taken.

Marco followed her to the bow, remaining at a respectful distance. He intuited the power of this moment and his role to come.

As *L'Étoile*'s engines slowed and the ship glided closer to port, Esther began to discern images. An imposing arched structure came into focus first. It appeared to be the target toward which the ship was aimed. Adjacent, to its left, was a massive multistoried building. Other smaller structures bordered these.

Motion forward. They drew nearer to the dock, and Esther began taking in details: a fortress-like structure, tall buildings, heavy concrete, carvings, wrought iron, paned glass windows.

No! Esther thought. There's something wrong. This is wrong. This is completely wrong! Everything is familiar looking. Too familiar. Almost recognizable.

The view before her revealed the edge of a city just like those in Europe. Exactly like cities she had left behind. Like the life she desired to leave behind.

Esther had traveled halfway around the globe—such a long way in distance and turmoil—only to arrive at a place indistinguishable from every location she had ever been.

She saw none of the vibrancy—the brilliance—the joyous cacophony of texture, shape, and color that had spoken to her senses and lured her to explore the makeshift stand on that long-ago evening in Köln. And there were none of the images of man, woman, or beast that had captured her soul. Not a hint of the magical, mystical draw. None of any of it. Anywhere.

Her thoughts raced—

What have I done? What was I thinking? How far did I have to run only to find myself in the very same place?

Without warning, Esther felt heavy, lost, baffled. The full weight of history bore its anguish and force down upon her. Turning toward Marco, she descended into his eyes full on and crumbled onto the ship's deck.

CHAPTER FORTY-THREE

The land is vast . . . and layered.
Encrusted with history.
Interwoven with spirit and deities, ritual and language . . .
Melded with truth and illusion, desire and despair.
Incongruent strata of color and texture
and sound and emotion:
silk on rag, gossamer on muslin, clear glass on cement,
fine crystal on jagged rock,
jewel on cow dung.
Riches beyond imagination; poverty of extreme proportion.
Human beings swaddled in luxury without care or want . . .
Straddling those with dismembered limbs,
disfigured bodies, leprosy, polio—
begging, pleading, imploring, tugging, following . . .
Stomachs empty, hands outstretched,
mouths open, eyes vacant.
Parts of this terrain are exceptionally raw, rough and exposed . . .
Other areas finely formed, molded and highly polished.
From all facets, it is a mirror from which your soul cannot hide.

. . . .

The smelling salts provided by the ship's doctor revived Esther, although she remained unsteady in equilibrium and thought. The delicate confidence gained over these past few hours, now gone.

"Do you . . . feel better?" Marco asked. "I do not understand. What happened?"

Esther could not respond with words, for the answers were not forthcoming from within. So she simply shrugged off the questions, avoiding his gaze by focusing on a weatherworn floorboard. Yet every so often, glancing toward the rapidly approaching port, her lips quivered and her chest restrained the ache that kept her heart at bay.

Esther did possess enough presence of mind to hand Marco the white slip of paper protected in her brassiere throughout the journey.

"Please, can you help get me to this place?" she appealed.

Marco unfolded the paper and saw written in decisive block letters the name and address of Bombay's Keneseth Eliyahoo Synagogue. The Zürich travel agent had provided this information. Concerned about Esther's safety and reasoning, most especially spurred by her inability to explain why travel to this most foreign of lands was of essential importance, the agent had done extensive research on lodging possibilities. He felt fortunate to have located what appeared to be a rational stopping place where perhaps this peculiar woman could get her bearings.

What better location but a synagogue for a Jewish woman alone in an unwieldy alien city? he had surmised. The rest must be up to her.

Esther had expressed appreciation for this extra effort, not having considered what would happen upon arrival in Bombay. It was the getting there that had absorbed her attention. Not what would take place from there and onward.

After the ship docked and bags were retrieved from their respective cabins, Marco gently guided Esther toward and then through the central arch of the stately Gateway of India. Midway, she stopped to gain a sense of its grandeur. The apex, at nearly eighty-five feet, soared above her tiny frame; the yellow Kharodi basalt and reinforced concrete enfolded her. Esther took a full inhale and, for one final time, turned and looked behind her, back at the ship, and the sea, and from whence she had come. In swift motion she relived all that had taken place. Then, with another, more cavernous inhale, she turned toward what was to come and moved through to the arch's opposite side. There she found throngs of people milling about on the esplanade.

"This way . . . this way . . ." Marco repeated loudly to ensure being heard above the din. Esther walked closely beside him, awed by the sizable crowd gathered all around. A mass of humanity, one indistinguishable from the next, encircled them.

They crossed the wide boulevard and headed toward an immense building.

"The famed Taj Mahal Palace Hotel," Marco announced, as though leading a tour.

This was the imposing structure Esther had seen from the sea that had sent shockwaves throughout her being. The potency of this place's European milieu remained disquieting. This area looks so much like many parts of downtown Köln or, even more so, Paris's business district.

Is this in actuality another place? Esther wondered. Is this what I have hoped for? Yearned for? How can my desired elsewhere be the same as everywhere? Is there even really an elsewhere—anywhere?

To her surprise, they did not enter the building. Instead, with Marco's direction, they turned the first corner. There stood a taxi stand and a block-long reach of compact black-and-yellow cabs in wait for fares, like bees in procession for nectar. For reasons Esther did not understand, Marco knew this city intimately.

His knowledge and ease made Esther more curious about this man, his history, and the reasons that brought him to this country. What implores him to return again and again? she wondered. Clearly, this is not his first visit.

But that conversation would have to wait. Little reserve energy remained for anything but sitting and looking and beginning to digest these new but uncomfortably common surroundings.

Marco slid into the backseat beside her. With the white sheet of paper in hand, he instructed the driver: "Please take us to this address—*Kripia humko iss pate pur lay chalaye. Sidhe aur Sambhal kar chalaye!* Drive directly. And carefully!"

This request was relayed in a singsong parlance distinct from any language Esther had heard before. Her interest mounted, but once more, any inquiry had to wait.

No words passed between the two during the drive. As the taxi drove on, Esther gazed out the window and took in the passing environment much as one would a slow-moving zoetrope. The structure of the buildings was, indeed, familiar. So her eyes strained to locate street signs or landmarks that were also recognizable. The city was dense; building jutted up against building up against building. European-style structures, some staid, others exquisite and regal, filled her view, as did a formal street plan and concrete sidewalks lined with storefronts. The people in view dressed in uninteresting, austerely styled suits and dresses. It was disconcerting—and disheartening.

"What have I done?" Esther mumbled under her breath, head shaking. "What have I done?"

They had barely traversed one full block when—the yearned for component—a subtle richness and vitality of color began to peek out between the far too recognizable buildings and along their edges. It became evident not everything was as first appeared.

Continuing one more block, the background's predominance of grays and browns began to unfurl. Like a multilayered quilt, divulging a deep, encrusted history that had been hidden at the port.

Color—rich, luminous, luscious, and occasionally garish color—became evident everywhere. It flowed out of windows and onto sidewalks. Graceful, raven-haired women—with thin bands of gold and jewels around their necks and through their ear lobes and pierced through one nostril—wore long flowing skirts woven with metallic threads and matching scarves echoing the seven colors in a rainbow and beyond. Vendors lined the streets, selling clothes made of fabrics like the ones seen at her exigent stand in Köln—cloths woven with mirrored glass, with fringe and sequins, beads and ribbons—others selling toys and dolls or books or baskets.

Large tubs spilling over with spices bordered a few storefronts.

When the taxi passed by these, a heat mixed with a subtle breeze of turmeric and cardamom wafted over her. In an instant, Esther began to savor, once more, the aroma and consciousness of purpose that had emanated from the rickety stand on that long-ago day, consuming her being.

Ah, she thought. Then—she beamed.

She observed the environs more and more closely. She became aware of signs, large and small, over doorways and on buildings and at street corners. Their beauty took her breath away. Esther understood these were written in some type of Indian lettering—she had seen similar things in the library book—although she could not find a relationship to any alphabet seen before. While there was no way to divine the meaning, the script emulated the most elegant, delicate embroidery. The beautiful flowing characters, each a unique symbol, captivated her. She envisioned creating tablecloths, napkins, or pillowcases with such graceful borders.

I must ask Marco about this, she reflected. There is so much—

Esther's streaming thoughts were cut off midstream as the taxi came to a screeching halt in the middle of the road. She looked around to see what happened but didn't locate a stop sign or pedestrian. Then a loud "moo" caught her off guard. A cow ambled across the street and their path. A second and then a third followed the first.

Marco turned to her. He smiled knowingly—and with amusement.

After that encounter, Esther saw cows everywhere. They dominated the streets and sidewalks and walkways—when there were sidewalks and walkways. This was an urban setting, no farmland or barns anywhere to be seen, yet these creatures seemed to wander without restraint or care.

Where are the farmers? Who owns these cows? This is something else I must ask Marco about, she mused.

Esther looked inside the car and noticed the driver's dashboard was covered with statuettes. A four-armed woman dressed in red sat cross-legged on a flower bed, and another four-armed figure, this one a man, painted all in blue, stood beside her. A third figure, all in gold, appeared to be dancing. Dangling from the mirror was a form with more arms than she could easily count. These were similar to the images she had seen in the Köln stand. However, there was not one of the elephant-headed man to whom she had been most drawn. Esther felt disappointed, but catching the driver's face in his rearview mirror took her aback. A joyous expression of content met her gaze. A light shone from his eyes.

"Curious, so curious," Esther whispered under her breath.

Turning her attention once more to the activities on the street, she noticed bizarre-looking men, sitting cross-legged against a tree, leaning against a wall, or walking slowly, either singly or in pairs. Long, thick locks, often flowing past their waists, covered these men's heads. Their bones seemed to extend beyond their skin. Mostly barefoot, some wore skimpy cloths, while others were swathed to their toes. Every man wore the same ochre-colored material. In all cases the exposed parts of their bodies were covered in what appeared to be ash. A few had decorated their faces with bold yellow and red paint.

"They are *sadhus*," Marco said, as though she had spoken this question and none of her earlier ones aloud. "Renunciates . . . holy men." He smiled broadly.

The driver made a sharp left and took them away from what had appeared to be a major thoroughfare. He turned right twice. Each turn took them on to smaller and narrower and bumpier and dirtier streets. He made one more left, and they came to a stop in front of a striking sky-blue-colored building. Three stories tall and delicately ornate, it was built in a traditional European style with highly detailed arched windows. The sign over the central window included the lovely embroidery-like script but also announced in Hebrew letters the synagogue's name.

It's exactly like a beautifully decorated wedding cake with layer upon layer of white frosting, Esther thought.

Speaking that unusual language again, Marco appeared to ask the cab driver to wait, came around to open the door, and walked Esther to the gated front entrance. A woman, in a long flowing dress and scarf identical to the color of the building's exterior, let them in. Her welcoming *"shalom"* echoed throughout the entryway. She beamed at Marco.

"I leave you in good hands," Marco said with his gracious smile, nodding in the direction of this woman.

Of course, thought Esther, they know one another. Nothing should surprise me with this man.

Before he turned to leave, Marco said, "If I may . . . I would like to take you . . . on an exploration tomorrow. I believe this adventure will please you. Would you be available?" Knowing full well she had no plans.

"You will be able to explore Bombay . . . at another time . . . in other ways."

The next morning Marco arrived promptly at nine, exactly when promised. Esther was waiting for him in the entryway on the narrow wooden bench, below the rustic balustrades and rich chandeliers, staged for this purpose. The pillars that bordered the room were nearly as colorful as the building's façade. She stood outside the sanctuary, where the congregation of fifteen or sixteen people had gathered for the daily recital of morning prayer. While she had been waiting for him to appear, Esther tried to pay attention to the service, but the runaway thoughts in her own head were loud and disjointed.

"Good morning . . . Good morning," he said jovially. "You are well?"

"Yes, thank you. I'm fine. I went to sleep immediately after I was taken to my room. I didn't realize how thoroughly exhausted I was. I only awoke a short while ago. I did have some breakfast. Not surprisingly, I'm disoriented. Although I must admit, for the first time since I was quite young, I'm feeling excited. This is such an adventure—a wonderful adventure. I'm finally feeling as though this is where I am meant to be. The reasons still elude me, but—"

"Perhaps today will provide . . . clarity," Marco responded. "Please . . . it is time we begin."

Heading toward the front door, they left just as the congregation recited the conclusion of their morning prayer.

Ani ma'amin,
be'emuno shleymo
Bevias hamoshiach, ani ma'amin
Bevias hamoshiach, ma'amin ani.
Bevias hamoshiach, ani ma'amin
Bevias hamoshiach, ma'amin ani.

Ve'af al pi sheyismahmeha
im kol zeh achakeh lo
ve'af al pi sheyismahmeha
im kol zeh achakeh lo
im kol zeh, im kol zeh, achakeh lo
achakeh lo bechol yom sheyavo
im kol zeh, im kol zeh, achakeh lo
achakeh lo bechol yom sheyavo.

. . . .

I believe
With perfect faith
In the coming of the messiah, I believe
I believe in the coming of the messiah
In the coming of the messiah, I believe
I believe in the coming of the messiah

And even though he may be delayed
Yet, still, I shall wait for him
And even though he may be delayed
Yet, still, I shall wait for him
Yet still, yet still, I shall wait for him
I shall wait every day for him to come
Yet still, yet still, I shall wait for him
I shall wait every day for him to come

Marco smiled. Ah, he thought, it is the *Ani Ma'amin* . . . a song of ultimate faith . . . of course . . . how fitting.

Without question . . . it is time . . .

CHAPTER FORTY-FOUR

Neti . . .
Neti . . .
Neti . . .
Not this . . . Not that . . . Not the other.

....

"Ah . . . yes . . ." Marco continued, "I knew love once. I did." Marco was seated behind the wheel of a small-sized, rather sleek black car devoid of icons or images save for a strand of prayer beads made from 108 *Rudraksha* seeds draped over the rearview mirror. The rosary held an unadorned, four-inch wooden cross and a much smaller, intricately carved sandstone mouse.

"A mouse," Esther queried, "how odd."

Marco merely smiled.

They had been driving for more than two hours when Esther finally broached the subject of his priesthood. Curiosity about him had taken reign, and she wanted to learn how Marco had come to follow that path.

At the beginning of the drive, Esther had been fully engrossed, looking at everything and absorbing as much as she could. She was fascinated by these most unusual surroundings. Everything was fresh and novel and different and astonishing. But instead of trying to discover more about the outside and what she was seeing or where they were heading, Esther asked Marco about Marco.

He said, "There is no question it was the kind of love . . . like what you described . . . what you shared with this man . . . with Tadeusz. It was . . . yes . . . a love unlike what most people experience in a lifetime . . . in many lifetimes . . . ."

At the mention of other lifetimes, Esther quickly turned her head toward him, quizzical. But she did not wish to interrupt. Most definitely, it was a question that must be set aside for later. She knew little about the lives of Catholic priests, and this revelation of a love and a passion fascinated her.

"This . . . I know . . . Of this I am in no doubt," he continued.

"Ah . . . Maria Elena . . . my beautiful . . . beautiful Maria Elena. *Cara mia* . . . she brought me such joy. She did. We had known one another since we were young . . . merely children. Since . . . what seemed to be the beginning of time . . . our time.

"There was never a question . . . neither by her nor by me . . . no . . . no . . . not then . . . that we would be together . . . always. For those years we were together . . . since the moment we met . . . we were each other's other half . . . the half completing the whole. The one that could finish sentences. The one who understood the other's thoughts . . . and very being.

"Such a glorious gift we had. And we both recognized . . . fully . . . that this was the greatest gift one can be presented within a lifetime . . . in any lifetime."

Esther's eyes widened.

"But . . . and this is such a huge . . . and remains . . . a genuinely wrenching . . . but . . . my needs . . . they changed . . . and my desires . . . grew expansive. No . . . no . . . I hear what you are thinking. No . . . not for the knowledge and the taste of another woman . . . or any woman.

"It was never about someone else. There has never been . . . nor could there ever be . . . another woman.

"It was the questions that began to possess me . . . questions that started to consume me. Everything became about questions . . .

and always questions seemingly without answers. These questions began to dominate me . . . pounding questions . . . of the unknowns . . . of here and now . . . and then . . . what? What then? And the whys. The fragility and elusiveness of life and . . . what began to appear as the mere illusion of life.

"The irrational always seeming to supersede the rational."

Marco inhaled deeply. "And . . . at that time . . . when it became evident the only thing clear to me was that nothing was lucid. Well . . . then . . . I knew I had to leave. Leave Maria Elena and everything we had known and shared and all we had meant to one another. It was no longer enough. She was no longer enough.

"No one person . . . even this person . . . this most significant person . . . was enough.

"I have come to understand . . . and of this I am confident . . . individuals have different paths to follow . . . and they must be responsive and respectful of their true nature. For us . . . for each of us in this life . . . there is not one . . . not just one particular way . . . the correct way . . . the only way . . . to follow . . . to pursue . . . to live. There is not just the Catholic way or the Jewish way or the path of the Hindu or Muslim . . . or . . . it goes on and on. There are many paths. They are all correct and all so beautiful. Each individual must follow his . . . or her . . . own way . . . toward our own truth… whatever this happens to be. And wherever this happens to take us. Even if it leads . . . seemingly . . . away from the person we hold most dear.

"It is important . . . so very important . . . to understand we are all . . . every one of us . . . on the same course heading in the same direction . . . just . . . perhaps . . . doing things a little differently . . . or even very differently . . . from one another. But for the most part . . . and this is so true . . . very much . . . each wanting the same things . . . no matter what we call it or no matter why we call it what we do.

"Ah . . . look around you. While much seems different and unusual . . . there are countless links between this culture and ours. Many connections . . . similarities . . . they are just not perhaps on the surface. There is much that is the same although much appears so very unusual . . . in any case . . . on the outside . . . or from the outset . . . at first impression. However . . . you must understand . . . this is only on the surface . . . and this surface is an illusion. And must be understood as only an illusion.

"Yet so sadly . . . so sadly indeed . . . there are too many . . . far too many . . . humans who believe that one way . . . their way . . . is the only way . . . is better than another. This I have never understood . . . as it is the same . . . we are all really the same. Just . . . perhaps . . . just a little bit different."

Marco sighed and turned to look at Esther—a fleeting sadness moved across his eyes.

"Ah . . . but I digress . . . I apologize . . . we were speaking of Maria Elena. *Il mio amore, la mia* Maria Elena . . . and me.

"I believe . . . I must acknowledge that not unlike your Tadeusz . . . who for a different reason . . . for another very different reason most definitely . . . left you . . . and devastated you more profoundly than can be articulated. I . . . too . . . hurt Maria Elena beyond measure. I shattered a belief and a knowledge she knew to be true. For this I still have profound regret . . . and sorrow.

"Yet I could not look back. I know I was called to this vocation . . . this is my fate. When this certainty became apparent to me . . . I moved to Rome and entered the seminary. I knew I must follow this path. I knew my life was to be one of service."

Marco turned and looked at Esther full on, almost falling into her eyes, and said, "I am here . . . now . . . at your service."

Heading further and further away from Bombay, they traveled the next hour or so in silence. Marco's thoughts were peregrine; Esther churned every syllable of what this man had said, grasping all too intimately Maria Elena's plight. Her heart went out to this woman she had never known but understood fully. Esther thought, too, of Sacha, back in Leiden, and wondered if she would ever find a way to recover from her wrenching loss of Claes.

The vast sum of new information to digest made her head throb. This, coupled with the steady, albeit bumpy, motion of the car, persuaded Esther to close her eyes and doze for short bouts. At these times, she imagined the ride grew smoother and a good deal faster, almost as though the car had taken flight to soar through the air.

During one of these periods, she roused to Marco speaking. Esther thought she heard him say, "Ah . . . Krauncha . . . *mushika* . . . my dear mouse . . . slowly . . . ever more slowly, please. Do not forget we have a precious passenger. . ."

"Pardon? Did you say something to me?" Esther asked.

Marco smiled his widest smile and emitted his heartiest laugh. "No . . . no . . . please excuse me for waking you."

Esther shrugged and closed her eyes once again. Questioning any aspect of this journey, its purpose or destination, did not seem necessary. It was apparent Marco was directed—on all levels. He drove without maps or compass, only with an abundance of persuasiveness impossible to ignore. Confident that where they were headed was a place she must see. An experience Esther had to undertake.

The last day on the ship, Marco had wholly won her confidence—heretofore an impossible feat. In truth, he had reawakened the trust buried on her fated wedding day long ago. If nothing else, Esther knew Marco's instincts were strong, his intentions virtuous, and their connection beyond explanation.

The route they traveled was one of gravel, dust, and ruts, with barely a dedicated lane available for each direction. Often the road would seem to disappear, no markings visible. Then everyone would fend for himself, larger vehicles dominating those of smaller dimensions. Marco constantly zigged and zagged to avoid potholes and people—men, women, and children, most seemingly of an age far too young to be alone, attempting to cross or walking alongside the road; men pulling two-wheeled carts packed to overflowing; people of differing sizes and shapes on two- or three-wheeled bicycles; and men and women balancing astonishingly bulky boxes or baskets or outsized pieces of wood or loads of bricks on the top of their heads or shoulders, like one might expect to see in a circus act. There were trucks and taxis and cows—many, many cows—wandering, by the looks of it, without caretaker or directed route—dogs, pigs, sheep, goats, chickens, and the occasional elephant ridden by men dressed entirely in white topped by bright headdresses—beautifully adorned elephants, canvases of marvelously painted faces and bodies, the likes of which Esther had never seen in the Wuppertal zoo.

With cloudless sky and the sun stalwart in one position, distance seemed impervious to time. It was not possible to establish how long they had been gone or how far they had traveled.

"Don't we need to stop for petrol," Esther asked after she spied what appeared to be another location for acquiring this requisite fluid just ahead on the road. Although not like petrol stations in Europe, these were demarcated areas that hosted large barrels with glass bottles and attached hand pumps. The one they neared had a small boy pushing, pulling, and jumping up and down. His full weight forced on a pump with a long hose connected to a standing automobile.

"Ah . . . we are fine . . . really . . ." responded Marco smiling. "Nothing to be concerned with. Please . . . enjoy the journey."

As a driver, Marco was skilled and attentive to the road's curious demands, but that fact did not engender the possibility of a truly pleasant or relaxing ride. Although Esther continued to doze off now and again, the heat, coupled with persistent humidity, was nearly unbearable. A thick mixture of dung and dirt hung in the air, blanketing everything. The fumes from the car endeavored to make Esther nauseous. Fortunately, the continual forward motion, steady or otherwise, generated a slight breeze that helped alleviate the symptoms.

At one point along the way, Marco turned to Esther and said, "In India you need only five things to be a most excellent driver: good heart . . . good brakes . . . good eyes . . . good luck . . . of course . . . and a good horn!"

With this, he threw his head back and laughed uproariously, eyes aglow with a mischievous crinkle.

Wide expanses of sandy brown jutted up against an equally vast hazy blue. The mostly barren landscape did accommodate tumbleweeds and bushes. The sporadic stunted tree filled out the vista in motion outside the car's windows. This scenery seemed to continue for kilometer upon kilometer. No substantial natural shelter could be seen, and no bodies of water. They had arrived in a desert of consequence, and as if on cue, Marco announced, "We have entered the great Thar Desert."

The landscape was mostly flat with the interruption of an occasional hillock. Every now and again, alongside the road or by a shrub or a tree or out in the middle of the distance, bright pockets of color would catch Esther's eye. Squinting tightly, a small-scale statue could be made out in a solitary stance or with two or more similar figures. Sometimes they were wrapped with ribbon in multicolored fabric in a robe-like fashion.

These seem to be more of those unusual images or icons I've seen everywhere, Esther mused.

Accompanying these statues were large and small piles of varying-sized stones layered upon one another. Often there would be flowers, solitary stems or bouquets. All dried to a crisp. Usually, parchment was attached to one or more of the figures with the graceful, embroidery-like script clearly visible on them.

These are like altars seen in every corner of a church, Esther thought, but to what—or whom? She could not begin to fathom their meaning.

Camels frequently appeared along their path, on occasion attempting to cross the road, thus ensuring Marco drove at a slow speed, at times almost a walking pace. Many of these regal animals had riders atop their pronounced humps. Or she observed one or two men walking to one side, taking care that the excessive loads carried on the camel's back did not come crashing down.

Every few kilometers, they passed what were most likely small villages, not more than a hundred yards or so from the road. But to call them "villages" was no doubt overstating, as these were merely groupings of three or four makeshift buildings. Now and then a tarpaulin or two would be staked into the ground, here or there, providing a modicum of protection from the merciless sun. There were always men—many men—all bearded, garbed in loose-fitting monochromatic clothes, with brightly colored cloths wrapped around their heads. Most often she noticed them lounging alone or talking in a group; sometimes one could be seen digging in the dirt.

But the women! Every woman she espied was hard at work—sweeping, tending fires, beating carpets and rugs, cooking, washing. A myriad of tasks, and always, it seemed, while nursing babies. It felt intimate and familiar to Esther's own experience many years before, although—different.

No matter how poor the area otherwise appeared, these women were dressed in dazzling textiles of patterns, textures, and colors—each wearing layers of three or four different materials that should have appeared discordant but, for reasons that eluded Esther, made perfect sense in this setting. These striking cloths covered heads and reached to toes.

Each woman wore at least one gold ring in a single nostril, usually the right side, dangling gold earrings, and one, two, or more strands of gold or multicolored beads around their necks, hugging throats or hanging down to waists. Without exception, one large red dot rested between their eyes.

My clothes are far too dull for here, Esther thought, looking down at her faded blue dress. When I have the chance, I must do something about this. It will be such fun to work with these colorful fabrics.

Then again, with her head shaking slowly and reflectively, thoughts drifting, Esther considered: Perhaps it's not my clothes at all. More likely, it is my skin itself that no longer fits me. I don't know when I've felt as though I were myself, that I owned myself—the self I was once and long to be again. This skin that covers me now is like an ill-fitting cloth, stretched far too tightly, painfully, across my chest and back. Yet, it sags around my ankles, droops at my knees, makes swooshing noises when I walk. Like a pair of exhausted overalls or a houseguest who has long outstayed her welcome.

And the skin on my face, which should shield and protect, well—it is not that it's aged or wrinkled, merely no longer familiar. The face I gaze at in a mirror does not reflect its true occupant. I must be honest with myself, Esther pondered, for really—truly—who the occupant is remains unknown.

This progression has not been as graceful as a snake that unhurriedly and deliberately slithers out of the old, the worn, like an ancient relic of an earlier civilization. No, this conversion has been a war, with countless battlegrounds and the resistance, my resistance, holding strong. On the surface anyway, the struggles are over; the arms put aside. The fields cleared and vistas arising anew.

What now stands between me—and me? Esther wondered.

What blocks the way to clarity and tomorrow?

When he glanced over and noticed how quiet and pensive Esther had become, Marco nudged her. He shared a warm, embracing smile as though he had heard the thoughts within her mind.

This man brought her back to the here and now, and Esther returned her attention to outward observations. She did her best to thoroughly digest everything she saw—continually looking. Not wanting to miss anything. In awe of these surroundings. So much was not easily comprehensible. Many questions remained to be asked.

"Ah . . . now . . . is the time for a bit of a rest," Marco said, leading the car off the road. Just to the side of the road, that is. No distinguishing signs announced a parking place or resting spot. No markers were represented.

When they finally came to a stop, Esther stepped outside to stretch her legs. She breathed deeply of the acrid and smoky dung-filled air and took in a 360-degree view of the setting. From what she could tell, there was no identifiable difference in this location from any of the views outside the car window these past many hours.

"Would you like some water?" Marco asked, handing Esther a canteen.

Marco had also brought what he called refreshments. Esther had to smile, for there was nothing of substance, just an assortment of cookies.

So childlike, she thought, but endearing.

"Please," he said with his now familiar broad smile. "Take one . . . or two . . . if you like. I am so very fond . . . of cookies."

"Do you miss her?" Esther asked.

Back on the road once more, her interest returned to their earlier conversation, a topic of precedence over the myriad questions about place and locale.

"Do you ever think of her, dream of her? Imagine what your life might have been like if you had taken the other path—if you had married her?"

"*Ma, fammi pensare* . . . Ah . . . I have to be honest . . ." Marco replied. "I do think of Maria Elena . . . and more often . . . than I probably wish to admit to myself." Marco's face expanded, deep smile intact. This time with a pensive breath.

"I think of her warm lush laugh . . . and the way her head would toss when she spoke . . . and those thick black curls that bounced off her shoulders with verve.

"I recall . . . vividly . . . her fixed curious gaze when she listened intently . . . and the many times . . . nearly every evening . . . when we would take long walks into the hills beyond our village and talk . . . talk about everything. But most especially when we discussed all the questions . . . 'the whys' and the 'for what reasons' and the 'I do not understands' of this world.

"Always . . . however . . . with no answers. Never any valid answers . . . in any case . . . not the answers I would ultimately seek. But we would talk for hours into the night . . . wondering . . . brainstorming . . . pondering . . . exploring . . . and grappling . . . always grappling . . . trying so hard to comprehend . . . absolutely everything.

"And as I say all this now . . . I realize Maria Elena . . . *il mio amore*. . . my beloved . . . truly . . . my other half . . . was the instigator . . . the igniter of this spark within me. This spark that would not lie dormant and simply smolder.

"I do not ponder . . . what if . . . for I had no choice . . . of this I am sure. I am clear of my purpose . . . my fate. Yet . . . I know . . . Maria Elena lives within me . . . always. One's beloved . . . one's immortal beloved never leaves. Whether this person is with you physically or not. No matter what occurs. No matter what takes place . . . on this . . . the physical plane. Regardless of how your story unfolds . . . this person remains with you for all time."

Marco turned and took in Esther's presence full on. "I believe . . . beyond question . . . you have been blessed to know what I am saying . . . and do understand this to the depth of your soul."

Esther froze as she realized he was speaking of Tadeusz. And, too, of her failure to come to peace with him, at long last forgive his actions borne of fear and immaturity. Uncertain how to respond, she remained quiet.

"Ah . . . and here . . . we have arrived," Marco said a few minutes later. He turned the key in the ignition to its off position.

Absorbed by Marco's comments, Esther had not noticed they had left the main road behind and driven into a desolate area. The setting was not unlike much of the land they had already traversed; there were no defined markings, signs, or structures. They were parked in a site more akin to the middle of nowhere than a desired destination. A few large bushes were scattered about, and a knoll could be seen in the near distance. No people or even animals could be found.

Marco, already out of the car, was rummaging in the boot. Holding a pair of dark blue pants made of thick denim and a pair of hiking boots, he came up to her and said, "Your dress has long sleeves . . . this is good . . . but the bottom is not right. Here . . . these are for you. I am sure they will fit. Please put these pants on under your dress."

Esther looked at him, dumbstruck. "What do I need those for? Where are we going?"

"Ah . . . my dear Esther . . ." Marco smiled broadly. "The adventure . . . only now begins."

CHAPTER FORTY-FIVE

Traveling to the core...
You (re-)
discover your center...
And all that has been...
lost...
forgotten...
or
cast aside.

....

The pants and boots fit perfectly, as though she had been seamstress and Abraham cobbler, using her feet as the mold. Esther tried not to be astonished. By this stage of the journey's progression, nothing about the experience or Marco should cause surprise.

All the same, Esther admitted to herself she was.

How could this be? she thought. How could any of this possibly be?

If she were to honestly reflect on her own actions of the past few months, they would be cause for wonder. The motivations that guided the course remained mystifying. Traveling to India without plan, direction, or guidance, let alone reason or rationale, could be summed up simplistically as the desire for escape—to flee past and painful history. Arrival in this country was solely due to intrepid impulse. After so many years of taking full command of everything and everyone, Esther was only now beginning to feel a release—a joyful liberation. This seemed to come about by relinquishing all responsibilities and giving herself over to this man she barely knew yet trusted more implicitly than any other.

Any other since Tadeusz. By some mysterious means, Marco alone had been able to melt her obdurate resistance.

And here, in what must be considered absolutely nowhere and the center of nil, Esther had followed him to a place indefinite and unconceived. Maybe they were traversing a westerly route or perhaps toward the north. This was not of import, as it was the midst of the vastest of deserts without path or guidepost. Only confident trust existed that this was the exact—and only—place to be.

Marco headed toward an extraordinary tree that grew beside the knoll. Eighteen meters tall with a massive trunk, it was covered in a halo of beautiful white flowers. Enchanting elongated pods, perhaps three centimeters long, grew out of many leaves. Esther had never seen anything like it.

This tree looks as though it has come from one of Miriam's fairytale books, she thought. It seems much more likely to be born from someone's imagination than to grow naturally from the earth.

As she ventured closer, a beguiling aroma encircled her.

"Ah . . . of course," Marco said, glancing back and noticing the quizzical look on Esther's face. "You have never seen a lebbeck tree . . . they do not exist in Europe. They are regal beings . . . do you not think? With the utmost grace and dignity . . . they are calming and healing. Very useful healers . . . the bark and the leaves . . . as well as the fruit. And their oils are all of medicinal value for so many issues.

"Her other name . . . this lovely one . . . she is called woman's tongue tree because of the constant motion and sound of the leaves. Like women . . . constantly chattering. Well . . . this just makes me laugh. And . . . as I am sure you have observed . . . I very much like to laugh!"

He then let out one of those comforting yet comical guffaws.

"Ah . . . on a more serious note . . . it does remind me of a most wonderful poem about another special tree . . . the Gingko biloba. Quite different from the lebbeck . . . but equally remarkable."

Without hesitation, Marco recited:

Dieses Baums Blatt, der von Osten
Meinem Garten anvertraut,
Gibt geheimen Sinn zu kosten,
Wie's den Wissenden erbaut.

Ist es Ein lebendig Wesen,
Das sich in sich selbst getrennt?
Sind es zwei, die sich erlesen,
Dass man sie als eines kennt.

Solche Frage zu erwidern,
Fand ich wohl den rechten Sinn.
Fühlst du nicht in meinen Liedern,
Dass ich Eins und doppelt bin.

. . . .

Leaf of Eastern tree transplanted
Here into my garden's field,
Hast me secret meaning granted,
Which adepts delight will yield.

Art though one—one living being
Now divided into two?
Art though two, who joined agreeing
And in one united grew?

To this question, pondered duly,
Have I found the right reply:
In my poems you see truly
Twofold and yet one am I.

Marco's eloquent delivery enchanted Esther. What surprised her was that she felt delight, a long-absent emotion whose return she welcomed. She recognized aspects of herself were returning. Those parts that had been integral to who she knew herself to be from earliest memories. She closed her eyes and drank in these words and the poem's message.

"Have you heard this before?" Marco asked.

Esther shook her head. "No. I'm not familiar with much poetry. Really none at all."

"It was written by one of the most glorious . . . enlightened writers and thinkers of all time . . . of any time . . . Johann Wolfgang von Goethe. Most popularly known as . . . Goethe. One of the few . . . true . . . masters."

Marco sighed, contented. Again, his wide smile.

"I am and have always been . . . will always remain . . . the greatest champion of writers and scribes . . . in any and all ways that I am able."

A foot or so beyond the tree, slightly to its east, at the edge of the knoll where the ground began to rise sharply, Marco came to a stop. He gestured toward an area surrounded by scree. At first evaluation, it appeared to be a huge pile of rock fragments and nothing more. But then, over to one side, peeking through the debris, Esther spotted a statue, just like those she had often seen along the route. Barely half a meter in height, this one was wrapped in sheer yellow silk tied with a red ribbon.

Before she had the chance to finally ask about the purpose of these figures, she spotted an entry leading inside the mass of stone and heard Marco say, "This way . . . this way . . . please," while bending more than in half to fit through the roughly triangular opening. It was, perhaps, not even one meter at its apex.

"I can't possibly go inside there," Esther cried out. "You can't be serious!"

"This is fine," Marco responded, the all too familiar smile dominating his face. "Truly . . . this is the way. Please come with me. It is safe. You will come to no harm . . . of this I can assure you. This is truth."

Esther stood outside the threshold for three long minutes, attempting to comprehend what moving forward entailed. The lone word—truth—reverberating in her mind—spurred her on. Standing to full height, closed eyes accompanied by a long exhale, as though preparing for a cliff's dive into deep water. No other thought or reaction or feeling took dominance, only a sense of peace—an unanticipated, profound quiet—resonated from her depth.

Crouching down, she followed Marco. She felt no fear now, only slight trepidation as she watched the dim light abate with each step forward. The air itself deepened, its color—an intensifying palette of smoke to platinum, silver to ash to slate, then *feldgrau* to arsenic and, finally, charcoal. At eight steps inward, Esther heard water splash, and she wavered. Only for a second, though as it happened, the water at its deepest point was no higher than her ankles, and the boots kept all moisture out. She persisted, doing her best to keep pace with the guide ahead of her. At seventeen steps, the ground beneath her was again dry, the water's source not revealed. Here, Esther was glad to find she could stand to her full height. She found herself enfolded in complete darkness, every crevice, texture, and contrast absorbed by any visible wavelengths.

She inhaled the pitch black's cool air, reveling in the fact that in lieu of encountering a confining, claustrophobic environment, an embracing generous room now welcomed her. There was an unexpected lightness and a wondrous tranquility in this new situation.

But this space only provided a respite. There was further to go, more to be discovered.

Esther became conscious Marco was at least three arm's length ahead and knew she must stay near. He did not tell her where to step or place her hand for balance. She understood this instinctively. His movements were assured, with confidence and knowingness. At first her paces were small and careful. One slow, considered step at a time became a pattern, each echoing the one before. Toes to heel—heel to toes—diminutive toes to little heel—each succinct movement precise and purposeful. It was as though Esther were measuring the length of a room, but it was in actuality the length of a life. Her life.

Within the darkness, Esther became aware of every breath. There was no longer distraction. Barely even sound. Though the soles of their shoes were not rubber, stillness predominated. Her thoughts within were elevated and intensely acute.

No hiding here. No running. And no secrets, most especially from oneself.

It would be easy to consider that my presence here is completely irrational, Esther thought. But is it really any more so than places I've been during these past many years? When hiding was the means to ensure survival.

Esther's left hand ran along a pitted, spongelike, textured wall—ostensibly to steady her, but it was more like a new lover's caress of discovery. Gently. Carefully. Without benefit of sight, her other senses were elevated, and Esther studied the space around her. Breathing in cool. Hearing stillness. She felt that the ground beneath her feet was irregular, the path winding with a slight but consistent decline.

These walls of jagged stone resonated with the assured temperament of possibility and transformation.

At different points along the path, the passageway narrowed or shrunk, and she had to bend or twist. In slow, steady motion they descended. Together they moved without haste. The deeper they went the surroundings remained mostly unchanged. The only evident distinction became a dampness—on the walls, on her clothes, under her feet, and, ultimately, in her heart. This path seemed to lead toward obscurity.

There was no possible way to turn around—and no reason to.

Esther continued to breathe through the dark. She felt there was no ending, and soon she no longer had memory of what had come before. No sense or possibility of time. While the space confined her physically, it liberated all her senses, most especially her powers of perception.

In this place, wherever this is, where it seems as though there is no change, I know full well everything is changing, even though it looks and feels exactly the same. These were the thoughts flowing through her mind.

This was a meditation in faith and in patience.

Confidence of trust—of Marco—was unquestioned. Going from the complete unknown to the truly mysterious should have caused uncertainty, if not anxiety, but moment by moment, the young Esther—the adventurous, fearless Esther, the Esther at her core—rebounded.

More than once she reached to the bottom of her dress pocket to tenderly caress dear Bubbe Royza's *kiddush* cup. The cherished possession that had traveled with her since she left Przeworsk—her constant—her sole constant. Esther innately understood that this cherished object, and only this, provided the bridge of connection and place.

From then—to now—to always.

Marco gently took Esther's right hand when the stones below became especially jagged and patchy. As soon as his hand, unexpectedly rough and calloused and thickly padded, touched Esther's, the spark of recognition resonated in her heart—a shared history and common path already journeyed together—wholly comprehending that this bond began long before their meeting on the ship. Knowing at the depth of her being this connection began in a park by the riverfront in Köln and—

She started.

—at this instant, Esther felt His truth.

Her hand squeezed His. She felt a slight twinge as the circulation lessened and no distinction remained between where one hand began and the other ended. They melded.

Is this the way it has always been? Esther thought in wonderment.

"You will not . . . have to do this alone," Marco said unexpectedly. "Never alone."

"But what?" Esther asked, confounded. "Why am I here? Why are we here? And where, exactly, is here?"

He did not respond; once more His concentration was inward.

Marco had no trouble providing direction and choreographing a path on the irregular rocks beneath their feet that could be traversed with ease. In a few places He lightly leaped, as though dancing; obviously He had negotiated this course many times before. As they moved onward, Esther saw that Marco kept His second hand face up, palm outward, which generated a pale glow illuminating the way ahead.

I didn't notice He brought a torch, Esther thought. It's hard to see clearly, but He must have one, for there's a ray of light flickering ahead.

Esther's thoughts began to race: was she seeing things that could not be real? It seems as though He's also carrying a rope and an axe—but each in a separate hand. How can this be, when one of His hands is holding mine? And I see the shadow of a flower on the stone wall. Like a lotus, so exotic. But that, too, can't possibly be real. The light must be creating shadows that are only illusions. More than one person would have to account for all those hands.

This place plays crazy tricks on my senses, Esther thought.

They continued on. The path beneath their feet grew increasingly irregular. Although no direction was evident, she felt clearly they moved in a large, circulating spiral. Esther became unsteady. She understood it had nothing to do with the misshaped rocks beneath their feet.

Time had evanesced.

Esther and Marco were in the deepest recesses of the cave when a clearing became visible in the near distance. The blackness began to relax its embrace from the passionate squeeze that had held them. Light and color converged.

They approached a space much like the grand ballroom of a palatial estate. Or the interior of a cathedral. The stunning stalactites and stalagmites that encircled them appeared as dancers floating above and below. A few seemed to extend their reach as though they strove to touch and be touched. Crystals and salt compounds emanated a kaleidoscope of shimmering lights, reflecting an expansive array of pearls and lace.

Suddenly—Esther's equilibrium shifted.

"This place looks impossibly familiar. But how could—?" She stopped mid-thought, mid-step, mid-breath.

In such an environment all becomes illuminated.

"I've been here before," Esther gasped. "I know this place.

"I've dreamt of this place. I'm sure of it. Only here. During the time when I thought I could no longer dream, when every night was dark and blank and empty. When only a few nights were broken by the possibilities that dreams offer. The few dreams I had then, during those awful years—throughout the war, and those before—all those years after Tadeusz—in Köln—they were of here. This place—I don't understand. How? How is this possible? What is this about? What is happening? Where am I?"

"Ah . . . my dear Esther," Marco said. His voice shimmered with an echoing timbre. "We are so close . . . nearly there . . . you will soon understand. Please . . . it will be lucid . . . clarity is your gift. For here is the center of all things . . . where your soul . . . all souls . . . meet. At this juncture is where the outer and inner worlds become one. It is where . . . all begins.

"Here . . . is the cavern of self . . . your self."

At that instant, Esther heard a drumbeat commence in the distance, faintly, echoing within the chamber's walls. Slow—cadenced—tapping. First of a lone drum, followed minutes later by a second, then a third and then others, impossible to distinguish how many or to ascertain their location.

Tablas—dayans and bayons—continuous, diffused, thoughtful tapping—tapping—tapping—

Escalating to an unrelenting, pulsating beat.

Pounding—throbbing—thumping.

Bells began to clang—gently. Conch shells blown. The hint of a rattle shaking, gaining energy—vitality.

Each frontward step increased the collective sounds twofold.

And then—like a mirage emerging on the horizon of a vast

desert space—Esther saw a sparkle of light from a candle glowing purposefully.

His silhouette took form.

He was manifest.

Seated on an intricately carved golden marble throne with His left leg folded before him, providing a resting place for His protruding belly, the figure towered above Esther at more than four meters. This elephant-headed man was draped in layers of luscious yellow and red diaphanous silk cloths. Countless chains of exquisite *mala*—each with 108 flawless beads—rested against His throat; garlands of red hibiscus flowers lay upon His chest. His four arms and hands seemed in constant motion yet without movement.

Before him were positioned three small clear glass bowls—two empty, one filled with water. Red and yellow joss sticks burned on either side. Fragrant smells of spices, woods, and herbs emanated from their incense. A pot of red paste lay to the right. Traces of recently perfumed air floated above, and freshly cut red roses, anthuriums, cardinals, peonies, dahlias, and calla lilies encircled him. A tall red candle had only just begun to burn. Mangos and coconuts lay in a bowl. A large rectangular ceramic platter spilling over with sugar cookies held center stage.

"Om Lam," Marco said softly, bowing before him and laying a second red candle down next to the first, along with a handful of marigolds.

Ah . . . my Esther. Your journey . . . is now realized.

As you now know . . . you have become clearly aware . . . we have been together for a long time . . . for a very long time indeed. It is my pleasure and my gift to assist and support you . . . to support all . . . whether it is understood that I am with you . . . or not.

For I am always . . . and have always been here for you.

Esther . . . my dear Esther . . .

The boundaries of your past are released. No barriers exist to your future . . .

Esther looked serenely into His eyes. She then turned in one full circle to embrace the surroundings. Have I fallen asleep? she wondered. Perhaps this is a dream. A dream like all the other times.

Ah . . . dear Esther . . . for you as for everyone . . . there is no real ending in the same way there is no real beginning. It is part of a continuum . . . merely a brief transition . . . and it is clear . . .

Your heart knows . . . and has always known . . . the way home . . .

Esther reached into her pocket and pulled out Bubbe Royza's *kiddush* cup. She laid it in front of him, just beside the second red candle. Her remaining link to this world, this life, the one object and its bond to memories that had sustained and supported her for these past many years, was offered—

—and released.

She lit the candle's wick, and the cavern immediately became enveloped in a rich rose hue.

Fulfillment washed over Esther. The long hibernation of self was over. The answers were before her. No questions remained. She began to let go—wholly—releasing all that had come before. Letting go of events and actions and experiences that had taken place in her life. In so doing she felt more alive and vital than ever before—more complete and full.

The one and only thing she did not leave behind—would not—could not—let go of—because love is all that matters and all that continues on—was Tadeusz. With forgiveness, and the cognition and the clarity that Tadeusz was and will—throughout time—remain her beloved, she fully embraced his being.

A true liberation—liberation of the spirit—was taking place. Wholly uniting Esther—with Esther.

Percussions and bells, hushed during His speech, resumed. This time—more powerfully and passionately—escalating in scale and tone—creating a high-pitched rumbling throughout—rising to an almost deafening degree.

The ground joined in the revelry and began to shake.

At the outset, this motion was barely discernible. Slight, seemingly insignificant vibrations reverberated through the earth.

But the movements grew rapidly stronger—more potent—with increasing force until the entire cavern shook dramatically.

At this, the drumming amplified—growing louder and louder. More insistent—more repetitive—strident—commanding—

Soon—all that was everywhere—all that was anywhere—was this sound and the reverberation of this sound.

And then—

—she slipped through the echo—on His arm—

EPILOGUE

The energy advanced—
    The ground continued to quaver and tremble, vibrate and roll—formidable and more vigorously with increasing vitality—

The persistent percussion matched the movement's intensity, expanding to an almost deafening scale. Thunderous drums and clangs—escalating excitement and ferment.

The environment elevated.

Climaxing magnetism. Pure—unbridled—energy.

Soon it was space overflowing with blessings and smoke.

Thick clouds of ash and soot and cinders rolled in like a giant swell crashing against the shore.

She appears—

—as an arresting exposed black form absorbing all frequencies of light while glowing brighter than any nearby star—the image of fierce magnetic beauty. She is constantly in motion: Her four arms, with clawlike hands and extended nails, flaying with swords and tridents, intoxicated red eyes emblazoned, hair disheveled and abandoned, lips smeared with blood, long sharp fangs protruding and tongue lolling. Her swaying skirt of human arms and garland of 108 human heads continuously in motion. Bedecked in corpses for earrings and serpents for bracelets.

She, alone, is the embodiment of disintegration and transformation.

Ah . . . Kali . . . Kali Ma . . . my beloved Kali . . . You have come. But of course You are here . . . for You are the most beneficent . . . and loving of us all.

Kali . . . they never know where We can be. Or ever so more importantly . . . who We can be.

Do you think a time will come when they will truly comprehend? Do You believe they can learn and accept?

That We are everywhere and always where We are most needed . . . even if it is not accepted that We are needed.

Do you think they will ever understand . . . what need even is?

Kali meets Ganesha's embracing gaze and smiles obliquely. Eyes sparkle. She moves close to Him. A knowledge and warmth passes between them. Left hands around waists, right hands held up, fingers intertwine, left feet swing to the side.

They dance.

ACKNOWLEDGMENTS

When a book travels a long and oft times circuitous route to publication—in this case eighteen years—there are myriad people to recognize who provided encouragement, sage advice, and the all-important humor and wit along the way. I extend heartfelt thanks for the support of all those noted below, and apologies that this list cannot be comprehensive.

First and foremost, I'd like to extend deep gratitude to my publisher, Brooke Warner, and her She Writes Press team, including project manager Caitlyn Levin, copywriter Jennifer Caven, and interior designer Tabitha Lahr; to my literary agent, Priya Doraswamy at Lotus Lane Literary, who remained invested and committed over the long haul; to Crystal Patriarche and Book-Sparks's innovative, strategic efforts to share my novel as far and wide as possible; and to my dear, longtime friend Michael Kellner, who brilliantly captured my tale on the book's cover.

I wish to acknowledge my appreciation for those who listened, those who encouraged, those who suggested, those who connected, those who cheered, those who read, and those who critiqued: Betsy Amster, Sasha Anawalt, Anne Bray, Cynthia Campoy Brophy, Anne Dubuisson, Karen Foster, Peter Gadol, Weba Garretson, Betsey Grady, Jack Grapes, Gilda Haas, Dharma Hernandez, Mead Hunter (my insightful first reader), David Kipen, Geralynn Krajeck, Adam Leipzig, Imre Molnar, Mary Jane Myers, Susie Norris, Laurie Owyang, Gary Phillips, Andrea Richards, Peggy Riley, Howard A. Rodman, Louise Steinman, Bill Stern, Janet Sternburg, Marie Unini, and Morrie Warshawski.

Many thanks to Terry Wolverton, a stellar teacher, who endeavored to launch me on the creative writing path; to my fellow writers in the Saturday morning Relax & Write group led by the inimitable Maia Danziger, who got me to do what others before had tried—namely, to put words on paper and read them aloud; to the wide-ranging, informative classes taught by discerning writers at UCLA's highly regarded Writers Program, of which I must single out Mary Yukari Waters—her ten-week course offered an in-depth overview that easily rivaled any top-notch MFA; and to the incredibly generous Kerry Madden-Lunsford, who appeared at the absolute right time to teach me exactly what I needed to know. In addition, I thank the Shoah Foundation Institute for Visual History and Education for the opportunity to do in-depth research.

Lastly, I am deeply indebted to my translators: Tine Kindermann (German), Rob Adler Peckerar (Yiddish and Hebrew), Emanuelle Batz and Aaron Paley (French), Ans Ellis (Dutch), Shashi Bhatter (Hindi), and Carla Fantozzi and Fabio Angelini (Italian). To Barrett Briske, who diligently researched the public domain status and necessary permissions of the many quotes, lyrics, and poems included in my novel, and to Coleman Barks, who generously gave permission to use his translation of Rumi's "The Guest House."

ABOUT THE AUTHOR

Judith Teitelman has straddled the worlds of arts, literature, and business since she was a teenager and worked her first job as a salesperson at a B. Dalton/Pickwick Bookstore. Life's journeys took her from bookstores to commercial fine art galleries to the nonprofit arts and cultural sector, in which she has worked as staff, consultant, and educator for more than three decades. Throughout this time, Teitelman continued her pursuit of all things literary, and over the years her writing has been published in a variety of formats and publications. *Guesthouse for Ganesha* is her debut novel. She lives in Los Angeles with her husband and three beloved cats.

Author photo © Anne Bray

SELECTED TITLES FROM SHE WRITES PRESS

She Writes Press is an independent publishing company founded to serve women writers everywhere. Visit us at www.shewritespress.com.

Light Radiance Splendor by Leah Chyten. $16.95, 978-1-63152-178-2. Set in Eastern Europe in the first half of the twentieth century and culminating in contemporary Israel and Palestine, *Light Radiance Splendor* shows how three generations of the Hebrew Goddess Shekinah's devoted mission keepers grapple with betrayal, love, and forgiveness.

Elmina's Fire by Linda Carleton. $16.95, 978-1-63152-190-4. A story of conflict over such issues as reincarnation and the nature of good and evil that are as relevant today as they were eight centuries ago, *Elmina's Fire* offers a riveting window into a soul struggling for survival amid the conflict between the Cathars and the Catholic Church.

Faint Promise of Rain by Anjali Mitter Duva. $16.95, 978-1-938314-97-1. Adhira, a young girl born to a family of Hindu temple dancers, is raised to be dutiful—but ultimately, as the world around her changes, it is her own bold choice that will determine the fate of her family and of their tradition.

Eliza Waite by Ashley Sweeney. $16.95, 978-1-63152-058-7. When Eliza Waite chooses to leave a stagnant life in rural Washington State and join the masses traveling north to Alaska in 1898 during the tumultuous Klondike Gold Rush, she encounters challenges and successes in both business and love.

Dark Lady by Charlene Ball. $16.95, 978-1-63152-228-4. Emilia Bassano Lanyer—poor, beautiful, and intelligent, born to a family of Court musicians and secret Jews, lover to Shakespeare and mistress to an older nobleman—survives to become a published poet in an era when most women's lives are rigidly circumscribed.

Tasa's Song by Linda Kass. $16.95, 978-1-63152-064-8. From a peaceful village in eastern Poland to a partitioned post-war Vienna, from a promising childhood to a year living underground, *Tasa's Song* celebrates the bonds of love, the power of memory, the solace of music, and the enduring strength of the human spirit.